SOUTHERN CROSS

GEORGE WALLACE

DON KEITH

SEVERN RIVER
PUBLISHING

SOUTHERN CROSS

Severn River Publishing
www.SevernRiverBooks.com

ISBN: 978-1-64875-578-1 (Paperback)

ALSO BY THE AUTHORS

The Hunter Killer Series

Final Bearing

Dangerous Grounds

Cuban Deep

Fast Attack

Arabian Storm

Warshot

Silent Running

Snapshot

Southern Cross

The Gibraltar Affair

Also by George Wallace

Operation Golden Dawn

Never miss a new release! Sign up to receive exclusive updates from authors
Wallace and Keith.

severnriverbooks.com

PROLOGUE

It was just past midnight. A thick fog, unusual for this time of year, had rolled in off the Río de la Plata River and blanketed downtown Buenos Aires in a dense, cottony shroud. Casa Rosada, the official office of the president of Argentina, was barely visible from the new homeless camp that had sprung up on the Plaza de Mayo, just across the street. A big, black Mercedes-Maybach S-600 Pullman limousine abruptly shot out of the main entrance to the pink-hued presidential palace, then turned and rocketed south on the nearly deserted Avenue Paseo Colón. The automobile's twelve-cylinder engine, the product of the finest German engineers, shoved the heavily armored vehicle up to more than one hundred kilometers per hour before even reaching and passing beneath the first red traffic light. A half-dozen motorcycle outriders, all dressed in black, their lights flashing and sirens blaring, cleared the way ahead for the black bullet.

Presidente Bruno Valentino Martinez gazed out through the limo's darkly tinted windows. He paid little attention to the mob of homeless people milling around their makeshift tents, or to those who had bedded down on the streets, unprotected from the elements. His self-proclaimed revolution was clearly having difficulties coming to grips with Argentina's failing economy. Martinez remained convinced these unfortunates were merely the inevitable fallout, the necessary victims of the change to a far more equitable socialist economy for his country. One that would soon benefit all the citizens, including these *gente pobre,* who were an unfortunate legacy of capitalism and the corrupt super-wealthy who had once enslaved them to satisfy their own selfish greed.

Instead of worrying about them, he sat back and enjoyed the limo's buttery-soft Moroccan leather upholstery and polished Macassar ebony trim as he poured himself a healthy glass of Fernet-Branca and Coca-Cola. The digestif, along with a fine cigar, was the perfect way to settle his stomach as he considered the volume of increasingly gloomy reports he had just received from his minister of finance.

The president decided to shove those revelations from his mind as well, to enjoy the ride, and to get himself into the proper mood for his upcoming journey.

It was a trip, after all, that would ultimately alter the history of the South American continent and, in the process, redirect the future of the Western Hemisphere.

Ψ

Capitán de Fragata Colas Lopez Alveras stood at the end of the long pier. The structure was empty save for one black shape, barely visible in the thick fog. The brand-new Argentine Navy submarine ARN *Santiago del Estero* sat low in the unperturbed waters of the inner harbor of the Mar del Plata Naval Base. Captain Alveras could just make out the burbling sound of the exhaust coming from his submarine's four diesel generators, but the exhaust smoke was erased by the fog.

He looked back toward the boat, where the crew was completing the final checks for an immediate underway. Lines were singled up and the shore power cables were neatly coiled on the pier. The pier crane was standing by, ready to lift away the brow as soon as everyone was aboard. Most importantly, the topside watch was dressed in neatly pressed dress white uniforms and looked properly sharp. That was not typical, but Alveras knew it would impress his guest.

The captain turned on his heel and marched smartly down the pier toward the Comando de la Fuerza de Submarinos building, the submarine force's headquarters. He glanced at his wristwatch. It would be a truly bad idea to be late. For the next week, his new submarine would be hosting Bruno Valentino Martinez.

El Presidente had risen to supreme power only a few months earlier. After losing Argentina's most recent presidential election, Martinez, along with his cadre of Army officers, mounted a bloody military revolt. The friendly media claimed massive voter fraud to justify the upheaval. Once the military took control, Martinez maintained the façade of leading a democratic republic, gradually assuming more and more control to—as he put it—"allow the people to control their government, the economy, and their future." But there were reports of numerous opposition figures mysteriously disappearing, of nosy journalists who had asked the wrong questions or written critical articles being assaulted and silenced. Then the government began the initial takeovers of private businesses, especially those owned by foreign companies.

Alveras was well aware of what was happening in his nation. It would be prudent for the submariner to remain on the president's good side.

As Alveras neared the headquarters building, the Mercedes-Maybach limo hurried around the corner and came to a stop in front of the graceless cement pile that served as the home of the submarine headquarters. The driver leaped out and raced around to open the oversized rear door. *Presidente* Martinez's head bodyguard emerged first, looked about, and then motioned to his leader that it was safe to step out.

The president climbed out, then stood tall. He was impressively resplendent in his Army general's uniform. Even Captain Alveras, very familiar with military officer puffery, had to admit that Bruno Martinez struck quite an impressive pose.

The submarine captain then had the secret pleasure of watching *Almirante* Anbessa Sepulveda, the chief of the general staff of the navy, and *Contalmirante* Pichi Espinoza, the commander of the Argentinian submarine force—Alveras's bosses several layers further up the military pecking order—as they practically quivered while snapping to attention before their new commander in chief.

Martinez waved them away, ignoring the assembled brass. He turned to Colas Alveras, clearly aware this was the man who was, for the moment, most important to him, and said, "Captain, your boat is ready to get under-way." It was not a question.

Alveras came to attention and answered, "*Señor Presidente*, we will cast off lines immediately after you are aboard." He glanced at his watch. "We will be submerged by 0600. But, sir, we do not yet know our course heading or destination."

Martinez waved his hand in dismissal. "I will tell you in due time, once we are submerged. The fewer ears that hear, the safer our secret and the more likely our mission is to be successful. Let us get aboard and see how this new toy of yours works." The president turned and stalked off toward the brow that offered access to the deck of the submarine, leaving his body-guard to lug his baggage.

Ten minutes later, the president, the captain, and the final members of the crew were safely aboard the ARN *Santiago del Estero*. Lines were cast off. A pair of small pusher boats pulled the sub away from the pier so that Alveras could point his vessel out into open water. The four twelve-cylinder MTU396 diesel engines hardly changed their throaty tone as the sub's single screw bit into the water, propelling the boat forward. From the bridge, Alveras directed his crew as they steered the sub out of the turning basin and around the inner groyne, then into the outer harbor. By the time he saw the outer mole through the early morning fog, Alveras could already sense the gentle roll of the open Atlantic Ocean.

A couple of kilometers east of the mole, the bottom dropped off sharply into the deep South Atlantic. That gave them plenty of water to safely submerge so they would have no worries about some deep-draft tanker suddenly emerging out of the fog and threatening to scrape their new paint job.

Once the *Santiago del Estero* was safely cruising at a depth of fifty meters under the South Atlantic, Alveras went looking for his very important passenger. He found *Presidente* Martinez sitting in the captain's stateroom, sipping espresso from a mug. The president was already dressed in blue submarine coveralls, but with his Army general stars pinned on and a name tag that read *Presidente Martinez*.

He looked up as Alveras entered, smiled, and said, "Your boat serves a good cup of *café en jarrito*. This trip may be more enjoyable than I imagined.

I have not been on your fine submarine before. I assume you could arrange a tour for me."

"Would right after breakfast be appropriate?" Alveras responded. "Our ship's cook, Carlos, makes the best *medialunas de manteca* in all of Argentina. They will melt in your mouth. And they are at their very best when eaten hot out of the oven."

Bruno Martinez smiled and answered, "You have discovered my sweet tooth. Right after breakfast, then. And I trust that you will be joining me."

Alveras nodded. "First, though, I must tell my helmsman which way to steer. What is our destination, *Señor Presidente*? I will have Carlos deliver a platter of hot *medialunas* as soon as I can tell the Navigator in which direction we are headed."

Martinez laughed. "I cannot believe that I am being held hostage over a plate of breakfast pastries." The president pulled out a chart from his valise and pointed. "We must be there in three days, at midnight. Such a voyage will allow us to test and see if the Brazilians built us the submarine they promised."

Alveras shook his head. Martinez had placed his finger on a point about twenty miles off the Brazilian coast just east of Rio de Janeiro. The captain quickly estimated that it was a distance of over two thousand kilometers from their present position.

"*Señor Presidente*, if we run at flank speed the entire time, we will just make that distance in three days. On a diesel submarine like this one, that means we will be surfaced for a great deal of the time to run our engines. Is this so important that we cannot go slower and more covertly?"

"*Capitán* Alveras, I was informed that the *Santiago del Estero* could remain submerged for over two weeks without needing to surface and that her maximum speed was something in excess of twenty knots. Have I been misinformed?"

Alveras again shook his head. "No, *Señor Presidente*. You were not misinformed, just not completely informed. Both statements are true."

"Then what is the problem, *Capitán*?"

"Both statements are separately true, but not combined. Our hydrogen fuel cell system will power the *Santiago del Estero* while submerged for up to three weeks, but only if we keep the speed below about four knots," the submarine commander explained. "Above that speed, the energy has to come from the batteries when we are submerged. After about three hours at maximum power, we need to use the diesels to recharge the batteries. That means we would have to run for four hours submerged, surface and run the diesels for about three hours, then dive and repeat. Does that make sense?"

Martinez nodded hesitantly, the slightest of frowns on his face.

"Yes. Yes, it does. *Capitán*, Argentina is placing its faith in you and the *Santiago del Estero*. I will only say that the future of our country hinges on my arriving at that meeting on time. Being a day late . . . even an hour late . . . is not acceptable. Now get your boat headed north and bring me the breakfast you have promised."

1

Cristiano Souza, the president of the Federative Republic of Brazil, angrily snapped the television off and slammed the remote control against the far wall of his spacious office. TV Globo Sao Paulo had been broadcasting a live feed from Washington, DC. The background scene behind the network's US correspondent showed a large crowd milling about in front of the Capitol building. Most of the crowd carried signs, but they were too far away and too out of focus for Souza to read the lettering. The talking head was babbling on about the American economy and how its perturbations ultimately and immediately affected the financial systems of all other countries of the world. The message was clear and especially maddening to the Brazilian president: what was good for the economy of the United States was good for the rest of the planet as well.

The damned prideful *norteamericanos* had not changed their stance in more than a century. Or was it *norteamericanas*? In today's politically correct environment, he could never be quite sure which gender usage was currently acceptable. What the hell did it matter? He had a fifteen-person media office to handle such fluff. But no matter what appendage dangled or did not dangle from between their legs, the politicians and bankers were all self-serving snakes.

Most recently, the imperious "leaders of the free world" had the audacity to strong-arm the International Monetary Fund into rejecting Brazil's legitimate loan requests to get them through a dry spell until the president's reforms could take hold. Then, they followed that up by influencing the World Bank into refusing to fund his bold plan to dam the Rio Paraguai to begin generating hydroelectric power and providing irrigation for the nation's crops. The reason? They claimed that the dam would destroy the "invaluable" Pantanal wetlands and cause incalculable environmental devastation. But the real reason was their animosity toward Souza and his regime after the government nationalized and took over dock facilities at most key ports in the country. And accepted a most generous loan from China to construct a massive airport and commodity-transport center on a portion of that otherwise useless swampland in the Pantanal.

Souza slammed his fist onto his desk. The place was nothing but a bog, a quagmire, fit only for capybaras and caiman. Why was it the business of the United States if he was finally replacing the greedy and corrupt capitalists and foreign corporations? If Souza's government was allowing the Brazilian people to begin reaching their potential? His plan would open thousands of hectares to agricultural development, but the two-faced *ianque* politicians were more concerned with securing green votes in Chicago than feeding *camponeses* in Passo de Lontra. Those starving peasants were his people, the backbone of his power. Though some—including the haughty United States—questioned the legitimacy of his election, Souza knew that regardless how he'd achieved the office, his people—the Brazilian people—would soon see his policies fundamentally change not only their own country but much of South America.

That thought calmed the president considerably. There was even a hint of a smile on his tanned and heavily creased face. It was time to teach the *ianque* politicians some respect. He had just the plan to do that.

Souza glanced at the mantle clock resting above the massive fireplace on the far side of his palatial office. The fireplace, of course, was fake. Fake, like so much of what had remained from former government leaders of his country, who had only been interested in power and self-enrichment in the name of "democracy." The fireplace's very existence in the mid-century modern Palácio de Planalto was jarring. Souza wondered which of his predecessors had the incredibly poor taste to have it installed. Probably the same forerunner who thought the massive mahogany Chippendale table made an appropriate work desk for the president.

The clock confirmed it was almost time for the president to go. He could hear the approaching clatter of the big VH-36 Caracal presidential helicopter as he walked out of the office. His aide/bodyguard, Pedreira, stood just outside the door, waiting patiently. He easily picked up two big bags at his feet and followed.

Pedreira had been with Souza for as long as the president could remember, ever since the bad days up in the mountains of Rondônia, hiding from those in the government who saw Souza and his ideas as a threat. Pedreira had shown up in the camp one morning, starving and near death. Taking in and nursing the *camponese* back to health was one of the best decisions Souza had made. The big man was utterly devoted to his leader and would, without any questions, do anything that the president asked. The two walked across the lawn to the waiting bird without exchanging even one word. Souza sometimes thought Pedreira must be telepathic. Just another of the man's many useful skills.

Minutes later, after they were strapped in and supplied with steaming cups of Black Tucano coffee, the helicopter smoothly lifted off—bad form to spill even a drop of the president's coffee!—spun around, and pointed its nose to the south. Their destination, the Base de Submarinos Almirante Castro e Silva, located on the Ilha de Mocanguê at the mouth of Rio de Janeiro's harbor, was almost three hours away. That would put them there just before their guests pulled into port and the historic meetings could begin.

Meetings that would one day lead to redrawn borders and a radically new axis of power in the Western Hemisphere.

Ψ

Guillermo Manuelito kicked the covers back and slowly eased out of bed to avoid waking his sleeping wife. Sunrise was still an hour away and he did not want to disturb her or his teenage daughters. He grabbed his clothes off the hanger where he had left them the previous evening and slipped quietly out of the bedroom. He put the coffee on to brew while he dressed, then grabbed a full thermos as he quietly scooted out the door into the warm, fragrant morning.

His battered old truck coughed to life, backfiring a couple of times before leaving a blue cloud of smoke in the pre-dawn haze. The flatbed had seen many kilometers of hard use, but it was all he had. He was confident it would successfully make the trip into Buenos Aries and then back home.

The gravel drive made a straight line through his ten hectares of olive trees. His great-grandfather had brought the first seedlings over from Italy and carefully nurtured them on this small plot of land a few kilometers out of Santa Teresa. His grandfather, and then his father, had managed a meager but comfortable life here, quietly growing their olives despite all the political and financial turmoil they had experienced over the years. Now it was his turn to protect the Manuelito hacienda. His wife had grandly named the place La Granja, "The Farm."

Everything he and his family had worked so hard to build and maintain was now facing serious risk. Not from insect pests, blight, or weather. Though Guillermo was up to date on all payments, the banks were suddenly calling each of his outstanding loans due. They declared that if he did not make full payment immediately, they would foreclose. All the way back to his great-grandfather, the Manuelitos had borrowed each year to nurture the crop, then promptly paid it back with the harvest, mostly through the same two or three local banks. Now, those same banks were threatening that his family would be turned out to wander the roads of Córdoba Province, begging for help. He knew it was not an idle threat. Three of his neighbors had already been evicted. And the few remaining bankers with whom he had worked so many times before had cried tears when they assured him it was beyond their control.

There was one positive thing, though. Guillermo's grandfather, Juan, had been shrewd with money. A survivor of the *juntas* and civil wars of the 1970s, Juan had learned the pain of monetary inflation the hard way. As a result, he had moved the family wealth—what little there was of it—out of Argentine pesos. Then, as did many of his countrymen, he occasionally made the short ferry ride across the Río de la Plata to Montevideo. The Uruguayan banks and the Uruguayan peso offered solid protection against the vagaries of his own country's monetary and banking systems. Those pesos represented the salvation he needed. They would satisfy the banker and save the Manuelitos' small *granja*.

The two-lane rural backroads had seen little maintenance in the last couple of decades, but they still managed to deliver Guillermo to National Route 9, the major artery connecting the country's verdant northwest with Buenos Aires. Traffic was heavy on the four-lane Camino Real del Perú. The low-angle morning sun was bright in Manuelito's eyes, causing him to squint as he did all he could to avoid plowing into the big rigs that clogged the road and seemed to be in such a hurry.

Traffic picked up even more as he neared the city, but it was not nearly so bad as he was expecting. Like in any major city, rush hour traffic in Buenos Aires was something to be avoided if at all possible. "The highways are so busy nobody travels them anymore," his oldest son often said with a laugh. Guillermo did notice something that was quite telling. On previous trips, he was accustomed to seeing new Mercedes and Fiat autos delivering suburban workers to downtown. Now there were far fewer of those. Instead, he saw older trucks and *tartanas*—clunkers—piled high with some family's meager possessions. Many of the cars' occupants, he knew, were homeless, dispossessed, in a quest for something or somewhere that offered hope.

National Route 9 ended at a T intersection on the border of Buenos Aries Province and the city limits of Buenos Aires, dumping all the traffic onto Avenida General Paz, the beltway that encircled the city proper. Manuelito worked through the maze and ended up eastbound, where he merged onto Avenida Leopoldo Lugones. From there, it was only a few blocks to the SeaCat ferry terminal, where the high-speed ferry would take him over to Montevideo. But traffic abruptly ground to a halt just as the big terminal buildings were coming into view.

Traffic police were shunting everyone over onto city streets, away from the terminal. It was unusual that these officers were heavily armed and decked out in full riot gear.

Guillermo cranked down his window and got the attention of one of the officers. He carefully explained to him that it was important that he get to the terminal.

The officer was having none of it. He impatiently growled, "The ferry is closed by specific order of *El Presidente*."

"But why?" Manuelito dared to ask.

"It is of no concern to you, *granjero!*" the cop responded, but then decided to take some mercy on the man in the beat-up old truck. "If you must know, disloyal traitors are using the ferry to sneak over to Montevideo to avoid our banking laws. They should be shot, if you ask me, but *El Presidente* is merciful."

"But I only need to visit with my aunt, who is very ill," Guillermo tried.

"I wish you the best for your dear aunt, farmer, but you will turn around and return to your fields now," the policeman told him.

Guillermo Manuelito nodded and quietly rolled up his window. He waited until he rounded the corner before beating his fist against the steering wheel. He had long feared this day would come but had continued to pray it would not.

Without the money to pay off the bank loans, the Manuelito hacienda would soon be gone. His first thought was that there was nothing he could do about that. But perhaps there was something else that could be done. Something to help change the course of these circumstances.

He pulled into a parking space at a convenience store, took his battered cell phone from the glovebox, and dialed a number from memory. When it was answered, Guillermo did not bother with a "hello."

"Balduino, this is Guillermo. I am ready to join the cause. *El Presidente* must be stopped, and I am ready to help."

Ψ

Admiral Jon Ward sat back, removed his reading glasses, and closed his eyes tight as he massaged the bridge of his nose. Damn, he hated having to use those glasses! But it was just another price to pay for growing older. And for the long hours spent reading densely typed intelligence reports just like the one he was finishing reviewing. Sometimes he wondered if the analysts were being paid by the word.

He stood, stretched, and walked over to stand at the window. From there, he could see beyond the brightly lit Pentagon parking lot to the long line of brake lights and the last of the tangled rush hour traffic on the Richmond Highway. The sun had already called it a day and did its usual disappearing act. The traffic jams would not affect Ward's day, though. By the time he would head home, both the parking lot and the highway would be virtually empty.

Ward sat back down, rested the glasses on his nose once again, and grabbed the report, picking up where he left off. So, the Argentine Navy had taken delivery of their new Brazilian-built submarine, the ARN *Santiago del Estero*. They were being very cagey about their new toy and its capabilities, leaving most of their previous allies, including the USA, entirely in the dark. Normally, that might have been mildly worrisome, but nothing to fret about. Maybe worth a cordial call to the Argentine Navy's head of intelligence, Admiral Ward's counterpart down there.

Not nowadays. The relatively new president of Argentina and his government had been spouting all kinds of socialist rhetoric, voting weirdly in the United Nations, and talking about their plans to defy colonialism and the domination of the western half of the globe by its lone superpower, the United States. The kind of rhetoric typically heard from tin-pot dictators in countries barely qualifying as "third world," who certainly were without the means or firepower to threaten anyone. There had also continued to be disturbing reports of back-and-forth talks involving the new Argentine president, Bruno Valentino Martinez, and Brazilian chief executive Cristiano Souza, along with both countries' military leaders and high-ranking representatives from China. Economic, diplomatic, and military discussions.

For Admiral Ward, this all meant that it would be prudent for the US to learn as much as they could before all that barbed oratory, the troublesome alliances, and those new submarines became a real problem. A starting point would be to check up on the nuclear submarine the Brazilian Navy was confirmed to be building. That boat should be almost ready for sea trials by now, too.

As Chief of Naval Intelligence, "learning" was Admiral Jon Ward's job.

He sat back and thought for a minute, tapping the desk with his fingertips. He was a former submariner himself and knew that any nation investing in such vessels had serious martial intentions. They were much

more expensive than surface warships and required extensive and specialized training for the men who crewed them. At the same time, they were far
easier to conceal and avoid prying eyes for those up to no good. Such ships
were the natural choice of any regime intending to build a more powerful
—and not necessarily totally defensive—naval force. The fact that these
two very large South American countries had been getting awfully friendly
with each other lately, just when socialists had grabbed power in both
nations, had raised one very large red flag for Ward. The development of
the submarines and the extent to which the Brazilians had kicked their
defense industry into high gear made it obvious they were worth serious
scrutiny.

Brazil was launching a new diesel boat every few months and making
huge strides on getting their long-dormant nuke boat to sea. When Cristiano Souza and his left-wing party took power, even the French had
abruptly cut them off from buying submarine technology. Brazil did not
miss a beat. Souza had simply turned around and began purchasing what
he craved from the Chinese, who were only too happy to fill the void.

Ward shook his head as he grabbed the secure phone and punched in a
number. It was answered on the second ring. "Fleet Forces, Admiral
Bradburn."

"Brad, this is Jon Ward. Glad to see I'm not the only one burning the
midnight oil on behalf of the red, white, and blue."

"Jon, good to hear from you. You, of all people, know how it is. If it's not
one problem, it's a dozen other ones. But something tells me you didn't call
to hear me bitch. What can I do for Naval Intelligence?"

"Brad, you been keeping up on what's happening in South America?"

"Yeah, Jimmy Riddell down at Fourth Fleet and Barry Acheson over at
SOUTHCOM are the guys on the pointy end of that spear, but I see their
reports. And it gives me considerable indigestion. Like bad Chinese food."

Ward glanced down at the report he had been reading. Bradburn had
clearly come to the same conclusions as he had. Troubling signals from a
largely forgotten corner of the world as far as the military was concerned,
all tied back to trouble with the economy and dangerous leaders using that
turmoil to grab power. It had been a while—if he did not count rumblings
from Venezuela and a couple of Central American dictatorships—since

there were any big issues down there. The last major dust-up worth reporting was the Falklands War back in the 1980s.

"Brad, I need to get a boat down there to snoop around and see what they can find out for us. You got someone?"

The line went quiet. Ward had just about decided that they had been disconnected when Bradburn came back online. "Jon, I had to check the boat schedules. I don't keep them in my head anymore. Senility is a terrible thing. But I got one candidate for you. *George Mason* is coming around for a yard period up in Portsmouth. We can just divert him from going through the Canal and have him take the long way around. We can have them on station in two weeks. That work for you?"

"Very convenient, actually. Sounds good. Thanks, Brad. And let's take in a Nationals game sometime. I still got season tickets behind home plate, five rows up. Watch the game on TV and you'll see those two empty seats most of the time."

"You miss going to the games with your boy, don't you, Jon? I run across his name in reports sometimes. Navy's keeping him hopping."

"Yeah, best SEAL I ever raised. He tells me the navy must think he's the only SEAL team commander they got. And yeah, I miss him. The wife would rather eat a bug than sit through a baseball game. She says the players spit and scratch too much."

"Okay, we'll do that game soon, Jon. And I'll confirm when *George Mason's* diverted."

Ward paused for a long moment. "Oh, and Brad, don't tell that skipper it was me that delayed his vacation for a few weeks."

Ψ

The flag suite of the Brazilian Comando da Força de Submarinos enveloped the entire top floor of an impressive granite building at Base de Submarinos Almirante Castro e Silva. The offices looked across a broad, tree-lined plaza, the Praça do Capitão Luís da Cunha Moreira, and past the Avenue Mello Marques to where several submarines were tied up along the pier. Just as the submarine base honored a World War II Brazilian admiral, the plaza honored the country's first naval minister.

As the host of this morning's meeting, Cristiano Souza arrived first, accompanied by his ever-present aide, Pedreira. The Brazilian president stepped into the empty room, quickly observed the position of the round conference table and the chairs around it, and then selected a seat with his back to the broad windows. It was a tactic he had learned early in his political career. It was difficult for others—friend or foe—to observe and decipher even the slightest of facial reactions if there was bright light behind him. Pedreira promptly set a cup of steaming coffee within the president's easy reach, then left the room to take up a position just outside the door.

On his way out, the aide held the door open and gave a nod to Bruno Valentino Martinez, the Argentine president, who strode into the room, helped himself to a cup of coffee at the urging of his host, and plopped down across the table from Souza. As he spoke a quick greeting to his counterpart, Martinez glanced around and noticed, with some concern, that the table appeared to be set up for three participants. At the third position, there was a legal pad and writing pen, a cup of tea, a glass creamer, and a dish filled with sugar cubes.

"Are we expecting someone else?" he asked, eyebrows arched.

Souza held his reply for a long moment as he took a sip of his coffee, watching the Argentine president over the rim of his cup. There was the barest glimpse of a smile curling his lips as he deliberately returned the ornate cup back to its saucer. Another acquired tactic, allowing a pause to keep anyone he was meeting with just a bit off balance.

"Bruno, my friend," he began, "I received a most intriguing call yesterday as I was making final preparations for our summit. Since you were submerged, I could not inform you of this communication. Our mutual friend Tan Yong called from Beijing. We had a brief but very interesting discussion. As it happens, Nian Huhu De, an official who President Tan describes as his 'special ambassador plenipotentiary,' has been secretly visiting the Chinese embassy in Brasília, attending to some business or the other." Souza's smile broadened as he again lifted the coffee cup and took a drink. "Extraordinary coincidence that such an important man would be in Brazil at the same time as that of our key meeting, do you not think?"

Martinez was not quite sure if the Brazilian leader was being sarcastic or sincere about such remarkable timing, not only of the ambassador's presence in the country but the president of China's telephone call to Souza. After a few seconds' pause, he opted for accepting Souza's statement as informative sarcasm.

Martinez offered up his cup in a toast. "And what, if any, will be the effect on our summit from this fortunate coincidence?"

At that precise moment, the door swung open and the Chinese ambassador sauntered in. Pedreira stood behind him, awaiting any sign from his boss that he should not allow entrance to this new arrival. Martinez gave him the slightest of nods. The aide shut the door behind Nian Huhu De, who glanced around the room, smiled, and made a perfunctory bow toward Souza. "*Bom dia, senhor presidente,*" he said in flawless, unaccented Portuguese. Then he bowed toward Martinez and told him, "*Buenos días, señor presidente.*"

Nian took his seat and purposefully pulled some papers from his briefcase, which he carefully arranged and then studied for a bit. Then he looked up at both leaders as he spoke. "President Tan sends his warmest greetings and gratefully thanks you for allowing a representative of the People's Republic to be a part of such a very important meeting. I know you have other matters to discuss, so I will be brief. However, I am certain that we will find we have many goals in common and that our nations can be of great assistance to each other going forward. Especially in implementing the steps you will formalize this day." He punctuated his words with a tiny sip of tea without touching the cream or sugar.

Martinez took the break in conversation as an opportunity. "Ambassador Nian, we are more than pleased to have you join us this morning, but I am curious. How did it come to your government's attention that this meeting was even occurring, much less what the agenda would be and how your nation might be a part of the discussions?"

"President Martinez," the ambassador replied, glancing at the Argentinian, a smile on his face. "You use a cell phone manufactured in Hangzhou. Your computer laptop was assembled in Quanzhou. Your country's entire communications infrastructure was manufactured in China and then expertly installed by our technicians. Much of the same is true for you, President Souza. Do you honestly expect us to not know what is happening in your country? And especially when those planned actions will have such a major effect on the world order?" The ambassador was still smiling as he shook his head. Then he added, "But your countries have nothing to fear from China or its leaders. We are aligned. We are your friends, allies opposing the same enemy. And there should be no secrets between friends, should there?"

Martinez and Souza looked at each other as Nian's statement sank in. They were both intimidated that China had been listening in on their conversations over what they believed to be secure circuits. But from what little Nian had shared already, it was obvious they had immediate, real-time access to the innermost workings of both countries. And that with China so deeply embedded in their communications infrastructure, there was nothing either country could do about such blatant eavesdropping.

The ambassador referred to his notes again before looking up. "I believe you will be pleased to know that President Tan has instructed me to inform you that the CCP will fully support your combined initiative to replace your existing individual currencies with a common one. I believe you call that currency the *inútil*. Our president respectfully suggests, however, that you immediately enter into discussions with Bolivia, Venezuela, and Cuba to bring them on board with this common currency. The leaders of those nations are already vaguely aware of what you are about to do, enthusiastically support the plan, and have a desire to be a part of it. And, of course, you will enjoy the CCP's support not only in establishing the common currency but in allowing the other countries to be a part of that effort. Such support coming in deep background, of course."

Both presidents had frowned involuntarily when Nian began his spiel. They were both nodding and smiling by the end. The whole *inútil* idea had admittedly been a huge risk for them and their regimes. But given the horrible economic conditions of their countries, such a move was essential. Without it, their initiative could never survive the machinations and meddling of the dreaded *norteamericanos*. Or the possible backlash from newly invigorated dissidents within their nations.

"We will need more than your country supporting us in the background," Souza countered. "To successfully revive our economic systems, we will need for the *inútil* to be accepted as a trade currency by key partners. Otherwise, some will see it as just another legal tender 'flavor of the day.'"

Nian held up his hands, palms outward, and shrugged. "But, of course! With your approval, we look to become a major trading partner for both Argentina and Brazil, just as we already are in Venezuela, Bolivia, and Cuba. Other nations in this hemisphere will soon be moving that way as well. The CCP will be happy to accept the *inútil* as the reserve currency for our mutual trades. If—or should I say when—you publicly bring our other three Latin American *compadres* into the fold, we will trade with them in *inútils* as well. That alone will be enough to rattle the very foundation of the US dollar as the world's standard currency."

The two presidents were now grinning broadly, no matter how hard they tried to maintain poker faces. In only a few sentences, the Chinese ambassador had just guaranteed the success of their currency endeavor, and, at the same time, had assured that the two presidents would not only soon be very rich—literally having the ability to print their own money— but would also be able to assume a major role on the world stage. And there was nothing the United States or the self-styled rebels among their own citizenry could do about it.

Nian cleared his throat. "But there are some conditions on which we must insist."

Smiles faded. A look of concern clouded both presidents' faces. The other shoe was about to drop.

The Chinese ambassador pulled papers from his stack and passed a sheet containing a short list of bullet points to each president.

"There are some strategic materials to which you have access, like lithium salts and niobium, and we look to be your exclusive customer for those. We are confident you have the labor to exploit these deposits and we are prepared to invest in those operations. Our major concern is access," Nian explained. "If China is to be your major partner, we need to ensure that our ships will be able to safely reach your ports without interference or harassment from other powers who may not approve of our exclusive alliance. We will, of course, help you expand your port infrastructures, more than doubling the size and capacity of those specific ones on the list. In order for this to work, we must be able to maintain our access to your ports through the Drake Passage and, eventually, to work toward controlling the Straits of Magellan, currently under Chile's jurisdiction. Unfettered access to these routes is, we believe, essential to ensure a beneficial and profitable trade partnership between our nations and to avoid disruption from the US. But we must rely on Argentina and Brazil to secure this access. We would hope your navies could accomplish this peacefully, but would also be willing and able to do so with force if you must. China cannot, at this point, appear to be too militarily aggressive. In the near future, yes, but not right now and not in this hemisphere."

With barely a hesitation, Nian progressed to his next topic. "And we think that Uruguay may become a true problem. They could easily and willingly become a staging base for the Americans to counter our efforts, should they dare to do so. And their democratic stance is a fly in the ointment to our broader efforts to bring the benefits of socialism to South America. We strongly urge that you make every effort to eliminate this annoyance."

Martinez and Souza nodded in tandem. This was all within their most ambitious plans. The Chinese government was making certain it happened, quickly and surely, and with an even greater chance of success.

President Souza was the first to stand. "Let us change our agenda immediately, Ambassador Nian. I believe my counterpart will agree completely that with this commitment from you and your government to the cause of the people and socialism, we should begin right here and now to put together our plans and agreements to make all this successfully happen."

President Martinez jumped to his feet and pounded the table with an open hand.

"Agreed!" he said, so loudly that Pedreira opened the door just enough to peek inside and make sure there was nothing wrong. He saw all three men vigorously shaking hands, pounding each other on the back.

Clearly, all was well.

Ψ

At that same moment, the submarine USS *George Mason* was steaming across the Pacific Ocean at a depth of three hundred feet, two thousand nautical miles due west of Panama. They were heading for the canal and then up the East Coast to Portsmouth Naval Shipyard in Kittery, Maine. The boat was scheduled for fourteen months of shipyard overhaul and modernization. That was fourteen months that the warship would be laid up, not available for service.

Brian Edwards, the skipper, was in his stateroom, pondering his future. He knew that this was his last cruise in command of this vessel. His relief would be waiting at the pier when they got to Maine. Edwards was destined to spend his last few weeks in command putting together the plans to tear his beautiful ship apart and rebuild her from bow to stern. At least in the meantime he could enjoy a leisurely cruise across the tropical Pacific and take advantage of a couple of great port calls in the Caribbean. Not a bad way to go out.

Jackson Biddle, the submarine's Executive Officer, stuck his head through Edwards' stateroom door. "Skipper, sorry to interrupt your thinking time, but the Eng has everyone ready in the crew's mess for the work package planning meeting."

Edwards shook his head and snapped out of his reverie. "Roger, XO. I've been looking forward to it." He glanced at the clock. "It's time to copy the broadcast. Why don't you go to control and supervise coming to PD. I'll go to the planning meeting. You can join us there after we have the broadcast aboard."

Biddle grinned, nodded, and stepped out to the control room. Edwards stood, stretched, and made his way for the crew's mess.

When the skipper arrived at the back of the crew's mess, he saw that Jeff Otanga and the other department heads had the first table cluttered with laptops and a labyrinth of cords and cables. Obviously, they meant business. The junior officers, chiefs, and leading petty officers sat around the remaining tables, equally cluttered with laptops, but still with enough room for mugs of coffee. The big-screen monitor was filled with the Gantt chart for the overhaul. Edwards stood and watched as he sipped his own coffee. The Engineer was already well into walking them all through the pre-overhaul testing phase, going over each step in detail.

Edwards leaned back against the bulkhead. This meeting was going to take a while.

Otanga was just getting into the intricacies of establishing plant conditions for switch gear testing when Jackson Biddle stepped up next to Edwards and handed him the message boards. He whispered, "Skipper, you need to read the top message."

Edwards flipped up the cover on the clipboard and scanned the page. His face broke out in a grin. This final trip might be quite interesting after all.

"XO, looks like we're going to have to miss our Caribbean cruise." That pronouncement interrupted the Engineer's scintillating presentation. Everyone's face turned toward Edwards as he grabbed the phone from a nearby bulkhead. "Officer-of-the-Deck, come to course south and ahead flank. And have the Navigator meet me in the control room. We're about to go someplace we've never been before!"

2

The rickety old bus belched black smoke as it labored up the steep mountain slope. It seemed all it could manage to do was just make it to the rocky, windswept summit of the Paso de Jama. The wheezing vehicle's slow crawl was leading to a traffic jam of impatient long-haul truckers lined up behind it along the narrow two-lane road. It finally lurched to a halt at the highest point of the pass, alongside a small tin shed that supposedly guarded the border between Chile and the Jujuy Province of Argentina. The high Altiplano desert stretched out below them in every direction. An endless sea of brown rocks and dust was alleviated only by far-distant snow-capped peaks.

A couple of Argentine border guards lazily checked the passengers' papers while the Chilean border guards lounged in the late afternoon shade. The passengers on the bus, mostly peasants and laborers in area mines, sat stolidly as the guards riffled through their documents. This was all little more than a formality. Still, both the passengers and the guards played out their parts as expected so it would be only the shortest of a delay.

Meanwhile, Thomas Jefferson Dillon, sitting in a window seat halfway back, passed the time by peering out through the dust-coated window at a bleak, brown landscape. There was not a hint of green or growing thing in any direction as far as he could see. Nothing except the green sign protruding from the rocks near the roadway that warned in Spanish: *Danger! Minefield!* Among other things, TJ Dillon was a retired US Navy SEAL, and his training required that he put such a dire and unexpected threat into context and assess how or if it might pose a risk to him or his mission. He decided it likely did not. The sign, and any potential landmines buried out there in the rubble, were probably left over from some of the many border skirmishes that Chile and Argentina had periodically participated in over the years.

Nowadays, Dillon was an operative for the US Central Intelligence Agency. And although the burly gringo did not fit in with the rest of the bus's passengers, the border guards did not seem to be any more interested in him than they were with anyone else on the bus. They were seeing more gringos these days, come to work in the region's thriving mining industry.

The stop at the checkpoint lasted five minutes. Then the bus continued a much easier part of the journey down the barren slopes into Jama, the tiny red-brick village waiting for their next stop at the base of the pass.

Off in the distance, Dillon could now see a most unexpected sight. There were broad expanses of blue water glistening in the bright sunshine. He knew these were the evaporative ponds for the lithium salts that had suddenly made this piece of remote real estate very important to the rest of the world. Over a third of the world's lithium, a crucial ingredient in electric vehicle batteries, was now being extracted from these mountains, and their apparently vast reserves promised a whole lot more. Promised fabulous wealth and potentially endless power for those who controlled the source of this soft, silvery metal.

The bus pulled over at a small truck stop and diner on the edge of Jama and parked among a collection of big rigs of all types. The passengers stood stiffly and piled off, then shuffled inside to find a meal. They knew that not getting off at Jama would mean several more hours on the road before the next small town. In the high Altiplano desert, it was best to eat at any opportunity in which food was available.

Dillon grabbed his knapsack and blended in with his fellow passengers as they made their way into the surprisingly shiny, clean diner. The room was full of truckers grabbing a late lunch before heading out on the road again. The aroma of freshly cooked food was almost overpowering. But TJ Dillon was not there for the food.

The moment he stepped inside, he quickly assayed the diner's customers. He spied four men sharing a table in the far corner of the dining room, drinking coffee and loudly discussing the previous night's Argentine national soccer team's narrow loss to some Middle Eastern country. Dillon knew the men could not have cared less about soccer. They were simply doing what a table full of truck drivers at an out-of-the-way restaurant would likely be doing so as not to stand out amid the other customers.

He also knew them only by their first names: Mateo, Felipe, Liam, and Ciro. They were probably cover names anyway. And their faces he knew only from photos he had studied at length. They were all in-country operatives for the Central Intelligence Agency. And they were expecting the American bus passenger.

TJ Dillon walked over, dropped his knapsack on the floor, grabbed a chair from another table, shoved it into an open spot, and sat down.

"That Julio! He could not kick a ball into the Pacific Ocean if he stood on the beach!" Dillon said, in perfectly accented Spanish. "No World Cup for us this time, I'm afraid."

As he spoke, he slid a photo across the table. It was a picture of an older man dressed as a local miner. Dillon lowered his voice and checked to be sure no one else was close enough to hear him.

"This is our target. He uses the name Manuel Viscosa now, but he is actually Josh Kirkland. Kirkland was once one of our agents, but he has long since gone bad. He and I crossed swords up in Venezuela a few years ago in a particularly nasty situation. He escaped and promptly went to ground. Deep underground. He has recently surfaced here and has set himself up as the local strongman, using some of his contacts from before and some especially deadly tactics. We want to take him alive, if possible. We can backtrack his contacts and probably take down a whole bunch of bad hombres. If we must, though, we'll do the world a big favor by taking him out."

Dillon glanced around the room. It still did not appear that anyone was giving them any special attention. The five men could still have been discussing the soccer match.

"So, if he is so well protected, how are we to locate and take him?" Liam asked.

"Kirkland—or Viscosa—normally stays close to home, down near San Salvador de Jujuy," Dillon explained. "He has a hacienda just outside town. He has it set up like a fortress, with some really sophisticated security technology and lots of hired help. Drugs don't have the kind of profits he is looking for anymore. He's gotten into mining lithium. Or at least taking advantage of those who do. Real tough nut to crack. But my intel is that he is heading up here, coming our way. He is supposed to meet and then ride along with some shipment that is important enough for him to slither out of his hole and come inspect the cargo himself. That shipment is supposed to clear the border tonight."

Felipe shook his head. "How are we supposed to sort one truck out of all the ones that cross the border here? Señor Dillon, this particular border crossing is far enough away from Santiago and Buenos Aires to make it very popular with anyone who wants to quietly cross the border. And all sorts of exotic cargo comes and goes through here all the time."

TJ Dillon smiled. "Felipe, that is exactly why Viscosa likes to use it. But this time, he is doing us a big favor. He is enough of an egotist to ship everything on his own Viscosa Trucking vehicles. You will not be able to miss the big red letters. *Viscosa Camionaje.*"

Mateo chimed in. "I'm guessing that just having the border guards nab him is not an option. And that is why you have invited us to the party."

TJ nodded. "You know the reason for that as well as I do. There is a real probability that the guards are on his payroll. And even if they are not, they are scared to death of him. That goes for patrols on both sides of the border. I don't think we can look for any help there. If they do get involved, their loyalty will be to Viscosa. Never doubt that."

He unfolded a small topo map and pointed to a spot about a mile from the border. There, the road made a sweeping curve so it was hidden from the border and made a sharp climb along the way, one that would slow any truck considerably. "I'm thinking that we throw a roadblock here and ambush Viscosa as he comes back with his haul so we can see what it is, too. That spot is far enough away and hidden enough that we should have our guy and be well clear before anyone is the wiser. You men bring the ordnance and comms gear?"

Felipe nodded. "Everything that you ordered is out in the pickup truck. M4s all around, Sigs for everyone, couple of AT-4s, a box of flash-bang grenades. We brought the intra-squad Rifleman Radios you asked for, too."

TJ stood and grabbed his knapsack. "Good. Let's roll. We need to be in place before it gets too dark."

The sun was falling below the mountains to the west when the group piled into the pickup and headed back up toward Paso de Jama. They found a narrow dirt road—really more of a goat path—that snaked upward and away from the highway. They hid the pickup there before climbing the slope to set an ambush a little higher up. Dillon sent Ciro further up the road to act as a scout and did a quick test with the new Rifleman Radios.

Then there was nothing else to do but remain hidden as they watched a steady stream of truck lights plying the narrow highway in both directions, up and down the mountain. It was well after midnight and the traffic had dropped to just the sporadic trucker trying to make up some time on the route when Ciro's voice crackled on Dillon's radio. A big rig with bright red *Viscosa Camionaje* stenciled on the side of the trailer had just cleared the border crossing and was barreling down the road in their direction.

Felipe and Mateo rushed out to throw a pair of spike strips across the highway before diving into the ditch and then scurrying back up a gulley. They had barely returned to their hide-holes when the approaching big rig's lights stabbed the darkness as it came around the corner and down-shifted to begin the turn and steep climb.

The truck hit the spike strips square on. They immediately shredded all eighteen of the vehicle's tires. The driver, caught unawares by the calamity, had his hands full bringing the rig to a stop without flipping it over the edge or oversteering and jackknifing.

But there was more than just the driver in the vehicle. As soon as the truck skidded to a smoky stop, four gunmen jumped down out of the cab. A wave of memory and anger flooded over Dillon as he caught a quick glimpse of Josh Kirkland directing his henchmen. It was like reliving that wild night in the Venezuelan jungle all over again.

Dillon also knew this was finally his chance for retribution. Before he could draw a bead on Kirkland, the man dropped and rolled beneath the truck trailer and then swung open the huge rear door. A dozen more gunmen jumped out, moving out in a well-ordered sweep, setting up a protective cordon around the truck. The simple ambush had suddenly developed all the makings of a desperate gunbattle. And Viscosa's men appeared both well-trained and well-armed for a skirmish. Intel had been flawed. Dillon expected only Viscosa, his driver, and maybe one shooter.

Dillon knew he had no choice but to rely on his own quartet of fighters. They had come highly recommended. He was about to find out if they were up to the task.

Just down the hill from Dillon, Felipe took aim with one of the AT4 shoulder-launched anti-tank weapons. The rocket arched across the narrow gap and slammed into the truck trailer. Its explosion rent the darkness, lighting up the night and reverberating against the mountainside like trapped thunder. The fire turned night into day on the lower slopes.

However, Viscosa's gunmen now had a point of aim. They sprayed the slopes with automatic weapon fire. The first burst chopped down Felipe, who had not had time to move. The other men ducked behind rocks to escape the lethal barrage.

Dillon's SEAL training kicked into high gear. He fired a three-shot burst, dropping one gunner, and then immediately scooted cross-slope before taking a second shot. Another quick burst, then he crawled down the hill another twenty feet. He kept looking for Kirkland, but the man had seemingly disappeared, probably under cover behind the burning truck or hiding in the black smoke.

Capturing the bastard was no longer his goal. Finding and killing him would signify success now. With only three of his shooters left, and one of them still in place as lookout back up the road, Dillon knew he was outmanned and had little time left.

Then Ciro called again over the radio. "Boss, we got company coming. The border guard is all ganged up and heading your way."

Damn! That was not what Dillon needed. Another dozen or so shooters rushing in to join an already very uneven gunfight. And there was no doubt whose side they would take. It was time to hightail it out of here. He keyed his throat mike.

"Guys, it's time to beat feet. Take Felipe with you if you can. Map shows a dirt road crossing five clicks due east. Muster there tomorrow evening, 2200 hours. *Buena suerte.*"

Dillon turned and scurried back up the slope, cursing himself the whole way. Last time they had tangled, it had been Kirkland who had scampered away, his tail between his legs, desperate for a place to hide.

This time, TJ Dillon was the one doing the skedaddling, running for his life.

Ψ

ETCM Dennis Oshley carried a quizzical look on his face as he stepped out of the chief's quarters. As *George Mason*'s Chief of the Boat, the grizzled old submariner thought that he had seen every trick a young sailor could pull, but this was a new one. He held up the special request chit and quickly scanned it again, just to make sure he was reading it right. He clearly needed to bring the submarine's Executive Officer in on this one. He could only hope the XO would not choke on it.

Oshley knocked on the XO's door and stepped inside. Jackson Biddle did not bother to look up from the pile of paperwork that covered his desk. Some of it spilled over to his bunk, and still more littered the deck.

"Hey, COB, whatcha got?" Biddle asked, eyes still on his pile of work. But he could somehow intuit the chief's puzzled expression and knew something was up. "I don't like that look on your face. It says this is going lead to my day going seriously sideways."

Oshley did not say a word. He just handed the request chit to Biddle. The exec gave it a quick read, tossed it on his desk, shook his head, and chuckled. "He can't be serious. Never heard of anything like it."

The COB shook his head. "XO, I'm afraid he is. It's the new 'Silent Service,' for sure. But I checked Navy Regs. There isn't any rule that prohibits it. Just the opposite, in fact."

"Well, get Petty Officer Rivera up here," Biddle grunted. "And might just as well get Petty Officer Roth, too. Let's hear what they have to say and how serious they are about this."

Machinist Mate Third Class Enrique Rivera was a young nuclear machinist mate from El Paso, Texas. He showed up outside the XO's door moments later, wiping grease from his hands with a dirty rag. His poopie suit was streaked with sweat and oil. He stood at attention as he knocked on the door.

Just as Rivera entered, Sonar Technician Third Class Julie Roth arrived. She was a shy young sailor from Newark, Delaware, serving her time as a mess crank.

She stepped into the XO's tiny stateroom and stood there next to Rivera. The COB did not miss the quick squeeze that Rivera gave Roth's hand as they waited, both still at attention.

Biddle picked up Rivera's request chit and waved it at the two. "Relax. Petty Officer Rivera, Petty Officer Roth, are you two serious about this?"

Roth blushed, but Rivera stood tall and forcefully exclaimed, "Yes, sir! Absolutely serious, sir. We've been dating for over a year now, ever since we met at sub school. We've been planning a wedding for a couple of months."

Roth nodded in agreement. "A couple of months," she confirmed.

Biddle shook his head, his brow furrowed. "What gives? Why now? And why this way?"

"Well, XO, here's the thing," Rivera explained. "If you remember our original schedule, we were supposed to be pulling in to Fort Lauderdale right about now. We had everything set up to get married there. Both our families were flying in for the ceremony. Then we both had a week's leave approved for the honeymoon. We had a stay booked in the Bahamas. We were going to meet the boat when it pulled into Portsmouth. But then everything got botched up with our new orders and our plans went out the window." Rivera and Roth looked at each other and smiled. "So, I did a little research. The skipper has the authority to marry us. We just want to keep the original wedding date we had planned. Which is tomorrow."

Biddle looked over at the COB. Now it was the XO who had the quizzical look on his face. Oshley cleared his throat and answered the unasked question. "He's right, XO. I went through the regs myself. This is all new stuff, as you can imagine. The only thing I found on the subject was in the MILPERS Manual. It says there that if they get married while they are both on the same afloat command, one of them has to transfer off the boat at the earliest opportunity. That's probably when we get to the shipyard."

Biddle pushed away from his desk and stood, scratching his head. "Alright, let's talk to the skipper. We'll see if he's ready to get in the marryin' business." He then looked directly at the couple. "But listen, regs or not, there ain't gonna be any consummation until you are back in port. You hear me? Roth, you stay in women's berthing and Rivera, you stay hot-bunking in the torpedo room. Got that?"

Rivera's eyes widened. "Sir, we've been real careful not to do anything onboard that ain't allowed. But I need to let you know that the consummation ship has sailed."

Roth blushed. "I think I'm about two months pregnant. That's why the wedding date is so important, sir. Both of our families are pretty old-fashioned about such things."

"Okay," Biddle said, shaking his head. "Let us talk with the skipper and get back to you."

Once the two young petty officers had left the XO's stateroom and headed back to work, Brian Edwards stepped out of the head that the CO and XO shared. As usual, the doors to their staterooms had been left open so that they could freely converse. The captain had heard the whole episode.

"Now, that was an interesting conversation," Edwards said with a chuckle. "I can't wait to hear what you two are recommending?"

The COB spoke first. "Well, Skipper, far as I can tell, it's a case of 'there ain't no rule against it.' But do we really want to go there? I can hear all the wisecracks about *George Mason* being the 'Love Boat.'"

Biddle added, "As close as I can tell from the regs, it's your call. Not a lot of precedent has been set yet, but you know it's coming. We do have time to call back to Pearl and get a JAG read-out. We can't be too careful in today's PC environment."

Edwards stroked his chin for a moment. Then he said, "They are a couple of good kids. Good sub sailors, too. I'm inclined to do the wedding. But I agree not to rush into this. XO, draft up a message to SUBPAC outlining the situation. Close it with: UNODIR I will proceed with performing the ceremony."

"And make an honest couple out of 'em, as we say back in Alabama," Biddle added.

"Yeah, honest couple," Edwards said as he ducked back into his stateroom. "Next thing you know, I'll be doing baptisms and funerals. Not a bris, though. I draw the line there."

3

President Cristiano Souza sat back, rubbed his eyes with both fists, and stretched his aching muscles. The chief executive of Brazil had been in meetings almost nonstop with Argentine President Bruno Valentino Martinez and Chinese Special Ambassador Plenipotentiary Nian Huhu De for more than two weeks. Serious, history-altering meetings. Such intense discussions had been physically and mentally demanding, but in the opinion of both presidents and the ambassador, quite fruitful. Now they all agreed that it was time to get back to their respective offices. After all, they did have nations to run. Nian had disappeared the day before, slipping back to Brasília and then onto an aircraft to Beijing. Souza and Martinez were enjoying one final meeting without the Chinese ambassador being involved with every action.

First, they would finalize and sign mutual agreements. Ones the CCP was not—so far as the presidents knew—aware of. Then they would set in motion steps that would reverberate around the world, especially in financial circles.

"*Meu amigo*," Souza said as he rose and stepped over to the bar to pour himself a glass of Brazilian wine. It was his favorite, the Pizzato DNA 99 Merlot.

"Bruno, may I pour you a glass of my country's finest?" he asked.

"Yes, thank you, though I note you do not have an Argentinian Malbec in your collection," Martinez answered, but with a smile. "You know we are the leading exporter of wine in South America, *sí*?

"Only because you have reminded me multiple times over the last few days, my friend," Souza shot back, sipping the wine and smacking his lips. "But now, we must no longer compare such things, as we are truly allies. This has been a very productive time. We have laid the groundwork for a mutually beneficial partnership between our countries that will finally enable us to compete against the so-called economic powers of the world. Let us solidify our agreement. That should require, maybe, some kind of letter or something."

Martinez smiled and took the wine glass Souza handed him. "Indeed, it has been productive, *mi amigo*. But I suggest that now is the time for action rather than more words. Words that could and likely will be used against us. We must coordinate our efforts and strike suddenly, before the *yanqui* bankers have any opportunity to react."

Souza nodded. Once again, Martinez had cut to the heart of the matter. Moves that would be this revolutionary must be accomplished swiftly and surely. "Yes, we will let them squeal like stuck pigs. By the time they begin to squeal, we will have set in motion these reforms to finally benefit our people, not the world's greedy nations and their predatory bankers and robber barons. I will instruct my people to be ready in one week." Souza held his glass of wine aloft, stood at attention, and proposed a toast. "To our mutual success and profit."

Martinez took a sip, then offered his own salute. "And, of course, to the prosperity of our nations and their long-suffering people!"

"Yes! Yes, of course. To the people," Souza replied, turning up the wine glass and drinking thirstily.

Ψ

President Stan Smitherman slammed the briefing book on the desk so hard that it skittered off and fell onto the floor, scattering papers all over the carpet of the Oval Office.

As they typically did, both Vice President Harold Osterman and Secretary of State Sandra Dosetti ignored the outburst and simply slid another copy of the briefing book onto the desk of the president of the United States. Smitherman's volatile outbursts were nothing new to either of them.

"What do those SOBs think they're pulling off down there?" Smitherman ranted, red-faced, pounding the desk with the heels of both hands. "It's a damn coup, a conspiracy, that's what the SOBs are trying to pull off," he spluttered. "Hell! I don't even know the right word to use! Can they really do something like this cow pucky?"

Sandra Dosetti, widely regarded as the "Secretary of State for Wall Street"—both from her career background and, lately, from her policies and actions as her nation's chief diplomat—leafed through her own copy of the briefing book. Then she pointed at each as she ticked off the entries.

"Issuing their own currency while simultaneously declaring the old official currencies null and void. Yes, that falls pretty much within the definition of the rights of a sovereign state. They can make dirt and gravel their currency if they want to. There are a whole lot of countries that have done something similar, but nobody nearly as important as Brazil and Argentina. The part about only allowing citizens to convert their old currency into this new"—she looked for the word on one of the pages—"*inútil* ... it's a bit of a stretch legally, ethically, and just about every other which way. But who's going to fight them over it, and where?"

"But Sandra," Vice President Osterman interjected, "what about this whole thing where they have declared they are nationalizing all foreign investments in Brazil and Argentina? Bad news for a bunch of our companies, I'd say. That hasn't happened since the communists took over in China and then Cuba. A bit with the oil companies in Venezuela, but not *every* foreign investment."

Dosetti held up her hand. "Harold, you are making my point for me. Actually, those are not the only examples since way back then. The precedence is there. Nobody's gone to war over it, though I'm sure there have been some stockholders and C-level executives getting paid in stock options who would have liked to murder a dictator or two. And as far as defaulting on national debt, Brazil and Argentina are past masters at that art."

President Smitherman was clearly growing even more frustrated. He groaned and slammed his fist on the arm of his chair. "Enough with the damned history lesson. I don't give a hill of beans for precedence. What are we going to do now about this crap those bastards are trying to pull down there?"

Dosetti cleared her throat before answering. "In the good old days, we would simply send this to the International Monetary Fund and the World Court. The international banks would block them from messing with international financing and stop any fund transfers. They would not be allowed to transfer these *inútils* for dollars, and that would make international trade impossible for them."

She paused for a second. Dosetti knew the boss would not like the "but" she was about to share. "But I'm afraid that ship has sailed. With all the trade sanctions slapped on various nations over the last several years, there is a whole community of countries that have left the dollar-denominated marketplace. China, Iran, and Russia are some of the major players."

Smitherman stared at the chandelier, then quietly said, "It sounds like our only option is to send in the Marines."

Ψ

The sun was just peeking over the horizon, painting the eastern sky in a spectacular kaleidoscope of reds and oranges. Jim Ward sat up in bed and smiled as he watched the show for a moment. Then he looked over at his new wife. Even with her hair mussed, she rivaled the beauty on display out the large window of their suite. He eased out of bed, careful not to wake her. Honeymooning at the Cauayan Island Resort, just off Palawan Island's northwestern shore, had been Li Min's idea. It was perfect. Their private thatched-roof bungalow looked out onto a pristine white-sand beach and turquoise blue water, a real-life image straight off a tourism poster, stretching all the way out to the horizon.

Ward stood at the window for a moment, smiling. They had not come up for air nearly enough yet to enjoy the spectacular view.

He glanced back at Li. She slept soundly. Ward quietly slipped on his swim trunks. He figured there was plenty of time for him to get in a couple-of-mile swim before he would have to finally put on clothes and keep a necessary appointment, heading over the short stretch of water to Palawan where he would meet up with the SEAL team he commanded. At least when he was not off getting hitched to and honeymooning with the woman he loved.

When he and Li had decided to get married, the young SEAL had stumbled onto the perfect boondoggle. In reality, it was more of a wedding present from his commanding officer. Conveniently, the Philippine Navy had requested some operational training from the US Navy for their own Naval Special Operations Command. Also conveniently, it just happened that their training grounds were on Palawan. And the window for the exercises nicely coincided with the last couple of weeks of Ward's honeymoon. That was how it happened that he was here as a guest of the Philippine Navy. It was even more fortuitous when Ward considered that this time, his dad—who just happened to be Admiral Jon Ward, Director of Naval Intelligence back at the Pentagon—had nothing to do with any of it.

Still, sweet as the deal was, he did have to leave Li for a few days to go crawl through some swamps with a bunch of other sweaty guys. But he suspected his new wife had a few duties of her own she would need to attend to. Her rather shadowy connections within the highest government echelons of the People's Republic of China required constant but very careful attention. And she was also a crucial clandestine operative for the Taiwanese government and, by extension, the USA. Jim and his father were two of the few in the world who knew about her unique position.

The seawater was bathtub warm, but the exercise felt good. He stretched out and assumed a long, rhythmic stroke, making good time. It was a mile up to Caverna Island, then another mile back. No strain for a Navy SEAL in top physical condition. Ward gave himself forty-five minutes to make the circuit. That allowed a little time to duck and dive to admire the colorful reef life that populated the brilliant coral beneath him.

The sun was well up, promising another warm, tropical day when he padded back into the bungalow, still dripping water. Li Min threw a towel at him in mock anger.

"Don't you dare track sand in here, frog boy," she growled, but could not avoid a laugh when she saw the look on his face. "Get in the shower and then take me somewhere for a great breakfast. I'm starving."

"Shower? You just want to see me naked." Ward retrieved the towel and swatted her with it. "Besides, you need to watch what you eat. I'm not having a fat *mama-san* for a wife."

Wards' cell phone buzzed but he first had to dodge the pillow she hurled his way with remarkably good aim. It was too early for his ride over to Palawan to be calling. A telemarketer, way out here? He was about to let it go to voicemail when he picked up the offending device and looked at the caller ID.

Bill Beaman.

Damn! Bill Beaman was his old CO in the teams and still one of his best friends, though they hardly ever got to see each other anymore. Bill had long since retired to purchase and run a bar on Exuma, in the Bahamas, catering to locals, former military, and an assortment of sketchy characters who all seemed to have stepped right out of a Jimmy Buffet song. At least he was a bar proprietor when he was not being called upon by various three-letter US government agencies. Sometimes for advice. Sometimes for something a bit more hazardous.

"Bill, if I owe you money, I ain't here. Please leave a message at the tone. Beep!"

"That the way you answer your phone when your oldest and best buddy calls to congratulate you on finally making an honest woman out of that girl of yours?" Beaman growled.

"Aw, man, you know it's great to hear from you," Ward shot back. "I think."

"I'm just checkin' to see if she's filed for divorce yet," Beaman said. "You finally found a girl that's blind to your many faults and still passes muster with your momma. That makes you the luckiest son of a bitch in the US Navy."

"Yeah, I'll admit it wasn't easy," Ward retorted. "Particularly with the lowlifes like you that I normally associate with. They'd scare off any normal girl. Fortunately for all of us, Li Min is far from normal. And we've been in a few skirmishes together, so she's seen me at my best and my worst."

"And remember, she knows how to kill you five different ways with a butter knife and shoestring," Beaman said with a laugh, then obviously shifted gears to a serious conversation. "Jim, you remember our old friend, TJ Dillon?"

"Yeah, sure. Thomas Jefferson Dillon. Former SEAL gone to doing underground work for fun and profit. Our paths have crossed a couple of times. What's that reprobate up to now? Probably still chasing that bastard double agent that got away from us down in Venezuela? I distinctly remember watching him paddling like mad down some Amazon tributary yelling what he was going to do with the traitor when he finally caught him."

Beaman replied, "Yeah, and oddly enough, that's why I'm calling. I remember that night very well. Josh Kirkland. That was the CIA guy who went rogue and was the one that got away from all of us. Which is damned embarrassing on its own. Well, TJ Dillon is one determined individual, I tell you. He has finally found Kirkland and he needs some help to bring him in this time."

"What I know about TJ, he must be desperate to ask for help."

"What I know about TJ, he just wants to be damn sure we get Kirkland this time and that we learn what that scumbag knows about the bunch of bad dudes in South America he's been freelancing for."

"Okay, so we're the cavalry riding to the rescue and trying to corral an over-aged, over-achieving rotten spook?" Ward asked. "When and where?"

"It seems that Kirkland has reinvented himself as a local strongman up in the Argentine Altiplano. And the people he's cozy with are way, way up the food chain. Not just druggies. Just about as mean but with far more fire-power than your usual coca smuggler. Kirkland's going by the name Manuel Viscosa now. The CIA—who has no love at all for this dude—has asked SOCOM for help taking him down. SOCOM is authorizing an off-books op to go in and take down Kirkland or Viscosa or whatever his name is."

"And I assume this off-books op somehow requires the services of a recently wed SEAL commander," Ward said, ignoring the frown on Li Min's face. "And a postponement of the stellar training we were about to give the good men of the Philippines navy."

"Damn perceptive, there, Commander," Beaman told him. "Sorry to alter your plans. Your team will have to teach the Philippine boys how to shoot straight without you. There are two first-class tickets waiting for you at Puerto Princesa Airport that'll get you and the new missus to Manila and then nonstop back to LAX. We'll meet up at WARCOM on Coronado in a couple of days," Beaman told him. "Really, Jim, I'm sorry to have to cut your honeymoon short. But there's lots more to this than grabbing some old turncoat and sending him off to jail."

"Sounds like your retirement is getting hosed pretty good, too." Ward laughed humorlessly. "Double-B, it ain't me that you need to apologize to. I suspect that Li Min will need more than a drink or two to forgive you."

"Tell her I'm sorry."

"Don't know if that'll work or not. Just remember, she knows how to kill you five different ways with a butter knife and a shoestring."

4

Capitán de Fragata Colas Lopez Alveras stood in the control room of his submarine, the ARN *Santiago del Estero*, and proudly observed his crew as they worked. A couple of weeks spent conducting exercises with the Brazilian Navy while the presidents of the two countries held their secret meetings had ultimately been a tremendous experience for the crew of the Argentine vessel. The learning curve had been very steep, the operations demanding and fatiguing, but Alveras was convinced he now commanded not only the most advanced, but also the best-trained submarine crew in all of his country's navy. He was also confident they would be ready to take on even the *norteamericanos* should they foolishly venture into Argentine waters. And from what his president and high-ranking members of the Brazilian Navy had told him, he was now convinced that was a real possibility.

Alveras watched as his navigation team plotted the latest GPS fix. They had made good time thanks to the warm southerly-flowing waters of the Brazil Current pushing them at an extra three to four knots, like a tailwind shoving an aircraft faster through the sky. But then things changed. That current met up with the northward-flowing Malvinas Current when they were off the mouth of the Río de la Plata. The chilly Malvinas Current brought waters up straight from the Antarctic. Now it was pushing back at them—like a headwind—at a couple of knots.

Alveras shook his head as he studied the plot. The current was unusually strong for this time of year. At this rate, it was going to delay their arrival home by several hours. Several hours later than what he had promised his president.

Speak of the devil.

"Our little sea cruise is about over, eh, *Capitán*?" Bruno Martinez asked as he strode into the control room. "I trust that we remain on schedule to still arrive in Mar del Plata by morning."

"*Señor Presidente*," Alveras snapped to attention and, despite his best effort, stuttered as he replied. "I regret to report . . . uh . . . that the sea currents are stronger than we anticipated. Our current ETA is tomorrow afternoon, about fifteen hundred local time."

Martinez shook his head and smiled. "That, of course, will not do. We must arrive by first light. I have important announcements to make and they must be precisely coordinated with President Souza and his own critical public pronouncements. You will make certain that we arrive at the time you have promised."

It was Alveras's turn to shake his head. "Sir, the only way we can do that is to surface and run at a flank bell all night. The meteorological report is unfortunately forecasting a major storm in this area for most of the evening. It will not bother us at depth, but it would be dangerously rough and very cold if we run on the surface. And that would be the only way to achieve sufficient speed to meet your schedule."

Martinez was not swayed. Again, he smiled. "Captain, sometimes comfort must be sacrificed. Please do what you must to arrive on time." The president turned and left the control room.

Alveras shut his eyes for a moment, then opened them again and gave the order to his watch officer. "Jose, surface the ship. Come to ahead flank. I will be in my stateroom putting on my foul-weather gear."

The submarine CO was just stepping into his puffy, bright orange, foul-weather suit when he heard the series of orders and felt the *Santiago del Estero* angling upward toward the surface. Almost immediately the round-bottomed submarine commenced to roll heavily, wallowing in the rough seas. Alveras was slammed against the outboard bulkhead and then, before he could recover his balance, he was thrown even harder against his stateroom door. By the time he had the suit zippered up and had grabbed his binoculars and gloves, he'd gathered what he knew would soon be several more brand-new bruises.

The captain made the long climb up the sail trunk to the bridge only to be slapped right in the face by a chilly wave as he emerged into the dim evening light. Yes, it was going to be a long, cold, miserable night.

The sun was setting to the west, partially hidden by low, scudding clouds driven to the north by the brisk wind from the polar south. The seas were running at three to four meters, Alveras estimated, two points off the port bow. Every third or fourth wave would break over the sail, burying him and the hapless lookout standing beside him in a deluge of ice water.

"Captain, Navigator," the bridge box blared. "Making turns for twenty-two knots. Plot shows nineteen knots made good—" The rest of the communication was lost as another wave broke over the sail, threatening to wash both Alveras and the lookout overboard and into the sea. When he sputtered and wiped water from his eyes, he could see the lookout dangling over the side of the bridge enclosure, held only by his safety harness. It took every ounce of the captain's strength to pull the young, wide-eyed sailor back into the bridge cockpit.

Alveras came to the realization that it just was not safe to have anyone on the bridge in this kind of weather. Someone was certain to be badly injured or worse. Ultimately, as CO, he was responsible for keeping his crew safe, just as he was responsible for accomplishing his mission. They would have to secure the bridge and depend on the periscope and radar if they were to safely race through the night. Reluctantly, he sent the lookout below and then followed him off the bridge, shutting and dogging the hatch before he dropped down into the control room.

Alveras did not even bother to remove his sodden foul-weather suit as he plopped down on a stool and gripped a stanchion to avoid being thrown across the room by the boat's constant pitching and rolling. He watched as more and more of his crew succumbed to seasickness and then exhaustion. But at least the submarine continued to race through the night toward their destination. If the waves did not damage them somehow, and if they managed not to collide with anything else dumb enough to be out braving this storm, they might just make it on time.

When dawn broke, the beaten, battered crew and the *Santiago del Estero* were at the mouth of the harbor of the Mar del Plata. The winds and seas had subsided with the rising sun, but the leaden sky promised the inevitability of more foul weather. *Capitán de Fragata* Colas Lopez Alveras was near utter exhaustion. He had spent the entire night leading his crew and struggling to keep them safe as they were bruised by the raging seas. Now it was time for him to make one more climb to the bridge and guide his boat until it came safely alongside the pier. Then he could finally rest.

Alveras barely remembered steering the *Santiago del Estero* into the harbor or the tugs pushing them firmly up next to the pier. From the bridge, he saluted *Presidente* Martinez as his country's leader, fresh from a night tucked snuggly in his bed, walked stiffly toward the brow to depart the ship.

"Fine work, *Capitán!*" the president said as he reached the brow, turned, and snapped off a sharp return salute. "I will make certain that someday the history books recognize you and your crew, and your brave and skillful contribution to the change in the world order."

But by then, the submarine's CO had fallen asleep, slumped in a heap over the bridge railing.

Ψ

"Fire in the galley! Fire in the galley!" The 1MC blasted out the urgent alarm.

Brian Edwards was shaken from a sound sleep by the announcement. As he leaped from his rack, the *bong! bong! bong!* of the general alarm began stridently sounding throughout the *George Mason*.

"Fire in the galley! Rig ship for fire! Fire in the deep-fat fryer!"

Fire! The most feared hazard for submariners, even ahead of flooding. The danger of a fire itself was bad enough, but just a small blaze could create enough smoke and deadly fumes to be a killer if the boat could not be quickly brought up near the surface and the toxic smoke vented overboard.

It took Edwards less than ten seconds to jump into his poopie suit, grab his EAB—his emergency air breather device—and dash to the control room. The air outside his stateroom was already heavy with the acrid smell of burning cooking oil. He pulled his EAB down over his face and plugged the air hose into a bulkhead-mounted fitting. He sucked in a couple of quick breaths then unplugged the hose and dashed to the next fitting to plug in again. A couple more breaths there, then on to the next one. By the time he got to the control room, the air was thick with dense, black smoke, hanging there like an oily fog. He could barely see the watch standers in the space.

The captain had to rely on memory as he felt his way across the control room until he found the command console. He called out, "Officer-of-the-Deck, what is the situation?"

Through the smoke, he heard Jeff Otanga's voice. "Skipper, we had a 4MC report of a fire in the deep fat fryer in the galley. No status on the fire yet. XO is laying to the scene. The fire main is pressurized. We've come up to one-five-zero feet, clearing baffles, ready to proceed to periscope depth. No sonar contacts."

"Thanks, Eng," Edwards grunted as he grabbed the 1MC mike and ordered, "Scene, report status of the fire."

There was a slight pause and then over the 4MC, he heard, "Conn, mess decks, torpedo room fire hose is working the fire." Jackson Biddle's voice was muffled by his own EAB. The exec took in a breath and then added, "Engine room firehose is back up. Three injured people."

Edwards frowned. Some of his people were hurt. And the fire was still burning.

Then, a few very long seconds later, Biddle reported, "The fire is out. No hotspots on the thermal imager. Zero visibility down here, though. We need to emergency ventilate before we overhaul the fire."

Brian Edwards knew the next part would be dangerous. Not as bad as a fire, but more people could still get hurt. Even at one hundred and fifty feet, he could feel the boat pitching and rolling with the waves above them. That meant when they got to periscope depth—the depth at which they could begin ventilating the smoke overboard—they would probably be facing state-five or state-six seas and experiencing wave heights of anywhere from ten to twenty feet. With everybody on board pretty much blinded by the thick smoke and their breathing apparatuses, and with heavy damage-control equipment strewn about all over the decks, it was a risky situation. And the hot oil in the deep fat fryer could easily splash out on someone, or worse, reignite.

But there was no other way. They had to get rid of all this smoke, even if only to make certain the fire was really extinguished.

Edwards grabbed the 1MC mike. "Heads up everyone," he announced. "We are proceeding to periscope depth to emergency ventilate. As you can feel, it's rough up topside. Find some place to hang on tight and don't let go unless you have to. And if you do, be damn careful." He released the push-to-talk button on the mike and turned to Jeff Otanga. "Officer-of-the-Deck, proceed to periscope depth and emergency ventilate the ship."

Otanga looked toward the ship control station, but all he could see was a wall of smoke. He called out, "Pilot, make your depth six-two feet. Emergency ventilate the ship. Raising number two photonics mast."

Chief Jason Schmidt, the pilot, repeated back the command. "Proceed to periscope depth and emergency ventilate, aye." Turning to Stanley Dewlap, the co-pilot, he quietly told him, "Hang on, Stan. This could be one hell of a ride."

Schmidt punched in the ordered depth of six-two feet on the ship control computer. He had to put his face right up against the screen to be able to see it. Normally, he would just sit back and let the computer guide the ship up automatically. But this was not normal. This time, he kept his hand firmly on the control stick, just in case the heaving, roiling seas were more than the computer programmers bargained for when they built the depth control algorithm.

"One-five-zero feet coming to six-two feet," Schmidt called out as the *George Mason* started its ascent. He used his shirt sleeve to wipe the smudges off the readout so he could see it. "One-four-zero coming to six-two . . . one-three-five . . . one-three-zero feet." At the whim of the waves on the surface, the submarine's nose was pitching up and down by at least twenty degrees. At the same time, the big vessel was rolling back and forth, port and starboard, by about the same amount.

"One-one-zero feet coming to six-two," Chief Schmidt yelled. The corkscrewing pitch and roll were becoming noticeably more violent, like a huge bucking bull. Everyone held onto something solid for support. Then, something heavy, something unseen but obviously not tied down, crashed hard into a panel.

Edwards winced. Hoped nobody was in the way.

Schmidt felt more than saw the depth control computer lock into the stops. As he had feared, the pitching ocean waves were too much for the software to control.

"Loss of automatic depth control!" he yelled. "Controlling in manual." His eyes on the panel, he alternately shoved and yanked on the stick, attempting to anticipate what the seas were going to throw at him next and what he could do with his ship's controls to counter the punches.

"Officer-of-the-Deck, I need speed," the pilot called out. The heavy seas were thrusting the sub to the surface. More speed was the only way to keep control. Otherwise, they could be broached, and that would leave them totally at the mercy of the ocean.

Jeff Otanga ordered, "Ahead standard, Chief. That's the most the snorkel mast will handle." If they went any faster, there was the danger of damaging the snorkel, a tube that would allow the smoke to be vented to the sea surface and clean air to be taken in.

"Yes, sir," Schmidt answered. "We may go flying anyway. Eight-four feet, coming to six-two."

Stan Dewlap's fingers danced across his control panel as if he was playing some exotic keyboard musical instrument. "Ship is prepared to emergency ventilate with the exception of draining and raising the snorkel mast."

"Depth six-two feet."

They were there, and it was an even rougher ride than anticipated. They could hear dishes and other objects crashing to the deck, and the grunts and groans of men in the control room who had long since begun suffering from seasickness.

Jeff Otanga quickly but carefully scanned the horizon with the photonics mast and the large screen display before he announced, "No close contacts." At least they had this section of southern sea all to themselves.

"Raise the snorkel mast and emergency ventilate the ship," Otanga ordered.

"Snorkel mast coming up," Dewlap confirmed. "Starting the low-pressure blower."

To a man, they felt their ears pop as the air pressure inside the submarine equalized with that outside, just above the surface of the ocean. Then they could feel the cold breeze as the main induction fan sucked in the clean-but-damp outside air while the low-pressure blower—really a big fan—shoved the nasty smoke and bad air out the exhaust mast. Soon enough the smoke had cleared to the point where they could see the extent of the damage. Even so, the submarine was still pitching and rolling far too violently for anyone to turn loose and do anything but stay safely secured.

After a bruising half hour of ventilating, the atmosphere inside *George Mason* was back to near normal. That is, except for the stench of burnt cooking oil that permeated everything and the oily sheen on every surface. Finally, the submarine was able to drop down to a much calmer two hundred feet and the damage assessment could begin.

A sweat-soaked Jackson Biddle, still wiping streaks of greasy soot off his face, walked into control, shaking his head. "Damn, I don't want to go through that again. The galley is trashed, Captain. The Chop and the COB are checking everything out. Figure we'll be living on cold cuts for a few days." The XO took a deep breath before continuing. "We got three injured people. Cookie and Svenson are down with smoke inhalation. Doc has them on oxygen and thinks they'll be okay."

The "Chop" was the boat's Supply Officer.

"You said three," Edwards said.

"Yeah, I know," Biddle replied. "Petty Officer Roth . . . I mean Rivera, now, since you married them and . . . well, she was 'mess cranking' when the fire broke out. Evidently the APC system didn't automatically function. She had to manually initiate it. In the process, she got burned pretty bad, but she still stuck around and discharged two cannisters of AFFF fire extinguishers before she was evacuated. From what I saw, if she hadn't done what she did, that fire would have been a whole lot worse."

"Mess cranking" meant she was helping to prepare and clear meals in the submarine's galley. The APC system was a specialized piece of fire protection equipment installed over a deep fat fryer designed to trip in the event of a grease fire, spraying the fryer with a layer of aqueous potassium carbonate that reacted with the grease, forming a thick "soap" layer that smothered the blaze. If it failed to trip automatically, it could be manually deployed.

"Wow!" Edwards muttered. "How is she?"

"We moved her to the wardroom. She's breathing but in a lot of pain. Doc has her sedated right now for the pain. And on oxygen," the XO reported. "He's checking to see if there are any other complications. She breathed in a lot of bad air. Skipper, we're going to need to MEDEVAC her."

Edwards nodded. "Yeah, let me figure out where the nearest port is that can handle a MEDEVAC. You and the COB go find Petty Officer Rivera and sit down with him. He's going to be upset with this. I'll go to the wardroom and see how she's doing."

Edwards stepped into what was normally the *George Mason*'s wardroom. The officer's dining room and lounge had been transformed into an emergency operating room. The Supply Officer, Ensign Jason Wordle, and the COB were laying out medical equipment on the small buffet. They looked up and nodded as the skipper entered.

The patient lay on the operating table under bright operating room lights rigged into the overhead. An IV was strung up, dripping saline solution into her arm while an oxygen mask forced life-giving O2 into her lungs. The Corpsman, "Doc" Scott, looked up from his examination as Edwards entered. He had been cutting away the burnt, charred remnants of her poopie suit, revealing bright red, heavily blistered skin underneath.

"How's she doing?" Edwards asked

Doc Scott shook his head. "Near as I can tell so far, third-degree burns to her hands and forearms. Looks like she got hit with a good bit of grease splatter. Burns to her face, anterior scalp, anterior torso. Some small burns to her anterior thighs. No surprise she was in a lot of pain. I'm surprised you didn't hear the screaming in control. I put two milligrams of morphine into her IV on a slow drip to help with the pain." He gestured toward the patient. "That seemed to cut the edge off pretty well."

Doc stepped back from the table, over to where the Chop and COB stood with Edwards. In a low voice, so that the patient, even in her drugged state, could not overhear anything, he said, "Skipper, what I am really worried about is her lungs. I don't know how much smoke or superheated air she breathed, so I don't know what damage there is. No way of telling, except to wait. And fluid loss is the other problem. The IV will help with that. She is in serious trouble. We could lose her or the baby if we don't get her to a real hospital real quick."

The CO had forgotten about the baby. *Hell of a way to spend a honeymoon*, Edwards thought as he headed back to the control room.

And a hell of a way to start a very mysterious new mission, too.

5

Guillermo Manuelito was in a real bind. The banks were demanding immediate repayment on the previous year's crop loans—even before the olives were ready for harvest and sale—and they were refusing to lend him a single peso to fund this year's crops. He owed only a few thousand pesos, but it might as well have been millions. He had no way to pay it. He had no money, at least not in Argentina, and he was being denied travel to where he could withdraw what he had saved. The banks were demanding payment immediately or they would be forced to foreclose.

He looked out over his beloved olive grove. God had been good. His trees were heavy with fruit. In a few months, he could easily repay the loans, but the banks were not giving him a few months. He had only until the end of the week to make payment in full and in the new currency, those *inútils* that President Martinez had unleashed on Argentina the previous week. Guillermo had no *inútils* and could see no way to get any. He and his family would lose La Granja, the modest acreage that the Manuelitos had farmed for five generations.

He opened the glovebox of his truck and took out the passbook for his account at the Banco Santander, the largest bank in Uruguay and arguably the safest financial institution in all of South America. He and his family had scrimped and saved over the years until they held almost forty million

Uruguayan pesos, a million US dollars at the current exchange rate. But now, with the border closed and foreign exchange in *inútils* considered a crime, that money might just as well be in a crater on the moon, not a couple of hundred kilometers away, on the other side of the border with Uruguay.

Manuelito tossed the passbook back into the glovebox, slammed its door shut, and smacked the steering wheel in frustration. He started the worn-out engine and headed down the road in a cloud of dust and smoke.

He had risen early after tossing and turning for most of the night, plagued by nightmares of his family joining those homeless hordes he had seen trudging down the Camino Real del Peru toward Buenos Aires in search of nonexistent hope. That alone had effectively prevented restful sleep.

But so too had the intrusive thoughts of a previous life. A life he had been determined to leave behind forever, regardless how skilled he had once been at the tasks it required him to master. The life of a conscripted soldier. But a life conflicted by his sworn allegiance to his country and his commanders, even if, in his opinion, few along the way deserved such blind and bloody loyalty. He had been a rebellious teenager when he was drafted, only too happy to leave his father's firm hand of discipline and the hard work in the groves behind. He had been surprised at how quickly he had taken to the military training; at just how much the violence appealed to him; at how easily he had picked up every nuance of combat. In fact, it had frightened him. That was why he was perfectly willing to go back home when the mandatory service program ended.

No, he would never regret stepping away from the lure of that life, he had long since declared to himself. To his wife. To God.

But now, here he was.

The dusty country road delivered Guillermo Manuelito to the equally dusty small *pueblo* of Cepeda. The farming community, barely more than a cluster of adobe farmsteads alongside the road, was surrounded by grain fields for kilometers in every direction. It was so quiet that dogs walked lazily down the middle of the dirt streets in search of shade and scraps of food while children played made-up games with no concern for the occasional vehicle that might pass through.

Manuelito steered his old flatbed into the gravel parking lot behind a battered brick building. The faded sign at the entrance read *Casa de la Reunión Sociedad Italiana*. A dust-covered Toyota pickup was parked under a big ceiba tree at the back of the structure. It was the only other vehicle in the lot. The tree's huge, spreading canopy shaded the truck and effectively hid it from observation.

Manuelito parked his own vehicle beneath the tree and quickly jumped into the passenger seat of the Toyota. Ricardo Balduino sat there in the driver's seat, calmly smoking a cigarette. Manuelito knew the man was a high operative—maybe even the top leader—in a shadowy resistance group. Some called it the *Movimiento de Resistencia*, or just the MDR. Having given up on the corrupt ballot box in frustration, his organization was determined to stop—violently, if necessary—what they saw as the destructive direction of the current government. And Balduino was one of the men with whom Manuelito had served during his brief army term. The only one who had kept in touch with him over all these years.

Balduino looked sideways at him through the smoke for a long moment without speaking. Then he reached beneath his seat, retrieved something, and tossed it to Manuelito. It was a pistol, a Browning Hi-Power 9mm, the same pistol the Argentine Army had issued him all those years ago. Manuelito caught it with one hand, instinctively slid back the action, and dropped the magazine into his other hand.

"You know the *pistola*?" Balduino asked. "Are you still any good with such a weapon, Guillermo? Or have your talents been lost after digging in the dirt for so long?"

Manuelito grunted as he expertly slid the magazine back home and engaged the safety catch. The single-action pistol was now double-safed, with both the catch engaged and the hammer down.

He laid the weapon in his lap and then answered. "It has been many years. The last time I shot one was during our *servicio military obligartoria* and I was a much younger man then. I learned to do many things in a short period of time then, as you well know, Ricardo." Manuelito smiled ruefully. "They taught us much, including how to aim and fire these weapons for maximum benefit and minimum waste of ordnance. I suspect they were constantly preparing us for our military's next coup. But then, the next year, it was all gone. They changed the law and removed the compulsory service requirement and I was back, as you say, digging in the dirt again. But they were good at teaching us. Some of us learned well."

"Let us hope that is the case," Balduino said, flipping his cigarette butt out the truck window. "And now you tell me that you are finally disheartened enough over *El Presidente* and his policies to put some of that long-ago training to good use, right?" Without awaiting an answer, he shoved the vehicle's shifter into gear and shot out of the parking lot, leaving a thick cloud of dust.

The pistol still on his lap, Manuelito held onto the door handle as Balduino slewed the old Toyota down a maze of dirt roads that bisected even more grain fields and the occasional small orchard. Nobody even gave the two farmers in the dirt-caked pickup a second glance. Balduino did not speak for the entire ride. By the time they approached the outskirts of the city of Rosario, the sun had followed its arc to a spot low on the western horizon.

Only then did Balduino slow, turning into the entrance of a ramshackle woodlot just south of town. A high wooden gate swung closed behind the Toyota. Manuelito could see that they were in a lot stacked high with wooden pallets, and that their truck was invisible from the street. Several semi-trailers were in various stages of being loaded with still more pallets, but there were no people to be seen. A pole shed with a rusty tin roof covered the machinery used for manufacturing the pallets out of raw logs. One corner of the area was filled with a tall stack of logs, waiting to be sawed, planed, and cut to length.

Balduino parked beside two nondescript gray panel vans. As he opened the door of his truck, five men spilled from the vans. Manuelito exited and shoved the pistol into his belt, easily accessible if he needed it. Balduino did not offer any introductions. It was obvious, though, that these were his men, more members of the MDR. It was best not to know names.

Balduino waited for them to join him at the tailgate of his truck, then spent a few minutes cryptically outlining their evening's mission. Without asking for questions, he motioned for them that it was time to be on their way. They all piled into the two vans and, at a leisurely pace to avoid any risk of attracting attention, headed down the road that led into the main business area of Rosario.

None of the men said a word as Manuelito sat on the floor in the windowless back of one vehicle. From there, he could just see out the bug-specked windshield. He was soon lost in the confusing and unfamiliar maze of city streets, with stoplights at every corner and heavy traffic. They passed through areas with many modern buildings and urban sprawl. Then through what looked to be industrial areas, bumpy streets lined with factories. He knew he could never find his way back to the lot and Balduino's pickup.

After more turns and twists than he could count, the two vans pulled up to a gate in a chain link fence that surrounded an industrial-looking brick building. Signs on the fence informed the world that this was the property of the Municipal Bank of Rosario. They carried the obligatory emphatic warnings that the area inside the fence was private property and that trespassers would lose all future birthdays. This gate was for shipping and receiving. It would only be open during normal business hours. Banking hours. And even then, only by previous arrangement. Visitors should use the main entrance on Arturo Illia Calle.

Manuelito was mystified. The building did not look like any bank he had ever seen. The neighborhood was an industrial area built up alongside a train yard and a shipping terminal on the Paraná River. Nothing looked like bank real estate, designed to impress depositors and borrowers. This place appeared to be a factory with an adjoining warehouse.

Balduino saw the confusion in Manuelito's eyes. "Do not worry, my friend," he said with a rare chuckle. "We are not knocking over a bank, as those *yanqui* gangsters love to say in the movies. This is nothing more than a printing facility. It is here that our beloved President Martinez and his minions are printing batches and batches of those hateful *inútils*. They are running a load of them inside there at this moment. Our job today is to destroy the presses and burn the building down to show them they cannot simply print worthless money and ruin the lives of so many of the people of our nation, all for their own personal benefit. It will only be a meager blow for the MDR, but hopefully it will be enough to show Martinez how the people feel and let him know we are willing and able to rise up and resist. As you will soon see, they do not anticipate any pushback from the people."

Bolt cutters made quick work of the lock. The gate swung open. Surprisingly, there were no guards or alarms. The two vehicles pulled inside the fence and toward the loading docks. Manuelito saw that several vans, very similar to the ones in which they were riding, were backed up to the loading docks and had their rear doors open to accept cargo. They appeared to be almost full already.

As the armed MDR fighters jumped from their own vehicles and rushed across the dock, the men who had been busily loading the other vans disappeared inside the building in panic. Manuelito and the rest of Balduino's team, carrying cans of gasoline, entered the structure and quickly spread out, then began pouring the fuel over flammable material and setting it afire. In such a large print shop, it was not difficult at all finding something easily ignited. In a matter of minutes, flames filled the building. Smoke and fire alarms were clamoring. Mayhem dutifully initiated, it was now time to depart, before the firefighters and police arrived.

As they rushed out the plant's big doorway and onto the loading dock, Manuelito pointed to the cargo vans still sitting with their back doors agape. "That is a gift that we cannot ignore," he shouted to Balduino.

Balduino smiled and nodded vigorously. "So, we knock over a bank after all! You take one of the vans. We'll grab the others. Hide the van on your farm. Keep the *inútils* and use them to help you solve your dilemma. We will contact you in a couple of days and arrange to get your truck to you. Follow closely, and we will lead you to a place where you will recognize your location. You have done well, my friend."

"I only spilled some cans of petrol."

"But by doing so, you have sent a strong message." Balduino snapped off a quick salute.

The procession of vans departed through the open gate at a leisurely pace and then turned through a maze of narrow streets that would eventually lead them toward the harbor freeway. They could see the flashing lights and hear the sirens behind them as they blended in with heavy traffic.

Guillermo Manuelito was almost within sight of his precious olive groves before he realized that the Browning 9mm was still stuffed into the belt at his right side, still easily accessible. Thankfully, it remained unused. But its presence confirmed for him that, ready or not, he had now taken a sharp turn down a new and dangerous road.

A road that would lead him to challenge those who in their evil quest for fortune and unbridled power would so brutally trample on the freedoms of the Argentinian people.

Ψ

The pilot made an announcement for passengers to check that all seat belts were fastened. The twelve-hour flight from LAX to Arturo Merino Benitez International Airport in Santiago, Chile, was finally reaching its destination. Commander Jim Ward stretched his back as he moved to restow his laptop beneath the seat in front of him, then looked out the window as the cabin attendant cleared away his cup of coffee. The big Boeing 787-9 Dreamliner swung inland, leaving the Pacific Ocean behind. They were passing over Chile's rugged, mountainous interior as the pilot dropped below the early-morning clouds. The high peaks of the Andes were still well to their east, but the ground below looked plenty steep and rugged to Ward.

Bill Beaman sprawled in the seat next to him, still quietly snoring, just as he had for most of the flight. Ward shook his head in wonder at how the retired SEAL could sleep through an entire flight, especially one as protracted as this one had been. At least Beaman would land in Santiago well rested.

Ward was surprised at just how great it was to be back on a mission with his former commander. Despite how clandestine and quirky this off-the-books operation was turning out, it was one that would put them back on the job together, way up in the Altiplano. Ward was also decidedly worried about what they might be about to face. That was the primary reason he had not been able to sleep on this red-eye flight. The mission had all the feel of a hurried pickup game. The "other agency" briefs in Coronado lacked a lot of detail. Not because they were unwilling to share. It was because they had little to tell them. And contingency planning was nil. Zilch. Nada.

To top it off, the assigned team had been pretty much slapped together quickly from people in San Diego who just happened to be nearby and available. Ward's normal team was still busy in Palawan, training the Philippine Special Forces, so he'd had to get shooters from SEAL Team Three and then run through some hurried exercises to try to gauge their skills and personalities. Sometimes personalities were more crucial than actual shooter skills.

At least they had a little time working together before real ordnance might start flying. The four shooters he chose were good, of course. Ward expected no less. But until things got dicey, he would not know for certain if they were up to the same standards as his own guys. Guys like Skip Cantrell or Tony Martinelli. He would soon find out. And that was what had him gazing out the window all night, watching the scudding clouds and the moon highlighting whitecaps on the ocean far below him.

Ward heard and felt the flaps lower as the plane came in on its final approach. He looked over just as the noise and bump caused Bill Beaman's eyes to pop open. The older SEAL stretched, smiled, and said as coherently as if he had been awake for hours, "Well, kid, it's just like old times, heh?"

"Yep," Ward shot back. "Pretty much. You sleep while I do all the work."

"Aw, come on kid," Beaman responded. "You know rank hath its privilege." Beaman chuckled as he pulled his seat to the upright position.

"Yeah, and your rank, old man, is officially civilian."

"An old man who can beat you up the side of any mountain you choose, whippersnapper," Beaman harrumphed. "Besides, we've usually entered new territory in far worse modes of transportation than business class, right?"

The jet's wheels kissed the runway. The pair were thrown into their seat belts as the big plane decelerated and then turned sharply onto a taxiway and proceeded toward the terminal. Traveling in business class at taxpayer expense did have its perks. One was being among the first to deplane. Ward gathered the rest of their team—Chief Billy Joe Hurt, together with SEALs Don Winston, Chuck Jones, and Gene LaCroix, had been scattered in seats farther back in the aircraft—as they came out of the jetway and then headed toward customs. They were traveling light, with only their laptops and what personal items they could stuff in a backpack. Their more "interesting" gear was in a shipping box down in the cargo hold. The box carried the Seal of the United States and was boldly marked as a diplomatic pouch. That meant it was exempt from inspection by customs or anybody else.

The six men walked down the concourse and through a maze of passages until they arrived at the large customs hall. If asked, they were in the country for hiking and fishing and visiting the usual sightseeing spots. They pulled out their tourist passports and were ready. Then they saw the long lines already forming at the only three open stations and steeled themselves for a long, long wait.

"Excuse me." A young man dressed in a short-sleeved sport shirt and khakis stepped up to the new arrivals. "I believe you are Mr. Ward and party? I'm Alston Jonas from the US embassy. Welcome to the longest and skinniest country on the planet. If you will follow me, we can skip all . . . this." Jonas waved toward the unending lines at the customs stations. He motioned for them to follow him out a side door, where he waved a plastic card at a guard, and then on through baggage claim and out of the terminal. A van conveniently awaited them at the curb.

As they pulled away, Alston turned and said, "Once again, welcome to Chile. Everything here is on Chilean time. It's only 0830 local and no one will be at the embassy before ten-hundred hours. I've taken the liberty of arranging a light breakfast for us at a little café that I know while we wait. I think you will enjoy it."

"What about our gear?" Chief Billy Joe Hurt was the team member asking. Hurt was the senior enlisted SEAL on this op. Hailing from the hills above the Tennessee River Valley near Huntsville, Alabama, he spoke with a heavy drawl. But Jim Ward already knew his speech was probably the only slow thing about him. With ten years' experience in the teams and several major missions under his belt, this was his first op as the senior enlisted operator. A bout of appendicitis had taken him away from his assigned team, but he was fully recovered, waiting to sync up with his team and go back to work. That made him conveniently available for Ward's rushed job.

"No worries. It's being delivered to the embassy," Jonas answered, looking at his watch. "It'll be there when we get there. I have a couple of people watching it the whole way. As I said, we're on Chilean time now. It'll take just a bit."

The van swung into traffic and smoothly merged onto Avenida Américo Vespucio. The modern freeway that formed an almost perfect circle around Santiago sped them to the other side of town despite the morning commuter traffic. Thirty minutes later, they pulled to the curb in front of a nicely appointed little pastry shop on a quiet, shaded street. As they walked up, they saw that two of the outside tables were situated away from the others and roped off, with a sign that read *Reservado*.

"Señor Jonas," the waiter called out. "I see your friends have arrived. Your tables await you." He waved the party over to the reserved tables.

"Mateo, *gracias*, perfect as always," Alston Jonas said as they all took seats. "Has Diego made *alfajores* this morning?"

"Indeed," Mateo answered quickly. "They are just coming out of the oven as we speak. Light and delicious, as always."

"A plateful for each of my friends," Alston Jonas told him. "And coffee all around. The way I taught you to brew it, not that awful Nescafe you serve the *turistas*." He laughed and waved at the other guests inside. The tables were mostly full. "Chileans prefer tea. They don't really drink coffee. They serve the tourists instant coffee. I had to teach Mateo how to brew real coffee and I even supplied him with the proper beans. Now he offers the best cup in all of Santiago."

Beaman looked across the table. "This is not the first time you have eaten here." What he was really asking was, you know and trust these folks not to be curious about a group of muscled young Americans taking breakfast with an official of the US embassy?

In a much lower voice, Alston answered, "You could say that, Captain. I frequently bring people here for discussions when I know they don't particularly want to be overheard or seen at the embassy. Mateo is to be trusted. Now, to business. TJ Dillon has messaged us. He will meet you in the little village of Socaire and update you on the...the situation. It is up in the Atacama Desert and about a fifty-mile drive from the Argentine border. We'll fly you and your gear up to Calama, the nearest town with an airport, this evening. Then you will have to drive down to Socaire. Let me warn you about driving across the Atacama. It is the driest desert in the world. There are places there that have never received rain. Ever. At least not since there have been people there. Pack plenty of water and be ready for anything. If you break down up there, it's a very real chance that you will die."

Alston had just finished speaking when Mateo arrived with a tray filled with steaming hot pastries, cups, and a couple of carafes of dark coffee. He put the tray down and presented the pastries with a flourish. "Señores, *alfajores* as you will only find in Santiago. A biscuit so light that we have difficulty preventing them from floating away. They are filled with *dulce de leche* so sweet you will think you are in heaven. And Señor Alston's own preferred coffee, of course. *Disfruta su comida.*"

And enjoy the meal they did. But Ward and Beaman kept exchanging glances over the rims of their coffee cups as the embassy man sounded more and more like a tour guide, jabbering on about this and that. For the most part, the SEALs ate, listened, and then ate some more of the signature pastries.

One thing was certain. This mission was growing odder and odder.

6

The *George Mason* rocked in the now much gentler sea swell near the surface of the Pacific as they took on message traffic and once again ventilated the ship. The smoky odor of burnt cooking oil was slowly dissipating as the sub drew in the fresh sea air, but the lingering stench remained. Replacing bad air with good inside the ship would help, but it would never totally remove the smell. That would not happen until they got back to port and could remove all bedding, clothing, and anything else that had absorbed the greasy smoke from the galley fire.

Dennis Oshley, *George Mason*'s Chief of the Boat, rapped on Jackson Biddle's door. In answer to the grunted "Enter," Oshley and the ship's Corpsman, "Doc" Henry Scott, stepped into the crowded stateroom.

The XO looked up from his pile of paperwork and promptly asked, "How are the patients?"

Doc nodded and answered, "Cooky and Svenson are fine. I restored them to full duty this morning. I'm concerned about Roth-Rivera. Her hands and arms were badly burned. I'm putting fluid in through the IV as much as I can, but she seems to be losing it through the burns and her lungs as fast as I put it in. Her urine output is still way below what it should be. We need to MEDEVAC her real soon."

"Doc, we're doing the best we can on that." Biddle tapped the screen on his computer. "We're waiting for SUBLANT to get back to us with all the arrangements. You got to realize that we are not exactly in a part of the world that is heavily trafficked by the US Navy." Biddle chewed his lip for a moment. "And what about the baby?"

Doc shook his head. "Well, that's the other problem. I've reduced her pain meds as much as I can while still keeping her comfortable. I've moved her from morphine to Demerol through her IV, but at a dose that only keeps the edge off her pain. And burns are about the most painful injury anybody can have." Now it was Doc Scott's turn to chew on his lip while the XO waited. "Look, pregnant women are not exactly my area of expertise here. Never got mentioned at the Undersea Medical Institute training in Groton. I really need a doctor to help out."

"You have all your questions ready if we get one on the line?" Biddle asked.

Doc nodded. "I'll admit, it sure would be helpful if we could come up on chat with the SUBLANT Medical Officer to get some advice."

"Well, let's go talk to the boss about it," Biddle said as he rose from his chair.

Dennis Oshley spoke up. "Before we do that, we need to talk about MM3 Rivera. You know, the husband."

Biddle nodded. "Yeah, I reckon so. How's he taking all this?"

"Well, the kid is pretty shook up," the COB answered, "as you might expect. Really concerned about his wife but damned determined to not let it get in the way of his standing watch. Right now, he's alternating between spending every minute with her and standing his watches back aft. He won't even consider coming off the watch bill, even though every sailor back there has volunteered to spell him. The kid hasn't slept since the fire."

Biddle stared down at his hands. "Damn! What are we going to do about him when we MEDEVAC her?"

The COB answered, "I'm recommending that we send him off, too. I spoke with the Eng. He's good with Rivera being . . . I guess that would be a HUMEVAC."

The COB hesitated for a moment. He obviously had something else he wanted to discuss but was struggling with how to approach it. Finally, he just blurted out, "XO, we have a real problem. We found out why the APC didn't trip. Someone had replaced the fusible link with a piece of wire. It looks like someone was purposely gun-decking the maintenance in the galley." He let that accusation sink in for a second before he went on. "And it looks like there was a lot of grease buildup and flammable material around the deep fat fryer. That's why the fire kept burning so hot even after Roth-Rivera tripped the APC."

Biddle shook his head. "What do the Chop and Cookie say?"

The COB shot back, "I'm afraid the Chop is so new and wet-behind-the-ears that he parrots whatever Cookie says. Cookie is saying that that area is Svenson's responsibility."

"Those are some pretty serious accusations," Biddle replied. "We're going to need a JAG Manual investigation, I'm afraid." He pushed back his chair and stood. "Let's go talk to the skipper."

The three stepped out to the control room where Brian Edwards sat, half-watching the crew as he perused the incoming message traffic on the command console. He looked up when he noticed the team marching across to where he was. And the serious expressions on their faces.

"Well, XO, you finally freed yourself from that wall of admin?" he asked with a chuckle.

"Admin-o-rama, I call it," the XO confirmed. "Sure as hell a lot of paperwork in the submarining business."

"Got a bit of good news, though," the skipper said. "Looks like we might have a galley back by morning. The Eng just reported that the electricians have rewired the controller for the dough mixer and the ovens are back up. Once they clear all the grounds on the electrical systems and the crew finishes field-daying the galley, we should be good to go. I don't know about you, but I'm way past tired of cold cuts for every meal. Though something tells me you guys are not here to discuss bologna sandwich recipes."

Biddle smiled. "Looking forward to pizza night tomorrow. But Doc here needs to come up on chat with SUBLANT medical. He needs some specialized advice for Roth-Rivera. And we need to talk about a MEDEVAC."

Edwards brightened. "News on the MEDEVAC just came in. The Chilean Navy—God bless 'em—will be sending out a ship to rendezvous with us. Lucky for us they have an LPD reasonably nearby." LPD stood for landing platform dock, a vessel primarily intended to transfer troops as part of an amphibious operation. "We'll meet up with them off Tierra del Fuego. They conveniently have a hospital facility onboard and a helo that can fly Roth-Rivera back to Punta Arenas. Gonna take us two days to get there. Now, let's get Doc up on chat so he can learn a little bit in the meantime about the female of the species."

Biddle maneuvered Edwards over to the side and quietly said, "Skipper, we're going to need a JAG Manual investigation on the fire and its cause. I'm going to appoint the Nav as the Investigating Officer."

Edwards, rubbing his chin, looked at Biddle for a few seconds. Then he asked, "XO, is there something about this fire that I don't know about?"

"Yes, sir. I have good reason to think there is. But I suggest we let the Nav find out for sure."

Ψ

Josh Kirkland—aka Manuel Viscosa—was in a deeply reflective mood as he rested in the expansive courtyard of his impressive hacienda. The shade of a tangerine tree shielded him from the harshest rays of a subtropical sun. The sweet citrusy aroma from the tree's star-shaped white blossoms filled the air, wafted about by a cooling mountain breeze. Nearby, a small stone fountain that was strategically placed in the center of the courtyard added a playful tinkling sound of falling water to the scene. This place was his usual sanctuary from the high-stakes tension he often encountered in the risky but lucrative path he had chosen for himself.

But today, Kirkland was not enjoying the relaxing setting at all. He was lost in thought, a mixture of worry and planning playing through his mind as he nursed a bottle of his preferred beverage, a Quilmes beer. It was not the only time he had found himself in a quandary about the next direction he should take. The first had come after he had risen into the higher ranks of the Central Intelligence Agency, chasing a long-held, clear-eyed goal of serving his country and the cause of freedom. Then, slowly, he'd realized the obvious. If he continued his path and lived through the journey, he would retire one day with a wall filled with plaques and a meager government pension, but with a world even more dangerous than it had been when he first joined the CIA.

That wasn't enough for him. He chose a different, darker path. One that offered him far more power, riches, and influence, but one that was the polar opposite to his original course. He found he was much more suited to it than he ever imagined, and that it actually held even more power, riches, and influence than he could have dreamed.

The risks were also more pronounced than he had anticipated, even with his experience in such things. The ambush near the Paso de Jama border crossing was a perfect example. The episode played over and over again in his mind like a bad movie. Especially one particular image, the fleeting glimpse of one shooter scurrying across the rocks, making his getaway. The face was all too familiar. An operative Kirkland had himself recruited out of retirement to serve the agency but who eventually came close to cutting short the former CIA man's new career path. It had culminated in another eerily similar mountaintop battle, that one in the Venezuelan jungle.

He took a long draw on the cold beer. Those were memories better forgotten. He was not surprised that TJ Dillon was still out there. And only mildly surprised that the bastard was still trying to chase down his old boss. That tenacity was one trait that had convinced Kirkland to bring the former SEAL to the CIA in the first place, for legitimate and worthy work. Now Dillon and his strong traits were coming back to bite Kirkland in the ass.

With Dillon involved, it was also not surprising that the ambush on Kirkland and his truck had been uncomfortably close to successful. No, it was more of a shock to Kirkland that he had managed to survive it. Dillon was that good. He rarely failed. Now he had—twice. And both times to Josh Kirkland's benefit. Odds were it would not happen a third time. He knew that he would need to take additional precautions to protect himself and to make efforts to eliminate that annoyingly persistent CIA operative once and for all. Especially now, when Kirkland was certain he was near the perfect setup in the perfect part of the world to cash in on all the years of scheming and skirting the law.

He finished the beer, barely tasting the pale gold brew. Even if he took out Dillon, the CIA was quite obviously too close for comfort. It was almost a sure thing that they would be able to track Kirkland down unless he solidified a buffer between him, his operation, and the Agency. The former agent decided that it was the time to utilize some of those deep tentacles he had so carefully established to burrow even farther into the Martinez government. He had done plenty to ingratiate himself with the president and his administration. Now that Martinez was making his big moves, solidifying his power, and striking deals with other nations who would assist in his lofty goals, Kirkland knew it was time to take his own advantage of the situation.

Yes, with the presence of Dillon and, by extension, the top US intelligence agency, the mantle of Argentina's new socialist government would afford him the cover and protection he required. It was time to exercise those carefully built relationships within the AFI—the *Agencia Federal de Inteligencia*—the arm of the Argentine government tasked with state security. He grabbed his cell phone from his shirt pocket and punched in a well-remembered number.

Juan Carlos Señorans answered on the second ring. "*Mi amigo querido, Señor Viscosa!* How may I be of service to you today?" Although he looked and sounded like the stereotypical oily politician, Señorans was anything but a benign public servant. Much as Kirkland had done in the CIA, the man had patiently, laboriously, and quite ruthlessly climbed up through the ranks of the old Secretariat of Intelligence, the infamous SIDE. When the terror and corruption of the SIDE finally became so notorious that it was necessarily disbanded, he jumped effortlessly and cleanly over to an even more advantageous position within the AFI.

Señorans literally knew where the bodies were buried, and he was blessed with both the complete lack of scruples and the *cojones* to leverage what he knew for his own nefarious benefit. Again, a resume strikingly similar to Josh Kirkland's.

The two men had first worked together in Kirkland's CIA days. Then, when Kirkland had the close call in Venezuela with TJ Dillon and eventually fled to Argentina, Señorans was the first person he turned to once he decided to establish his exile and begin building his new life and enterprise there. They quickly determined that both their styles and their business interests overlapped in what could be a mutually beneficial way. Kirkland/Viscosa's extralegal activities required top cover from the AFI. Señorans was glad to meet his needs in exchange for a share of the profits and the promise of future partnerships.

"*Mi amigo*, Juan Carlos," Manuel Viscosa began. "It has been too long since we have shared a beer. We must remedy that."

"Indeed, we must," Señorans answered, "but I am sure you are aware that I am saddled with considerable duties here in Buenos Aires lately while you enjoy the life of a leisurely *ranchero* up there in the peaceful mountains. But I agree. The next time you are in the city, we must have that beer and compare notes on our various adventures."

Viscosa chuckled. "That is just why I called. I find that it is necessary for me to come down out of the mountains. I want to discuss with you a particularly annoying gnat that requires swatting. There are also a few other items of mutual benefit that we should discuss. Do you have time on your calendar, say . . . tomorrow? I will fly down in time for a late lunch and an ice-cold beer at, say, three o'clock?"

There was only the slightest pause on the other end of the connection.

"For you, my friend, I will clear my calendar," Señorans answered.

Ψ

Brian Edwards brought the *George Mason* to the surface five miles off Isla Noir, the desolate and deserted island situated seventeen miles off the coast of Chile's Magallanes region in the very far south of that shoestring country. The submarine skipper scanned the dark, mountainous speck of land through the photonics mast video camera, but he could not discern a single sign of life there. Now he understood why a rough English translation of "Isla Noir" was "do not go there." It must have really looked foreboding to the seventeenth-century sailors trying to beat their way around Cape Horn. Even today's sailors were cautioned to stay well clear of its windblown and rugged, rocky cliffs.

Those same cliffs could serve a useful purpose today. They would provide a bit of a lee—a shield from the driving wind—that would make the perilous personnel transfer just a tiny bit safer for all involved.

Edwards zipped up his orange exposure suit, grabbed his binoculars, and made the long climb to the bridge. When he stuck his head above the bridge coaming, the wind promptly snatched his ball cap off his head and sent it sailing aft. There, it mixed with the waves that were churning over the submarine's main deck.

"Damn! Another perfectly good hat sacrificed to the sea gods," he ranted to no one in particular.

The wind and the waves were driving in directly from the west. Since South America extended farther south than either Australia or Africa, the water and sea had plenty of open ocean in which to gather tremendous power as they circled the world before slamming into the obstacle represented by the Chilean coast. Fortunately, on this day the waves out in the open water were only fifteen to twenty feet high and the wind was about thirty knots, nowhere near what they could be when a real blow kicked up.

"Eng," Edwards yelled to Jeff Ortega, even though the Officer-of-the-Deck stood right next to him on the bridge. "Get us in to about two miles off the beach. We'll need to snuggle up as close to those cliffs as we can."

"Captain, XO," The bridge box speaker blared. "In comms with the *Sargento Aldea*, the Chilean LPD, on channel sixteen. They're twenty miles north of Isla Noir. They just launched a helo, heading this way. Answers to Flight Six-Seven on channel sixteen. ETA ten minutes."

Edwards grabbed the mike and answered, "Roger. XO, contact Flight Six-Seven and tell them that this will be a transfer from the bridge. No way we could put anyone on deck in this weather. And XO, make sure Doc has the patient ready for transfer."

Edwards looked up and saw that the high rocky cliffs now seemed to be looming directly above them. They were not, of course, but it certainly felt as if the submarine was dangerously close to solid, unforgiving land. Before he could say anything, Jeff Ortega reported, "Skipper, two miles off the beach, coming to course two-zero-five to parallel the coast, dropping speed to ahead one-third."

They heard the roar of the Chilean Navy Cougar's twin turbines before they could see the helicopter rounding the eastern cape. Then the bridge-to-bridge radio crackled, "US Navy warship, this is Flight Six-Seven. How do you want to do this transfer? We have a doctor onboard, ready for your patient."

Edwards grabbed the bridge-to-bridge and answered, "Flight Six-Seven, this is US Navy warship. We will transfer from the bridge. Two passengers, one stretcher case, one in harness. On course two-zero-five, speed four. The wind is directly off the bow. All masts and antennas coming down. Request you lower your basket. We'll need to disconnect and take it below-decks to put the patient in."

Meanwhile, Ortega ordered all masts and antennas lowered, as promised, and then made sure that the crew was ready to conduct the transfer just the way they had drilled so many times before. The Chilean helicopter moved up alongside the sub, into a position where it was flying parallel to the bridge, but thirty feet off the port side. The side door slid open and a basket stretcher was lowered out until it dangled several feet below the bird. Slowly, continually adjusting for the wind, the pilot edged over until Edwards could reach up and grab the basket with the grounding rod. The electrical potential between the chopper and the submarine could be lethal, so the grounding rod was essential. The skipper and Ortega unshackled the basket and passed it down below. The Cougar then moved away to take station a few hundred yards away from the submarine.

It took the better part of ten minutes to securely strap the injured and sedated Julie Roth-Rivera into the basket stretcher and then hand her back up the trunk and finally to the bridge. A worried and nervous Enrique Rivera, already wearing a transfer harness, followed his new wife up the trunk.

Flight Six-Seven sidled back up to the *George Mason* until the helo was hovering directly above the submarine. Edwards grabbed the hook as it was lowered and immediately attached it to the stretcher. After checking to make sure it was secure, he signaled to the helicopter winch operator to raise it. The basket lifted away and swung in space as it was pulled up into the waiting helicopter. A couple of minutes later, it was Enrique Rivera's turn to be lifted away to join his wife on the hovering bird. They were still reeling him in as the Cougar turned north.

The bridge-to-bridge crackled again. "US Navy warship, Flight Six-Seven. Two pacs safely onboard. The doctor is with your patient now. He has directed us to fly to the Naval Hospital at Punta Arenas. She will be in the burn unit at Armed Forces Hospital Punta Arenas. *Buenaventura*. Flight Six-Seven out."

Edwards keyed the microphone. "Flight Six-Seven, very well done. *Muchas gracias*." He turned to Ortega and said, "Eng, come to course south and ahead full. And let's get back deep, where we damn well belong, as quick as we can." With that, the skipper dropped back down the ladder.

Twenty minutes later, the *George Mason* was at a depth of four hundred feet, heading southeast through the Drake Passage around Cape Horn at a flank bell. Even the world's most feared and roughest stretch of ocean was pleasantly calm beneath four hundred feet of seawater.

Now they could turn their thoughts to whatever it was that was so important that it had radically diverted their trip home.

7

The Argentinian Agencia Federal de Inteligencia was conveniently located just across Avenue Rivadavia from the Casa Rosada, the nation's famed pink presidential palace. The expansive office of Juan Carlos Señorans occupied the entire corner of the agency's fifth floor, overlooking the street below and the main entrance to the imposing edifice across the street. Josh Kirkland—who would only be known as Manuel Viscosa for the duration of this meeting—was dismayed by the open placement of the country's spy agency across the street from the palace. But he had to admit, the visual was impressive. And maybe the juxtaposition sent a thinly veiled message that the nation's chief executive and its intelligence organization operated closely and effectively.

Viscosa stood and stared out the window. He was so caught up in the vista he hardly noticed the door open behind him.

"Impressive view, yes?" Señorans said as he entered the office and stepped to the ornate sideboard that took up most of the wall at the back of the room. He quickly poured a drink and handed it to Viscosa. The amber liquid half-filled the Glencairn whiskey glass. "I seem to recall that you have a weakness for Scotch whiskey. I believe you will find this one suits your taste. It is a twenty-five-year-old Laphroaig."

Viscosa took the snifter and swirled it around before taking a deep sniff.

"You can positively smell the peat," he crooned. "A truly fine Islay Scotch." He took a taste, then noticed that Señorans had not yet joined him. "Are you not having one?"

Señorans smiled. "Manuel, my friend, your taste for fine Scotch only shows your *norteamericano* roots. For me, I find that Argentine whiskeys set much easier on my palate." He held up a bottle with a gold-lettered black label. "This La Alanza whiskey is Patagonia's finest. Much smoother than your peaty concoction."

The spy chief sat down in a deeply tufted red leather club chair and waved Viscosa to the matching sofa.

"Now, my friend, let us discuss business before we enjoy dinner this evening. I have reserved a private dining room at Don Julio's for us." Señorans sipped his whiskey, took time to savor it before swallowing, and then continued. "First, let us discuss this matter that so urgently brought you down from your mountain paradise. Then we can entertain a business proposition that I think will be exceedingly profitable for us both." He nodded for Viscosa to begin.

"Don Carlos, thank you for your willingness to see me on such short notice," Kirkland/Viscosa started. "In earlier meetings, I told you about some adventures from my previous life and how a certain three-letter agency from up north would seek to disturb my peaceful semiretirement here in your beautiful country." He sipped at his Scotch as he pointedly switched from history to current events. "A few weeks ago, we were moving some supplies across the border up at the Paso de Jama crossing. It is a quiet, out-of-the-way place, located high up in the Altiplano. The perfect place to attract very little interest from road pirates in a simple transport that was hauling machine tools from the port of Antofagasta to the mines up in the Altiplano."

Señorans snorted and shook his head. "Don Manuel, you, of all people, should not underestimate us. We are very aware of the weapons shipments that you have been smuggling into Argentina. We have some knowledge of the ambush up there. But are you saying that the American CIA, your old employer, conducted the ambush of your truck? That would be a major incursion into our country."

"Oh, there is no doubt the CIA was responsible for the ambush. That is not the worrisome part. The problem is the man I identified as the attack leader," Viscosa continued, leaning forward for emphasis. "He is a retired SEAL who I personally recruited back when I worked for the agency. His name is TJ Dillon, and he has taken it as his personal quest to end my freedom, my enterprise, and, I know, my very life if he can. He must be stopped, and I am asking you to give me top cover while I find and eliminate him."

Señorans nodded. "I will send a message through back channels to the *norteamericanos*. We will make it clear that clandestine CIA operations in our country are considered a hostile act and proper responses will be made if they do not cease immediately. The fact we know they have an operative working here should be enough to chill their efforts. If this Dillon persists, we will be only too happy to end his exploits down here, violently if necessary." He smiled and saluted with his almost-empty glass. "But listen, my friend. The proposition I have for you may take care of your little problem while at the same time making both of us very wealthy men."

Viscosa settled back. "I am listening. I am certainly interested in becoming more wealthy. Otherwise, I would have simply kept my humble government job in the USA and be drawing my pension by now."

"We want you to greatly expand your little operation as it pertains to the lithium business."

Señorans walked over to the sideboard, poured himself another snifter of whiskey, and refreshed Viscosa's, too, before continuing. He was well aware of the effect his mention of lithium would have on his guest. The former American spy remained quiet.

"As you know, that corner of Argentina, Bolivia, and Chile is called the 'lithium triangle.' Something like eighty percent of the world's lithium reserves are buried there, the greatest part of it in Bolivia. At this point, Bolivia barely mines any lithium at all, and Argentina hardly scratches the surface. But Chile—Chile is the world's second-largest producer of the mineral that has suddenly become so precious to electric vehicle battery manufacturers. Thanks to some new economic and trading partners, we have only recently received the necessary resources to greatly expand our production and assist Bolivia with theirs, if they are smart enough to allow us. My friend, I need for you to use your very special talents to stop the Chilean production of lithium cold while we ramp up and become the primary source. Can you imagine the strategic position we will be in if the world—and especially the nations in this hemisphere—have no choice but to come to us for this invaluable commodity?"

Viscosa smiled. "From what I hear, you already have an exclusive customer."

Ψ

Capitán de Fragata Colas Lopez Alveras marched into the Comando de la Fuerza de Submarinos headquarters and up the broad staircase to the admiral's conference room. After the guard checked his name off the list and swung the heavy door open, Alveras stepped into the room only to find it filled to near overflowing. There was one seat left available at the table. All of the strap-hanger seats along the walls were already occupied. He nodded to a few headquarters staffers who he recognized, and several officers that he knew to be the captains of the few warships in the Argentine Navy that could actually go to sea, should they be required to do so. However, most in the crowd were unfamiliar to him. Then he noted that all these strangers were dressed as civilians, including most of the people seated at the conference table.

When he greeted the civilian to his left with, "*Buen día, soy Colas Lopez Alveras,*" the stranger replied, in Portuguese, "*Bom dia, Capitão Alveras. Eu sou Capitão Bruno Ribeiro.*"

Alveras quickly concluded that the "civilians" in the room were in fact Brazilian Navy, probably dressed as civilians so as not to raise undue interest should someone notice so many Brazilian naval officers congregating in the Argentine submarine headquarters. That would surely raise a lot of unwanted interest, not only in the military of other countries in the region but in offices much farther north.

Before the two naval officers could start any conversation, the door to the admiral's office swung open. Someone called "Attention!" As everyone jumped to their feet, *Contralmirante* Pichi Espinoza, commander of the Argentine submarine fleet, marched briskly into the room, accompanied by another man dressed in civilian attire. As everyone settled back into their seats, Admiral Espinoza, speaking Spanish, the lingua franca for the room, introduced the man standing beside him.

"Gentlemen, I would like you to meet Vice Admiral Eduardo Barbosa of the Brazilian Navy. He will be commanding Task Force Southern Passage, the first of several joint operations between our two navies. Fellow warriors, our presidents have given us the chance to make history. We, Argentina and Brazil, will soon be asserting our strength to assume our rightful positions as economic and military leaders on our own continent. Certain of our neighbors, as well as the United States, will not be pleased, and we anticipate they will attempt to interfere with our future shipping routes. With this in mind, the task force's initial mission will be to restore the Straits of Magellan to Argentine rule for the first time since Chile illegally took possession of that vital region almost two centuries ago. I will now turn it over to Admiral Barbosa, who will further explain the operation."

Eduardo Barbosa stood and glanced around the room before he began to speak, also in Spanish, looking into the faces of those standing there. "Our plan is simple, and we believe it will be successful if properly executed. The men in this room will assure that is the case. Our combined fleet will force our way through the channel from the east, eliminating any resistance we might encounter. Meanwhile, the Argentine Army and Air Force will effectively cut traffic along the only two highways into the Magallanes region. At that point, we will finally have control over a major portion of the commerce that passes through, as we rightfully should. For too long, colonialists and the USA have tried to force their will on us. That will soon cease. We will finally control our rightful territorial waters."

An area map appeared on a large flat-panel display that occupied one wall of the room. A blue arrow sliced through the Straits while a pair of red ones swooped down from the Argentine border cut across the eastern plains at the southern tip of the South American continent.

"There is much planning and coordination yet to complete," the Brazilian admiral continued. "We will consult with some of you as we formulate those final plans. However, the battle fleet will muster at the Ushuaia Naval Base on Tierra del Fuego in one month. Air support for the operation will fly out of Ushuaia Naval Air Station. Ship and squadron commanders should plan on independent sailing to the naval base with no radio traffic so we do not alert any outside interest. Stealth and surprise will help assure our success, which is the primary reason submarines will be a major part of the operation."

The large area map was replaced with a chart of the Straits of Magellan. Barbosa continued, "While the surface and air forces are mustering down south, two units will get underway immediately and take station within the Straits. The ARN *Santiago del Estero* with Captain Alveras in command will penetrate the Straits and patrol the waters between Isla Carlos III and Isla Dawson. Captain Alveras will guard the doors against any Chilean ship silly enough to challenge us."

The group laughed as Alveras rose and nodded, acknowledging his task.

"The other unit will be our nuclear submarine, the *João Cândido* with *Capitão de Fragata* Ribeiro in command. The *Cândido* will take station off Punta Arenas to monitor any activity from the Chilean navy base there." Boxes appeared on the chart to show the patrol areas for both submarines.

"Now, if there are no questions . . . ?"

There were none.

"Captains, return to your ships and immediately begin making preparations. Your sailing orders will be sent to you. Dismissed!"

As they rose to leave, Alveras offered his hand to Ribeiro. "Captain, it appears that we will be working together. Good hunting."

Ribeiro returned the handshake and said, "And good hunting to you. I am afraid I have a little farther to travel to my boat than a short walk down to the dock. The *Cândido* is tied up at the Rio Grande Naval Station." He glanced at his watch. "And my flight leaves in an hour. I am sure we will soon have the opportunity to compare notes. But now, if you will excuse me . . ."

Ribeiro grabbed his satchel and hat as he rushed out the door.

Colas Alveras watched his counterpart go, then left the headquarters building and slowly walked toward the pier where the *Santiago del Estero* was quietly moored. His mind was lost in all the details that needed attention before his ship would be ready to go to war.

War. That was something he and his crew had never actually faced before. He was convinced they would be ready for the challenge.

It was his job to make certain they were.

Ψ

The rudely jangling telephone roused Guillermo Manuelito out of a deep, deep sleep. He instinctively sat up in bed and groped about in the pitch blackness for the handset. Something told him this was no wrong number. His wife only stirred and grumbled something incoherent before rolling over and immediately going back to sleep.

Manuelito could hear static and rustling background noise on the phone's earpiece. He blinked, cleared his throat, and finally said, "*Hola.*"

"Guillermo, you must escape immediately." He recognized the distinctive voice of Ricardo Balduino. "It is obvious that we have an informant among us. The Federales have already ambushed and murdered several of our people tonight. They are on their way to La Granja. You must move fast. They will be there in less than an hour."

The cobwebs of sleep were no longer muddling Manuelito's mind. He knew he must think clearly and act quickly. "My family," he grunted. "I must get them out."

"We will make arrangements. Call this number when you have escaped and are certain you are in the clear." There was only a moment of silence. "Good luck, my friend. I am sorry this has happened."

Then the line went dead.

Before Manuelito could even replace the old-fashioned telephone handset on its cradle, the light in the room suddenly snapped on. His wife was out of bed and hurriedly dressing. "I will wake the children and get them moving," she said, her voice strong but with a slight quavering from fear. "And I will pack some food."

A part of Manuelito's mind marveled at how Abril could think of food at a time like this. How perfectly like a wife and mother. The rest of his mind was already finalizing the details of their escape plan. One that had already been in planning from the first day he decided to join Balduino's revolutionary cadre. And had intensified since their recent assault in Rosario.

He reached high up to the closet shelf and pulled down the box where he had carefully hidden the Browning Hi-Power pistol and the extra ammo. He slipped the weapon into his waistband and pocketed the ammo. Almost as a second thought, he grabbed his trusty old bird gun, an ancient 20-gauge, double-barreled shotgun he used to keep the doves from devouring his olive groves. Not much firepower, but it was the only other firearm he had. And it certainly made enough noise to perform its primary function.

He ran out into the house's small kitchen. His wife and children were there already, waiting for him. He ushered them out to the ancient flatbed truck parked near the rear door of the house. But as they loaded up, he looked into the distance. He could see headlights coming down the road toward the farm. This time of night in this area, he knew at once who it was that was approaching his home. The hated Federales were only about a mile away and it was a certainty that they had blocked the one road out of La Granja.

He needed something to keep the Federales preoccupied while he tried to slip the family out through the groves. Then he noticed the van parked beside the *granero*, where he had left it after returning to the farm from Rosario. Inside, it was still stacked full of *inútils*, his government's virtually worthless paper money. Grabbing the shotgun, he blasted two shots into the vehicle's fuel tank. Gasoline gushed out of the myriad holes the bird-shot had made and poured out onto the ground. He flicked a match onto the spilled fuel but did not have time to confirm if it had caught. He gunned the flatbed out into the maze of olive trees.

The night was still very dark, but Manuelito did not dare turn on his own headlights as he barreled down between the squatty trees. Only a few were more than ten meters tall. Fortunately, the rows were arrow-straight, but the branches still slapped the windshield as the truck bounced along uneven ground. He kept the gas pedal mashed to the floor, willing the old truck to move as fast as it ever had.

Manuelito risked one glance at the side mirror in time to see a Federale car skid to a stop by the *granero*. Just then the van exploded with a terrifying bright blast, lighting the night sky and showering the police car with shrapnel and burning debris.

The final row of trees ended at a fence line separating the grove from a deep drainage ditch along the perimeter. Manuelito skidded the truck around the corner and aimed it down the path between the trees and the fence. At the end of the row, he blasted through the wire fence and bounced up onto an old dirt farm lane. The lane wound through farm fields for several miles before it ended at a gate opening onto Ruta Provincial 23, a road that had probably been paved at one time in its distant history. Now it was only a rutted back road with tall weeds down its center and along each side.

The Federales were far behind them. Unless they did something to attract attention, or if the federal police had anticipated this backdoor route, Manuelito guessed he and his family should be able to slip away. Only now did he dare to turn on his headlights and drive at a more normal pace, like a farmer up early to get on with his long day's tasks.

He continued to drive as he dialed his cell phone. The MDR leader Ricardo Balduino answered on the very first ring.

"*Gracias a Dios*, you have escaped!" Balduino exclaimed, clearly pleased. "Listen closely now. We have made arrangements for your family. You know the old Arenera Arroyo Pavon, the abandoned horse arena at the base of the Pavon River canyon? Meet us at the parking lot. We have a boat ready to take your wife and children down the Pavon and then on down the Paraná River. They will be safely in Uruguay by this time tomorrow."

Manuelito closed his eyes as he breathed a sigh of relief. His family would be safe. That was what was really important. But it also would allow him to do what he now knew for certain that he must. He had unfinished work. President Martinez and his cronies had already robbed him and his family of all that they had built over the generations. Built through sacrifice, hard work, and financial risks. The latest political leader of Argentina was robbing thousands of other families of the same heritage as they had Guillermo Manuelito, all out of personal greed and an insatiable lust for power.

The olive farmer smashed his fist hard against the truck's dash. His wife stared at him wide-eyed. She had rarely seen him so enraged.

"Ricardo, *mi amigo*," he spoke into the cell phone. "It is well past the time that we rise up and stop these bastards. We will make them pay for what they are doing to the people of Argentina."

8

Jim Shupert checked the *George Mason*'s position on the ECDIS, the submarine's electronic plotting table. The "X" plotted just inside a box labeled "OPERATING AREA." When he looked up from the display, he noticed Bill Wilson, the OOD, studying the passive sonar display on the command console with a slight frown on his face.

Shupert called out, "Officer-of-the-Deck, the 0800 posit shows you inside the ops box. Recommend slowing to a two-thirds bell and conducting an ASW sweep in accordance with the night orders."

Wilson held up his hand, his eyes still stuck on the sonar display. "Just a second, Nav," he responded. "Sonar is just picking up a contact on the fat line. This guy looks very interesting."

The TB-34 "fat line" array was a 1,400-pound, 240-foot-long passive acoustic sonar sensor. It was being towed behind the submarine by a 2,400-foot-long cable. Shupert quickly moved over to where Wilson stood and looked over the OOD's shoulder.

The Sonar Supervisor, STi Josh Hannon, announced, "Officer-of-the-Deck, new sonar contact on the TB-34 towed array, designate Sierra One-Two-Seven, best bearing zero-three-one. Or Sierra One-Two-Eight, bearing three-two-nine. Recommend course change to the southwest to resolve ambiguity and open track."

Wilson glanced over to the array of computer screens that was usually Hannon's haunt. The senior sonar operator stood hunched over, intently studying the myriad displays that his team was busily leafing through. Hannon nodded in response to some report from one of his team before he looked around at Wilson.

"Officer-of-the-Deck, recommend you turn now!" he said with considerable urgency in his voice as well as his words. "Based on tonals, this guy is a probable submerged sub, and he's closing. Fast. Best guess of range is eight thousand yards."

Another submarine? Suddenly finding an unexpected, submerged contact meant that counter-detection was now a possibility, or a collision, which would be even worse. Either could ruin their day.

Wilson jumped into action. "Pilot, left full rudder, steady course two-six-zero," he ordered. Grabbing the 1MC microphone, he announced throughout the boat, "Captain to the conn. Station the fire control tracking party."

The big sub quickly swung around to the new course. Jason Schmidt, the pilot, called out, "Steady course two-six-zero, ahead full," as the last of the fire control tracking party slid into their seats, ready to track this new arrival, figure out who he was, what he was doing, and where he was going.

The CO, Brian Edwards, and the XO, Jackson Biddle, showed up at the same time. The XO was still chewing a bite of his morning pastry. Edwards went right to the command console where he began studying the sonar display. Biddle grabbed a headset and started directing the fire control tracking party.

Wilson reported, "Skipper, new sonar contact on the TB-34. Probable submerged submarine based on tonals. I maneuvered to the southwest to resolve ambiguity and open track."

"Okay, slow to two-thirds. We don't want to make any more noise than we need to. If he doesn't know we're here yet, I'd sure like to keep it that way."

Josh Hannon announced, "Array is stable, regain Sierra One-Two-Eight, bearing three-three-one."

The contact was to the northwest and drawing aft, going astern of the *George Mason*. Biddle called out, "Track Sierra-One-Two-Eight, drop Sierra

One-Two-Seven." The guy to the northwest was the real contact, the other one the ambiguous bearing.

Edwards looked over to where Hannon stood. The sonar supervisor continued his report. "Skipper, he's displaying tonals from a typical nuke sub. I'm getting a 100-hertz line, probably from reactor coolant pumps, and a suppressed 30-hertz line that looks like a minor shaft rub. He sounds something like those new French *Barracuda*-class boats, but not really. This guy is a submarine for sure, but not one I've ever heard before."

Edwards shook his head. What was a mystery nuke boat doing down here in the South Atlantic a couple of hundred miles off the southernmost Argentine coast? Who was he, and what was he doing sailing around way down here? More importantly, was he friendly? And had he also detected the *George Mason*? The real quandary was, what should the *George Mason* do now?

Too many questions. Damn few answers.

Edwards stood tall and stretched his back. That always seemed to help the thought process. Then he called out, "Attention in control. We have an unknown nuke sub, designated Sierra One-Two-Eight, now bearing three-three-five and drawing aft. I intend to dance around behind this guy while conducting TMA on him as we work our way into his baffles. Once we have a good, solid tracking solution, I intend to close him to gather sound-pressure-level data on him. Set counter-detection range at five thousand yards, safety range at three thousand."

He glanced over at the weapons control console where Aston Jennings sat. "Weps, the torpedo in tube one will be the self-defense weapon. Make tube one ready in all respects except for flooding or opening the outer door." That would make sure that they were only a couple of seconds away from being able to shoot in self-defense if they really had to. Though there was no reason yet to consider the other sub to be hostile, Edwards and his crew had to prepare for whatever might happen.

Jackson Biddle eased over to where Edwards stood. He quietly asked, "Skipper, you sure you want to do this? Not in our OPORD. SPLs are real tricky and can be downright dangerous."

Edwards nodded. "Yep, XO. I know. Let's call it the option of the on-scene commander. That would be me. Chances are this guy is friendly, but he could be Russian or Chinese, too. Either way, if there is an unknown nuke boat sniffing around down here at the bottom of the planet, I think it's best we find out all we can about him and get that info back home to the boss so they can noddle it through. Agreed?"

Before Biddle could respond, Jeff Otanga, supervising the solution from the ECDIS tactical display, called out, "XO, we got a leg. Recommend a maneuver to course three-zero-five."

Now that they had an initial bead on the other vessel's course and speed, the *George Mason* slowly spiraled around behind the unknown sub, keeping it just forward of the *George Mason's* baffles—her sonar blind spot —and drawing aft while the American sub worked deep into the other boat's baffles. All the time, they worked on a wide range of trial solutions based on the contact's bearing and received frequencies. As Brian Edwards had repeatedly drummed into his team, those two pieces of data were the only truths they could rely on when doing a passive sonar approach. Every-thing else was just guesswork.

It took most of the morning and some intense work refining their solu-tions, but finally all the trial results narrowed down until they had a course, range, and speed that tracked accurately.

After sitting behind Sierra One-Two-Eight for half an hour to verify that the solution was dead-nuts accurate, it was time to move in closer and gather the SPL data. It all sounded very simple. They would simply draw in close to the other sub, taking a position just aft of his beam and just on the edge of his baffles. Then, as they recorded all the sound data at a known distance and bearing, they would slowly slide back before crossing just a few hundred yards astern of the sub they were tracking. Then they would move up on the other side and repeat the process. If everything worked as planned, the solution was, in fact, "dead-nuts accurate," and if the other sub cooperated by not zigging or counter-detecting the *George Mason*, they could then have accurate recordings of the other boat's noise profile. The resulting data would give the eggheads back at NAVINTEL what they needed to calculate this particular sub's acoustic signature, essentially its ID.

Everything needed to work as planned. It rarely did.

Edwards deftly maneuvered the *George Mason* forward along the mystery sub's port side until he was just aft of midships and two thousand yards away. Then he slowed by one knot to allow their quarry to move forward as he slipped toward the other sub's stern.

Everything was going smoothly as the *George Mason* slid back toward the target sub's stern. The anonymous submarine was cooperating, staying on a consistent course and speed. The all-important digital data was piling up in the sonar system's hard drive.

Then things changed.

"Captain, underwater comms from Sierra One-Two-Eight," Josh Hannon called out. "Can't make out what he's saying, but there must be someone else around here he wants to chat with."

That bit of eavesdropping threw a huge monkey wrench into the whole operation. Edwards had no choice but to stop the SPL process and open out, putting a safe distance between Sierra One-Two-Eight and the *George Mason* until they figured out what was going on and who else might be joining the party down here.

"All stop." That would put distance between the *George Mason* and the tracked submarine while also allowing them to remain as quiet as possible.

"Captain, I have underwater comms, bearing two-six-four," Hannon called. "This is not coming from Sierra One-Two-Eight. It's somebody else. No sonar contact on that bearing, though."

Somebody else was talking, but *George Mason* could not hear anything but the comms from the third guy. He had to be close, inside ten thousand yards, to be heard.

"Shit," Edward muttered under his breath. "This is getting way too complicated."

"What'd you say, Skipper?" Biddle asked.

"Nothing," Edwards answered. "Just trying to figure out what to do next. Any good ideas?" The XO, eyes wide, shook his head. If there were two boats already in this herd, how many more might show up? And what the hell were they doing in this typically deserted patch of chilly ocean?

Jeff Otanga reached up just then and turned the volume of the underwater telephone speaker up loud enough so he could hear it. "Skipper, they're talking in Spanish. *Gracias, Mama!* My mother always insisted we learn our home language so we could talk with our relatives from the old country." He listened for a moment. "We got two subs rendezvousing. The distant one is . . . " He trailed off as he strained to hear more. ". . . she's the *Santiago del Estero*, I think he said. It's really hard to hear for sure with all the biologics. The one we've been trailing is the *João Cândido*. They're heading down to the Magellan Straits. They are saying they'll meet off Faro Punta Dúngeness in five days. That's all I heard."

"That's plenty," Edwards said, then added, "*Muchas gracias*."

Biddle had already jumped to the command console and was furiously typing. After a few seconds, he stepped back to stand next to his captain.

"Skipper, you ain't gonna like this. The *Santiago del Estero* is a *Scorpene*-class sub that the Brazilians sold to the Argentines last year. It's a second-generation *Scorpene*, with a fuel cell AIP system. But here's the corker: the *João Cândido* is Brazil's new nuclear boat. Intel still maintains that she is at least a year away from being operational. Though we just heard her right over yonder, so I reckon she's out of the barn."

Edwards rubbed his chin. This was a real bind. The Brazilian *Scorpene* boats, built on contract from a French design, were state-of-the-art diesel-electric boats. They were good submarines, a really challenging adversary should they ever be used against the USA. They were just as quiet as the *George Mason* when they were operating on the battery, and they sported a modern air-independent propulsion system to boot.

The *João Cândido*, on the other hand, was a total unknown. There was no way to figure out the capabilities of that boat or the tactics to use against it since she was supposedly not even in operation yet.

"Okay, this is what we'll do," Edwards said, summoning up a lot more decisiveness in his voice than he actually felt. "XO, draft up a message back home. Tell them what we have down here, send them all the data, and tell them that we intend to shadow these two all the way down to the Straits. Mr. Wilson, put us eight thousand yards astern of *João Cândido* once we get a good read on her. Stay there while they move south and sing out if anything changes." He glanced at his watch. "Now, since these two bastards so rudely interrupted my breakfast, I'm going to the wardroom for lunch."

As usual, Jackson Biddle relied on his Southern roots to sum up the situation. "Looks like we got ourselves a bagel in a bucket of grits for damn sure!"

Ψ

"Ladies and gentlemen, the president!"

Everyone in the crowded Cabinet Room jumped to their feet as President Stanley Smitherman strode with apparent purpose through the big double doors. He was closely followed by Vice President Harold Osterman and a gaggle of aides. Smitherman moved to stand behind his seat, a high-backed brown leather armchair placed at the center of the broad mahogany table. Osterman sat down in a far less impressive one on the president's right, well aware it would be bad form to also remain standing and steal his boss's thunder.

Smitherman glanced around the room. The large space was packed with people. It seemed that the members of the president's cabinet had mustered every assistant, advisor, associate, and any other strap-hanger they could corral to show up and indicate their importance and attention to the nation's business. The Secretaries of Agriculture, Labor, Education, and Transportation had no idea why they were required to be present, other than to appear busy and purposeful to the press, who were assembled in the back of the chamber. Most of the executive branch participants had already been told they would be dismissed after the first part of the meeting, just after the media representatives had been sent out.

The president, as well as his other key cabinet members, also knew that someone—and likely several dozen of the unnecessary attendees—would rush to leak everything that was said in his opening remarks. But the second part of the meeting would require a much smaller and more close-lipped crowd.

Smitherman allowed a few minutes for the press to get the obligatory footage of him looking presidential for the evening's primetime newscasts before making a few opening statements about the current important legislation he championed, which was being blocked by members of Congress from the opposition party. As he spoke, aides handed out stacks of papers with charts and graphs that put the proper spin on each measure that was so crucial for the nation's economy, the national defense, and equitable treatment for each American. He also declared his final statements to be "off the record" for the press, but he was confident the leakers in the room would make sure they were promptly public knowledge. Then he signaled to have the reporters shooed out and the doors shut. He ignored shouted questions from some of the more aggressive journalists as he chatted with those closest to him. Then, several of the aides—referring to printed lists—proceeded to clear the room of all the other attendees not required for the actual purpose of this gathering, ushering them out a side door.

Only then did the president take his seat, symbolically assuming the level of the others remaining in the meeting room.

Smitherman deliberately opened his red leather briefing book, the one with the gold presidential seal stamped on the front, and studied the first insert with apparent great interest. Only the vice president and the Secretary of State knew it was the first time he had seen it.

"Folks," he began, with just a trace of his distinctive West Texas drawl. "Y'all have seen the joint announcement from the presidents of Brazil and Argentina. They've lost their ever-lovin' minds down there! It seems that their efforts to destroy the world's economy weren't enough. Now Presidents Martinez and Souza appear to be bent on flexing their military muscles, too. I have called this meeting to solidify what our reactions will be. We need to show the world we're going to be firm and decisive before every little ole nation on the planet decides to get uppity. And American voters . . . citizens . . . will know we're on top of this thing. Let's see where we are and what we need to do. First off, Secretary Ibatomboo, where is Treasury with our response to their issuing that bogus fiat currency of theirs? I forget what they call it."

Juanita Ibatomboo, the first transsexual Black woman to serve as Secretary of the Treasury, stuttered nervously as she answered. She still felt far more comfortable in her Berkeley classroom than in the Cabinet Room. "Uh, Mis . . . Mister Pres . . . President, they call it the *inútil*. Once China accepted it as a reserve currency a couple of weeks ago, several African nations followed Beijing's lead. Now India and Russia have both agreed to fluidly trade in *inútils*."

"What the hell we doing about it, then?" the president interrupted.

The Secretary of the Treasury swallowed hard. "Sir, we locked all of Brazil's and Argentina's accounts held in US banks, but that didn't have much effect. There simply is not much left there. The non-NATO countries have refused to cooperate in the effort. That leaves us stuck on where to turn next regarding the currency."

Smitherman shook his head and pursed his lips. He could not believe the incompetence of this woman. He would never have appointed her to a cabinet seat if he had not needed the support of her backers for his second-term run. The polls showed she had actually made a difference in the outcome of the election, delivering a few precious percentage points from California and New York.

"Well, dammit, Madam Secretary," he growled, "Come up with something. Something that works and something that doesn't leave us looking like we don't know our ass from our elbow. And try not to piss off China and Russia in the process. We promised the voters we'd calm down the tension with those two and I, by God, intend to do it."

The Secretary of the Treasury closed her eyes and tried to breathe normally.

Smitherman turned to Secretary of State Sandra Dosetti. He was confident that she would be prepared with a good plan that attacked the problem from every angle. But he was also afraid of her. She was a conniving politician and damn smart. And she was going to be the first female US president or die trying.

"Secretary Dosetti," he said. "Please tell me you have something for us."

Dosetti flipped open her own briefing book, a thick loose-leaf file. She thumbed through it until she came up with the page she wanted.

"Mr. President," she said, her voice betraying her New York heritage and Ivy League education. "We have prepared a response to present to the United Nations Security Council protesting Brazil and Argentina's clear violations of international law and reminding the world of their treaty obligations. Their untenable claim to all waters out to a thousand miles off their seacoasts—something they call a 'protected exclusion zone,' where they have declared they will forbid all shipping or overflight without their prior permission—is a clear violation of the United Nations Convention on the Law of the Sea. And that is an accord that both countries signed a long time ago. They apparently took this move directly from China's playbook, ignoring international law and claiming vast areas of the oceans as their sovereign territory."

"Sandra, let's leave China out of this, okay?"

She looked up from her notes. "But Mr. President, they—" The look on the president's face told her she should follow his lead on this. "Okay. There's no enforcement teeth in the accord anyway. We must note as well that our case for invoking the 'law of the sea' on this matter is weakened since we have not yet signed the UNCLOS agreement ourselves."

"Won't China just veto any action we ask of the Security Council?" Vice President Osterman queried.

Dosetti glanced over at the veep. The barest hint of a smile crossed her face. "Of course, but we will at least be on record, and our response will show the world that we consider Argentina and Brazil to be the aggressors. China vetoes anything we propose anyway. Which brings me to their second claim. As a reminder, both Argentina and Brazil simultaneously declared that all of South America south of fifty-two degrees south latitude is the rightful territory of Argentina, based on some shaky historical claims. That takes in a lot of Chile, including the city of Punta Arenas, about the only town of any size down there, and a bunch of sheep and oil and gas wells. But it also takes in the Straits of Magellan, one of the world's key shipping routes. The Chilean ambassador has already presented us with a request for military and political assistance in refuting this declaration and, if either country tries to test the limits of their authority to make this claim, we would be obligated to support them, including shooting back."

"Go to war in South America? Jesus!" Smitherman turned to his new Secretary of Defense, Sebastien Aldo. "Mr. Secretary, where is the fleet? Our closest assets?"

This was Aldo's first cabinet meeting, but he had come prepared. He looked over his shoulder at his aide who passed him a file.

"Mr. President, the *Gerald Ford* battle group just entered the Mediterranean Sea for their regularly scheduled Sixth Fleet deployment. We have already turned them around and have them steaming toward the South Atlantic. The Secretary of the Navy as well as the Chief of Naval Operations are recommending that we do a well-publicized 'freedom of navigation' operation down the South American Atlantic coast, challenging this unlawful declaration early and showing the world we will not allow it to stand. I concur with that recommendation."

Smitherman looked over at Osterman, who smiled and nodded. Smitherman said, "Good, let's go ahead with this 'freedom of navigation' deal, but look here. Stay as non-provocative as possible. Nothing within five hundred miles of the coast. We'll make our point and maybe the dumbass sons of bitches will be smart enough not to shoot at us."

Aldo's aide handed him a second file. The SecDef glanced at it before looking up.

"Mr. President, one more thing of which you should be aware. We currently have a submarine, the *George Mason,* operating off the Argentinian coast way down by the Magellan Strait. They were on a routine patrol when they reported that they encountered and are shadowing two submarines down there."

Smitherman frowned, then slammed his hands down on the mahogany table. His face went crimson, the veins on his neck bulging.

"This meeting is adjourned! Right damn now. Clear the room. Only the vice president and the Secretary of Defense are to stay."

The gaggle hurriedly vacated the meeting room with puzzled expressions on many of their faces, then quietly shut the doors as the last of them left.

"Goddamnit, Sebastien," Smitherman roared. "Just what the hell are you doing authorizing covert submarine operations without my approval? I should fire you and arrange a nice little suite for your ass in Leavenworth for such insubordination."

Aldo's mouth fell open. Osterman held up his hand.

"Calm down, Stan. Seb didn't do anything wrong, and certainly nothing we can't recover from. That's what our subs do. Investigate anything out of the ordinary. Let's just call this one off and send them back on to whatever their original mission was before they got curious about the boats they saw down there. Okay?"

Smitherman, now visibly calmer, nodded and said, "Seb, get back to the Pentagon and make damn sure they pull that submarine off its wild goose chase before they do something dumb. I want a report back by this evening that this *George Mathis*, or whatever its name is, is steaming to wherever in hell it was originally headed. Understand?"

Secretary Aldo nodded and headed for the door.

Once Aldo was gone—and only the president and vice president were in the room—Harold Osterman looked over at Smitherman.

"Stan, what was that all about? Seb doesn't need your approval for what that sub is doing. Neither does any other warship we got floating around out there. It sounded like they were doing something pretty valuable, trying to figure out whose subs those were and what they were doing running together. Lots of possibilities and all of 'em bad."

"Harold, I got a phone call just before this meeting," Smitherman answered. "It was Tan Yong. You may have heard of him. President of China? Seems his nation is looking for a quicker shipping route from his country to Buenos Aires. Hard to believe it looking at a map, but the route from China to Argentina and back is considerably longer and more expensive through the Panama Canal than it is around the ass end of South America. Plus, they don't have to worry about all the yahoos hiding in the bushes, counting every ship and taking note of the cargo when they go through the canal. They want to go through the Straits of Magellan as part of a new trade deal they cut with Brazil and Argentina so they can haul all that beef and whatever kind of grain they grow down there back home, and be able to deliver toys and fireworks and cheap cell phones to the good folks of South America."

"Mr. President, I don't think we'd mess with them hauling beef and Happy Meal toys through the Straits of Magellan," Osterman said. "As long as that's all they're transporting."

Smitherman looked sideways at him. "They may decide they want to haul some other stuff down there. Stuff they'd prefer we not see. We know they're building seaports and airports and have a deal to provide some military equipment to both countries. Look, Tan warned us to stay well clear. I'm sure we can keep an eye on them from a distance and raise a stink if they really start shipping fighter jets and tanks and missiles to our Latin American friends."

"I don't know, Stan. What if—?"

The president held up a hand. "You don't understand. They're cashing in a chit, Harold. I assume you remember all that 'help' Yong gave us during the re-election campaign. We'd have been toast without him. Well, now it appears that the bill is coming due. And the price so far is pretty low, way I see it. They could be asking a hell of a lot more. We don't need some Captain America sub skipper getting in the way down there and start shooting. We can let Argentina and Brazil screw things up with their economy on their own and they won't need our help doing it. It'll just be a drain on China eventually, too, and that's a good thing for us. We are damn sure not going to do anything to help Chile besides to complain and pontificate at the UN and in the media. Something you and me are damn good at, in case you forgot. Is that quite clear?"

"That gives China cart blanche right here in our hemisphere," Osterman said.

Smitherman sat back and relaxed a little. "Dosetti can do all the State Department striped pants diplomacy she wants and put on a good show. She's good at that. It ain't gonna change nothin'. That incompetent Ibatomboo will ultimately screw up whatever she tries and give us a fine scapegoat when the feces strikes the oscillating device. The press will go easy on her or him or whatever it is, for obvious reasons. Tan Wong said that he didn't care one whit about that thousand-mile exclusion zone. If the South American tin-pots want to make a big deal over it, he's okay with us doing whatever we need to. That leaves us the chance to save face, if it should ever come to that."

Smitherman reached into his coat pocket and extracted a couple of cigars. He tossed one to his VP.

"I don't know," Osterman said, deftly catching the cigar midair. "Lots could go wrong. It does give Tan and the CCP a big foothold down there if they decide to exploit it. The other side of the aisle will have a field day if word gets out."

The president lit his own cigar and took a big puff. "A bridge we can cross if we have to. Later. Much later. If Tan gets all serious down there, or if the dictators press this claim of territory from Chile, we can tariff and PR 'em to death, come up with some fancy sanctions, all kinds of nasty stuff, but with nary a shot fired. Meanwhile, if there's really ever a dust-up about this thousand-mile thing, it could be good for us. It only takes attention off all the stuff they're blaming us for, our own miserable economy up here and the crime rate in the big cities and the hosed-up airline system and . . ."

Smitherman stopped to take a long, satisfied draw on his cigar.

"I only hope you're right, Mr. President," Osterman responded. He was having trouble getting his cigar lit.

"I think I am. This is how dealmaking works, buddy. China gets something. Wild-eyed South Americans realize they're only going to screw it up worse than ever if they don't come crawling back to the good old USA with hats in hand. We get something. And . . ."

"And?"

"And we all stay friends."

9

Manuel Viscosa grunted as he sat down, breathing hard. He was mildly surprised that he found it such hard work to suck sufficient air into his lungs, even if they were up in the high mountains above the Atacama, likely near 13,000 feet above sea level. He remembered a time—back when he was Josh Kirkland and worked for the CIA—when he could charge up hills like the Andean mountains all day without his body protesting. Even when his was primarily a desk job at the Langley headquarters, he kept himself in top shape and often accompanied operatives on tough missions, just so he could see firsthand what was happening. It soon became a personal thing for him to directly and personally oversee the more critical operations. Somewhere along the line, though, he was beginning to think he would soon be too old for these kinds of adventures.

"Do we need to take a break, *Jefe*," Ildefenso Vargas chided him. "Maybe call for you an Uber?" Viscosa's lieutenant had all the cockiness of youth. He also sported a brash, bold recklessness that Viscosa found useful for jobs such as this. At times, though, the kid became annoying, edging close to impertinence. This was one of those times.

Viscosa took a sip of water and gazed upward at the barren rock stacked ahead of them. It seemed to reach all the way to the heavens. The narrow path they were following wound back and forth interminably upward until it finally disappeared in a saddle between two peaks. It would take his little group all day to hike up to the unmarked pass through the mountains. There, they could make camp in the natural shelter offered by the mountains on either side. It would still be another two days of rugged hiking over the high promontories to their destination. The Chilean border was up ahead somewhere, but in the wilderness around here, it was nothing more than a meaningless line that someone had drawn on a piece of paper. There were no signs or fences, and the nearest border guard was probably standing in a tiny patch of shade at the Route 51 crossing, fifty miles to the south, cursing his luck for drawing such thankless duty.

Viscosa took a few more deep breaths of the thin air and slapped his knees. It was time to get moving again. His back ached as he stood. He groaned as he picked up his pack and rifle and threw his *ruana*, the local indigenous version of a poncho, over the pack, both to conceal it and for warmth. When he pulled his flat, broad-brimmed, black hat onto his head, he was just another Atacameño walking in the mountains with his tribe, looking for grazing grounds for his llamas. At least it would appear so from a distance.

Vargas and the rest of the team were already up the trail, setting a fast pace. Viscosa had to push hard just to keep up. Alpenglow was painting the higher peaks in gold when they finally reached their intermediate destination, the mountain pass. Viscosa was not sure he could have made it another kilometer. He slumped down, totally exhausted, then barely had the energy to chew a piece of jerky and eat a couple of sweet *alfajores* biscuits. The sugar rush and resulting crash did help him fall into an exhausted sleep without the benefit of tent or sleeping bag. Not even the scurrying of leaf-eared mice—one of the few animals tough and stubborn enough to live here—disturbed his sleep.

Ultimately, the prediction of it taking two days of hiking to reach their ultimate target proved to be a hopeful estimate. It was past noon on the third day when Viscosa finally lay behind an outcropping and looked down on the lonely pumping station. It was one of six such facilities recently constructed and brought online way up there in the high-desert mountains. The station's purpose was to pump lithium-rich brine up from wells nearby and then send it down to the concentrating fields that littered the flat desert floor miles below.

The new installations had been the cause of a great deal of angry confrontation between the local Atacameño people and the mining companies. This method of lithium extraction required huge quantities of precious water here in the driest desert in the world. Many weather instruments in the area had never recorded measurable precipitation. The indigenous people—the few who were tough and stubborn enough to live here—decried the loss of their water and the inevitable pollution from the residual salts left over from the extraction, usually dumped in ugly piles without regard for its effect on people, animals, or agriculture. Demonstrations in the local towns had turned violent. Four people had recently been killed in the tiny native village of San Pedro de Atacama when the Chilean police opened fire to disperse the crowds protesting the pumping stations and settlement ponds.

Viscosa recognized this as the perfect opportunity to throw a big monkey wrench in the Chilean lithium industry. And to take a crucial first step in his promising partnership with Juan Carlos Señorans of the Argentine intelligence agency. Viscosa's men in Chile had already moved large sums of money and arms to the more radical elements among the locals. With that help, the locals would be able to do the small, dirty jobs. But now was the time to deliver a major blow if he really wanted to get things rolling. Viscosa had decided that this was another of those operations important enough for him to personally lead the assault team. Ildefenso Vargas had pushed back mildly, assuring his boss he and his squad could handle the job sans supervision. But it took only the cold, scathing look on the face of Manuel Viscosa to confirm that the boss had already made his decision.

"Then I will use this as my first opportunity to show you my capabilities in the field, *Jefe*," Vargas told him.

"See that you do," Viscosa/Kirkland shot back.

The station was little more than a large concrete building housing the massive pumps. An adjacent metal structure contained a couple of large diesel generators, and the roof was covered with solar panels, all to provide the electric power needed to operate the pumps. A dozen wellheads dotted the barren valley surrounding the station. A couple of dirt-crusted pickup trucks were parked adjacent to the side building housing the generator. They appeared to be the only transportation in or out of this dusty, godforsaken outpost. A single large concrete pipe, running beside a windblown dirt road, snaked all the way down the valley toward the concentration fields below.

It appeared his intelligence info was valid. Only a few men operated and maintained the machinery, and they did double duty by guarding the station from the local rabble-rousers as well. Right now, though, the operators-slash-guards were playing a vigorous game of one-net soccer on a rough pitch scraped out of the rocks and dirt beside the main building. Viscosa counted five men. He sat and watched as Vargas moved his assault team into position to launch the attack. The mountainside was barren, providing little cover for a true stealth approach. But with so few defenders, there was no point in waiting for darkness. At least, that had been Ildefenso Vargas's recommendation. Viscosa was not so sure, but he decided to allow his squad commander a bit of leeway.

Vargas's squad was barely halfway down to the station when one of them was spotted. By the goalie. They were at least halfway ready for an attack. Their weapons were neatly propped up against the soccer net. In seconds, they had grabbed their rifles and, assuming the worst, opened fire.

Even so, the firefight was lopsided. Vargas's men were trained killers. They immediately picked off a couple of the guards too slow to find cover. Then it was a matter of locating each of the others and then concentrating their firepower on each when he popped up to shoot or scrambled for better protection.

The last of the station personnel apparently recognized the hopelessness of his situation. He tossed his rifle aside and made a mad dash for one of the pickups. Miraculously, none of the bullets found him. He managed to get inside, cranked up the engine, jammed the battered old truck into gear, and spun out of the compound in an eruption of dust and gravel. He made it a hundred meters down the road before one of the squad members finally took time for careful aim. His rounds found their target, smashing into the back of the guard's head. The windshield was immediately covered with blood and brain matter. The truck weaved a couple of times and then crashed hard into the concrete pipe.

The short, one-sided fight was over.

By the time Viscosa had lumbered down the mountain, Vargas and his men had placed explosive charges around the pumps and the diesels. It took a few more minutes to sabotage each of the wellheads. They were climbing back up out of the valley when the charges detonated with a breathtaking *whoomph!* The rolling pressure wave reverberated across the canyon walls like thunder, a phenomenon never heard before in this realm.

Viscosa pulled Vargas aside.

"That man should never have made it to the truck," Viscosa said. "Let us be certain we do not suffer such questionable marksmanship the next time." Then he smiled at his sweat-soaked lieutenant. "Ildefenso, we have five more of these to destroy. They may or may not hear about what happened here, so they could be expecting us. Might I suggest we hit the next one at night?"

Duly chastened, Vargas nodded and, without so much as a smile or a thanks for the good suggestion, walked back up the slope.

Ψ

Jim Ward steered the five-year-old Toyota Land Cruiser, a rental, through the desolate high desert. He checked his rearview mirror. Other than Billy Joe Hurt and his ancient Subaru Forester a hundred yards back, the road was empty as far as he could see in both directions. Just like the landscape that surrounded them. Nothing moved except some dust devils kicked up by the never-ceasing winds. Though the SEAL team leader had traveled the world during his service to his nation, Ward had never seen a land so devoid of life, both flora and fauna. Even the harsh Horn of Africa had been nearly a tropical rainforest compared to this moonscape. Nothing but blue sky overhead, shades of gray and brown in every direction, and a road that was little more than a long, black line stretching arrow-straight to both horizons.

Just when Ward was certain the highway would carry them right off the end of the earth, Route 23 took a drop into a narrow, high-walled canyon

and made a sharp left turn to shoot down into another rocky canyon appropriately named Valle de la Muerte, "Death Valley." They then climbed
again, swept through a pass in the surrounding hills, and ultimately
descended into the only green spot that Ward had seen since leaving
Calama a couple of hours before. The town of San Pedro de Atacama
consisted of a cluster of adobe dwellings surrounded by a few hectares of
green fields. And here, it was obvious that tourism had found the Atacama,
or at least as deep into the Atacama as San Pedro. Tour buses sat double-
parked, diesel engines running, all along the widened roadway. Every other
house was advertised as either a hotel, hostel, or a bed-and-breakfast. But
they all looked the same; low, flat-roofed, dun-colored mud-brick buildings
with a couple of struggling chañar trees offering some meager shade.

Checking his map. Ward decided this town would be a good place to
top off their gas tanks and make sure they had enough water. The next stop,
Socaire, was another fifty miles down Route 23 and across more totally
open country. TJ Dillon had already warned Ward and his SEAL team that
Socaire did not even have a gas station, so they would have to tank up here.
He pulled over at a station where Route 27 separated from 23 and then
vanished toward the east, where it eventually pierced the Argentine border
on the other side of the high mountains.

The locals attending the station were abuzz, and perfectly willing to
share with these gringo tourists the source of their commotion: the news of
the recent attacks on the much-hated brine-pumping stations that had
been so odiously placed in the hills above their town, robbing them of
precious water. When Jim Ward asked who might have done such violent
damage, the attendants reported that it had certainly been some of the
more radical elements of the Atacameño people. Maybe some from right
around here. They had finally taken matters into their own hands and
destroyed several of the facilities rather than continue to protest peacefully
to a deaf federal government. Maybe now the miners and the authorities
would realize the effects of wasting the people's precious water and
polluting their sacred land just to leach out the lithium, the "white gold"
the greedy mining companies craved.

The retired SEAL, Bill Beaman, had been riding in the second car with
Billy Joe Hurt, getting to know the chief who would be the enlisted team

leader. Now, with a concerned look on his face, he pulled Ward and Hunt aside.

"Guys, I recommend we stay close together from here on. And keep your head on a swivel. This may be ecotourist country, and we may appear to most of these folks to be *turistas*, but down the road we'll be in open desert again, away from civilization. We know from our briefings that the locals around here are pretty worked up. Out there in the desert, they may not be too good at differentiating between money-grubbing miners and good, honest SEALs playing in their sandbox."

Ward chuckled. "Got you, old man. But my gut is telling me there's more to this story. I don't see TJ calling us down here to check on local hotheads who are blowing up pumping stations. Local law would be handling that. Kirkland's at work here. I'd bet on it."

Beaman answered, "My rather aged gut is telling me to be ready for trouble, whoever's causing it. And it don't really matter if it's some irate local guys or Josh Kirkland out here building his crime empire one explosion at a time. A bullet is a bullet, no matter who shoots it. Now, let's get rolling. I'd sure like to be in Socaire and meet up with TJ before sundown."

The sun was just dropping below the horizon when the two vehicles rolled into the little town. Neither Ward nor Beaman expected what they saw when they pulled in. The main road was blocked by the Carabineros de Chile, the country's national law enforcement agency. At least a dozen green-and-white police cruisers lined the road, lights flashing, leaving only a narrow corridor for traffic to snake through once each vehicle had been searched and the papers of their occupants examined. A helicopter with the same green-and-white paint job sat idling in the middle of a nearby soccer pitch.

Ward's main worry was how they might explain to the Chilean police all the firepower they were hauling in the back of the two SUVs. Then he spied a familiar figure. TJ Dillon was standing next to an officer who appeared to be in charge.

Dillon grinned when he saw the SEALs and waved them over. A policeman obligingly guided them into parking spots off the main roadway. Still, Hurt and Ward made certain to lock the car doors. As they approached, Dillon grabbed Jim Ward in a bear hug, and then did the same with Bill Beaman.

"Gawd it's good to see you two frogs again! It's been too darn long!" Then he stepped back. "Excuse my manners. Let me introduce you to *Teniente Coronel* Juan Perez-Garcia. He commands the Atacama regional office of the Carabineros de Chile. Juan, these are the SEALs I've been telling you about. They may look ragged, but they won't bite. Captain Bill Beaman is the grizzled old guy, and the youngster there is Commander Jim Ward."

The smartly uniformed officer snapped to attention and rendered a sharp salute. "Captain Beaman, Commander Ward, welcome to Chile. *Señor* Dillon has told me much about your work together. I am sorry that you are seeing our beautiful Atacama under these circumstances. It seems that our local Atacameños have decided to take the law into their own hands and the results have been tragic, to say the least. So far, we have found thirty men murdered at a half dozen brine pumping stations, and the facilities at each have been completely destroyed. We must find the perpetrators and bring them to justice, and we sincerely appreciate you and the US government offering to assist us in this effort. Now, if you will excuse me, I need to see that my men are pursuing all leads. It has been a long, hot day here and, as you know, attention to detail can suffer in such conditions."

Perez-Garcia stepped away to confer with his sergeant.

Beaman looked at Dillon and snorted. "Josh Kirkland. This is his bag of alpaca shit."

Dillon nodded. "Agreed, and if it's Kirkland's work, he's already well on his way back across the border into Argentina. We've learned he has quite the spread over there. And lots of friends in the upper echelon of the government to help him maintain his lifestyle."

Ward shook his head. "Motive. What's his motive for hiking over here and knocking off some pumping stations? Lots of work for not much outcome, and we hear he's making plenty of coin with his usual products."

Dillon rubbed his chin for a second before he answered. "Jim, we already know that Kirkland has found himself a role in the Argentine lithium mining business, which is getting considerable investment from our friends in Beijing. These pumps over here in Chile were the key source for the Chilean extraction effort, which has been doing really well. Plenty of customers around the world and, so far, China has not been one of them. China is real cozy nowadays with the new regime over in Argentina and royally pissed off at Chile. Some of our folks believe—and I agree with them—that Kirkland's role is to use his network and considerable down-and-dirty assets to help knock off the competition. The Atacameños are just convenient patsies getting the blame. And truth is, they don't mind this nasty stuff at all so long as it supports their cause. So, we'll not be getting much help from them. To the contrary, they'll probably do what they can to get in our way if they suspect what's going on."

"So, what's our move, TJ?" Ward asked. "We got a couple of rental cars full of weapons and some guys who know how to use them."

"Despite what the good *Teniente Coronel* thinks, our mission is to take out Kirkland, not solve these murders and terrorism cases. Even if he doesn't have a damn thing to do with all this mayhem over here, Kirkland still deserves our attention. I think we need to beat feet and cross the border to his headquarters to reintroduce ourselves to the son of a bitch. If we drive hard, we may be able to get out in front of him."

Bill Beaman gave Dillon a hard look. "How much of this is personal, TJ? And how much is because we really need to get this slimy bastard? You've been chasing this dude for a long time . . ."

"BB, you gotta know I wouldn't risk the lives of you and this team on a personal axe I might have to grind," Dillon shot back. "This guy's neck-deep in some really bad stuff, and it's lots more than running dope. Top-level political shit that will cause a lot of people to get hurt or killed and maybe —and I'm not exaggerating—lead to a shift in power and influence in this hemisphere that directly threatens the USA. We probably won't stop that just by taking Kirkland out, but it would do some damage to their plans."

They noticed Perez-Garcia was heading back their way, accompanied by a much shorter man.

"I had to ask, TJ," Beaman said. "We have our orders, and we'll follow them, but it always helps to know all the angles when lead flies."

"Of course, you did. And I'll tell you more when I can. It'd curl your hair if you had any left."

The shorter man was wearing a red-and-white striped *ruana* over a wool shirt and jeans. A woven *Chilote* cap covered his head. He was the picture-postcard image of one of the rough-hewn llama herders of the region.

"This is Jose," Perez-Garcia said. "He is our ears in the Atacameños. Jose was telling me a story of a gringo pretending to be an Argentine, a man named Manuel. It seems that Manuel has been very generous in supplying money and weapons to the Atacameños who are so upset about the lithium industry. I suspect if you could interrogate this Manuel, you might learn who has been responsible for all the atrocities over here. The description of this 'Manuel' sure sounds like that Josh Kirkland that you have been inquiring about."

"Thank you for that valuable information," Beaman said, then looked at Dillon and Ward. "Let's grab some chow. I'd say we have a hard night's drive ahead of us. And a dicey job to do when we get where we're going."

10

The main dish on the dinner menu was Brian Edwards' favorite, fried shrimp with a generous cupful of Cookie's special extra-horseradishy cocktail sauce. The skipper would have enjoyed it even more if he had a green salad to go along with it instead of the three-bean concoction—all three varieties from tin cans—but the *George Mason* had been at sea for weeks now. Fresh greens or anything else not from a can or the freezer were only a distant memory. Submarine chow was supposed to be the best in the US Navy, and usually was. But at the end of a long cruise that had already been unexpectedly extended, the choices became necessarily limited.

Still, the ice cream sundaes were the perfect topper and helped make up for what was lacking. So did a cup of espresso to finish it off.

After dinner, the junior officers hurried off to attend to various tasks, but Edwards found he had some time on his hands before the scheduled wardroom training at 1900. He stepped into the galley and poured himself a second cup of espresso, then pulled the wardroom cribbage board down from its shelf.

"XO, you up for a game?" he said as he set the board down on the table between them. "Cut for the deal."

Jackson Biddle looked up from the file he had been perusing while he sipped his own coffee. He knew that he had been trapped. There was no easy way to turn down a game of cribbage, the traditional game played aboard submarines. Always a popular seafarers' game, it had been brought to America by sailors aboard whaling ships way back in the eighteenth century. The XO nodded and grabbed the deck of cards. He cut an ace of diamonds to Edwards's three of spades. Good start!

Shuffling the deck and starting to deal, the XO smiled. "The cut portends your ultimate defeat, Skipper."

"Quit the early gloating," Edwards laughingly shot back. "He who gloats last, gloats best."

"I don't remember the phrase quite like that."

"Yeah, well, I kinda like it the way I said it," Edwards answered as he picked up his hand. He threw two cards into the crib and then cut the deck for Biddle to turn the starter.

"Well damn, Skipper, look at that," Biddle chortled as he threw a jack on top of the crib and promptly moved his peg two holes down the board. "And so it begins. I sense a rout."

"Remember what I said about gloating early?"

The play proceeded through several more hands, with the XO slowly pulling ahead of his captain. Biddle had turned the final corner and was halfway down the last row with Edwards still finishing the next-to-last row. Biddle dealt the hand.

Edwards picked up his cards and saw four fives and a jack. He smiled broadly. Twenty-nine points, the highest hand possible in cribbage. And the rarest one, too. In all his years playing the game in the wardrooms of many different submarines, he had never been dealt a perfect hand. He had never even seen one. All he needed to do was keep the XO from pegging out, and the game was his.

The phone under the table by his seat abruptly buzzed. Both men jumped. The phone was a direct line to the Officer-of-the-Deck. Edwards grabbed the handset and answered.

"Captain, Officer-of-the-Deck, sir," Jim Shupert said. "We lost Sierra One-Two-Eight, the Brazilian nuke."

"How'd we manage to do that?"

"He zigged and it looked like he was doing a baffle clear. I opened up a couple of thousand yards to avoid counter-detection. Then we lost him when he went above the layer. I have come up and started a lost-contact search."

The Brazilian submarine they were shadowing had moved up toward the surface and had gone above a depth at which the sound velocity changed sharply. "Above the layer," sound waves were bent upwards by the effects of both sea pressure and surface warming playing against each other. Below the layer, the water was essentially isothermal, and only pressure affected the sound waves. This caused them to bend down. The two phenomena combined to leave a shadow zone at the layer that sound waves did not penetrate. The submarine below the layer could not hear the other boat above the layer and vice versa.

"I'll be right there, Nav," Edwards told the OOD. The perfect cribbage hand temporarily forgotten, he put the phone back in its cradle, rose, and was out of the wardroom before he called back to Biddle. "XO, you'd better come, too. We could be busy for the next bit."

In the control room, he found Jim Shupert bent over the sonar display, the tip of his tongue out the corner of his mouth and a puzzled look on his face.

"Nav, this had better be good," Edwards said. "You just called me away from the first perfect cribbage hand I've ever been dealt. What you got?"

Biddle, standing behind the skipper, grinned.

Shupert looked up and shrugged. "Skipper, we haven't regained Sierra One-Two-Eight yet. Best we can tell, he suddenly slowed and came shallow after running steady since we first acquired him. Best guess is he's copying comms. I'm working my way down his track to the last known datum and then I'll start a spiral search."

Edwards nodded. Shupert was following the standard lost-contact protocol.

"Officer-of-the-Deck," the sonar supervisor called out. "Active sonar bearing three-one-six. SPL plus thirty-eight. Less than fifty percent chance of detection. Four-point-five kilohertz. Equates to a Thales UMS-3000 active sonar, carried on *Scorpene*-class submarines."

So, the other submarine in this threesome, the Argentine diesel boat, had decided to start using their active sonar for some reason. Normally, a submariner would not use active sonar for the simple reason that it advertised to a very broad audience precisely where he was located in a very large ocean. That alert reached out twice as far as he could expect to get a return from, too. What was happening here?

Jackson Biddle was bent over the ECDIS tactical display. "Skipper, the active sonar bearing is in the general direction of where we have just been getting hints of the Argentine boat."

"Any guess on a range?" Edwards asked.

The sonar supervisor piped up. "Best guess is twelve to fifteen thousand yards. We'll get a transient hit every once in a while, so he is reasonably close, but still no good passive detection. The transients are designated Sierra One-Four-Six."

Edwards nodded. The guy had been transiting all along with Sierra One-Two-Eight—the Brazilian submarine—so it made sense that he might stay pretty close to his buddy until they got to wherever they were going and did whatever it was they intended to do.

"Skipper, picking up loud transients from Sierra One-Four-Six," the sonar supe called out. Sure enough, a bright, broad white line was developing on the trace. The sub was doing something, and it was loud.

"Captain, Sierra One-Four-Six has commenced snorkeling."

Edwards looked at the sonar trace and then at the tactical display. Then he said, "If everyone else is up on the roof, it's a good time for us to go up and grab the broadcast. Officer-of-the-Deck, proceed to periscope depth and copy the broadcast."

Ten minutes later, all the message traffic meant for the *George Mason* was onboard and receipted for. And so far as they could tell, the other two submarines were still unaware they had anyone following them.

Jackson Biddle was leafing through the downloaded material while Brian Edwards worked to regain the Brazilian nuke boat. The Argentine diesel boat was still snorkeling, likely charging batteries and taking in fresh air. Her broadband sonar trace was still painting a broad swath off to the west.

"Skipper, you ain't gonna believe this." Biddle sidled up to Edwards and spoke in a low voice. "Priority message from SUBLANT. We are ordered to immediately break off and proceed at best speed to Portsmouth. They want us to come home and right damn now. The really strange part is that they are directing that we delete all sonar information and message traffic we have gathered on these two contacts and to make no further reports. It's almost like they don't want anyone to ever know we were down here this far south or that we had any encounter with these two guys."

"That is strange," Edwards agreed. The skipper rubbed his chin, thought for a moment, then said, "They say to destroy the recordings. No orders there to not back up data for safekeeping, right? See that we retain a backup disc on everything and then have the originals destroyed. Keep the backup in your safe, XO. I have a gut feeling that it may come in handy later." He then turned to Jim Shupert and ordered, "Officer-of-the-Deck, come to four hundred feet, course north, and ahead full."

The CO, the XO, and the OOD all carried deeply bewildered expressions as the *George Mason* nosed down into the deep and did a decided about-face.

Ψ

Scintillating scenery was hard to find. The little two-car convoy wheeled along Chilean Route 23, winding around volcanic peaks and past stark white salt flats. It seemed that nothing green grew this high above sea level in these desert mountains. Except for the paved highway on which Jim Ward, his SEAL team, Bill Beaman, and TJ Dillon traveled, man had left no stamp on this place at all. They may as well have been driving across the surface of Mars. This was virgin rock, altered only by wind and sun since the day the mountains were born. A full moon and a sky littered with more stars than Ward could count illuminated the scene so that it seemed almost as bright as day.

With the highway angling steeply up, the two rental SUVs wheezed and groaned as their engines tried to suck in enough oxygen from the thin air to support combustion. Ward sympathized with the straining motors. The high altitude had long since given him one splitting headache.

It was only a little over seventy-five miles from Socaire to the Argentine border at Sico Pass. At normal altitudes, and with no small-town speed traps to fear—or even small towns—the drive would have taken about an hour, but above fourteen thousand feet and thanks to the twisting mountain roads, it would require more than two hours before they would arrive at the border crossing.

When they got there, the Chilean border guards, obviously expecting them, waved them right on through. The overhead sign announced that they were entering the "Argentine Republic." It also marked the end of the paved highway. Argentine Route 51 would be a dirt track for the next two hundred miles. Ward was rethinking the strategy of driving to get out ahead of Josh Kirkland and his men, assuming they were the ones who had done all the damage to the Chilean lithium pumping stations and mines. Maybe hiking the more direct route up and over the mountains would have been quicker after all. But with all the firepower they were carrying, it would not have been an easy walk.

And who knew? Maybe they would catch up with them somewhere on this lonely route, scooting back to their lair to take stock and gloat over what they had done.

The Argentine National Gendarmerie guards—the force primarily charged with guarding the country's borders and frontier—waved Ward into the inspection station a hundred meters beyond the border sign. They were clearly not as accommodating as the Chileans had been. The SEALs had sidearms ready and were poised to grab rifles should there be a need.

Except for one old pickup, likely the transportation for the poor SOBs who drew this lonely, isolated duty, there were no other vehicles parked at the sheet-metal building. It was not surprising that there were no other travelers here since it was just now three in the morning and this spot was certainly a remote crossing far from any well-traveled stretch of highway. Ward would have been amazed if there had been anyone else crossing at this early hour. And he was relieved that was the case. Should there be a challenge from the two guards, it would be best if there were no witnesses to the inevitable solution to that problem.

"Stay alert, frogs!" Dillon told them as he jumped out and walked toward the little building. "This ain't the tourist welcome center, you know."

Five minutes later, the CIA agent returned and slid back into the SUV. He signaled Ward to drive on as the barrier bar blocking their way slowly rose ahead of them. One of the guards grinned and sharply saluted as they passed by.

Once they were through and back on their way, Ward glanced at Dillon and raised his eyebrows with the unspoken question.

Dillon chuckled. "That was five thousand of Uncle Sam's dollars that won't show up on the expense report. Or I expect on the official books of those two crossing guards. Those gendarmes will be eating high on the hog for the next few days, compliments of the good folks of the USA."

The road down from Sico Pass—if calling the rock-strewn dirt path a road was not too much of a stretch—crossed over the most desolate land that Ward had witnessed yet. Starlight reflected off washed white rock as far as he could see on either side of the road. Ahead, the route sloped sharply down to where it met the deep gray of a dried lakebed. One that had likely not held water in centuries.

The sun was little more than a bare glimmer on the far eastern horizon when the team finally pulled into the tiny mountain village of San Antonio de los Cobres. The pueblo consisted of little more than a few single-story adobe houses and a collection of metal buildings to support the copper mines up in the surrounding mountains. The raw metal hidden in the high mountains was the only reason for this village's existence.

Dillon checked his GPS and said to Ward, "Route 51 turns right here. Go straight. That'll put us on Provincial Route 70."

Ward saw nothing more through the windshield than another dirt track heading straight up the valley. This stretch made the rutted and stoney Route 51 look like an interstate highway. Was this an actual government-maintained road? As if to confirm his thoughts, a battered and rusty sign said they were now on *Ruta Provincial 70*, with an arrow that pointed in the direction they were headed.

Even before Ward could complain, TJ Dillon explained, "It's a shortcut, Jim. Fifty miles shorter and over an hour quicker. Shorter and quicker are better, right?"

Ward shot Dillon a withering look. "Maybe so, but if you think I'm going to make fifty miles an hour on this goat path, you've been sampling the local drugs. Betcha the rental company is going to keep our deposit when they see how we've abused their fine vehicles."

The one-lane dirt track took them up high mountain valleys, alongside salt flats that had once been shallow lakes before succumbing to the arid climate, skirting around long-extinct volcano cones. Then, suddenly, the track ended at a T-intersection. They had met up with National Route 52.

Ward whipped the dust-caked Toyota onto the paved highway and shot eastward. The newly paved highway felt like smooth velvet after the rocky path they had just traversed. Then they encountered a dizzying stretch of radical switchbacks. The tortuously twisting road sent them climbing steeply to fourteen thousand feet or more and then careening down the other side, just as steep and even more treacherous. And there was traffic now, a steady flow of big-rig trucks, either laboring up to the Paso de Jama border crossing or flying back down in the same direction as the SEALs were going. The trucks kept Ward on his toes. It seemed that the ones ahead were riding their brakes, while the ones behind them had none. They could smell hot brake pads and the exhaust from the big diesel engines as they used lower gears to try to keep from hurtling out of control down the slopes. All along, the twisting, turning highway descended through narrow canyons with steep mountain slopes and the occasional well-used runaway-truck escape ramps on either side. Ward hung on for dear life around each screaming hairpin turn, doing his best not to be shoved off the road by one of those eighteen-wheelers.

The village of Purmamarca sat at the end of Route 52 where it joined National Route 9. Literally translated from the local Aymara language, Purmamarca meant "town in an uncivilized land." As Ward looked out the dust-streaked windshield, he decided this adobe village was quite appropriately named.

But it was civilization. It had a gas station that appeared to be open for business. As they slowed to match the speed of several of the trucks, Ward turned to Dillon.

"TJ, how far to San Salvador de Jujuy?" he asked.

"About forty miles," Dillon answered. "Why?"

"Then it's time to get gas, some chow, and stretch my aching back," Ward answered. "I've been sucking either dust or diesel exhaust for way, way too long. I'm hungry, and the gas tank is below a quarter full."

"And I thought today's SEALs were a tough lot." Dillon ignored Ward's frown. "OK, we'll fill up and let you guys get a soda pop and a Snickers if you'll be good boys the rest of the trip."

Ward steered the Toyota into the cramped parking lot of the rustic little truck stop/cantina and eased up to the gas pumps. Bill Beaman did the same with his SUV. Ward had just crawled out of the Toyota, stretched, and told the attendant to fill it up when he glanced over at the doorway of the cantina.

"Men, stay put," he said. "Stay in the car."

Dillon, Beaman, and the rest of the team quietly eased their doors back shut and settled back. A group of men—eight or nine of them—were just sauntering out of the little establishment, evidently having finished their meal. They seemed more interested in joking with and picking at each other than they were in the two cars sitting beside the gas pumps behind them. They walked over to the far side of the lot and piled into a pair of well-used vehicles parked there.

Something in the way those men carried themselves had raised Jim Ward's antenna. These were not mining engineers or geologists. They were hard men. Combat trained men.

Then, as Ward bent lower to hide behind the gas pump, he saw another man exit the cantina and double-time over to climb into the driver's seat of one of the vehicles. That man glanced around quickly, warily, but also failed to notice the two SUVs.

Josh Kirkland. Damn! It was Josh Kirkland.

An older, grayer Kirkland, but Ward would recognize that smirk anywhere. The two vehicles cranked up and were back on the highway heading south before Ward could even speak. He looked back at Dillon and Beaman.

Dillon was the first to speak. "Was that the rat bastard I think it was?"

"As a matter of fact, it damn sure was."

"Forget breakfast, boys," Dillon said. "I think we just saw somebody we need to have a little chat with."

11

The Brazilian Navy's flagship, the helicopter carrier *Atlântico*, cautiously steamed up the Bahía Blanca Channel toward Argentina's largest navy base, Puerto Belgrano. Although Bahía Blanca literally translated to "White Bay," it clearly was not named for the muddy brown water that filled it. The murky stuff did a good job, though, of hiding a maze of ever-changing mudbanks that threatened to ground the huge vessel. By the time the *Atlântico* completed her transit from the clean open waters of the Argentine Sea to the dirty water where they dropped anchor abreast of the navy base, the captain and the Navigator of the big ship were bathed in sweat from the effort.

Capitão de Mar e Guerra Tomás Diego-Moreira had already declined the Argentine Navy's offer to moor his ship alongside the pier in the naval base's inner harbor. There had not been a deep-draft ship inside that breakwater in many years. It was unlikely that Argentina would have spent the resources to dredge the muck and silt that deep when their few destroyers that typically used the harbor drew only half as much as did the *Atlântico*. Despite rumors that the suddenly generous Chinese were willing to loan Argentina enough money to do the job in exchange for being able to station some of their own ships there at certain times of international tension, it had not yet been accomplished. Meanwhile, swinging at anchor out in the channel might be a minor inconvenience for everyone, but it was far better and less embarrassing than having to summon a bevy of tugs to ingloriously pull his ship out of the mud.

A signaling gun on the harbor breakwater blasted out a fifteen-gun salute in honor of Vice Admiral Eduardo Barbosa of the Brazilian Navy, Commander of Task Force Southern Passage. The *Atlântico* flew the vice admiral's three-star flag from its main yardarm.

Although Captain Diego-Moreira was far more concerned with getting his ship safely anchored without running aground than he was with the pomp and pageantry involved with a flagship entering a foreign port, he knew full well that he would hear from Vice Admiral Barbosa if the proper protocol was not punctiliously handled. He breathed a quick sigh of relief when the *Atlântico*'s signaling gun roared out a salute in reply and the Argentine Naval Ensign fluttered up on the port main truck.

The anchors had no more than splashed down into the hazel-hued water when a lookout spied a motor launch getting underway from the pier outside the Comando de la Flota de Mar, the Argentine fleet headquarters. The launch was flying the Argentine CNO's flag and would now be identified as the "Admiral's Barge."

Diego-Moreira quickly sent two messengers off. One was to inform Vice Admiral Barbosa that the Argentine admiral was on his way. The other was to warn *Atlântico*'s XO to get the sideboys decked out in dress whites and the ship ready to receive a four-star admiral in the proper way. Fortunately, it would be twenty minutes before the barge pulled alongside. By the time Argentine *Almirante* Anbessa Sepulveda climbed the boarding ladder, all was in readiness aboard the carrier. The boatswain piped him aboard, the sideboys rendered honors, and the seventeen-gun salute roared out across the harbor.

Vice Admiral Barbosa greeted Admiral Sepulveda with a warm handshake. The pair promptly disappeared into the flag cabin.

Life returned to normal on deck. Except for the steady stream of small boats shuttling Sepulveda's considerable staff aboard, that is. Diego-Moreira could only shake his head in disbelief. All of these junior officers and senior enlisted personnel, crowding his ship and getting in his way just so three truly ancient Argentine destroyers could steam along with the

Brazilian Navy on this mission. There were already half a dozen modern Brazilian frigates and three amphibious ships steaming around out there in the Argentine Sea. Three old rust buckets did not seem to be worth the effort. Neither did having all these staffers cluttering up the decks of his warship.

Diego-Moreira told himself that he clearly did not grasp the realities of international diplomacy. Nor could he fathom what this current mysterious set of operations with Argentina might be about. He was only a salty old sailor. Sailors followed orders. That was precisely what he would do.

He turned to the business of getting the *Atlântico* back to sea, where she belonged, without getting her stuck in the mud.

Ψ

Jim Ward was eons past being frustrated. Josh Kirkland—aka Manuel Viscosa—and his team had simply disappeared. Bill Beaman, TJ Dillon, Ward, and his SEAL team had raced out of the little gas station in Purmamarca and gave hot pursuit of Viscosa's SUVs. The thug only had about a five-minute head start when they swerved out onto National Route 9. It was a heavily traveled major highway that connected La Quiaca all the way up on the Bolivian border with Buenos Aires, twelve hundred miles to the south. But most important to Jim Ward, the road was a direct shot down the Rio Grande valley to San Salvador de Jujuy, where it passed Viscosa's storied hacienda.

At this time of year, the Rio Grande was little more than a muddy little trickle snaking its way through the mountains before it joined the Río Lavayen and helped to irrigate the farms around San Pedro de Jujuy. There were only a couple of roads, little more than jeep trails, branching off the road. According to Ward's detailed maps, they dead-ended after they climbed a few miles up to some played-out mine or a long-forgotten abandoned mountain cabin. There was no way that Viscosa and his henchmen might have disappeared up one of those goat trails to nowhere.

But disappear they had.

Ward and Dillon put their heads together and decided that the best option would be to head on down to Viscosa's hacienda and see if they had somehow gotten there already. If not, the son of a bitch was in the wind once again.

It was dark by the time they climbed the hills up out of the mountain town of San Salvador de Jujuy toward Hacienda de Viscosa. From an overlook three miles away, the place appeared to be empty. No vehicles in the parking area just inside the gated entrance. The only light shone from the gatehouse, which also appeared to be unmanned, while the great house itself was totally dark.

As the two scanned the hacienda from the convenient ridgetop, Dillon whispered, "They had to have turned north out of Purmamarca and headed toward the Bolivian border. Like a couple of non-quals, we made an assumption based on no evidence at all, that they were headed home. Looks like we were a hundred and eighty degrees off course."

Ward nodded and ruefully responded, "Yep. So now what, bossman?"

"By the time we get to the border, they could be anywhere, blowing up stuff," Dillon answered. "I'll kick my contacts in Argentina and Bolivia and see what turns up. Meanwhile, we sit here and wait. This is the one place we know they'll eventually show up."

"Eventually, huh?" Bill Beaman—even more cynical than the typical retired SEAL despite his years running his bar on the beach in the Bahamas—stood behind them. "Don't remember hearing the term in BUD-S."

"Whiskey hotel foxtrot oscar," Jim Ward responded immediately, already working on his own cynicism. "When hell freezes over."

"If you guys got a better plan, I'm ready to copy," Dillon shot back.

"Naw, we'll just camp out here in the nice cool mountains while we wait, I reckon," Beaman said with a broad grin. "Anybody ready for s'mores and a peppy singalong?"

Ψ

"Officer-of-the-Deck, picking up multiple broadband contacts to the northwest," Josh Hannon called out. "I'm counting at least seven. All are pretty much on the same bearing, give or take a degree or so. All contacts held on the conformal array."

Jeff Otanga punched up the sonar broadband display on the command console. "Yeah, I see what you're saying," he answered. "Any idea on range?"

Jim Shupert was standing back by the ECDIS, checking out the navigation situation. The most recent orders for the submarine USS *George Mason* had been to proceed to Portsmouth at best speed. Other than that, the command had been pretty open-ended. Neither the change to their OPORD nor their assigned submerged transit lanes had been sent back down to them yet. Shupert knew that the ship's Commanding Officer, Brian Edwards, was playing very loose with standard procedures, and he had a good idea why. The skipper felt it important to see if he could figure out what these two subs from two different countries were doing way down here at the bottom of the world. Likely nothing sinister, just playing submarine, but it was certainly worth investigating. The fact that somebody way up the command tree wanted to pull them off the trail and abruptly bring them home only made it more curious.

In truth, without assigned submerged waters or a valid OPORD, they should be transiting on the surface pending receipt of that information. But since they were nearer the South Pole than the Pentagon, and likely the only submarine within a thousand miles—with the exception of the two South American boats now in the Straits of Magellan—Brian Edwards felt submerged operations were warranted. His "official reasoning" was that since he had not yet received the new OPORD, he was still operating under the old one, the one that sent the *George Mason* to surveil the Argentine coast. With that in mind, the Nav was being extra cautious.

"Eng, I'd put max range at fifty miles," Shupert chimed in. "We're fifty miles off the Fondeadero Delta. The Puerto Belgrano Naval Base is up there. That's where all the Argentine Navy surface ships are homeported, and we don't want to give them indigestion if they figure out we're down here watching them."

Hannon replied, "That explains what I'm hearing, then. I can make out several frigates or destroyers and a couple of heavies. Picking them up on the wide aperture array. Ranges look to be between forty and sixty thousand yards."

"Heavies" were vessels larger than destroyers, typically aircraft carriers or large amphibs.

"Okay, let's go over and take a look," Otanga said. "Pilot, left full rudder, steady three-two-five. Ahead full."

The *George Mason* changed course smartly and surged ahead. Otanga was reaching for the phone to call Edwards when the skipper walked into control.

"What you got going on, Eng?"

"Skipper, I was just calling you," Otanga answered as he put the phone back down. "Sonar is reporting multiple broadband contacts around bearing three-two-five. That's the bearing to a major Argentine Navy base. Sonar classifies them tentatively as surface warships. They are distant, twenty to thirty miles."

The captain pondered the report for only a moment. "Well, let's mosey on over and see what's going on that might bring so many out to play," Edwards said. "Nav, make sure to keep us outside the twelve-mile limit. The coast snakes around a lot here. Eng, station the fire control tracking party. With this many contacts, we're going to need the first team up here."

It took more than an hour to close the surface ships enough to go to periscope depth to take a look. By that time, they had sorted out the contacts enough to determine they had at least five frigates or destroyers and three heavies steaming together in formation. The small guys were steaming in a loose circle around the heavies, but they all were holding station fifteen miles off the coast.

Edwards worked the *George Mason* around until he was between the surface ships and land. That was so any noise from the *George Mason* would be masked by the surf and other in-shore clamor. Plus, the surface ships would be less likely to look for a sub from that direction.

"Pilot, ahead one-third. Make four knots by log. Make your depth six-two feet," Edwards ordered. As the sub angled up, he called out, "Raising number two photonics mast. ESM, coming to periscope depth. Heads up for any threat emitters."

As the mast slid up, he shifted the command console to the photonics mast video. With the mast still underwater, it flickered from darker blue to a lighter blue color. The mast broke clear of the water and the picture on the screen glimmered with sunlight. Edwards quickly swung the mast around. Ships littered the surface to the horizon. None was close to the

George Mason. The nearest vessel was a frigate six thousand yards away, slowly heading out to sea and opening. Edwards was looking at its after-port quarter and could clearly make out the smooth sides and enclosed masts of a modern stealth frigate.

He proceeded to swing the mast around, pausing for a second at each ship, calling out "range, mark," on each as he pushed the button for the photonics mast's built-in laser range finder.

"Conn, ESM, completed initial search. No threat contacts. Hold three TRS-4D electronically scanned arrays equates to Brazilian *Tamandaré* frigates. A Type 997 Artisan surface search radar equates to an *Atlântico*-class LPH. A DRBV-21A search radar equates to a *Foudre*-class LPD. Sending bearings to fire control."

Each ship and its position data would be designated as a "target," but there were certainly no plans to shoot at anybody.

Edwards dropped the photonics mast back down, below the surface. He then punched up the recorded video to play on the large screen monitor. "All right, everybody, let's take a look at what we have floating around up there. This scene is complicated enough, like Saturday afternoon at the lake, so we need to figure it out before I stick the pole out of the water again."

Edwards, Biddle, the Nav, and the Eng huddled around the monitor, reviewing what they had just recorded. They quickly identified three Brazilian *Tamandaré* frigates, the most modern and dangerous ships in the Brazilian fleet. Quick, versatile, and heavily armed, each one could be a true threat to a submarine if angry. Then they saw the *Rademaker*, an older destroyer the Brazilians had purchased from the British a few years before. This was a good-sized ship with a lot of punch. There looked to be a couple of amphibs beyond the frigates, but it was hard to get a clear identification on those vessels.

They would need to take another look to confirm what they had seen, and also to locate and ID the heavies.

Edwards drew Biddle aside. "XO, step into ESM and talk to them about reporting ESM contacts when we are making an approach. I don't really need a complete list of everything they are hearing. Only if there is a threat. The rest can wait until rush hour's over."

Biddle nodded and was starting to leave when Edwards stopped him. "And XO, be nice."

Edwards allowed ten minutes to elapse before going back up to periscope depth to take another look. He glanced at the ECDIS tactical display to visualize what he could expect to see when he popped up the mast. In the interim since the last look, they had maneuvered to the mouth of the Bahía Blanca, just at the twelve-mile line, still barely in international waters. It was time to take another look.

Edwards raised the photonics mast and spun it around. The battle group was still pretty much where they had left them, but he could also see that there were more ships coming down the channel from the navy base. Edwards watched as the *Atlântico* LPH followed by three really old destroyers steamed by, no more than a thousand yards away. He could plainly see the people on deck and the broad streaks of rust down the sides of the destroyers.

Edwards dropped the photonics mast and scratched his head. "Well, it looks like most of the Argentine Navy has come out to play, and a big part of the Brazilian Navy is already here for the party, too. Let's open out a couple of hundred miles and then tell the boss what we stumbled upon. Eng, get me deep and two hundred miles off the coast. XO, let's review the video again and draft up a message to send back home."

Both the CO and XO had puzzled expressions on their faces. Nothing wrong with a couple of friendly nations joining up to practice war. But typically, when they did, they told everybody else ahead of time to avoid any unwarranted speculation. Nobody had mentioned any such exercise to the *George Mason*.

Well, figuring all this out was the job of Naval Intelligence, and they were pretty good at it. Most of the men on the front line knew that the last two Directors of Naval Intelligence —Admirals Donnegan and Ward, both former submarine skippers—had done spectacular jobs when given the data they needed. It was the task of Edwards and his crew to gather that information so the folks back in the Pentagon could have a better chance of making the right call.

Edwards and Biddle stepped back to the skipper's stateroom to begin composing their message.

Ψ

Guillermo Manuelito jerked awake, instantly wide-eyed. It took a moment to adjust to the different surroundings, to not awakening in his familiar bedroom back at La Granja with the warm body of Abril, his wife, snuggled next to him. Giving him a morning kiss. Rising without complaint to go start his coffee and breakfast while he got ready to go out to work the groves. The flood of emotions overwhelmed him when he realized that the hacienda was no more, that the family he loved so much was now far away from him. But at least they were safely in hiding somewhere in Uruguay. He, on the other hand, was only marginally secure, in what Balduino called a "safe house." He didn't know how accurate that description really was, or how long it might apply. Or how much his family worried about him as he pursued what he saw as his new calling to be a freedom fighter.

The place was actually nothing more than an ancient adobe farmhouse on the outskirts of the town of Río Segunda, many miles north and west of his former family olive farm. The house backed up to a small, muddy stream, barely ankle deep, that someone in antiquity had rather generously named the Río Segundo, the Second River. The locals had long since dubbed the little creek "Río Enclenque," the "Puny River."

Guillermo stretched and peeked out the window at the new day. The sun was still well below the eastern horizon, but it was growing lighter. Years of farm work had geared his body clock so he would be up and at work by this time each day. "Waste sunlight, waste money," his father had warned. And only two things justified being in bed when it was daylight outside. Illness was one. The other only created more mouths to feed.

He could hear Ricardo Balduino rustling about in the next room. The rebel fighter was an early riser, too. Today they would be moving to another safe house, using daylight and open roads for cover. In this area, anything moving at night created suspicion. They had been hiding in this place long enough already. Possibly too long. They needed to move closer to the next planned strike to help the cause of liberation for their people.

"*¡Buenos días!*" Ricardo called out. "I hear you coming to life in there. *¿Listo?*"

"Yes, I have been ready. Ready while you were still snoring and dreaming of all the girls you claimed to have conquered while I was making an honest living."

"Claimed? Claimed?" Balduino allowed himself a rare laugh.

After leaving his family alongside the Pavon River, Ricardo had driven him in a circuitous route all over northern Argentina. They hadn't spent more than a few hours in any one place until Ricardo was quite sure the hated Federales were not hot on their trail. Then Ricardo brought him to this farmhouse.

They had been hiding here for a week without anyone even coming close. Their next move would take them somewhere north of Cordoba. Ricardo said something about an important meeting there tomorrow night, assumedly about another mission.

Something out the window caught Guillermo's eye. Something among the trees, down by the river. He could not be sure what he had seen. It was nothing more than a hint of motion out of the corner of his eye.

Wait. There it was again. Yes, something big was slowly making its way through the brush. Something trying to move quietly and remain hidden but definitely coming their way.

Then, confirmation. A covey of *perdices*—Argentine partridges— suddenly burst from the low brush. Startled, their distinctive, high-pitched calls shattered the peaceful quiet of dawn. The fleeing birds disappeared over a fence row to the east.

Guillermo clearly saw the camo-clad man, spooked by the birds, hastily dashing behind a tree. The man carried a scoped long gun. That was not a weapon for bird hunting. Simultaneously, several other men ducked for cover to each side of the first gunman.

Manuelito grabbed his Browning Hi-Power, checked that the clip was full and chambered a round. The 9mm was locked and loaded, ready to go. Ducking low, he moved out the door and across to Ricardo's room.

"We have visitors," Manuelito whispered as he entered. "Shooters moving in down by the river."

"How many?" Balduino asked, not really surprised, as he picked up his own automatic.

"From the movement, several," Manuelito answered. "I only saw one for sure, but signs of more. Wearing camo with a rifle. I'm guessing at least a half dozen."

"We are going to need some more firepower," Balduino said between clenched teeth. "At least more than these pop guns."

He jammed his pistol into his waistband before grabbing a Remington 1200 shotgun from beneath the bed and tossing it to Guillermo. He then grabbed his FARA 83 automatic rifle and several spare magazines.

The pair duck-walked into the kitchen. Out the rear window they could see six men in camouflaged dress crouched down, moving across the field that separated the farmhouse from the river. The men were about halfway across the hundred meters of open ground, keeping well spread out as they converged on the house and what they assumed would be its sleeping occupants.

Balduino looked sideways at Manuelito, then took careful aim and fired off one round. His bullet dropped one of the attackers. The figure did not move again. The rest immediately fell to the ground and started shooting. Rifle fire spattered the house, shattering the kitchen windows and splintering the door. It appeared most of the return fire was not coming from the men hunkered down in the field. It emanated from a stand of trees along the riverbank.

"Snipers," Balduino said. They were obviously there to give the assault team cover fire.

"Ricardo," Guillermo shouted over the fusillade. "You concentrate on the snipers, then. The ones down by the river." He pumped the action on his 12-gauge. "I'll handle the ones in the field."

As he moved to the bedroom where he could get a better angle on the assault team, Manuelito heard Balduino deliver several three-shot bursts toward the more distant shooters. The attackers had quickly realized that the return fire was now aimed at the snipers, so they continued their advance on the house, slithering across the field. Unfortunately for them, the grain had already been harvested and all that was left in the field for cover was some low stubble.

Also bad for them was the fact that Manuelito knew to remain patient and allow them to get much closer, well within range. Then he aimed at the nearest attacker and blasted him with a round of double-aught buckshot.

Blood exploded from where the man's head had been. Manuelito pumped the action and took aim at the next one. He fired again, scored a fatal hit, and then immediately ducked as automatic weapons fire peppered the window from which he was shooting.

It was getting hot quick!

He rushed back into the kitchen to find Balduino on the floor, leaning against a cabinet, clutching his side. Blood welled up around his hands. He looked at Manuelito and groaned, "They hit me, *amigo*. Lucky shot."

There was no time to field dress Balduino's wounds while fighting off the assailants by himself. Assuming they even had a realistic chance against the overwhelming odds. Manuelito made an instinctive decision. He blasted off two more shotgun rounds downrange, then grabbed the wounded MDR leader and helped him to his feet. It was time to run. He was just lifting Balduino when the back door crashed open. He blew away the entering gunman with the shotgun as the door swung open and then half-carried, half-dragged Balduino over what was now a blood-spattered corpse.

The truck was parked very near the back door of the house. Manuelito opened the driver's-side door and shoved Ricardo over to the passenger seat, ignoring his agonized groans. Then he slid in behind the wheel. In anticipation of just such a hurried departure, the keys were already in the ignition of the battered pickup. It cranked on the first try. Thrusting it into gear, he spun it around on the gravel and shot off down the country lane, which ran the opposite direction from where the shooters were coming. All the time, he sprayed 9mm rounds with his left hand to discourage pursuit as he drove and shifted gears with his right.

An Iveco Daily delivery van, proudly painted out with the logo of the Grupo Especial de Operaciones Federales, blocked the lane where it turned onto Ruta Provincial C-45. A lone guard was waving, signaling for the truck to stop. Then, when Manuelito kept coming, the soldier raised his rifle and pointed it directly at the driver.

The guard hesitated. It was a move that proved fatal for him.

Manuelito gunned the engine even as he aimed a couple of pistol rounds at the man. Then, just before he collided with the van, he turned sharply. His front bumper hit the guard squarely before striking the rear quarter of the light van and shoving it out of the way. Manuelito fought to control the pickup. It slid off the far side of the road and then skewed back up onto the blacktop of the main highway. There was an eruption of dirt, dust, grass, and gravel.

He kept his foot on the accelerator and skipped second gear, going straight to high. Amazingly, the road ahead was clear, and the old truck seemed to be steering and running just fine despite the collision. As he sped away, Guillermo Manuelito knew he needed to put distance between them and the assault team. Hopefully, the van was immobilized. That would give him some time, but radio waves traveled much faster than this vintage pickup. There would be trouble coming to meet them.

He needed to get Balduino to a doctor. There would be one somewhere in the vicinity who was on the side of the cause, but Ricardo would have to be conscious and able to direct him, either to the sympathetic doc or to someone else who could give directions.

Finally, he would have to locate another vehicle. By now, the Federales would certainly be looking for this particular old, white truck with the badly damaged left front fender and ugly assortment of bullet holes.

12

"Conn. Maneuvering, reactor scram! Request rig for reduced electrical. Answering 'all stop.' Cause not known." The urgent announcement from the 7MC speaker blared into Bill Wilson's ear.

In his mind, he ran through the immediate actions to take in response to a reactor scram, an emergency shutdown where some of the control rods had slammed into the core, stopping the fission reaction in a nuclear reactor. Turning to Jason Schmidt, the on-watch pilot, he calmly but forcefully ordered, "Pilot, answer, 'All stop.' Make your depth one-five-zero feet. Right full rudder, steady course zero-nine-zero."

First step was to stop using steam, to save it for emergency use if needed, while employing as much residual speed as possible to coast up closer to the surface in case they needed to go there in a hurry.

Wilson yelled over to the sonar supervisor, working to keep his own voice calm but firm. "Clearing baffles to the east. Coming to one-five-zero feet." Then he grabbed the 1MC microphone to speak to everyone aboard the *George Mason* and ordered, "Reactor scram! Rig ship for reduced electrical. Casualty assistance team, lay aft."

He could feel the ship planing upward as it lost speed. The compass rose showed the bow moving around from the north to point toward the east. The control room grew noticeably quieter as the co-pilot killed all electrical loads that were not absolutely necessary. Things like the air conditioning and most of the vent fans.

Wilson glanced over to see Brian Edwards casually standing across the control room from him, beside the co-pilot, scribbling in a notebook. He could never quite understand why the skipper still insisted on actually writing notes, pen on paper, when it was so much simpler just to record on a notepad computer.

It was the first and only indication that this reactor scram was a drill. Not that it mattered. When the rods hit the bottom, the reactor was scrammed for real. They really needed to get the reactor back up and online, or going home would be very hard and very slow.

Wilson reported, "Skipper, Maneuvering reports a reactor scram. No known cause yet. Answering 'All stop,' coming to one-five-zero feet on course zero-nine-zero."

Edwards glanced at his watch and replied, "Very well, rig for delayed scram recovery."

Wilson grabbed the 7MC mike and ordered, "Maneuvering, conn. Rig for delayed scram."

With this order, the engineers would take action to conserve as much steam in the ship's steam plant system as they could in order to save residual power for emergency use. Meanwhile, they'd troubleshoot to determine whatever problem had caused the scram, and then work to correct it—hopefully quickly. All the electrical loads would be shifted from the steam-driven turbine generators over to the battery and the turbines secured. Then they would be running on battery power, just as submarines had done for most of the century prior to the development of the USS *Nautilus*, the first nuclear-powered vessel.

The engineers would also shift propulsion from the main engines to the tiny, electrically driven emergency propulsion motor. The EPM could drive the *George Mason* forward at a couple of knots but in the process, it used a lot of valuable battery power. That was why it was only turned on if absolutely needed.

With the engine room rigged for delayed scram, all power on the sub would be assumed by the battery until Bill Wilson could get them up to periscope depth and light off the emergency diesel generator. He would do that as soon as sonar had completed the baffle clear, and when he knew for sure what contacts might await them up there on the surface. Surfacing submarines had ruined the day of more than one fishing boat, and that created a great amount of paperwork.

With the diesel generator running, they would have an hour to fix whatever had caused the scram. If they could not complete the repairs within that one-hour time limit, they would need to fully shut down the reactor and then bob around at periscope depth until they could finish the repairs and do a complete normal reactor start-up.

There was another motive to make haste while floating about on the ocean's surface. Only a small number of people on planet Earth knew where the *George Mason* was located. There were plenty of good reasons to keep it that way. The longer they floated around up there in plain sight, the more difficult it would be to keep that secret.

"Steady on course zero-nine-zero, speed point-four knots and slowing. Depth one-five-zero feet," Jason Schmidt reported just as Josh Hannon called out, "Completed baffle clear. One new contact, Sierra One-Two-Nine, bearing one-three-seven. Wide aperture range one-four-thousand yards. Contact just lit off, classified warship, probable *Niterói*-class frigate."

Hello! Brian Edwards quickly stepped back to the command module and studied the sonar display for a short moment. Then he grabbed the 1MC microphone and announced, "Secure from scram drill! Commence a fast recovery start-up."

Within fourteen thousand yards of a potentially hostile warship—particularly one with anti-submarine warfare capabilities—was no place to be running engineering drills, and certainly no place to stick up the snorkel mast and light off the diesel generator. The captain's sudden order was also the first confirmation that all this emergency activity was only an exercise.

The fast recovery start-up was an emergency procedure developed soon after the tragedy of the USS *Thresher* (SSN-593), which was lost with all hands in April of 1963. Fast recovery allowed the engine room and the reactor to be rapidly and simultaneously brought back online as long as certain safety criteria were met.

The 7MC almost immediately blared back with, "Commencing a fast recovery start-up. Latching control rods."

It only took a few seconds for the reactor operator to latch the control rods and then to begin withdrawing them from the core until the fission process had resumed and the reactor was once again critical. Then he carefully monitored the reactor until the core was producing enough heat to make steam.

The 7MC soon announced, "The reactor is at the point of adding heat."

With that confirmation, the engineers could start using steam to bring the main engines and the turbines back online while the reactor operator continued to carefully withdraw the rods to heat the reactor core back to normal operating temperature. The Officer-of-the-Deck could then use the main engines again if he really needed them, but only at a reduced speed. That would slow the recovery considerably. Bill Wilson chose to wait, since there was no reason not to remain exactly where he was in the ocean for a bit longer.

The engineers brought the first turbine generator back online. The electrical operator then shifted the electric plant to a half-power lineup on that turbine and took the load off the battery.

"The electric plant is in a half-power lineup on the port turbine generator. Answering bells on the main engines," the voice on the 7MC proclaimed.

That was Bill Wilson's cue. He grabbed the 1MC and announced, "Secure from reduced electrical." Immediately, he heard the vent fans spool up and felt the welcome cool air on his face and arms. And he now had enough propulsion to drive the ship. "Ahead one-third," he called out to the pilot.

"Okay, Mr. Wilson," Edwards said. "Let's go up to periscope depth and see this guy who dared to stumble into the middle of our engineering drills."

Wilson wiped the sweat from his brow and responded, "Yes, sir. But at least he gave us a few new things to practice." Turning to Jason Schmidt, Wilson ordered, "Pilot, make your depth six-two feet."

The George Mason swam up closer to the sea surface until the photonics mast showed them a crystal-clear blue sky and an empty, darker-blue sea. Empty except for a small ship just at the horizon to their southeast.

"Conn, ESM, picking up a twelve-megahertz surface search radar, classified a Terma 'Scanter Mil.' Also picking up an S-band air search radar, classified as RAN-20S. Best bearing one-three-five. Neither are threats. Both systems are carried on *Niterói*-class Brazilian frigates."

Wilson grabbed the 21MC mike and answered, "ESM, conn, aye. We hold a frigate visually and on sonar on that bearing. Sierra one-two-nine."

Everything agreed. Just more unanticipated naval activity way down here. But what was a Brazilian frigate doing hanging around just off the Uruguayan coast, anyway?

Then it got even more crowded.

"Conn, ESM, receiving a second Terma Scanter and a Furuno nav radar on bearing three-three-one."

Wilson spun the photonics mast around to look down that bearing. Nothing visible out there but blue sea and sky. Hannon shook his head. Sonar could not yet hear anything on that bearing either.

"ESM, conn. We don't hold anything on that bearing. Designate this contact as Echo-two. Possibly another Brazilian warship."

And the boss wanted them to leave this fun party just as it was getting going?

Brian Edwards idly scratched his chin as he pondered just how much longer he and his submarine could dawdle down here before having no option but to skedaddle as ordered.

Ψ

Argentine President Bruno Martinez sat back and stretched. It was a beautiful Monday morning in Buenos Aires, and he was feeling especially chipper today. Perhaps it was the morning sun playing on the flowers in the gardens below his balcony. Maybe it was the café con leche and plate of *medialunas* his personal chef had served. Most likely, it was a truly memorable night with his new, beautiful, and quite skilled *amante*.

Martinez was not sure. Then again, he really did not care. His recent moves were having all the desired effects, and most were lining up exactly as his friends—especially his Chinese and Brazilian friends—had predicted.

The door from his office out onto the private balcony unexpectedly swung open. Daniel Campos, his *asistente de oficina,* swished out, his cerulean blue jacket and mauve shirt vying with the flowers for color and flamboyance.

"*Señor Presidente,* the Uruguayan ambassador is in the outer office, and he seems to be in a feisty mood. He is most insistent that he speaks directly with you. He says the matter is most urgent. I did not know what to tell him, I'm afraid."

Martinez frowned. This infrequent moment of peace and happiness was hopelessly shattered. He had to remind himself that his utterly incompetent assistant was not only the son of the Minister of the Economy, but also the *amante* of the Chief of the Army. Both were powerful men and vital allies. Especially now that the plan was well in motion.

Bruno Martinez took a final sip of coffee and wiped his lips without replying to Campos. Then, after carefully folding his napkin, he rose and looked for a moment out onto the flower garden.

"Well, have the cook clear this, then," he finally said, waving at the remnants of his breakfast. "Then show his excellency, the ambassador, into my office. Let us see what the old windbag finds so very important that he must interrupt my busy morning."

Martinez walked across his spacious office and took a seat behind the massive mahogany desk. Its top was clean. No papers or documents. The credenza behind Martinez was flanked by the flag of Argentina and the presidential standard. Above the credenza hung a life-sized portrait of Martinez's father wearing his full-dress uniform as a general of the Argentine Army. This was an office meant to impress, not one where work got done.

The massive oak outer office doors swung open. An older, short, balding man marched through the doorway and walked purposefully toward Martinez. From behind him, Daniel Campos announced loudly, "*Señor Presidente,* his Excellency Marcel Díaz-Acosta, the Uruguayan ambassador."

Martinez rose, smiled, and offered his hand across the desk to the clearly agitated diplomat. Díaz-Acosta ignored the handshake and snapped to attention. The man's face was florid with repressed anger.

"President Martinez, I deliver a message from President Félix Mendez, representing the people of Uruguay."

Martinez glanced toward Campos and gave him a wave. "Leave us, please, Daniel." As soon as the door swung shut behind his assistant, the president turned to the ambassador and asked, "What is this message you are so determined to deliver in person?"

Marcel Díaz-Acosta bit off his words as he spoke. "The government of the Oriental Republic of Uruguay forcefully protests the actions of the Federative Republic of Brazil and the Argentine Republic in establishing an illegal blockade of our ports and in closing our borders. These actions constitute acts of war. I am officially informing you—in person—that we are protesting your actions before the United Nations and the Organization of American States. We further demand that you raise the blockade and reopen the borders immediately, or we will necessarily invoke the protective measures available to us."

"Mr. Ambassador," Martinez answered, his voice intentionally calm and soothing, "I have no knowledge of any overt blockade of your ports. As necessitated to maintain peace and security, our two countries have instituted a protected and lawful exclusion zone inside a thousand miles of our borders. It is unfortunate that you view this as a blockade of your ports. As we see it, this offers an excellent opportunity for your nation to join Brazil and Argentina in the defense of our borders." President Martinez changed his voice so that it became noticeably hard and unforgiving. "Otherwise, Mr. Ambassador, you must accept the fate of a tiny mouse caught between two giants. Tell President Mendez that he either joins us in our noble efforts to finally repel the colonialists and anti-socialists, or there will be troops on his borders in one week."

Ambassador Díaz-Acosta's face was no longer red with anger. It was pale white with fear.

13

"What the holy hell is going on down there?" President Stan Smitherman growled. "We gonna fool around and get caught up in this little territorial skirmish or what?"

Sitting across the Resolute desk from the president, Sebastien Aldo and Sandra Dosetti squirmed uncomfortably in their straight-backed side chairs. The commander in chief did have a reputation for treating underlings every way but gently. The Secretaries of Defense and State were very familiar with their subservient positions, so there was no point in complaining. They also knew Smitherman expected to be informed of every development and morsel of information that might prove useful, whether or not he actually paid any attention to the data. Or bellowed about being blasted with so much minutiae when he was trying to run a country, for God's sake.

Harold Osterman sat back comfortably on one of the facing overstuffed couches in the office, enjoying the president's scolding. He took a sip of his coffee and smiled. It was good not to be directly in Smitherman's line-of-fire for a change.

"Wh–wh–what's the problem, Mr. President?" Aldo stammered. "We have kept you and your staff informed. Everything is going according to plan. The *Gerald Ford* battle group reports that they arrived on station, seven hundred miles off Natal, in the state of Rio Grande do Norte, Brazil, and have commenced steaming down the coastline—five hundred nautical miles out, as you directed—to show our defiance of their ridiculous thousand-mile limit."

"Yeah, about time," Smitherman said with a grunt. "What's that smarmy bastard Souza up to anyway?"

The Secretary of Defense nervously riffled through his notes, looking for a particular page, found it, then answered, "The Brazilian Air Force sent out one of their early warning birds, something called an Embraer R-99. It flew around a bit and tried to order the *Ford* out of the disputed waters. A pair of our F-18s played escort until the Brazilian aircraft got tired and went back home." Aldo looked through his notes again while the president blew cigar smoke rings. "Satellites are showing a patrol craft leaving harbor from the Natal Navy Base. ETA to the *Ford* is about noon tomorrow, DC time."

"One lousy patrol boat ain't gonna do crap against the *Ford*," Smitherman replied. "We know it. They know it. I told y'all, it's all bluster, distracting us from that currency mess they're trying to pull off. Which they won't, by the way. You sure there ain't no other Brazilian Navy ships headin' that way?"

"No, sir, none," Aldo answered firmly. "We estimate all their big stuff is down south, either in that bunch the *George Mason* stumbled on or enforcing their blatantly illegal blockade on Uruguay."

Osterman chimed in then. "Speaking of our wayward submarine, where's that damn loose cannon by now?"

Aldo looked at his notes yet again and flipped a couple of pages, unwilling to rely on his memory when performing for the president and vice president. "Latest traffic from them says they are heading north off the Uruguay coast. They are also reporting contact on a couple of Brazilian frigates patrolling off the coast fifty miles east of La Palma, likely in support of the blockade."

Smitherman vigorously shook his head back and forth, then leaned forward. "Look, that damn submarine seems to always be getting in the way down there. Damn thing's gonna screw around and get some shootin' started or give Brazil and Argentina a reason to blow up at us!" The president slammed his fist onto the desk for dramatic emphasis.

"Easy, boss," Osterman told him. "Remember your blood pressure. Doc warned you at your last physical. Don't go getting excited." Osterman thought for a few seconds before adding, "Besides, that sub's not doing anything but reporting to us while they come on back up to Portsmouth for refit. He's not affecting anything the Brazilians are doing. The Argentinians either. None of them know he's there. And Tan Fong sure as hell doesn't know he's there watching all the shenanigans—"

Sandra Dosetti interrupted with a wave of her hand. She was looking at her phone in the other. "By the way, the Uruguayan embassy has just sent through diplomatic channels an official request for military assistance in ending Brazil's blockade. They also delivered an official request to the Organization of American States and the United Nations Security Council for an immediate meeting and a call for votes to invoke mutual defense accords. How do you want us to deal with that, Mr. President?"

"One thing at a time," Smitherman dictated, his cigar now forgotten. "First, on that submarine, make sure the thing keeps moving north while it's still our little secret. Once it's well north of Brazil, I really don't give a damn where it goes. Just keep it busy until this all blows over and everything is replaced in the press cycle by something else that draws better ratings and clicks and shit." Then, looking at Secretary of State Dosetti, he went on. "Look, China will veto anything we or Uruguay propose in the Security Council. The OAS will argue back and forth until the cows come home, and nothing will ever happen with that bunch."

"Maybe so, Mr. President," Dosetti responded. She held up a piece of paper. "But just remember, the OAS charter, Article 28, says, 'Every act of aggression by a State against the territorial integrity or the inviolability of the territory or against the sovereignty or political independence of an American State shall be considered an act of aggression against the other American States.' It doesn't say that the act of aggression can't come from an OAS member. A blockade is an act of aggression. So, what do we do if the OAS can actually align enough members against Argentina to start shoving back with bullets and torpedoes?"

"Sandy . . ." Smitherman knew Sandra Dosetti despised being called Sandy. "I want you to do what the State Department does best. Dither, duck, dodge, and fart around without making any substantive statement about anything. Keep all those other OAS ambassadors arguing and speechmaking and grandstanding until this shit is long forgotten. Most of them have never been on CNN before. They'll love the bright lights. That's what I want you and your bullshit artists to do. Got it?"

"Yes, Mr. President." Her face was a deep red. With a wave of dismissal, Smitherman rose and headed off toward his study. He stopped to look back at his two cabinet members and veep. "All right, you two have your instructions, now get busy. And do a better job of keeping me up to date on everything, how about it?" Looking to Osterman, he said, "Harold, I just got a great bottle of Pappy Van Winkle's Family Reserve. Really smooth sippin' whiskey. Wanna join me for a taste before dinner?"

Ψ

A long line of heavy haulers loaded with Leopard 1 main battle tanks from Brazil's Sixth Army Division clogged the westbound lanes of the Osvaldo Aranha Highway, BR-290, where it snaked out of Porto Alegre. The roadway ran arrow-straight for one hundred and twenty-five miles before reaching a major split. There, half of the transports turned south, taking BR-153 to the border crossing into Uruguay at the tiny town of Aceguá. The rest of the convoy continued on, driving farther west to the much larger subtropical city of Sant'Ana do Livramento, which straddled the Uruguayan border. A couple of miles outside both towns, the heavy haulers dropped off their massive main battle tanks. The armored behemoths lumbered off, spouting smoke and sending up billows of dust as they took up positions where their cannons overlooked the key border crossings.

Another column of tanks clogged the busy BR-116 heading from Porto Alegre southwest down to the river town of Jaguarão, another border crossing point. Here too, the armored vehicles took positions threatening the line that marked the border between Brazil and Uruguay.

The arrival of the tanks was merely the beginning. Within the next few hours, the Brazilian Army moved more troops and vehicles into position at points along the Uruguayan border. Their total number of soldiers and tanks along the border constituted more than three times the force of the entire Uruguayan Army.

At the same time, the Argentine First Armored Brigade moved their Tanque Argentino Mediano—medium tanks—from their base in Tandil, south of Buenos Aries, up to threaten the strategic bridges on the Uruguay River at Fray Bentos and Nuevo Paysandú. Additionally, the Argentine First Army Division shifted troops and infantry fighting vehicles down from their base at Curuzú Cuatiá to the border crossing at Salto. After those moves, the Argentine forces deployed on the border constituted a force that was more than twice the size of the Uruguayan Army.

With little fanfare, and without a single shot fired, the Argentines and the Brazilians took position, dug in, and sat there, daring anyone to challenge them.

Uruguayan President Mendez pleaded with the United Nations, the Organization of American States, and personally to US President Stan Smitherman for assistance and protection from the combined threat sitting poised on his borders. There were many speeches at the UN and OAS, but nobody took any vote or moved for action, other than issuing pleas for no hostilities from any of the three parties. President Smitherman offered only the suggestion that Mendez take it up with the relatively new heads of state of the other two nations, see what they really wanted, and not provoke any kind of dangerous military response. A response in which civilians, in addition to military personnel, might be injured or killed. Besides, Smitherman explained, the US had obligations in other parts of the world and was not prepared, economically or militarily, to become involved in a "minor border dispute way down there the other side of the equator." Best they settle this little dust-up among themselves.

Meanwhile, traffic and commerce into and out of Uruguay from Brazil and Argentina came to a virtual halt. Citizens began to feel the pinch within only a few days.

Ψ

Argentine Navy *Capitán de Fragata* Colas Lopez Alveras carefully eased his submarine up to periscope depth. Even down here at the bottom of the world, ship traffic was thick. The heavy, deep-draft container ships and tankers would be very unforgiving of a tiny submarine that might suddenly pop to the surface in front of one of them. They had no brakes, of course, and such massive vessels could hardly take evasive measures. The only thing to do was to hide behind one of the many tiny islands, back in one of the deep fjords, when trying to come up to periscope depth to see what was going on.

The trip down from Mar del Plata in the company of the Brazilian nuclear submarine *João Cândido* had been uneventful until they rounded Punta Dúngeness. There they separated, and Alveras guided the *Santiago del Estero* deep into the Straits while the *João Cândido* conducted a detailed surveillance of the Bahía Felipe and then Punta Arenas.

Alveras's orders were simple. He was to take the *Santiago del Estero* far up the Paso Froward and guard the door against any Chilean interference. Any interference at all. He had asked for confirmation that this meant sinking any military vessel from Chile that might attempt to pass. Affirmative, he was told. Any warship in the Straits would be knowingly challenging the new declaration regarding rightful Argentine territorial waters. They would have to be shown the threats against such an unlawful incursion had been no toothless bluff.

Once in the Straits, the water was plenty deep, but the channel itself was twisting and narrow. The large commercial ships transiting these routes frequently gave Alveras little choice but to abruptly go deep to avoid being run over. It took almost three days from the time they entered the Straits until they were in their assigned patrol area. Three days of winding through narrow channels surrounded by granite cliffs on either side. Three days of almost being run over by giant tankers and then having to try to get back to periscope depth again without being scalped by a tanker or freighter. Alveras felt that it was his duty to always be in the control room under such conditions, always ready to instantaneously take whatever action he needed to keep his ship safe and on the job. He was exhausted.

Once they had the *Santiago del Estero* safely behind some unnamed island in the middle of the channel between Peninsula Brunswick and Isla Santa Inés, Alveras at last felt it was safe for him to go to his tiny stateroom and nap for a few minutes. After giving his watch officer instructions to remain hidden behind the island and to call him if he saw any Chilean warships, Alveras finally allowed himself to go lie down.

The captain was sure that his head had just hit the pillow when his phone buzzed angrily, breaking his deep sleep. The watch officer reported a large Chilean amphibious ship escorted by a frigate had just rounded the island. The two were heading down the channel, boldly steaming in newly declared Argentine waters.

Alveras rushed to the control room and grabbed the periscope. He quickly identified the *Sargento Aldea*, a landing platform dock (LPD) and the largest ship in the Chilean Navy. The other vessel was the *Capitán Prat*, a frigate that the Chileans had not so long ago purchased from Australia. The two ships were steaming in company, the frigate leading the larger amphib. They were close enough that Alveras could see people out on the LPD's flight deck, evidently enjoying the late afternoon sunshine despite the chilly temperatures at this latitude.

He quickly called his submarine to battle stations and readied the torpedoes in tubes one and two. The Italian Black Shark heavyweight torpedoes in each tube were the ideal weapon for this situation. The battery-operated torpedoes' fifty-knot speed could easily outrun either target, and the three-hundred-and-fifty-kilo warheads on each weapon had the ability to quickly put either vessel on the bottom. The only thing that concerned Alveras was how the torpedoes' active sonar would handle the narrow, granite-walled strait. Would the inevitable reverberation blank out the sonar return and confuse them? He decided not to risk it and chose to use passive sonar instead. Not as accurate or sensitive, but immune to the reverberation problem.

In the three minutes that it took to get the *Santiago del Estero* battle-ready and the target solution refined enough to shoot, the two targets had opened the range by almost two kilometers. That was of no concern. The Black Shark torpedoes had a maximum range of over fifty kilometers before they ran out of power.

Alveras took an observation on the *Sargento Aldea*. The solution in the fire control system closely matched what he was seeing through the periscope. It would be almost impossible to miss. He launched the first torpedo directly at the broad stern of the LPD. High-pressure water flushed the torpedo out of its tube. As soon as the weapon sensed it was clear of the nest, the electric motors started driving the contra-rotating propellers. The torpedo quickly gained speed and dutifully turned toward the *Sargento Aldea*.

"Captain, sonar reports torpedo running normally," the watch officer said. "Fire control has good signal on the wire."

Alveras nodded, but he was already working on the frigate. He wanted to get that torpedo in the water before the first one exploded and warned the frigate that they were under attack. He took an observation on the *Capitán Prat*. Again, the fire control solution agreed completely with what he was seeing with his own eyes.

"Fire tube two at the frigate," he calmly ordered.

Once again, high-pressure water forced the torpedo out of the tube. The electric motors sent the weapon speeding toward the unsuspecting frigate.

"Normal wire continuity on second weapon," the Watch Officer reported. "Sonar reports second weapon running normally."

The Fire Control Petty Officer called out, "First weapon has enabled, slowed to passive search."

Alveras lowered the periscope and looked at the computer screen. It showed the first weapon heading straight for the *Sargento Aldea*. It had to traverse another thousand meters—that would take less than one minute—before it would then detect the presence of the LPD and begin to chase it down.

The waiting was interminable. There was nothing for Alveras to do but calmly watch it all play out on the computer screens like some extremely lethal video game. He found himself clutching a periscope lifting rod with white knuckles. A quick thought passed through his head: The two deadly torpedoes launched from his submarine were still tethered to the boat by thin wires. With an order, he could divert them, abort their mission.

But he did not even consider such a thing. He had his orders. He would obey them for his president, for his country. For the Argentine Navy.

"Second weapon has enabled, slowed to passive search," came the report.

Then the Fire Control Petty Officer called out, "Detect! First torpedo detect." The torpedo had found the *Sargento Aldea*. The device would now make sure the target satisfied its logic circuits. It would, of course. Then the torpedo would close in for the kill.

142

GEORGE WALLACE & DON KEITH

"First torpedo acquisition. In final attack."

Alveras quickly raised the periscope. The two warships still peacefully steamed down the channel, unaware of the threat lurking beneath them.

Assured it was doing what it had been programmed to do, the first torpedo armed its warhead and charged in. Its course took it to just beneath the *Sargento Aldea*. When it sensed the ship above it, the warhead detonated.

The explosion instantaneously drove the giant warship upward and generated a huge pocket of high-pressure gas beneath the doomed vessel. Just as quickly as the gas pocket generated, it collapsed, dropping the *Sargento Aldea* back into what amounted to a hole in the water, breaking its back.

Only the bow and the stern remained above the surface, each cocked at odd angles and sinking quickly. Alveras could see men sliding off the ship's decks, falling into the cold water, arms and legs flailing.

"Detect! Second torpedo detect."

Alveras spun the scope to look at the frigate. He saw the stern squat down in frothy white water as the ship's twin gas turbines drove its screw up to maximum speed. The ship was also turning as it sped up, both to go to the aid of the vessel it was supposed to be protecting and to dodge any weapon that might be aimed toward it.

It was already too late.

"Second torpedo acquisition. In final attack."

Just like the *Sargento Aldea*, the torpedo broke *Capitán Prat*'s back. The two halves of the frigate rose high in the water and then disappeared below the surface as if shoved down by giant hands. On the surface of the strait where two proud warships had sat just moments before, nothing remained except flotsam from the wreckage and a few survivors, swimming furiously, struggling to reach the shore.

Now there was only one other chore. It was time to tell Comando de la Fuerza de Submarinos what had transpired here.

It was then that another odd thought entered the mind of Captain Colas Lopez Alveras: This was no game. No practice exercise. For the first time in his long career, he had just sent men to a watery grave.

He shook his head to clear it. He had followed his orders, done his job.

The one he had spent decades preparing for. He had struck a blow for his country, for its people.

So why did he have such a throbbing pain in the pit of his stomach?

Ψ

Li Min Zhou's cell phone beeped a perky alert. The private phone's number was known only to a very select group of people. When she picked it up, she saw she had a text message demanding her attention.

Li was sitting on the terrace of her penthouse apartment, watching the sun set over the hustle and bustle of busy Taipei on the island of Taiwan. She had been enjoying a rare unprofessional moment, sipping from a glass of her favorite chardonnay and wondering where in the world her favorite man, her husband, Navy SEAL Jim Ward, was on this fine evening. Married life was still new to both of them, and their chosen work did not lend itself to settling down into any kind of newlywed routine. He was already away on some clandestine mission he was not allowed to tell her about and, as per usual, was totally out of communication.

But she had little room to complain. Her own double life assured that she, too, had secrets she could never share with her husband. Fortunately, he knew just enough about her spy activities to know not to ask questions or to resent it when she remained quiet. After all, they had first met and then courted as part of some very hairy missions in which both of their duties coincided.

She pushed buttons on the cell phone's keypad to unlock it, knowing that the text would not be from Jim. No matter how much she wished it was so. He would not use this number. Or require such a complicated scrambling algorithm just to tell her he loved her and missed her terribly and list the naughty things he would with her when he returned home. The text was encrypted with an immensely complex and secure advanced 256-bit system. Someone had calculated that it would take the world's most powerful supercomputers a million years to crack the AES code. But Li Min's phone deciphered the text message in a few seconds. The message appeared to be a grocery list, complete with vegetable prices.

She stretched as she stood, picked up her wine glass and phone, and stepped back inside her apartment. Then she took the innocent-looking list and carefully, but manually, transcribed it onto a laptop computer on her kitchen table, a machine that was air-gapped from all possible communications paths. Another algorithm on the laptop transposed and commuted the letters and numbers into an intelligible message, a message from a source well placed within Chinese President Tan Yong's inner circle.

Min Toa had been Tan Yong's most trusted personal aide for many years. He had been an agent for Li Min Zhou and her elaborate spy network for even longer. He was offering verifiable proof that Tan Yong had been providing monetary support to US President Stanley Smitherman, both personally and for his campaign—in return for the president's cooperation on a number of occasions and issues.

Would Li Min find that information useful? For a price?

She smiled as she quickly crafted an ad for cat litter, then uploaded it to a website in Beijing. She should have an answer from Min Toa in the morning.

Ψ

When the news broke of the sinking of the *Sargento Aldea* and the *Capitán Prat* by an unidentified submarine, the world south of the equator erupted into pandemonium. Shockingly, two Chilean warships, which had been involved in peaceful activities in what had long been recognized as their own territorial waters, were now fractured hulks scattered along the bottom of the Straits of Magellan. In only a few horrible moments, the lives of more than a thousand people had been lost in those frigid waters.

The world press automatically assumed that the submarine that had set loose such deadly havoc was from the Argentine Navy, despite President Martinez's loud protestations. But the Argentine president did add that he certainly would have ordered such an attack if he had his own warships in the area, because those Chilean vessels were challenging the rightful seas belonging to Argentina and its people. And that would no longer be allowed.

Regardless of who did the deed, scores of ships that had been routed through the Straits quickly changed their plans to take a longer route to their original destinations, opting to either use the stormy Drake Passage—almost to Antarctica—or turn north and make for the Panama Canal. Quite a few of them simply turned around and headed back to their port of origin.

There were exceptions. Ships flying the flag of the People's Republic of China steamed blithely on, seemingly without hesitation, continuing to their destinations without fear of challenge.

Chile's ambassador to the United Nations announced before the hastily assembled Security Council that Chile had suffered an unprovoked attack by Argentina and that a state of war now existed between the two countries. He demanded UN protection under Article 35 of the organization's charter from the naked aggression his country had suffered at the hands of the dictators of Argentina and Brazil. He loudly protested not only the brutal and unprovoked attack but also the recent ridiculous declarations regarding sovereignty across the lower reaches of the South American continent. The Uruguayan ambassador rose in solidarity, decrying the threatening Argentine-Brazilian alliance and urging the UN to send troops or to demand that the organization broker peace negotiations immediately, before more lives were lost.

It was all for naught. China, of course, vetoed any such action before the Russian Federation or Brazil—a temporary member of the council—had the chance to do so.

Meanwhile, as the diplomats argued, the combined Brazilian-Argentinian battle group, Task Force Southern Passage, serenely steamed westward through the chilly waters of the Straits. Once they arrived at the city of Punta Arenas, the ships dropped anchor in the quiet harbor as if they owned it, then immediately began to blatantly disgorge troops and equipment.

The first wave of six Blackhawk troop transport helicopters flew directly to Presidente Carlos Ibáñez del Campo International Airport, twenty kilometers north of the Chilean city, where the Brazilian Marines jumping out of the choppers were greeted with wide-eyed amazement. The airport was under Brazilian control in minutes. Not a shot was fired. That is, except for the one short burst when a Marine forgot to safe his rifle when he propped it against a urinal while using the terminal

restroom. When it fell and discharged, one soap dispenser paid the ultimate price.

Twenty minutes later, the first C-130 bearing the markings, distinctive
wings-and-red-cap emblem of the Argentine Air Force, landed. A steady
stream of both cargo and combat aircraft followed it. By the end of the day,
the airport was a fully functioning Argentine Air Force Base.

EE-11 Urutu and VBTP Guarani amphibious armored personnel
carriers ferried combat troops from the amphibious warships to the piers
under the protection of the warships' guns. The troops and their armored
personnel carriers mostly had the streets to themselves. The civilian population had wisely decided to shelter behind locked doors and drawn drapes
until they could gauge what might be going on. The first platoon that came
ashore roared up to city hall, where the mayor promptly surrendered the
city to them. Even the marine guards protecting the Base Naval Punta
Arenas simply laid down their weapons, opened the gates to the facility,
and then disappeared.

By sunset, all of Punta Arenas was firmly under control of the task force.

Further north, at the border separating Argentina from the Chilean
Magallanes region, a battalion of Tanque Argentino Mediano tanks led
columns of vehicles down the two highways that crossed the border.
Swarms of Brazilian AS550N attack helicopters flitted about, searching for a
target worthy of their efforts and ordnance. They found none. The Chilean
border guards did not even bother to offer token resistance. At the Paso
Integración Austral crossing, they obligingly left their weapons behind as
they piled into a pickup truck, a cloud of red dust behind them as they sped
south, leaving it up to those at a much higher pay grade to sort things out.
The guards at the Paso Laurita Casas Viejas crossing merely swung open
the gates and surrendered. The invading troops told them to go home to
their families.

Well before the fleet arrived, *Capitão de Fragata* Bruno Ribeiro had
steered the Brazilian nuclear submarine *João Cândido* down into the Inútil
Bay. That would put him well out of the way, allowing the surface ships of
Task Force Southern Passage to proceed unimpeded on their cruise to
Punta Arenas. More importantly, he wanted to make sure that no overly
eager Watch Officer on one of those surface ships might detect the subma-

rine and mistake it for one from Chile. Even though he'd been given a chunk of water assigned for the exclusive use of the *João Cândido*, and all the task force had been warned that there was a friendly submarine nearby, Ribeiro elected to be very cautious. It would not be the first time that some trigger-happy captain shot first and asked questions later when a submarine was suddenly discovered, especially in the heat and excitement of what might well be his first real battle.

Ribeiro cautiously guided the *João Cândido* to periscope depth and popped the periscope up so that it barely broke the surface of the calm water. Only little ripples in the protected bay washed over the scope. He spun the scope through a complete circle. Task Force Southern Passage was safely swinging at anchor over in Punta Arenas, across the channel from him. The remainder of the normally busy waterway was eerily empty. There were not even any of the usual fishing boats skating across these waters.

Satisfied that he was alone in this little patch of the bay, Ribeiro raised the communications mast so that he could talk to Vice Admiral Barbosa and receive any updates to his orders. Almost immediately a message appeared on the comms screen: The *João Cândido*'s services were no longer required inside the Straits of Magellan. He was to proceed immediately to the eastern entrance of the Straits from the South Atlantic Ocean and begin patrolling off of Punta Dúngeness. In the process, he was to report any warships attempting to enter these recently reclaimed waters.

Then, once the report had been made, he was to attack them.

Ribeiro blinked hard, sucked in a deep breath, lowered the periscope, and calmly ordered that they assume a course to head north and then east, to Punta Dúngeness.

14

Li Min Zhou once again reviewed the files that Min Toa had been so keen on selling and delivering to her. His price had been exceedingly steep, but she was now sure that if the information was accurate, what it disclosed would be invaluable. Stunning. And downright toxic. The difficult question would be how she might best leverage such a blockbuster set of data. There was also a niggling worry in the back of her mind about why Min Toa had chosen this time to offer up his wares when some of it dated back several years.

The files she was reviewing revealed a long and sordid history of US President Stanley Smitherman's secret negotiations with Chinese leader Tan Yong and members of his staff to support Smitherman's rise to political power, both financially and with covert actions to sway elections and discourage challengers. There was also apparent proof of exactly what Smitherman had offered up to China in exchange for such help. Li Min gasped at the extent of the treachery. Calling it treason grossly understated its length and breadth. That was not all. Harold Osterman, the current vice president and presumably Smitherman's eventual successor as chief executive, was also implicated, and had been involved in the mess almost from the beginning.

As nearly as she could tell, the trail of covertly recorded videos, emails, complicated currency transactions through myriad banks and shadow companies, and recorded phone conversations were incontrovertible proof of Smitherman's deceit. Almost equally as troubling as the man's greed and betrayal of his country was his unbelievable stupidity. Or maybe it was his arrogance, leaving himself so open to discovery or blackmail. It was also mildly surprising to her that the Chinese were so willing to go along with the mess, knowing just how difficult it would be to keep it under wraps due to Smitherman's carelessness. Tan was just arrogant enough to assume there would be no repercussions for them, even if the thing blew up. Both men were confident they were untouchable, and it was well worth a few weeks of bad press coverage for the return they were getting on their investment.

Li Min shook her head. This was almost too much to deal with. But deal with it she must. How? One thing was sure. She needed to take this to the one person, the one American, who she most trusted to properly juggle such a hot potato. That person was Admiral Jon Ward, Director of Naval Intelligence, who just happened to also be her new father-in-law.

She glanced at her watch and did some quick calculations. The time difference between her Taipei apartment and Ward's Pentagon office was twelve hours. Since it was 1830 here, it was 0630 in Washington, DC. Chances were Admiral Ward—he would always be "Admiral Ward" to her for official business, even though he insisted she call him "Dad"—would already be in his office, on his fourth cup of coffee and hard at work. And certainly his faithful flag aide, Jimmy Wilson, would be guarding the door and screening incoming telephone calls, even at that ungodly hour.

She decided to take the chance she was correct, that he was there, and hit the speed dial button on her phone. Jimmy picked up the call on the second ring. "Office of the Director of Naval Intelligence. Lieutenant Jimmy Wilson. This is not a secure line."

"Lieutenant, I need to speak to the Admiral."

Wilson immediately recognized her voice. He knew not to identify her over an open line. "Yes, one moment please."

She heard a couple of clicks and then, "How's my favorite daughter-in-law?"

"Good morning, Admiral—uh, Dad. How's Mom?"

"Doing well. You know she's teaching a botany class as an adjunct at Georgetown this term? I know she sends her best."

Ward knew already this was a business call. And Li promptly got to it. "I wanted to let you know that I have some wedding presents for you to take a look at. They're too valuable and delicate to trust to normal shipping, I'm afraid. It's good to have such generous friends willing to share with us."

Conscious that their call could possibly be intercepted, and even though such a chance was infinitesimal, Li Min always had a way to phrase her request so Ward would know the conversation was more business than familial. Discussing wedding presents seemed to be a relatively innocuous way to get that message across.

"Can I send a courier to pick them up?" Ward asked.

"These particular gifts will likely be family heirlooms one day," she replied. "I would feel most comfortable if I personally handed them over to you so you could judge for yourself how to take care of them. I could also tell you more about each one."

She could almost hear the gears meshing in Admiral Jon Ward's head. She had already told him enough for him to deduce that whatever she had to give him was hot enough that she could not use her normal routing for important or time-sensitive information. That would have been either through the American Institute in Taiwan, which served as the de facto US embassy, or even by using a dedicated courier. This batch was hot, indeed.

"Well," he said, chuckling. As usual, he had instantly made a decision, a trait that had stood him in good stead when he had once served his country as the Commanding Officer of a US Navy submarine prior to his high-echelon desk job. "You know, I'm due for a sweep through the Orient anyway to check on a few things, and I do need to see the family home in Taipei." She could hear him punching keys on his computer. "Let's see . . . looks like there's a twelve-thirty ANA flight out of Dulles. If there's a seat left and I hurry, I can just make it. I'll have Jimmy book me on it. It arrives at Taiwan Taoyuan International tomorrow at noon."

"You allowed to fly on a foreign carrier?" Li Min asked. "ANA is a Japanese airline. To hear Jim tell it, your travel rules are really strict lately."

Jon Ward grunted. "Well, Jim isn't a flag officer yet. I need to see those gifts and hug the daughter I never had, right? Besides, some rules can be waived for expediency. And by the way, they serve a killer bento box on their long-haul flights."

"I'll meet you at the airport. Give Mom my love."

Ψ

Brian Edwards was seated at his desk in the cramped space that constituted the Commanding Officer's stateroom on the *George Mason*. Jackson Biddle sat at the tiny settee that folded down to form Edwards's bunk. Dennis Oshley sat uncomfortably on an even tinier fold-down stool. Uncharacteristically, the stateroom door was shut.

"XO, COB," Edwards began, "have you both seen today's message traffic?"

The CO did not wait for an answer. He pulled up the offending message on the computer screen on his desk. The orders directed the submarine to immediately break any contact it had with Argentine or Brazilian warships, or "any other vessels or targets you may currently have under surveillance." Then they were to destroy "any and all contact logs dealing with all such encounters and to immediately set course for Portsmouth Naval Shipyard at best speed." Additionally, the *George Mason* was to avoid all contacts until back in US territorial waters.

"Something's hinky here," Edwards said. "This is the second time in as many weeks that we have been pulled off a target, ordered to forget all we may have seen, and then told to make best speed home. And it is the second time that we have been told to destroy all evidence of the contacts we have had occasion to observe. I'm no conspiracy theorist, but guys, it's looking to me like somebody is trying to hide whatever is going on down here. Of course, we'll follow the orders to the letter. XO, destroy all the primary logs—but while you're at it, make and keep a backup in your safe along with all those submarine contact logs we scuttled but kept backups of before."

Biddle nodded.

Dennis Oshley shrugged his shoulders and shifted on the little stool. "I'm with you, Skipper. I've been on the boats a long time and I sure would like to know what's going on. Especially after those reports we got about the two Chilean ships sunk in the Strait. We all know the chances are damn good that the guy who did that dirty deed was one of the subs we met up with down off Argentina. Or maybe both. You know, once we started tracking and reported unusual submarine activity way down there, I would have bet my left nut we would've been assigned to continue to track it and try to figure out what was going on, right?" The COB frowned and rubbed his chin. "Besides, we might've been able to do something. Maybe saved a bunch of lives."

"You're right, COB. I'd love to know," Edwards said ruefully. "Not so long ago, we would've been on them like glue. But as always, we do what we're told, even if we don't like it. Ours is not to reason why. Ours is but to do and die. Alfred, Lord Tennyson. 'Charge of the Light Brigade.'"

"Really?" Biddle said with a slight grin. "I thought my hero, Bear Bryant, said that."

The CO stared at the grounds in the bottom of his coffee cup for a moment. "Look, no reason to ponder. For now, let's get the Nav up here and plot out the best route home, one that keeps us well off the Brazilian coast and out of the shipping lanes so we don't accidentally get caught up in another mystery they won't let us solve. And, of course, not a word about this to the crew, okay?"

Both men nodded just as the skipper's phone buzzed.

"Captain, Officer-of-the Deck." Bill Wilson's distinctive high-pitched voice immediately gave him away. "We got a problem. The Engineer is reporting a failure of the main shaft electromagnetic bearings. They're troubleshooting right now, and I've shifted propulsion to the SPM."

The SPM—the "secondary propulsion motor"—was a small electric outboard motor that could be lowered from the after main ballast tank and put to use when needed. It was trainable so it was most often employed to shove the submarine's stern around when careful maneuvering was required, such as when operating in tight quarters or while docking the ship. It could also propel the boat when the main shaft was not available for use, but only at very low speed.

There wasn't much Edwards could say to Wilson other than, "Very well." He placed the phone handset back in the receiver, turned to Biddle, and relayed the OOD's report.

"XO, lay aft and see what's going on. I confess, I never did like those newfangled magnetic bearings. Trying to levitate something the size of the main shaft of a submarine with a bunch of magnets just ain't natural somehow. Then sticking one of them out into seawater is just asking for trouble. Get Bill Wilson a relief as OOD. He's the E-Division Officer and this sounds like it's going to be his problem to solve."

Biddle nodded, but chuckled. "Skipper, despite your Luddite tendencies, you gotta admit the bearings have been damn quiet. And not having a lube oil system has really been a nice thing for us, too. Look, it's probably just a blown fuse or something simple like that. But I'm on it." The XO ducked out of the stateroom and stepped quickly toward the engine room.

The sub's Engineer, Jeff Otanga, was more than capable of handling this problem, but an extra set of eyes never hurt. Besides, until the issue was identified and fixed, they would be limited to about two knots forward speed. That would not win many submarine races.

Dennis Oshley rose stiffly from his stool and stretched. "Skipper, I figure I'll mosey out to control and make sure everything is runnin' smooth. Help the QMs lay out the new track, but at two knots, making 'best speed,' it's gonna take us a while to get to anywhere."

After the COB left the stateroom, Brian Edwards forced himself to sit back and think. As complicated as a nuclear-powered submarine was, and with all the systems it took to keep one fully functional, it was inevitable that things broke. And there were no convenient repair shops or submarine-parts stores in the middle of the world's vast oceans. In situations like this latest one, there was not much for him to do until his people had figured out the problem and had a solution ready for him to review, which he was confident they would. If the captain jumped into the problem right now, it would deprive his team of a chance to sharpen their expertise. It would also take several reviews out of the chain, additional opportunities to catch mistakes or recognize solutions. He had learned from other skippers under which he had served that it was usually better for the CO to stay out of the way. For now, he would read up on those damn mag bearings so that he could speak intelligently when Jeff Otanga and Bill Wilson ultimately brought him their own findings and a suggested course of action.

As he clicked away on the computer, looking for the right documentation, an interesting thought flashed into his mind. What had the XO said? "Making 'best speed' of two knots, it's gonna' take us a while to get to anywhere."

Wait. Maybe this problem was a good thing after all. The *George Mason* was the only US warship within several thousand miles of the Straits of Magellan. When the shit inevitably hit the fan down there, they would be the only submersible vessel situated to take action for days. And that convenient fact was due to that damned failed bearing.

"Luddite indeed," he said to himself with a broad grin, then went back to pecking on the keyboard, searching for the documentation.

15

Admiral Jon Ward sat in his daughter-in-law's penthouse apartment high above the hustle and bustle of Taipei. The views in both directions—downtown to where the Xindian and Dahan Rivers formed the Tamsui, or up toward the forest-shrouded Tiansheng Mountain—were certainly awesome, but Ward had hardly noticed. Nor had he taken the opportunity to catch up with Li Min on her or his son and their recent activities. It appeared that Jim and Li saw even less of each other than the busy admiral and his own spouse, but there was no time to commiserate. This was a business meeting. His attention had been entirely riveted to the computer screen on the table in front of him ever since she had booted it up and he started scrolling through documents, transcripts, and photos. One after another, each even more incredibly damning than the last.

He audibly groaned as he read the information on the screen, his fingers angrily punching the keys. He finally stopped, sat back, and took a sip of his now-cooled tea.

"You have to be kidding me!" he growled. "All this, it's friggin' impossible! How could somebody smart enough to get elected president of the US be enough of a dumbass to do all this and then leave such a complete trail of evidence? Just how sure are you that this stuff is legit?"

Li Min Zhou sat across the table from Admiral Jim Ward. She was only half-tasting her own cup of tea. She answered slowly, deliberately. Obviously, she believed the documentation to be real or she would never have alerted Ward. "The source is as reliable as it comes. My operative has been one of Tan Yong's most trusted aides for many years. This person is privy to pretty much everything of importance happening in Zhongnanhai. Nothing goes in or out of Tan Yong's office without it being routed through this person. I did check some of this through other sources without raising any red flags. So far, everything jibes. Everything. As you can see, this file has been under development for some time. Probably since it all started."

Ward nodded. "Yeah, I see some of these documents go all the way back to when Smitherman was a junior senator. And before Tan was president, too. Looks like each guy was grooming the other for bigger things. But why is your guy—or gal—finally coming forward with this atom bomb of a dossier now?"

Li Min shook her head. "I don't really have a definitive answer for that. My high-placed source certainly doesn't need the money. I keep tabs on the person's various bank and investment accounts, and they qualify as those of a very rich person. Even so, what you have there on that thumb drive cost me a billion yuan. That's almost 140 million US dollars."

Ward whistled. "Not cheap, that's for sure. But they say data is the new currency."

"Especially when it indicts the president and vice president of the United States in what amounts to treason," Li Min agreed. "But to further answer your question about its timing, I did get some information from other sources in Beijing. It seems that my reliable source has been making frequent visits to the top oncologist at the Peking Union Medical College Hospital and has stage four pancreatic cancer. The prognosis is that it is terminal, and the patient has less than a year to live. This may be a case of big-time conscience clearing. And maximizing the inheritance for the spouse and some lucky kids and grandkids."

"Sounds plausible. But are you sure that's the motivation?" Ward queried.

Li Min took a sip of her tea as she considered her answer. Then, with a slightly crooked smile, she answered, "No, not necessarily. Or maybe only partly. I strongly suspect President Tan Yong is either behind this or is allowing it to happen. Either way, I'm convinced the information is valid. There is simply too much stuff here, and it all checks too closely to known facts, to have been made up. Even so, you will need to have your experts vet this and see if anything has been doctored, of course. A few errors or false evidence and your press and the president's political party will shoot holes through the whole thing, even if it is otherwise ninety-five percent bulletproof."

"Of course," Ward responded. She was right.

Li took another sip of tea and paused for a second before continuing. "My guess is that Tan Yong has decided your President Smitherman has morphed from being an asset to becoming a liability for Tan and the CCP. This is his way of disposing of that liability. As an added benefit, it throws the US into absolute turmoil when it hits the media. That could be coming at a very convenient time for President Tan."

Ward closed the computer and put the flash drive in his pocket, then leaned forward, a worried look on his face. She had seen that very same expression on the face of her new husband as he prepared to go off on some super-secret but hazardous and complicated mission he could not even hint to her about. He was his daddy's son.

"Li, if that's the case, does this mean China is finally putting the whole plan into motion? Setting off a media and political frenzy in the US so they can implement whatever it is they've been planning to do to claim superiority on the world stage?"

"No way of telling," she told him. "You can expect Tan Yong and the CCP to play the long game. Remember, we Chinese think in terms of decades and centuries, not weeks or the next election cycle. I think they are expanding their Belt and Road Initiative even deeper into South America, just like they're doing in Africa and the South Pacific. From Tan Yong's perspective, South American raw materials like lithium and iron ore are vital. And they need the markets to sell all the stuff they make. For all that, they need ships and shipping lanes."

Li Min took a sip of tea while she organized her next thoughts. "You Americans look at China's economy as something monolithic and unstoppable. It's not. Tan has some serious problems he has to resolve. China has a population of one-point-four billion souls and an aging demographic.

The workforce is getting smaller as expectations are inevitably rising. He has to maintain economic growth. Stagnation is failure."

"I'll include him in my prayers tonight," Ward said sarcastically. Li ignored him and went on.

"He has a cash flow problem. All those Belt and Road projects cost money. The raw materials to keep China's manufacturing efforts churning costs plenty, too. Money on a massive scale. Trillions of yuan. Tan could easily paint himself into a financial corner that he can't get out of. I think what we are seeing here is him maneuvering to stay out of those corners until all this seeding starts to grow crops."

"Yeah, the bastard," Ward said quietly.

"Bastard indeed." Li Min took a breath. "I sound like I'm teaching a master class on Chinese grand strategy, and I know you know most of this, but with China nothing is simple or straightforward. I think there is a very real possibility that Tan is tying up loose ends with this move to deep-six Smitherman. And there's just a bit of desperation in what he is doing."

"Smitherman. The other bastard."

"Your commander in chief, remember."

"Don't remind me," Ward responded, frowning. "Especially after I've just waded through all that manure you gave me."

"Look, that Argentine attack on Chilean naval vessels in the Strait fits right in with Brazil and Argentina's open flirtation with China. As do all the goofy economic and military moves by those two South American coun-tries of late—which are only goofy from the typical Western viewpoint. From Tan's perspective, they make perfect sense. He needs easy access, and those two tin-pot dictators are more than willing to go get it for him in exchange for power and money. And more money. Then he can use the materials on that thumb drive in your pocket to distract the world from what he's doing. Brazil and Argentina's leaders don't care about any of that. They have their own desperate reasons for going along with Tan."

Ward stood, shaking his head. "Thank you, Li. I need to get back to DC as quickly as possible. I gotta decide where to go with this crock of hooey. I do know leaving it on the doorstep of the *New York Times* is not the right solution."

Li Min looked at her watch and told him, "There is a KAL flight in a couple of hours. My driver can have you at the terminal in an hour. There will be a first-class ticket in your name at the counter."

Ward stepped over and gave his daughter-in-law a quick hug and a distracted peck on the cheek. "Next time I visit, let's plan on something a little less dramatic. Maybe dinner and a little sightseeing with Mom and me. And if you see that lug of a husband, tell him to call his mother."

Li Min laughed. "Thanks, Dad. I sure will. When he gets finished playing frogman, that is, and remembers that he's a married man now and navigates his way back home."

By the time Jon Ward was comfortably seated in the back of Li Min's Maybach S-Class limo, his mind was racing at warp speed. The flash drive was burning a hole in his pocket. The revelations on that little device were so massively volatile that they would absolutely spread chaos far wider than just the downfall of two politicians. Somehow, it had now become Jon Ward's job to decide how to handle it safely and properly, without causing quite so much collateral damage.

The car had just glided onto Highway 4 in Taoyuan City, smoothly mixing with the rush hour traffic, when Ward made up his mind what his initial step would be. He grabbed his cell phone and punched in the number for his Pentagon office. Jimmy Wilson picked it up on the first ring.

"Good morning . . . that is, good evening, boss. What can I do for you?"

Just as he started to answer, Ward's phone hummed. Another call. The caller ID said it was Li Min.

"Hold one, Jimmy. Call on the other line from somebody far prettier than you." He punched the "Accept" button.

"Dad, I made a couple of calls. There will be a Gulfstream G-650 waiting for you at the general aviation terminal. I've texted details to your driver. You'll need to refuel in Anchorage, but the flight time is a little over sixteen hours. Way better than that twenty-seven-hour slog you were going to make on KAL. Mom'll appreciate you not being so jet-lagged."

Ward laughed. "Thanks. That's what I call first-class service. I'm beginning to think that having a daughter-in-law is way better than having a son."

Ward shifted back to Wilson.

"I got upstaged by Mrs. Admiral Ward, I presume," the aide said.

"No. And I ain't telling you who it was, so quit fishing. Jimmy, I'm on my way home. Call the SecDef's office. I need to meet with Secretary Aldo first thing tomorrow morning. Tell them that this is extremely urgent and that it has, well, the highest priority that you can think of."

Ward could almost see Jimmy Wilson nodding. "You got it, boss. Sounds hot."

"Jimmy, you can't even imagine how hot."

Only then did it occur to Ward that he was not on a secure line. Oh, well. If anybody had intercepted his little cell signal in the middle of Taipei traffic, let them figure out what the hell was going on. Anyway, the Chief of Naval Intelligence knew one thing for certain.

When it came right down to it, even Ward, the man who was supposed to know every damn thing and to comprehend it all, really did not have a clue on this one.

Ψ

Vincente Díaz, the recently elected president of Chile, was shocked and dismayed. At first, he thought his close and very dangerous neighbors had only been testing him. But now, not only had the unholy alliance of Argentina and Brazil treacherously attacked and sunk two of his navy's warships, they'd had the audacity to do it in Chile's home waters. A mere few thousand meters from Chilean shoreline. There had been no warning, and there had been no assistance to the sailors left floundering in the icy waters after the vicious assault. The *Sargento Aldea* and the *Capitán Prat* were both gone, along with almost fifteen hundred young sailors and officers.

His government was still appealing to the world for aid and assistance as a result of this unprovoked attack—with a puzzling and disappointing lack of specific response, merely eloquently spun cries of dismay and promises of humanitarian aid, then silence—when the other shoe dropped. The combined Argentine-Brazilian fleet steamed into Punto Arenas and invaded his country, boldly claiming it as Argentine territory, while the Argentine Army stormed across the undefended border that separated the Magallanes region from its neighbor to the north, Argentina's Santa Cruz

Province. He hardly had time to take notice of the blockade Argentina and Brazil had simultaneously thrown up on the other side of the continent around Uruguay. He knew there had to be a connection, though.

President Díaz met with his military leaders only to find that he had very limited options available. The rugged, mountainous wilderness, cut through by hundreds of deep-sea fjords, made an impassible barrier for Chile's outnumbered army to even reach the invaders, let alone launch a counterattack against them. Then his admirals briefed that two of his four submarines were out of commission for maintenance and that with one frigate gone, they only had three frigates that could quickly be made ready for battle. Even so, those vessels were all currently operating around the naval base at Iquique, almost four thousand kilometers to the north. It seemed that the very geography of Chile was conspiring with his new enemies to defeat him. And even if his naval assets were fully available and close enough to challenge the invasion, the two attacking nations had already demonstrated in deadly fashion that waterways in the region would be difficult to traverse.

President Díaz recognized that even if he could somehow get his small fleet down to the Straits, they would be hopelessly outnumbered. Additionally, with the loss of the Punta Arenas airport, there would be no way to effectively provide any air support. The admirals convinced him that any military response they might muster would be nothing more than a suicide mission.

"How long will it take to get our submarines down there?" he finally asked, grasping at straws, determined to do something to fight back.

"If they steamed at a flank bell on the surface all the way and then pulled into the little base at Puerto Montt to refuel, they could probably enter the Straits in a week."

Díaz looked around the room at each of the hopeless faces of his top military advisors. No one seemed to have a better idea.

"Send the submarines," he ordered. "We have no better option."

Ψ

Guillermo Manuelito took two steps back, farther away from the window, but still with an unobstructed view of the street outside. Despeñaderos was just another dusty farm town and nothing more. Most everyone here worked at trying to claw a meager existence from the hard, dry ground, or in some other business associated with agriculture. The activity on the town's narrow streets was predictably governed by the sun. At dusk, most of the byways quickly became deserted. That is, except for those that led to either of the two local cantinas. People were simply too exhausted to be out roaming around at night, except maybe for a stiff drink before bedtime to help them sleep. That was why Manuelito felt confident he could finally leave the tiny, rundown, single-room apartment that had served as his hiding place for the past couple of weeks.

With no one in sight, he slipped outside but still kept to the shadows as he moved. The simple buildings occupying lots along Parana Street mostly housed small machine shops and truckyards. The lone exception, the apartment building where the olive-farmer-turned-revolutionary had gone to ground, was left over from more prosperous times. Manuelito turned left onto Calle Argentina. The businesses on this stretch seemed a bit more prosperous. Several offered quick loans provided by sketchy land agents. Others sold staples like flour, maize, lard, and sugar, or necessities such as rope and hand tools.

Three blocks down, just before Calle Argentina reached Avenue Vélez Sarsfield, lay Manuelito's destination. Looking about, seeing not a soul, he abruptly ducked down a narrow drive to the back of the sprawling adobe building, and rapped three times on a heavy oak door that opened into the alley.

Doctor Sergio Cruz, dressed in a white lab coat, cracked the door open and glanced out into the darkened drive. Recognizing Manuelito standing there, he quickly ushered him inside, then shut and barred the door.

Manuelito had found Dr. Cruz's little, out-of-the-way medical practice quite by accident. He had been madly driving the old pickup away from the ambush as the wounded Ricardo Balduino bled out on the seat beside him. Almost by instinct, he came upon Despeñaderos, the nearest town of any size. Avoiding what passed for the main street through the town, he happened to turn down Calle Argentina. The small *Consultorio Médico* sign appeared before him as if by magic. He jerked the steering wheel hard to dash down the narrow alley, then screeched to a stop. There was no way of knowing if the doctor here would be sympathetic to two men—one gravely wounded—who had just shot it out with government troops. Or if he was even equipped to treat such serious wounds. But Manuelito had no other option. Even if they were captured, Balduino would surely die very soon without medical treatment.

Doctor Cruz immediately recognized the problem; not just that Balduino had been shot but also that the pair were on the run, trying to escape the Federales. He helped carry the wounded man into his small surgery while his assistant went outside and made the battered pickup disappear. Manuelito had no idea where it had gone but assumed it would be abandoned in some hidden arroyo.

The good doctor told Manuelito he would put him in touch with the local MDR. They would find him a safe hiding place while the doctor treated Balduino until he either died or was able to travel. Again, Manuelito had no choice. He had to trust that the man who soon knocked on the medical office door was part of the MDR, not an agent of the government.

All this had occurred a couple of weeks earlier. Now, Balduino was finally healthy enough to be moved. Manuelito sensed that it was time to find a different hiding place, distant from Despeñaderos. His local contact gave him cryptic directions to an MDR enclave in the high mountains, up near San Salvador de Jujuy. It served as headquarters for the rapidly growing group organizing to oppose the latest Argentine government.

The wounded fighter was still not well enough to walk on his own. Doctor Cruz and his assistant helped carry Balduino outside to a waiting Fiorino panel van parked in the driveway. The ubiquitous van was the perfect vehicle for the long drive north. It would blend right in with all the other delivery and work vans plying the backroads in these parts. And Balduino could lie in relative comfort on a mattress from Dr. Cruz's clinic for the thousand-kilometer drive up into the mountains.

Bypassing larger towns and main highways, Manuelito's circuitous route bounced through the arid foothills and a few dusty cattle towns that time had forgotten. So had most cartographers. The villages were small and anonymous, with no welcome signs or street names. The land outside of the towns provided little more for scenery than cacti and desert shrubs, barely enough vegetation to support a few head of cattle and the tough native critters that had somehow survived here for millennia.

Balduino slept peacefully in back as the kilometers clicked by. The few other vehicles that Manuelito met on these backroads looked very much like the one he now drove, work vehicles moving between towns or rancheros hauling cattle to market, no longer trying to make money to feed their families but to pay the steep new taxes or tributes to the corrupt local officials following the lead of the new administration in Buenos Aires.

It was well past midnight on the third day when Manuelito finally arrived at his destination, a few kilometers outside San Salvador de Jujuy. He had almost missed the turn off Ruta Provincial 3 onto an unpaved path that led up a narrow defile marked with a faded, crooked sign: *Valle Escondido*. Manuelito chuckled. Hidden Valley, indeed. Even expecting the turn-off, which was marked precisely on the otherwise cryptic, hand-drawn map, he had passed it twice before finding it.

A couple of kilometers up, the twisting goat path ended at a high iron gate. An armed guard appeared from nowhere to swing the gate open while two others kept their weapons at the ready, aimed directly at Manuelito. Holding his breath the whole time, he deliberately pulled the van through the gate into the courtyard of an out-of-the-way hacienda. More guards, without saying a word, carried Balduino into a small but well-equipped dispensary. Then they led Manuelito off to a tiny bedroom. There, the guard who had shown him to the room snapped to attention and gave Manuelito a sharp military salute.

"*Usted es un héroe*," he said. "You are a hero."

"No, only a simple olive farmer who wants nothing more than to have the people in control of their lives and country, not the tyrants," Manuelito told him.

The guard nodded respectfully then left, easing the door closed behind him. Exhausted, Manuelito dropped, fully clothed, onto the cot. He instantly found sound, dreamless sleep.

16

The brain trust aboard the USS *George Mason* was meeting again. Brian Edwards sat in his usual seat at the head of the wardroom table. XO Jackson Biddle sat on his skipper's right, across the table from Jeff Otanga, the Engineering Officer. Bill Wilson sat a little farther down. His laptop was open and he was leading the conversation. Chief Sam Sharkey, the electrical division leading chief, sat next to Wilson. At the moment, the big-screen monitor at the foot of the table was showing a complicated diagram titled "Simplified Schematic Propulsion Shaft Magnetic Bearing Controller."

"Skipper," Wilson started, "we've been troubleshooting the shaft bearing system. We've completely checked out both of the forward radial and thrust bearings in shaft alley. Since the aft radial bearing is out in the mud tank, we have checked everything about it that we can do remotely. The good news is that the bearings all check good."

Chief Sharkey chimed in. "Tech manual calls for visual inspections, clearance checks, and continuity checks. Inboard bearings look great. The outboard bearing checks fine electrically, so it ain't the problem, either."

"Did the bearing failure cause any damage?" Biddle asked.

"None that we could see," Sharkey answered. "The auxiliary bearings are designed to handle a mag bearing failure and it looks like they worked just as they are designed to do. Otherwise, we'd be puttering along on the outboard all the way home. We might get there by Christmas if we swim in the right current."

"So, it sounds like you're telling me that the problem is in the controller, not the bearings themselves," Edwards said. "What does that mean as far as getting it fixed?"

"Damn good question," Chief Sharkey shot back. "Tech manual ain't much help in the troubleshooting department, and nobody on my team is an expert on these mag controllers."

"Well, we're sure not gonna be able to sit here on our thumbs while we zoom along at two knots," the CO growled. He looked around the table and shrugged his shoulders. "Ideas? Time to shine, guys."

It was Bill Wilson's distinctive high-pitched voice—the trait that had long since earned him the nickname "Squeaky"—that responded. "Skipper, the engineers at NAVSEA and at the shipyard could certainly be of some help. Suggest we come up on chat and see what they might have to say on the subject."

Edwards looked over at Biddle and frowned. "A deployed submarine up on something called 'chat' to ask for help. Maybe I *am* a Luddite, but what in hell is the world's foremost submarine service coming to?"

Ψ

Bill Beaman slowly climbed the hill to where Jim Ward sat waiting beneath a small tree. As the elder retired SEAL approached, Ward stood and stretched. He had just spent the past six hours in the scanty shade of a thorny acacia, staring down at Viscosa's silent and obviously deserted hacienda. After a couple of weeks of watching the empty great house with no sign of Viscosa or any of his henchmen, each of the SEALs now took a six-hour watch. And so far, they had come up with squat. It had been a fruitless and very boring time spent high up in the Andes, watching dust blow about all day and shooting stars going crazy, crisscrossing the amazingly full sky above them all night.

On the bright side, though, they had agreed that a permanent campsite up here was sure to attract unwanted attention. The team had settled on checking into a nice little out-of-the-way hotel in the tiny town of Salta, some eighty kilometers to the south. That was just far enough away to not raise undue suspicion among the wrong people about a bunch of strange men prowling around town. But it was also close enough for them to easily commute to the ridge above the estate. They all agreed that it was an almost civilized way to run a stakeout, even though the room TVs only had access to eight channels and they were all in Spanish.

"You may be older and uglier than ever," Ward told Beaman, "but you're still a sight for sore eyes. My ass end is aching more than usual from sitting on all this gravel."

The retired SEAL laughed. "You young whippersnappers just don't have *la paciencia* of your *ancianos. ¿Verdad?*"

It was Ward's turn to laugh. "Practicing your Spanish again? Maybe if we stay down here another twenty years, you might learn enough to order a bag of taco chips. Maybe you can get some young *señorita* to give you lessons while it's your turn to watch Viscosa's, or Kirkland's, or whatever-his-name's place."

"Well, about that," Beaman answered. "TJ finally got a couple of calls back from some folks. Seems our boy Kirkland or Viscosa was up in Bolivia after all. And he's been busy. TJ's contacts say that he was making deals with some people up there to ramp up lithium production and ship it out through Argentina. The guy is in the storage battery material brokerage business now. Apparently, he gets a healthy kickback for his efforts in negotiating the deals and violently eliminating any competitors along the way. Obviously pays better than cocaine and grass. He's due back here in a couple of days so he can sit around and count his money, I guess."

Beaman slumped down in what little remained of the shrub's shade.

"So, we just keep on sitting up here watching nonexistent grass not grow?"

"Nope. There's more. The Argentine Movimiento de Resistencia has made contact with some of TJ's operatives. They're reaching out for some help from Uncle Sugar. Dillon is calling us down off this stakeout, so maybe you'll quit your bitchin'. We're all heading up to someplace called Valle Escondido to meet with a team of MDR fighters. They're apparently some pretty serious guys." He jumped back up and swatted at Ward. "Grab your crap, Commander. TJ wants us to meet up at some place named El Burgués Food and Beer down in town. Then we'll drive out to this Valle Escondido place and see what's up."

The two men quickly policed the area until it appeared no one had ever been there before. Then they headed down off the hill.

A burger and a beer sounded really good about then.

Ψ

The chief of staff, Margaret Brenton, ushered Admiral Jon Ward into the Defense Secretary's private office, then waved him toward the bright yellow settee off to the side. Ward did not sit. He remained standing beside the couch while Brenton grabbed a couple of cups of coffee already poured, steaming and waiting for them on the sideboard. She handed one to Ward and quietly sipped from the other.

"Thank you," he told her. "I needed this."

"I understand you take it black and strong," she said. "I hope this fits the bill."

"Take it from an old submariner. You cannot get it too black or too strong, ma'am. Thank you." He tried not to wonder how she knew such a detail about him.

Secretary of Defense Sebastien Aldo stood at the window, his back to them, staring out at the Potomac River, seemingly deep in thought as they entered. He turned and quickly walked across the broad expanse of blue, deep-pile carpet to greet Ward with a sideways smile and an offered hand. Ward found Aldo's grip firm and slightly assertive. Unlike most politicians with whom he dealt. That was mildly reassuring. And somehow confirmed the good things he had heard about the SecDef.

"Admiral, your reputation precedes you. I've been looking forward to meeting you since I came aboard, but our paths have somehow not yet crossed. For that, I apologize. Blame it on the Air Force. They kept me hopping for most of the quarter of a century I was their property. I will admit that I was little surprised by the urgency your office conveyed when your aide requested this meeting. He did not, however, provide any information as to the nature of the discussion."

Ward answered with a bit of his own sideways smile. "He didn't have any details to relay. I was returning from Taipei when I called the office to set this up. I only told my aide that it was of the very highest priority to see you in a private meeting and that it should take place immediately after I landed back in DC." He glanced over at Margaret Brenton meaningfully. She appeared sharp, attentive. "When I show you the information that I am carrying, you will understand the urgency." He again looked at Brenton. "And the need for the utmost security."

Aldo nodded before he answered. "Yes, the sense of urgency was adequately conveyed. I cancelled several engagements to be able to honor your request, Admiral. As to security and privacy, Margaret here is my chief of staff. She is privy to anything that I see, hear, or know, and has a clearance at least as high as yours. We will proceed with her sitting in."

Aldo waved Ward to a seat on the settee and took one of the yellow upholstered armchairs for himself. Brenton took the other one.

Jon Ward opened his computer case and pulled out the flash drive Li Min Zhou had given him. "This drive and the information it contains came into our possession from a very reliable source in China. This source has almost unfettered access to the very highest levels of the CCP. The data herein has been very thoroughly vetted. We have extremely high confidence that it is valid and truthful. Otherwise, I would not have asked you to rearrange your busy schedule for me, Mr. Secretary."

Brenton interrupted sharply. "Source? Just who is this source, and how reliable are they really?"

Ward looked her in the eye and answered quietly but firmly. "I am not at liberty to disclose the source's identity. Not even to you. The person's life would be in immediate and grave danger if anything even inadvertently leaked out. And even if the source should somehow survive, the person would no longer give us access to the most valuable intelligence you could imagine. Our agreement with this person has been absolute in this regard. This I can tell you. Previous information from this source has been critical in several operations that proved to be vital to our national security. And it has always been true and accurate."

Margaret Brenton pointedly cleared her throat. "This is the SecDef's office, Admiral. There is no higher level of security anywhere in government. Before we can judge the value, reliability, and importance of this . . . this information you bring, we must know the source."

Ward shook his head. "Ma'am, with all due respect, that is not happening. If that is required in order for me to—"

Aldo held up a hand. "Margaret, let's first see what Admiral Ward has brought to us. Then we can decide if pressing for the source is necessary or not."

Only then did Ward boot up his laptop, insert the flash drive, and set the device down on the coffee table in front of the two. Then he carefully walked Secretary Aldo through some of the evidence Li Min had gathered from her Chinese source. It took several hours—with breaks for more coffee and trips to the bathroom just off the main office—but after the first few items had been brought up on the screen, Aldo had called out to ask his secretary to cancel his meetings for the balance of the day.

Both Aldo and Brenton were visibly shaken by the depth and breadth of Smitherman's greed and criminality, and by the clear evidence confirming not only the president's guilt but his obvious indifference about leaving such an incriminating trail. Each new document revealed another layer in the expanding scheme to enrich and empower the man at his country's expense, without regard to its effect on international relations.

And the trail led straight to Tan Yong, president of China.

As they finished digesting the last file, Aldo, eyes wide, shook his head. "Admiral, this is ghastly. Absolutely unprecedented. Do we know of anyone else who might have had access to any of this?"

"Just the three of us, my source, and the operatives in China who helped gather it," Ward answered. "I needed to bring this straight to you because I don't know what the next step should be. And I believe you are someone who will know how to handle it from here. Frankly, it falls outside the realm of my office unless it becomes a military matter. All I know is that as sloppy as the perpetrators have been, there is a real danger some of it could leak into the hands of the press, and who knows how it might get spilled should that happen. Or what effect it might have on the country and how we are perceived by the rest of the world, friend or foe."

Aldo nodded. His face was pale. "Smart thinking, Admiral. This is a criminal, diplomatic, and political matter. Not a military one. At least not yet. Let me take it from here."

That was exactly what Jon Ward wanted to hear. The long meeting was finally over. Exhausted, the admiral slowly stepped from the SecDef's office and walked around the Pentagon's E-ring to his own digs.

As soon as the door closed behind Ward, Secretary Aldo turned to Margaret Brenton and said, "Get Sandra Dosetti on the private line. Tell her that I am on my way to Foggy Bottom. We need to meet. And call my car around."

He held the little data storage device between his thumb and forefinger, away from his body, as if it were a snake that might suddenly strike out at him. As he waited for his car, he once again stepped to the office window and looked out at the Potomac, but his thoughts this time were a million miles away.

Ψ

Capitán de Fragata Luis Alvite leaned against the bridge fairing, enjoying the sunrise over the Andes, the Technicolor show taking up most of the sky far to the east. The sea air was invigorating, and the deep blue skies promised another day of calm seas and smooth sailing. He sipped his cup of Nescafé, enjoying the mild tang and rich aroma as he gazed out toward the horizon, deep in thought. Occasionally a wave would break over the submarine's rounded bow, sending a shower of sea spray up his way. But with well-practiced ease, Alvite ducked below the fairing, keeping himself reasonably dry and his coffee untainted by seawater.

The *O'Higgins*, one of two *Scorpene*-class submarines in the Chilean fleet, was racing south, ordered to locate whatever enemy warships were infesting Chilean home waters in the Straits of Magellan. Then, he and his crew were to attack them. They were not alone in this mission, though. The *Carrera*, Chile's other *Scorpene*-class submarine, was a couple of miles off the *O'Higgins*'s starboard beam, heading south as well.

The two modern diesel submarines had been built in Spain for the Chilean Navy. For submerged operation, they featured a unique air-independent propulsion system that used ethanol and liquid oxygen to drive a small steam turbine plant. By combining the AIP plant with the submarine's massive main storage battery, these boats were capable of higher speeds while submerged. They could travel almost as fast as a nuclear boat, but for only a couple of hours. By then, the battery would be exhausted and need a recharge. They could recharge the battery either slowly by employing the AIP plant, or much more rapidly by using the sub's diesel engines.

While the submarines' performance numbers were impressive, their one significant drawback was their slow transit speed on the surface. When not submerged, they could only do about twelve knots. On the plus side, they could do those twelve knots for a very long time. With full fuel tanks, the subs could travel more than six thousand nautical miles without refueling.

"*Capitán*," the Officer-of-the-Deck said, disturbing the skipper's reverie. "Engineering reports that the battery charge is complete."

Alvite nodded toward the OOD and responded, "Very well. Signal the *Carrera* that we are diving. I am going below. Have all hands lay below and submerge the ship."

He then turned and dropped out of sight through the open hatch. Two quick blasts from the diving klaxon soon followed. The lookouts and OOD slid down the ladder, the OOD pausing to swing the hatch shut above him before dropping on down into the control room. The *O'Higgins* slid smoothly below the surface, gliding down to one hundred meters and, at the same time, accelerating to better than twenty knots.

Alvite had carefully calculated the shortest transit time they could make in the two submarines' dash south. By running submerged on the battery and AIP system at flank until the battery was exhausted, and then surfacing and continuing the sprint southward—but at only twelve knots with the diesels while they recharged the battery—they could average almost fifteen knots. That would save them almost a full day in getting down to Puerto Montt. There, they were to refuel and resupply. The downside of being in such a hurry was that they would arrive with both the liquid oxygen and the ethanol completely exhausted and, since they had not topped off their fuel tanks before departing Iquique, they would also be very low on diesel fuel.

The bean counters at naval headquarters protested the unnecessary expenditures for expensive fuels and urged a slow, economical transit, but Luis Alvite had been adamant about not worrying about cost on this mission. For him, this job was personal. His younger brother, *Primer Teniente* Jorge Alvite, had been aboard the *Sargento Aldea*, one of the ships sunk by the bastards in their vicious and unwarranted attack.

The last Luis had heard, Jorge was still listed among the missing. But whether his brother was dead or alive, the sub captain was determined to get on station as soon as possible and see that someone paid the price for what they had done.

Against his country. Against his family.

This mission to the Straits of Magellan was not a neat, cold, impassionate set of orders. It was a vendetta for *Capitán de Fragata* Luis Alvite.

Ψ

Jackson Biddle stuck his head into Jeff Otanga's cramped stateroom. "How's it going, Eng?"

The Engineer shared the tiny sleeping and workspace with Bill Wilson and Jerry Billings, two of his division officers. The two junior officers were very aware that sharing a stateroom with the Engineer meant that not only were they immediately available for whatever task he might need done, but the stateroom was really his and they were just sort of allowed to use their racks there when they required sleep. For that reason, both Wilson and Billings made themselves scarce.

The Engineer was deep into reading up on magnetic bearing controllers. The chat with the NAVSEA engineers had not resulted in any conclusive plans to repair the failed controllers. Safely ensconced in their offices—located on solid ground in the Washington Navy Yard—they had taken all the data the *George Mason* could provide and then admitted they would have to study it and get back to the semi-stranded submarine. But they had sent links to several tech manuals that they thought might be helpful. Otanga was slogging his way through them. So far, they had been of no help whatsoever.

Otanga looked up from the computer screen. "XO, I'm not sure. All this theory is pretty simple, but I'm not seeing a way clear to fix our problem." He took a swig of his coffee and grimaced. It had gotten bitter and ice cold.

Biddle swung the other chair around and plopped down next to Otanga. "Okay, what we got so far?"

Otanga pulled up a screen and started to explain. Biddle held up his hand. "You don't need to run through all the theory to me. What I didn't learn at the academy, I got force-fed at MIT. What I really mean is, what are our alternatives?"

"As I said, it's all pretty simple. The shaft itself is held up by a magnetic field. The position sensors send feedback to the controller to move the shaft to keep it centered. For the thrust bearings, they sense the fore and aft position and keep that centered too."

Biddle thought for a second and then asked, "What's the difference between the shaft bearing and the turbine generator bearing controllers?"

"Just a matter of size, as far as I can see," Otanga answered. "The shaft is a whole lot bigger than the TGs, so the field strength has to be a whole lot higher."

"Well, couldn't we just work out some amplification and use one of the TG controllers in place of the shaft one?"

Otanga slapped his forehead. Then he did some quick calculations.

"XO, that may just work. You know, you might be a genius. But if anyone asks, I'll deny I ever said it. Let's go talk to the skipper."

17

The business that had brought Josh Kirkland/Manuel Viscosa to Bolivia was about to be successfully wrapped up. The Bolivian consortium, badly strapped for cash and woefully short on mining expertise, was only too willing to accept Viscosa's magnanimous offer. His team, backed by Chinese muscle and money, would be most happy to extract the lithium from the vast Uyuni salt flats. Then the suddenly very valuable commodity would be trucked and shipped by rail from the landlocked Andean country, the longer route through Argentinian ports instead of across Chile, then down through the Straits of Magellan—now under control of the Argentine Navy with help from Brazil—and ultimately across the Pacific to feed the hungry battery factories in China. The cost for all this "help" would only be half of the gross revenue realized. And, of course, the "protection" came at no additional charge.

Viscosa had to chuckle. The Bolivians, unsophisticated in the ways of the world, actually thought they had negotiated a good deal for themselves. After all, the lithium had little value to them if it remained underground. Reality would rear its ugly head and bite them soon enough. But for now, Viscosa knew that he had a long drive ahead of him, down out of the high Andes to the restful solitude of his beautiful hacienda outside San Salvador de Jujuy. And from there, he would be able to watch from poolside as the initiative he had set in motion finally came to lucrative fruition. Years of dabbling in drugs, weapons, human trafficking, and other illicit commodities, beginning with his days while still working at the US CIA, had not allowed him to achieve the power, influence, or riches he sought. Now he was about to realize it all with a perfectly legal product, even if his methods for reaching this pinnacle were not exactly socially acceptable. And among his first purchases would be that of a high-end business jet aircraft. He also figured he would have time to update his flying skills and renew his pilot's license. Then he could fly himself anywhere on the planet he wished to go. But he'd still keep a crew on retainer should he prefer to keep himself otherwise pleasurably occupied on the journey.

Viscosa/Kirkland was gleefully calculating how many accountants he would have to employ just to help him keep track of his money and precious metal accounts when his cell phone interrupted the happy reverie. It was Juan Carlos Señorans, head of Argentina's Federal Intelligence Agency. The country's top spy dispensed with any greetings.

"*Señor* Viscosa, I have immediate need for your band of *rufianes armados*," he began. "We have information that the Movimiento de Resistencia has established a major headquarters somewhere near San Salvador de Jujuy, practically your neighbors there. They have simply grown too large and too effective so that they now pose a real threat to our government, and at a most inopportune time. We have reasons to question the loyalty of some in our own military and fear word of any action we might take against the MDR would be leaked beforehand and prevent success. It would be of tremendous assistance to the cause if you and your operatives would find this headquarters and crush the MDR once and for all."

Viscosa held the cell phone to his ear as he awkwardly steered down the twisting mountain road with his free hand. He smiled broadly as he swung the big SUV around a sharp curve and then answered, "Juan Carlos, my friend, my 'armed ruffians,' as you call them, are at your service. Since our task in Boliva has been successfully completed, they are now at loose ends and need something . . . something profitable . . . to occupy their time and attention."

The tone of the voice on the other end of the call stiffened noticeably at the not-so-thinly-veiled expectation of payment. Was his Federales providing protection for Viscosa from the *yanqui* CIA not payment enough already? But Señorans knew the lay of the land. Viscosa's greed was a powerful lever, one that he could rely on, and the former CIA agent's assistance was always money well spent. "Manuel, you will, as always, be amply compensated. But understand one requirement: there can be no survivors."

Ψ

Sandra Dosetti stood, a questioning look on her face, as Sebastien Aldo was ushered into her office. She impatiently waved her assistant back out as she guided the Secretary of Defense to a seat.

"Okay, then, Sebastien, what in hell is so hot that we have to meet on such short notice and without any prior documentation?" she queried irritably. "And so quietly?"

"Sandra, you are not going to believe what just got dropped into my lap," Aldo told her as he plopped down, pulled out the flash drive, and held it up for her, as if she could intuit what data was on the device just by looking at it. "The head of Naval Intelligence just gave us the tool we need to get some things done." She motioned to the computer on her desk and followed him over. He plugged the drive into a port. "The information here absolutely documents and proves a long, long list of dirty deeds that scum Smitherman has pulled off in conjunction with China and some others. There are emails, documents, correspondence, banking transactions . . . all vetted and verified. We put this in the right hands in Congress not only will he be impeached, but he'll spend the rest of his days in a super-maximum-security cell somewhere hot and dusty. And so will his veep."

Dosetti scrolled through the files, eyes wide, whistling in disbelief at some of the tape labels, copies of scrawled notes, and email chains.

"Jesus! The arrogance is unbelievable," she said. "The bastard must actually think he's untouchable to be involved in all this and . . ."

The Secretary of State abruptly sat back in her chair and steepled her fingers beneath her chin. A sudden thought had come to her. A few moments of silence passed. Aldo knew her well enough to remain quiet until she verbalized whatever she was so actively scrolling through in her mind.

Finally, she spoke. "Sebastien, I have a better idea. We need a private meeting with the president. Just the three of us. The president can put it to Osterman any way he pleases. Look, Stan Smitherman likes to play power politics. So, let's ram some power politics right up his rather ample ass."

Ψ

The sun had fallen below the western horizon as Luis Alvite guided his submarine, the *O'Higgins*, through the narrow channel that separated Isla Grande de Chiloé from the mainland. From his vantage point on the bridge, he could look back and see the running lights and yellow flashing submarine ID beacon on the *Carrera*, their sister Chilean sub, a mile astern. Fortunately, the navigation channel was well marked. He only needed to keep the red buoy lights on his starboard side and the green ones on the port to remain out of trouble. Alvite allowed himself the barest hint of a smile. Lately, he rarely smiled.

The channel into Puerto Montt was littered with hundreds of small islets and rocks that lurked menacingly just beneath the surface. And this place was well known for the dense fog that could quickly descend and obscure everything in thick, gray wool. But tonight, he could easily see lights winking at him from houses strung like beads along the necklace of shoreline, and the headlights of the few cars making their way along the road that ringed the water.

It was almost midnight by the time the two Chilean submarines were moored at the tiny Puerto Montt Naval Base. Tanker trucks were already waiting in anticipation of the submarines' arrival. Big hoses snaked across the pier and were connected to the boats as soon as they had been safely tied up. Alvite was concerned about simultaneously loading the extremely volatile liquid oxygen while also taking on highly flammable ethanol and diesel fuel. Just one small leak or inadvertent spark could leave the boats and a great deal of the pier and base swept up in flames. He was also worried about the possibility of sabotage. Those who had been vicious enough to attack and sink two Chilean ships without warning could also have placed saboteurs in other key places, such as here on this pier. However, there was no other option but to quickly fuel the submarines if they intended to remain on schedule on their trip further south.

Alvite stepped across the brow and onto the pier. He took in a deep breath of cold air as his legs adjusted to the stability of solid ground beneath him. He had deliberately not checked to see if there was word about the fate of his brother, Jorge, who had been listed as missing from one of the two Chilean naval ships sunk in territorial waters. Somehow, it was better not to know, even if the news had the slightest chance of being positive.

Bluish-white mercury vapor lamps illuminated the area in a harsh, bright light. The pier and narrow causeway connecting it to the shore were unusually crowded with people and trucks vying to quickly offload stores onto the newly arrived boats. He did not pause to watch all the activity. Alvite eased past the tanker emblazoned with large green letters that spelled *Oxígeno Criogénico*. A thick layer of frost was building on the valves at the back of the tanker. Clouds of condensate wisped up around it. The ethanol tanker was parked next in line, just behind the liquid oxygen, with its hoses also unfurled down to the twin submarines.

As Alvite hurried along, he found the base headquarters building, fittingly the first one at the head of the causeway. A staffer directed him to a small meeting room where the captain of the *Carrera* and his team were already seated.

Without so much as a greeting, Alvite unrolled a navigation chart of the Straits of Magellan and surrounding waters. Both COs had been there before, but not often, and certainly never while the area waters were occupied by hostile warships.

"My plan is pretty simple," Alvite began his brief. As the senior officer, he had been designated as the mission commander for this two-sub operation. "We will continue our transit south just as we have been doing so far. We will submerge abreast of Isla Duque de York." He pointed to a blob of land fronting the Pacific Ocean, amid a scattering of other islands and fingers of water. "That is about a thousand kilometers from here. When we get to Isla Desolación, the *Carrera* will go on the north side of the island

and enter the Straits by the northern route, the one used by most sea traffic. *O'Higgins* will stay on the west side of the island and continue south."

Alvite paused and traced out the path with his finger. The captain of the *Carrera* watched attentively, then nodded.

"Yes, go on, Captain."

"The *Carrera* will search the strait southbound along the usual transit route while the *O'Higgins* will go through the passage south of Isla Furia. The *O'Higgins* will enter through the Canal Cockburn and then the Canal Magdalina. Since *O'Higgins* has to transit an extra two hundred kilometers, *Carrera* should conduct a slow ASW search down the Straits. A four-knot search will take two days. That gives the *O'Higgins* twelve hours to get in position and thirty-six hours to search." Alvite again pointed at the chart. "We will use the seventy-one-degree, ten-minute longitude line as a mutual interference boundary. Neither one of us should approach within a kilometer of the line, nor shoot across it. Please remember that their diesel submarines are very similar to ours. There is really no way to differentiate using only sonar. If you detect a submarine on your side of the boundary, it is the enemy, and you will be free to shoot."

The captain of the *Carrera* stroked his chin and observed, "*Capitán* Alvite, if I did not know better, I would think that you are using my submarine to flush out our quarry and herd it down to where you will wait in ambush."

Alvite's face was devoid of expression as he nodded and said, "That is exactly what I have in mind. Any submarine that crosses the boundary will be shot. I fully intend to avenge my brother and all the other sailors we lost."

Alvite gazed around the room, looking each officer directly in the eye. No one had any doubt that this was a serious mission, to be followed to the death. Luis Alvite took a deep breath and went on.

"Assuming neither of us locates any of the hostile vessels after the two-day search, we will rendezvous off Isla Dawson and work together up to Punta Arenas and then on to the northeast, out past Point Dúngeness, into the Atlantic." Alvite's finger traced the route on the chart. "If we reach that far without encountering any opposition, we will take stations to guard the

Straits, *Carrera* back at the western entrance and *O'Higgins* near Point Dúngeness. Any questions?"

The CO of the *Carrera* said, "If we find any other Argentine or Brazilian warships, what are our orders?"

Alvite gave a dry chuckle. "We will sink them. Any other questions?" There were none. He did notice the color had mostly left the faces of the *Carrera* contingent. He looked at his watch. "It is three hours to first light. We will be underway at zero-six-hundred. Good hunting, gentlemen."

With that, he turned and strode out of the room, back in the direction of the pier and his submarine, her tanks full, appetite sated, ready for war.

Ψ

TJ Dillon sawed the steering wheel of the big Land Cruiser back and forth as he guided it up the winding, narrow road. As had others before him, Dillon considered Valle Escondido—a true hidden valley—to be well named. As hard as it was to find, it was even more difficult to navigate. The MDR had chosen this for their headquarters because it was not only an out-of-the-way spot but one that could be easily defended. No unwelcome visitors were going to pull off a surprise visit up this road. Approaches from other directions would be over steep, rough, rugged terrain.

The road ended at a high stone wall. A heavy iron gate was the only access to the ancient two-story *casa* just visible through the entrance. A pair of guards stood inside, the muzzles of their rifles pointed ominously toward Dillon's SUV. He leaned out the driver's window and shouted the password. The gate creaked open so that he could swing the SUV through and into the courtyard. Following closely behind, Billy Joe Hurt guided his Forester in. The heavy gate immediately swung shut behind the Subaru with a solid clank.

In the courtyard, heavily armed men were rushing about, apparently oblivious to the two newly arrived vehicles. Some were loading up into a couple of old pickup trucks. Others were slipping out the gate in squads of six or eight at a time and disappearing up into the hills that surrounded the hacienda. Although the men looked more like a ragtag assortment of misfits than they did military troops, they still moved with the air of experienced fighters on a mission.

Dillon was just climbing out of the Toyota when a man stepped down off the *casa*'s wide *terraza* and walked over. He held out his hand. In slow, halting English, he said, "Welcome to the headquarters of the Movimiento de Resistencia. We appreciate your assistance. I am Guillermo Manuelito and until our leader recovers from his wounds, I suppose I am the one in charge. But I confess I am only a simple *olivarero*, hardly qualified or well trained in conducting battle. You have arrived, as they say in your Western movies, just in the nick of time."

Dillon met the man's firm handshake and made introductions. "I'm TJ Dillon. The grizzled old coot over there is Bill Beaman, a former Navy SEAL pulled from retirement to help with our efforts down here. The kid is Jim Ward, commander of the SEAL team." Nodding toward the SEALs climbing out of the Forester, he went on. "And those four characters are a SEAL fire team. We heard that you needed some help. But if anyone ever asks, we were never here."

Manuelito responded, "We certainly do need help. And we need it right now. Our lookouts down in San Salvador de Jujuy have just reported several trucks loaded down with heavily armed men are headed this way. We have no idea how they learned of this headquarters, but we know they are on their way to eliminate it and us as a threat to the new government in Buenos Aires. We fear that Manuel Viscosa and his hired thugs are coming to do the dirty work of the Federal Intelligence Agency. This Viscosa, who some say is actually a *norteamericano*, is the local *jefe del crimen*. I think your movies would call him a 'mob boss.' Anyway, he is in bed with the Federales. The AFI has discovered that we have established a headquarters here and they are planning an attack to wipe us out and—"

"Wait," Dillon interrupted. "Did you say Viscosa is coming along with the attackers?"

"That is what we have heard. He is an arrogant man and prefers to directly oversee the more important and lucrative missions of his *matones*."

Dillon and Ward looked at each other. Dillon could not suppress a smile. A smile of anticipation.

"Where do you want us?" Ward asked. "This Viscosa character is the reason we are here in the first place."

Manuelito pointed back over his shoulder, to a ridgeline that overlooked the hacienda. "I do not have any shooters to put up there. My best advisors tell me that Viscosa may well try a flanking attack over that ridge while a smaller diversionary force approaches up the main road. If he can control that high ground, we will be *patos sentados*, sitting ducks, down here. Our resistance to tyranny will be over and I am not sure there would be anyone else to take up leadership of the fight for freedom."

It took the SEALs five minutes to unload the two vehicles and saddle up for the hike up the steep slope. After an hour of tough climbing, bushwhacking most of the way through thick undergrowth, SEAL Chief Hurt had his team dig in along the ridgeline. Down the backside of the mountain, they had a clear view to a path of a road that snaked up alongside a narrow valley. The path stitched its way back and forth along the slopes up to a small pass that probably dropped into a valley on the other side.

They were, indeed, just in the nick of time. The SEALs were still digging in when Ward spied a dust cloud billowing up from somewhere down near the bottom of the mountain. Minutes later, three flatbed trucks could be seen, crawling purposefully up what passed for a road. There appeared to be at least a dozen heavily armed shooters riding on the bed of each truck.

Hurt tapped Don Winston on the shoulder and pointed at the lead truck. Winston nodded and settled the bipod for his M82A3 fifty-caliber sniper rifle into the dirt and quickly sighted on that particular vehicle. The laser range finder showed the distance to be just over a thousand meters, a relatively easy shot for Winston with this rifle. It was well below the advertised effective range of around eighteen hundred meters. Winston had regularly scored hits out at better than two thousand meters.

"Chief, you want me to take out the third truck after I hit that first one?" he asked as he slid the box magazine into place and cycled a round into the chamber.

"Winston, do I need to tell you to wipe your butt after you take a dump?" Hurt growled, his slow North Alabama drawl dragging the words out. "'Course I want the third truck hit. And then, if it's not too much bother, could you put a round in the middle one to boot?"

Winston ignored the chief, squinting at the computer as he input the range, downslope angle, temperature, and adjustment for a slight crosswind. After dialing in the compensations on his Leupold Mark 4 scope, he centered the crosshairs on the lead truck's hood, specifically to a spot eighteen inches back from the front and a foot to the near side. His actual target was the engine block under the hood.

He took a deep breath, let half of it out and gently eased the trigger back. The big gun roared and bucked as the seven-hundred-grain bullet left the barrel at almost three thousand feet per second. The bullet's journey would take less than a second. It would be three seconds before anyone down on those trucks would even hear the shot. By that time, two more rounds would be flying, heading for the other two trucks. Sure enough, each of the bullets tore through an aluminum block, reducing the vehicles to so much useless metal.

Winston shifted his targeting to the fighters that were now baling off the trucks. By the time Viscosa's thugs had dived for cover, three bodies hung from the bed of the first truck and another lay still, bleeding out in the dust.

Chief Hurt scanned the scene with his 7x50 binoculars. The three trucks were smoking hulks and not really suitable for cover. He could see some of the fighters scurrying off to their left, staying low and behind whatever cover they could find, but paralleling the path down the mountain. Other fighters were doing the same but heading upward along the edge of the road. There were several gullies that emptied out onto the road in each direction, snaking up the slope and providing cover all the way to the ridgetop.

One thing was obvious. These guys were well disciplined, properly trained for the task. Despite having just been ambushed, not one of them was panicking, wildly slinging lead up the hill at a shooter they could not see while giving away their own position. Instead, they were moving out to flank and encircle whoever had shot at them.

"Don, good shooting," Hurt told Winston. "Do your best to try to keep them heads-down and scrambling." Turning to the other two SEALs, he said, "Jones, LaCroix, make your way down the ridgeline to the head of that gully." He pointed to the first ravine that would likely offer the attackers cover all the way up. "Make those climbers uncomfortable for as long as you can." Turning to the officers, he continued, "Commander Ward, I suggest you and I move over to that gully up the road and do the same. They'll be coming out the top of the chute sooner or later." He handed his binoculars to Bill Beaman. "Captain, can you spot for Winston? And Mr. Dillon, you provide cover fire here in the middle."

Dillon nodded as he picked up his MK 17 SCAR H assault rifle. He slid a 40mm grenade launcher on the lower Picatinny rail and the fire control unit onto the upper rail. He was ready to rock and roll. A narrow gully, full of brush, ran all the way up the slope, ending directly in front of his position. If Viscosa's men came at them—and Dillon was reasonably sure they would—that would be the most likely route.

"Same tactic as the Japanese in World War II on islands in the South Pacific," Bill Beaman noted. "They'd use those ravines like staircases to move up and down the bluffs."

Jim Ward and Chief Hurt moved off to the left, crouching, keeping to the backside of the ridge so their movements were hidden from the men down below. When they had traversed a hundred yards or so, they peeked over the ridgetop. Ward used his rifle scope to glass the gully. Sure enough, he could just make out movement a couple of hundred yards downslope, but he would not yet have a clear shot. He signaled to Hurt that they should take positions on either side of the gully to engage the shooters as they climbed up closer.

By then, they could hear the rip and tear of automatic weapons fire from the direction of the hacienda below and behind them. It sounded as if Manuelito and his MDR fighters were heavily engaged back there. The mercenaries, or *matones*—"hoodlums," as Manuelito had called them—climbing the slope toward Dillon and the SEALs had likely intended to flank the hacienda and catch the MDR in a classic pincer movement. It would have worked had the SEALs not foiled that plan. Dillon knew they needed to deal with this aspect of the assault quickly and effectively so that they could charge back to help Manuelito with the other arm of the nutcracker.

Further down the ridgeline, Jones and LaCroix were also setting up at the head of another gully to catch the *matones* taking that route. They had just found good fighting positions when the MK 82 roared again. Someone downrange had remained in the open for a split second too long. This time, the fifty-caliber shot was answered by a smattering of returned small arms fire. That was followed closely by a blast from a 40mm grenade and several 7.62mm rounds from Dillon's SCAR H. The battle was on, at least in the middle ground at the crest of the ridge.

TJ Dillon was still scanning downrange, searching for his next target, when he saw a burst of smoke and flames from a point near the attackers' lead truck. He instantly knew what that was. Someone had launched an AT4 projectile—a lightweight, man-portable, shoulder-fired weapon—at them. He immediately shouted a warning as he dived for cover, landing on top of Bill Beaman amid the rocks and brush along the backside of the ridge.

The 84mm round was nothing more than a visible blur as it arced up toward them and then fell just short of where Don Winston lay in the dust. The resulting blast tore the MK 82 sniper rifle from his hands and flung it several yards away. Burning hot metal fragments from the exploding projectile ripped through the SEAL's body.

He died instantly.

Dillon swung his binoculars around in time to see the shooter down below as mercenary discarded the AT4 tube and scurried for cover, aware the launch would draw fire. Dillon took aim and fired a couple of shots, but it was hopeless. The son of a bitch was well beyond the effective range of his assault rifle. No point wasting ammo he might desperately need shortly.

Bill Beaman slithered down to where Winston lay. Confirming the SEAL was dead, he crawled over to retrieve the sniper rifle. But it would be of no use. The blast had severely damaged it. He tossed it aside and moved back to where TJ Dillon waited.

"Well, brother," Beaman muttered. "Looks like it's you and me holding the middle. You think us old farts can do it?"

Dillon snorted. "Never underestimate an old fart armed with an assault rifle," he said as he slammed a fresh magazine into his SCAR H. "And a severely pissed-off one, to boot."

Small arms fire broke out to their right. Automatic weapons ripped and tore the air from somewhere down the slope, interspersed with single shots from Jones and LaCroix. They seemed to be holding their own against the shooters who were climbing up the gully in their direction, occasionally firing in the general direction of the hidden SEALs.

Over to the left, a 40mm grenade explosion reverberated off the mountains. Jim Ward had used his grenade launcher to good effect, dislodging half a dozen *matones* who had made it up near the top of the chute and were hiding behind a pile of rocks. Billy Joe Hurt splattered them with well-aimed fire as they scurried to find safer cover. Four of the *matones* did not make it. They lay dead, sprawled across the scree.

Viscosa's men moved inexorably up the slope. Although the SEALs had the advantage of holding high ground, the *matones* had vastly more firepower and numbers going for them. That gave them an advantage. They had begun a pattern, likely part of the plan should they come under fire before reaching the top of the ridge. Several of them would liberally spray the ridgeline with withering gunfire while their mates scrambled up the slope and found adequate cover. Then they repeated the process, hopscotching up the gullies toward their goal. A dozen or more *matones* lay sprawled on the rough ground, but Viscosa's men still had numbers on their side. They could lose a dozen more and likely be able to overrun the hard-pressed SEALs.

Jim Ward dared to raise his head to assay the situation. What he saw stunned him. Or, actually, who he saw.

"TJ, you won't believe this," he muttered to Dillon over his intra-squad radio.

"Tell me, brother!"

"It's Kirkland. He's coming up the hill with the rest of his scalawags!"

It was true. Manuel Viscosa—aka Josh Kirkland—was following his team up the gully that led to Jim Ward's position. He was pushing and prodding, waving and shouting, urging his fighters to hurry and make it up the ridge. And it was working. They were almost three-quarters of the way up the slope and coming quickly. The ridge was only one big push away.

"Damn egomaniac!" Dillon answered back. "If you want a job done right, though . . ."

Viscosa certainly knew that if he could take the ridge here at this point, it would be a simple matter to roll up the other outnumbered fighters along its spiny top. They would have only twenty yards to charge across, but those yards were pretty much in the open, devoid of effective cover.

But Viscosa did not know that those fighters he was about to face were US Navy SEALs, four active-duty, two retired, but all powerfully motivated. Even more so after the loss of their squad mate.

Viscosa stationed a pair of machine gunners to furiously stitch the ridgeline with fire, effectively forcing Ward and Hurt to keep their heads down while he sent the rest of his *matones* boldly charging, zigzagging up the open slope. They might well have made it if the slope had not been so steep. The two SEALs who were dug in there were able to knock the charging shooters down as they scrambled up the grade, this time firing wildly.

But then, both SEALs were hit by bits of that random fusillade. Jim Ward was slammed backward with a round through the upper body. At almost the same time, Chief Hurt was hit in the right side of his chest.

With the return fire from directly above them suddenly stopped, Manuel Viscosa rose and sauntered on up the slope to join his men. That was when he saw who had been so effectively deterring his attack team.

"Damnation! Who do we have here?" he said with a broad grin and wide, mocking eyes, even as he waved his men on to challenge the other shooters along the ridge. Jim Ward was in pain, barely conscious, unable to respond to the man he knew as Josh Kirkland. "Why, it's the young Ward! God's gift to the US Navy. Too bad your running mate Dillon isn't here to join the party." Viscosa pulled his Glock 17 and aimed at a spot directly between the eyes of the prostrate SEAL.

Ward braced for the shot that would end his life and thought of his parents. Of Li Min. As always, she had kissed him goodbye and instructed him not to get himself killed. Both knew that was a promise he could not necessarily keep, but he always made it anyway. So did his folks. Especially his dad.

"I truly wish I had the time to savor this moment. We've seen the movies where the villain talks too long and gives the hero a chance to do something noble. But we have a job to do, so I think I'll just finish what I should have taken care of that time up in Venezuela."

The shot rang out sharply, echoing off the uncaring nearby mountains. Viscosa stood there, staring down at the SEAL team leader, then glanced, puzzled, at the pistol in his hand.

He had not yet pulled the trigger. The shot had come from some other gun nearby. He dropped the Glock to the ground then staggered sideways, as if he was still intending to carry on, to lead his men as they continued their highly profitable assault.

Then, suddenly, he fell to his knees, his hands clutched to his chest, blood spurting out between his fingers with each heartbeat before he abruptly pitched forward onto his face. The remaining thugs watching the mini drama play out suddenly broke and, now leaderless, fled wildly back down the slope.

TJ Dillon, pistol still in hand, and Bill Beaman ran from the brush and over to the fallen SEALs. Once they confirmed the few surviving attackers had run away, they began assessing and bandaging the men's wounds. Jones and LaCroix joined them.

"Reckon we oughta go after those guys?" Jones asked Dillon.

"I'd say they won't quit running until they get home, wherever the hell that is," TJ answered. "They just saw their boss take a round to the old ticker. Looks like the snake just got its head cut off."

"Thanks to your good shootin'," Beaman said.

"I've practiced that shot in my head a million times. It felt good to finally make it for real," Dillon quietly responded. "The planet just got a hell of a lot better off with that bastard gone from it." There was still sporadic fire from the other direction, back down the mountain at the resistance HQ. "Let's get the wounded and Winston back down the trail and we'll help those guys chase off the last of the attackers."

Beaman glanced over at Dillon.

"Okay, TJ, but you're the one that gets to tell Li Min and Mrs. Ward that you got their brand-new husband and precious baby boy all shot up. I've already had that assignment a couple of times and I ain't sure I'm forgiven yet."

Dillon grinned. "Maybe you'll verify I saved their guy's frog ass in the process. And take the edge off the news."

18

Chief Sam Sharkey was elbows-deep into the controller cabinet, and it was pretty much the same position that he had been in for the past twelve hours. The pinouts for the amplifier cards had turned out to be significantly different for the replacement cards removed from the port turbine generator. Modifying the wiring in the tightly constrained cabinet was infuriatingly ticklish and required him to contort his body into painful shapes just to see what he was doing and make the proper connections. Whoever designed these components obviously never anticipated a repair job at sea. The myriad of different colored wires resembled a quite decorative rat's nest. There was no way that he would ever get the cabinet door shut, let alone make it look nice and neat.

"How's it going, Chief?" It was LCDR Jeff Otanga, *George Mason*'s Engineering Officer.

Sharkey groaned as he pulled the rest of his frame out of the cabinet, leaned back on his haunches, and then slowly stood, stretching his aching back as he did so. Otanga handed him a steaming cup of coffee.

"Thanks, Eng." Otanga took a slow sip. "Lord knows I needed that. Life would've been a hell of a lot easier if some design engineer hadn't stuck the bearing controller in a frame bay under an air-conditioning plant. My back feels like a stale, overcooked pretzel."

"Colorful description and likely an apt one," Otanga responded. "But please tell me you about have it buttoned up."

The chief electrician took another sip of coffee and sat down heavily on the steps that led up to the reduction gears. He looked up wearily at Otanga, "Mostly. I've about wrapped up installing the cards. Unless I really screwed something up, we should be able to energize this mess in an hour or so. Then, if I didn't bugger something up in there, and we don't release large amounts of sparks and black smoke, it's just a matter of aligning everything and fine-tuning the positioning."

"How long you figure that'll take?" Otanga asked.

Sharkey chewed on his thumbnail for a moment, considering his answer. "Okay, if all goes well, alignment should take a couple of hours. The fine-tuning will be ongoing for several days, of course. We'll need to station a watch back here, monitoring the shaft position and adjusting the gains as necessary while we answer bells on the main engines." He took another long sip of the coffee. "Speaking of gains, I really need the amplifier gain values before I can do any alignments. We get anything from the engineers at NAVSEA yet?"

Otanga laughed drily. "Chief, it's a three-day holiday weekend back in the world, you know. You don't really expect them to come into their nice cozy offices and generate those numbers for us on a government holiday, now do you? I expect we'll be stuck creeping along on the SPM at two knots until at least Tuesday morning." Otanga turned and headed out of the compartment. "I'll go forward to brief the skipper. And I'll suggest he bug NAVSEA again to get us those gains whenever they decide to come back to work."

He found Brian Edwards and Jackson Biddle standing in *George Mason*'s control room in heavy discussion about whatever they were looking at on a screen. Edwards waved Otanga over.

"Eng, just the man we need. Looks like somebody at NAVSEA put in some overtime hours after all. The amplifier gain settings just came in, along with a suggested alignment procedure and an emergency operating procedure."

Otanga quickly skimmed through the message. "Appears to be just what we need. I take back some of those ugly words I was muttering about shoreside pukes. Chief Sharkey's almost ready to button up the cabinet. Probably four more hours on the wiring to finish the work and wring it out, then figure eight hours for alignment. So, knock on simulated wood, we could be able to answer bells on the mains by the midwatch."

Edwards nodded. He knew full well that Otanga had taken Chief Sharkey's most conservative estimates and then padded them generously as a "just-in-case" to cover any unexpected contingencies. He had done the same thing often enough when he was an Engineer. Best case, they might be back on the main engines right after lunch.

"Skipper, remember that we tore the bearing controller off the port turbine generator. It'll stay out of commission until we get back. We'll only have one turbine generator," Otanga reminded Edwards. "That's going to limit us to about sixty percent reactor power. A good full bell is about the most we'll get."

Edwards nodded.

That he understood. But he was pondering another issue. The problem with the ship's propulsion system had provided a good excuse to not hasten home as ordered. To remain in the area where some truly interesting things were taking place. Activities that absolutely called for them to stay there and monitor. But for some reason, they were not being allowed to do so.

Thanks to some go-getter at NAVSEA, that fortuitous excuse for lingering had just evaporated.

Ψ

US Secretary of State Sandra Dosetti ignored Stan Smitherman, seated behind his desk, watching her as she marched into the Oval Office and promptly took a seat on the blue- and gold-striped settee as if the president had invited her to do so.

Secretary of Defense Sebastien Aldo hurried to keep up with her, ignoring the wide-eyed stare of the president, and then sat down next to her.

Smitherman finally stood up from behind the oak Resolute desk, an astonished look on his face. He was not at all sure what was going on here. Dosetti and Aldo had arrived at the White House together, unannounced and uninvited. And unscheduled. Sloppy as he was with most things presidential, Smitherman was usually a stickler for keeping to the schedule his personal secretary, Martha McGinnis, built and maintained for him. She refused to allow him to be otherwise.

This time, though, the two members of his cabinet had simply shown up, marched into the outer office where Martha kept guard, and told her that despite not having a spot on the morning's agenda, they were there to meet with the president on a matter of utmost importance. And she should rearrange her boss's calendar to accommodate them because the meeting would take place now and it should not be a very long one at all.

"But he has a photo op with the Girl Scout cookie people in an hour, and—" the secretary began, but Dosetti held up her hand.

"Martha, you will immediately announce us to President Smitherman," Dosetti said. Aldo nodded to affirm that was his request as well. When she did as told, and when the door to the Oval Office opened, Aldo and Dosetti unceremoniously marched right on through without being invited and took their seats on the settee facing the startled president.

"Sandy, Seb," Smitherman sputtered. "What is the meaning of this? I didn't . . . there are protocols. I'm damn busy . . . you can't just barge in here at your convenience and convene a damn meeting with the damn president of the United States, you know."

It was clear Smitherman had anticipated a leisurely morning. His suit coat was draped across a chair. His necktie was coiled in a pile on the desk and his shirt was open, unbuttoned halfway down the front revealing a patch of gray chest hair. He had not even yet installed his trademark steerhorn cuff links. His shirt sleeves were loosely pulled up to his elbows. And there was a water glass on the desk, half filled with what appeared to be whiskey, right next to a coffee cup.

"Oh, do us all a favor for once and shut up, Stan," Dosetti shot back. Smitherman looked as if someone had slapped him in the face. "You best get your butt back in the chair and listen for once in your life. When I—we —" She nodded in the direction of the Secretary of Defense next to her, but it was clear this was her meeting and that she intended to run it. ". . . when *we* want you to speak, we will let you know."

The president's private secretary was already in the process of quietly backing out of the room. She eased the door shut. Martha had no intention of being anywhere near this meeting or bearing witness to any of the proceedings. This one appeared to be the kind that might one day be subpoena-worthy.

"Now, since you claim to be so busy, I'll get straight to the point." Dosetti pulled a flash drive from her jacket pocket. "Stan, you can take a look at the contents of this drive at your leisure. It contains a pretty complete history and indisputable proof of your dealings with Tan Yong. Not all of it is on this drive, mind you. We have much, much more. Even so, this right here is more than enough to convict you. The payoffs, the shady deals, the bribes, you name it. We have enough solid evidence to get you and your shadow, Osterman, impeached and convicted and made the guests of some nice federal retirement home—probably Leavenworth—for the rest of your natural life. Maybe they can arrange adjacent cells so you two can hold hands through the bars."

Smitherman was clearly stunned. But his first instinct was to deny, deny, deny. "What the hell are you talking about? Have you gone stark raving mad? You two had better get your asses out of my office and go somewhere to sober up before I have the Secret Service boot you out onto the street."

Sebastien Aldo cut him off. "Stan, stop with the threats already. You had better listen to what Secretary Dosetti is telling you. We have literally terabytes of absolutely undeniable proof of your corruption, mostly with China but with some other interesting characters, too. The evidence has been vetted and verified ten ways to Sunday, even as we have been careful to avoid it being leaked. If even a fraction of this stuff falls into the wrong hands, you and Harold are toast. Your Chinese friends have sold you out. Maybe accidentally, maybe on purpose. I don't know which, and it really isn't important."

"Can't be . . ." was all the Leader of the Free World could manage to say. His face had gone sickly pale. Then, with what little breath he seemed to have left, he asked, "Is this a coup, Seb?"

"No, but if it was, it would have been self-inflicted by your actions, Mr. President," Aldo answered, but immediately felt bad about saying "Mr. President" out of habit.

Dosetti jumped in. "Look, we are just arrogant enough to believe that what we are doing is for the good of the country. And even the world. Even you have to know that the Chinese will sooner or later want to cash in their chit for all the money they've invested in your corrupt ass. And it'll be far more than allowing a tariff to expire or to look the other way when they take over the economy of some third-world country."

"But listen to us, Stan," Aldo continued. He almost felt sorry for his soon-to-be-former boss and longtime friend. "Listen well. We are here to offer you a deal that will keep you out of jail and maybe able to retain what little dignity you may have had. And, of course, enough of those millions you have ferreted away offshore to keep you from having to go on welfare."

Dosetti tossed the flash drive in Smitherman's direction. It landed heavily on the desk pad in front of the president like a brick, as if it weighed pounds instead of a few ounces.

"Take a look if you want," she offered. "You can have your experts check it out, but that's probably not a really good idea. It would be real difficult to keep this kind of crap under wraps if you sicced the CIA, NSA, or even the FBI on it. You've stepped on enough toes at all three places that they would be over at CNN or Fox News and in the offices of the opposition leadership in a flash."

"There's no way..." Smitherman was obviously still in denial.

"Want an example?" Dosetti asked. She sported a sly grin. They were about to deliver the real haymaker, a misdeed a political animal like Stan Smitherman would instantly recognize. "An example that by itself would likely be enough to get you hanged for treason if not just for pure, unadulterated stupidity. How many millions did you get funneled to your political action committee before your last campaign, every penny of it directly from Tan Yong and the Chinese Communist Party?"

Smitherman's already pale face turned even whiter. "My PAC? How . . . ?"

"Does the figure of one hundred and seventy-six million dollars sound about right? Delivered through one hundred and seven different LLCs and dummy S-corps, including Minnie Mouse Millinery, Who's on First Inc., and Mountain Oyster Culinary, among others. Enough money to have a standing order to automatically have dibs on and snatch up every TV commercial slot available on every network and local affiliate that counted before your opponent's ad agencies even knew they were there? And bribe your way to exclusivity on several social media sites? 'Freeze 'em out strategy,' I think you called it. You even bragged to us about how expensive it was, and how grateful you were to have such generous donors 'among the working American middle class.'"

Smitherman's jaw dropped. Not only did Dosetti know about the under-the-table cash, but she had also hit the actual amount dead-on and even named a few of the companies formed specifically to cover the trail. The president glanced at the flash drive on his desk, then closed his eyes and sat back in his chair. Realization had clearly set in. They had the goods on him, the far better hand. There was nothing to do now but to fold, to see what the pair wanted. Time to cut a deal, as always. But this time, he had few, if any, bargaining chips left on his side of the table. Dosetti and Aldo had successfully—and brutally—called his bluff.

"Okay, what the hell do you want?"

Dosetti tried not to allow even a glimmer of a winning smirk on her face. She failed.

"Stan, it's very simple. We want you and Harold out of here. As far from the office of president and vice president— from Washington, DC—as physically possible. Sebastien and I will take over here."

"So, it is a coup," Smitherman said.

Dosetti ignored him. She was on a roll. "We want to do it while raising as little suspicion as possible, but some of that will be inevitable. We all just have to keep our stories straight and have as few people as possible know what's really happening. The news cycle will move on soon enough. All the shit going on down in South America will help us in that regard." She leaned forward on the sofa and tried to look her president in the eye, but he still had them closed. "Okay, Stan, here's how you're going to do it. Your vice president is going to have a sudden medical emergency that requires that he resign from office immediately."

"Harold's in fine shape," Smitherman muttered. "Runs five miles every . . ."

"Don't sweat the details. I really don't care what his problem will be, but we'll sell it hard enough it'll be believed. Maybe terminal hemorrhoids. At any rate, you will immediately appoint me as your new VP. We easily have the votes in both houses of Congress to get me confirmed. Then, as soon as I take office, you will invoke the Twenty-Fifth Amendment and resign for personal reasons."

"Personal reasons?" Smitherman asked softly. Dosetti and Aldo could hardly hear his words. He had the look of a totally defeated man.

"We have plenty of time to come up with something the talking heads will believe and propagate for us. And Stan," Dosetti continued, "until we get this transition all in place, you will do or say absolutely nothing without first clearing it with us. That starts with you like Thin Mints and Do-si-dos best." She caught the confused look on his face. "Girl Scouts. Cookies. You'll meet them shortly for a photo op. If either of you go off-script, we'll see to it that some of that evidence on the thumb drive gets seeded to the most fertile ground. Is that quite understood?"

Smitherman finally opened his eyes, picked up the flash drive, looked at it as if it was a poisonous snake, then threw it back down. He did not nod, nor did he even glance at the triumphant pair sitting across from him.

"First order of business is to get Harold out of here immediately," Dosetti ordered. "Tell him whatever you want about the evidence we have but be sure he understands what happens should either of you not do precisely as you have been told. He's welcome to meet with either of us if he doubts any of this or has questions about how the plan will work. But the first thing is for him to pack his bags. I will be taking his White House office, and I expect it to be vacant and available by the end of the week. Clear?"

Smitherman nodded.

Dosetti and Aldo rose to leave. The Secretary of State paused to look back over her shoulder at the president.

"Stan, just in case you get any smart ideas, we have a number of copies of those files hidden around in convenient locations for quick release. You could never find them, much less destroy them. For once, do the smart thing. Stow that drive somewhere where nobody else will find it. Flush it down the shitter if you want to. I—*we*—don't care. But be sure you step aside the way we have it laid out. Plan the design of your presidential library, start making speeches at a quarter-mil per, and sign a lucrative book deal. You won't necessarily need the money, but you'll meet some really fun ladies on the book promotional tours and get to tell some of your tall tales when you're on TV with Kimmel and Colbert. Understood?"

The president again had his eyes tightly closed, his bleached-out face screwed up in a pained scowl, slumped limply there in his big chair. To Dosetti and Aldo, it almost appeared as if he were dead.

They did not bother to check his pulse. He was defeated, not deceased, and that was close to the same thing for President Stanley Smitherman.

The two marched on out of the Oval Office, shutting the door with finality behind them. But not before they caught a glimpse of the president, coming back to life, sitting up, and draining the whiskey from the water glass in one big gulp.

19

Vice Admiral Eduardo Barbosa stood on the bridge wing of his flagship, the *Atlântico,* and watched the steady flow of merchant ships steaming past where the Brazilian Navy's most powerful warship swung at anchor. In fact, his entire battle group, grandly named "Task Force Southern Passage," had been quietly anchored there, just off Punta Arenas, for over a month. Except for a few minor skirmishes up in the mountains, the fighting had pretty much come to a halt. The Straits of Magellan were securely in his hands, under control of Brazil and Argentina.

There was one big difference, though. Normal commercial traffic had resumed, but now almost all of the ships on this route flew a Chinese flag.

Despite the success of his mission and the lack of drama so far, Barbosa was uneasy. His ships had been down here, at the southern end of the world, far away from their logistic support, for too long. He had already sent the ancient Argentine frigates back to Puerto Belgrano before they broke down and required a tow to get back home. He knew he should get his own fleet back home to Brazil before the same thing could happen to them. The fact that no one had challenged his fleet's presence also contributed to his unease. Neither the *norteamericano*s nor the still relatively capable Chilean Navy seemed to have reacted at all.

He saw that *Capitão de Mar e Guerra* Diego-Moreira, the Commanding

Officer of the *Atlântico*, was standing just inside the pilot house. Barbosa beckoned to him.

"Tomás, signal the fleet to prepare to get underway. All except the *Bahia* and the *Tamandaré*. They can stay here and support the forces ashore where there might still be some fighting. And the submarines. They will stay and guard the Straits. Meanwhile, we will sail at first light."

Diego-Moreira responded, "At once, Admiral. Do I tell them the destination?"

Barbosa half chuckled. "That is the subject of your second message. Message Comando de Operações Navais and tell them that we are departing Punta Arenas. Our mission here is complete. Commander Task Force Southern Passage recommends that we return to home waters for upkeep and maintenance."

Diego-Moreira nodded. "It will be good to head home. But the *norteamericanos* don't seem to be much of a threat. They just steam back and forth five hundred miles off our coast. Why should we be concerned with them?"

"Tomás, my friend, that is something for President Souza and the Joint Staff to worry about. It is our task to get our ships relocated to where they are useful and wait to do what we are told."

Ψ

Sandra Dosetti sat in the Oval Office, reading through the PDB. To maintain all appearances of normalcy, Stan Smitherman still sat behind the Resolute desk. Dosetti had chosen the settee in the middle of the room. The big office was filled with an uncomfortable silence as she skimmed the papers in a large, spiral-bound binder.

The President's Daily Brief, the all-source intelligence compendium, was developed and delivered to the president every morning, whether he ever got around to reading the material or not. Today's PDB began with a lengthy treatise on the reactions from various governments round the world to Harold Osterman's sudden resignation as vice president due to unspecified medical reasons. Unspecified to protect the privacy of the vice president and his family. The brief also noted the submitted appointment and request for a quick vote of approval for the Secretary of State to fill out

Osterman's term. Most of the remainder of the briefing was devoted to the ongoing crisis in South America.

Dosetti slowed her rapid scan of the thick document and read several pages more carefully. She stopped, thought for a long moment, and then spoke. "Stan, we need to get more involved in the Brazil-Argentina thing. We should move that carrier battle group down off the Uruguayan coast. And I see that we have a submarine down there, too. Let's put them to work."

Smitherman roused himself from the lethargic funk into which he had settled of late. "I don't think that's a good idea," he offered, but without much enthusiasm.

"Stan, I didn't ask for your opinion," Dosetti shot back without even looking up from the document. "Move the carrier battle group, *now*. And get on the phone with the president of Uruguay to give him your full support. His name is Mendez. Félix Mendez."

She then looked up when Smitherman did not do or say anything. There was a waspish bite to her tone. "Get moving, Stan."

Smitherman closed his eyes for a moment, a look of pain on his face. Then he picked up his phone and asked Martha McGinnis to kindly set up two calls, first with the Secretary of Defense and then with the Uruguayan president.

Ψ

Jeff Otanga knocked on Brian Edward's door and stuck his head in. "Skipper, we completed alignment on the shaft bearing controller. All sat. We're answering bells on the main engines now. The procedure has us stay at ahead-one-third for a couple of hours while we do some fine adjustments and then we'll slowly step up the bell, checking the bearings at each new speed."

Edwards looked up from the report he was reading. He smiled broadly.

"Great news, Eng! And perfect timing. We just copied the broadcast. Looks like we're not going straight home after all. Our tasking has changed. We're to stay down here off Argentina and sniff around, as we should have been doing all along. Let's go find the XO and figure out what kind of fun we're about to have."

"He was in control talking with the Nav when I walked through,"

Edwards pushed his chair back and rose. "Perfect. Let's get going before somebody way up the chain changes their mind yet again."

The group was soon gathered around the ECDIS navigational display table. It showed the *George Mason's* current position four hundred miles east of the Uruguayan coast.

Edwards held a tablet with their new orders pulled up. "Looks like the *Gerald Ford* carrier strike group is moving this way, too. They're going to take station off Uruguay. We need to pedal real hard south so we aren't underfoot when they get here. I'm thinking that we mosey on down to Mar del Plata. That's the Argentine submarine base. If they're about to do something else ugly, you gotta figure our bubble-head counterparts will be involved somehow. They sure as hell were in the Straits of Magellan."

Jim Shupert looked up. "Boss, you may want to look at something a little different here." He punched up the latest intel report on the tablet. "According to this, it looks like that battle group we saw heading for the Straits is back out in the Atlantic again. Latest satellite imagery has them just rounding Punta Dúngeness and heading north. I'm thinkin' maybe we should go cut them off before they get close enough to the *Gerald Ford* group."

Edwards bent over the ECDIS display and ran the cursor down to the mouth of the Straits. Thirteen hundred nautical miles. "What's the ETA to intercept that bunch if we follow the Eng's retest plan?"

Shupert, the Navigator, and Otanga, the Engineer, put their heads together and started punching buttons. It took a few minutes and some discussion, but they finally looked up, obviously satisfied.

"Skipper, if we take an intercept course now and assume that the battle group is heading north at twenty knots, and if our patch holds, we should meet them about two hundred miles south of Mar del Plata," Otanga reported.

Edwards looked at the pair's numbers and smiled. "That works. Nav, what's the recommended course?"

Shupert hit a couple of buttons on the ECDIS and answered, "Recommend course two-one-zero."

Doing his best Patrick Stewart impersonation, Edwards—ever the *Star Trek* fan—said, "Nav, make it so."

Ψ

Cristiano Souza, *Presidente da República Federativa do Brasil*, sat back and listened as the ABIN briefer droned on and on, citing needless details about which the president cared little to nothing, backing them up with a screen filled with more boring data, charts, and graphs. The young man was a rising star in the *Agência Brasileira de Inteligência,* the Brazilian Intelligence Agency, and was probably a very good analyst, but as a briefer he served much better as a powerful sleep aid.

Souza was having a very difficult time staying awake, much less paying attention. The daily intel briefing was the first thing on the president's schedule today and the previous night's *festa* had lasted into the wee hours. Pedreira, the president's faithful aide and bodyguard, had anticipated the situation and had a carafe of dark black coffee at the ready, but it was not going to be of much help this morning.

The president was on the verge of waving off the brief, dispensing with whatever else there might have been, when the young man's next topic abruptly got his attention. "Our agents in Montevideo report that President Mendez has formally requested that the *norteamericano* Navy employ assets to protect Uruguay's sea lines of communications from interference from what Mendez terms the 'illegal Brazilian naval blockade.' Our analysts report that there is nothing new in this latest such request, but unlike previous ones, which were ignored, as we expected, the *norteamericano* president promptly assured Mendez that he would grant his request. Indeed, the *Gerald Ford* carrier strike group has been confirmed as heading there now at all due speed. And, in the words of the *norteamericano* ambassador's response, they will do 'whatever is necessary to break the blockade.' They are citing such action as part of their obligation as part of the OAS charter. My next slide details that agreement and—"

Souza suddenly sat up, immediately awake and wide-eyed as he interrupted. "Where is this US strike group now? We have been assured there would be no . . ."

The briefer blinked, thought for a moment, then flipped forward in his deck to a new slide on the screen. It was an aerial photograph of the ships, each vessel trailed by long, white wakes. "This is an image from our latest overflight. The *norteamericano* ships are currently five hundred miles due east of Recife. They are on a course that heads straight to Montevideo and are making a speed of twenty-five knots." He glanced at his notes. "Their ETA is just under five days."

Souza viciously slammed his fist down on the table. His coffee cup jittered across the polished surface and would have fallen to the floor if Pedreira had not deftly caught it in the nick of time.

"Damn that slimy bastard, Smitherman!" Souza growled. "It is as I have been told. Once purchased, you can never trust an *ianque* politician to stay bought." He struggled to calm himself, to look presidential, even though there were only three of them in the room. Then he asked, "What naval forces do we have available that we could employ to rebuff this aggression from the *norteamericanos*?"

The briefer again flipped through his notes before he answered. "Navy Operations Command reports that they have four frigates and three diesel submarines that can deploy in twenty-four hours. Anticipating your orders, sir, they have already ordered an emergency deployment. The rest of the fleet and our nuclear submarine are all down in the Straits of Magellan. Admiral Barbosa had already ordered the surface ships home, but the *João Cândido* nuclear-powered submarine has been instructed to remain in the south to continue to control that route."

Souza turned to Pedreira. "Get the Navy Command on the phone. I will order Barbosa's fleet to stay south of Buenos Aires under the cover of the Argentine Air Force. He is no match for the *norteamericano* fleet. Then we send the *João Cândido* up to threaten the *ianque* carrier. The *norteamericano* move could all be for show and is merely the bastard president quieting some of his many critics. But if not, if he has reneged on his promises, we will see if *Senhor Presidente* Smitherman actually has the balls to risk his shiny aircraft carrier, or if he will turn away. With either reaction, Pedreira, you and I will forever be heroes of the long-suffering people of Latin America. And we will ultimately prevail."

Ψ

Martha McGinnis, Stan Smitherman's personal secretary, stuck her head in the door of the vice president's White House office, just around the corner from the Oval Office, where Sandra Dosetti had ensconced herself after Harold Osterman's surprise "medical problem." The former Secretary of State did not have to remind herself not to get too accustomed to these digs. She would be moving to much grander accommodations soon enough.

"Excuse me, ma'am. The Secretary of Defense is on line one. He says that it is urgent that he speaks with you."

Without thanking her, Dosetti grabbed the phone and punched the button for line one. "Good morning, Sebastien. So, what's so urgent on such an otherwise fine morning?"

Sebastien Aldo paused a beat, then answered. "First of all, congratulations, Madam Acting Vice President. I see that Smitherman has made it official and requested Senate confirmation. The 'acting' part will be dropped in a few days, I'm hearing."

Dosetti allowed herself a dry chuckle. "Yes, he has requested that the Senate expedite confirmation. Rather eloquently asked, if I may say so. After all, I wrote his script myself. And we're ready to drop the other shoe, right?"

Aldo allowed the comment to pass, then went on. "Sandra, the main reason for my call is to discuss with you some information that we just received. The *Gerald Ford* carrier strike group is moving south, exactly as we ordered. They will be off Montevideo in five days. When the Brazilian Navy detected the move, they immediately protested, as we anticipated, and they informed our strike group commander that if he approached the coast within two hundred miles, it would be considered a hostile act and dealt with accordingly."

"Seb, just what do you think they mean by 'dealt with accordingly'?" Dosetti asked.

"Don't know for certain," Aldo replied. "But I suggest we be prepared for the worst. There could be some very serious shooting. We'll make sure to give the admiral the rules of engagement that allow for an early determination of the need for self-defense. We don't want any sea lawyers muddying up the waters and allowing the Brazilians to land the first punch."

"Agreed," Dosetti answered. "This could not have played out any better, Seb. A good dust-up down south gives us a tailor-made crisis to keep the attention of Congress and the media while we jettison Smitherman and Osterman. Who was that politico that said to 'never let a good crisis go to waste'? Well, this is our good crisis. And we'll come out of this as heroes, not just to the US but to the people of Latin America. US military might applied not for our gain but for the good of poor, oppressed people everywhere. Some of them may actually believe it."

"You could well be right," he agreed. "But let's hope, if it comes to hostilities, few lives will be lost on both sides."

"That goes without saying. Body bags and flag-draped coffins are really bad PR." Then she had another thought. "Seb, what's the name of that submarine we have down there?"

Aldo responded immediately without having to look it up. "That's the *George Mason*. I'm looking at an update right here. They just reported that they have completed emergency repairs and are testing their main engines."

"Perfect. Make sure they know what's going on and that they're covering the strike group from the south."

Ψ

Capitão de Fragata Bruno Ribeiro stood in the control room of the Brazilian Navy nuclear submarine *João Cândido* as he carefully read the message a second time. He could not help but smile. Life for him and his crew was about to get very interesting after all. The previous day, Admiral Eduardo Barbosa had ordered him and the *João Cândido* to guard the backdoor to the Straits of Magellan while Task Force Southern Passage headed home. That assignment promised to be both tedious and boring, offering no opportunity to demonstrate his abilities and expertise, no chance to further his career within his country's navy. Other than to demonstrate that he could perform even the most mundane duty without complaint or loss of attention to detail.

Now everything had changed.

Just when he steeled his crew to the fact that they would be spending time down here in these storm-tossed waters with nothing to do but gaze at the occasional Chinese merchant ship ploughing through the cold, steel-gray seas, these new orders came in like an answered prayer. Navy Operations Command decided that the *João Cândido* would much better serve the needs of Brazil by running out ahead of Admiral Barbosa's task force and intercepting the *norteamericano* aircraft carrier that was reportedly steaming south with hostile intentions.

Ribeiro checked the plot on the chart table. At the moment, Admiral Barbosa and the Task Force were two hundred miles ahead of the *João Cândido* and heading north at twenty knots. His nuclear-powered submarine could make a little better than twenty-six knots. That meant that he should overtake Barbosa somewhere off Puerto Deseado. By the time the sub reached the Río de la Plata, they would be over two hundred miles out ahead of the Task Force. The *norteamericano*s were not expected to arrive in the area for twenty-four hours after that. This would allow plenty of time to scout the area out and make plans for an ambush before the US ships could even catch their breath from their long run south.

Ribeiro smiled once more as he issued the series of commands that would send them hurrying northward. He then ordered that the torpedoes and fire control system on his warship be checked out and groomed for impending action.

Few career Naval Commanding Officers ever had the opportunity to strike an actual blow with the weapons they carried, to repel a threat to their country. It could be that he was about to be given that chance.

Captain Bruno Ribeiro intended to make the most of it.

Ψ

Guillermo Manuelito, TJ Dillon, and Bill Beaman rested easily on the

MDR casa's broad veranda as workers labored to repair the last of the battle damage. Bullet holes still pocked the adobe walls of the rebel stronghold and the iron gates lay mangled and twisted, torn from their hinges during the barrage by Manuel Viscosa's mercenaries. Most of the wreckage had already been hauled away. Several wounded fighters sat nearby, soaking up the healing powers of the warm afternoon sunshine.

Manuelito reached into an ice chest and pulled out three bottles of Quilmes. One at a time, he popped the tops on each and handed the frosty bottles to his fellow warriors.

Beaman tipped his bottle toward the MDR commander in a salute and took a long, thirsty pull on his beer. Then, smacking his lips in appreciation, he looked at the bottle with the distinctive blue and white label.

"Damn, this tastes great! Feels good to just sit here and relax," Beaman sighed. He took another sip. "I'm starting to develop a real liking for Argentine beer. If it didn't cost an arm and a leg to export it to Exuma up yonder in the Bahamas . . ."

Manuelito tasted his. "Sí, my country has several centuries' experience brewing cerveza. It is something we have definitely gotten right. Maybe with help from some of those Nazis who escaped Patton and Eisenhower and came here." He chuckled and added, "But my Italian ancestors demand that we try the vino tonight. Our troops liberated a case of fine Bonarda from Viscosa's hacienda. The bastard might have made some really bad choices in life, but he had a taste for the best fruit of the vine, at least. Though the grapes are native to Italy, the taste is truly Argentine. We will have a bottle with dinner this evening."

"Ah, the spoils of war," Beaman said, stifling a burp.

Manuelito watched a cloud scud across the sky for a moment, apparently lost in thought. Then he continued, "I pray for the day when I can go back to tending my olives with my family and spoiling my grandchildren, and you can go back to your beach bar, my friend."

Beaman lifted his bottle in a toast. "May that day come very soon."

"Si Dios quiere," Manuelito responded. "Our fight appears to finally be spreading now. Word of the Battle of Valle Escondido seems to be lighting the embers of a fire. Many, like me, who would never have considered taking up arms against their country's political leaders have been pushed to do so. MDR fighters seized the city hall at Alta Gracia down in Cordoba Province, taking the mayor and *el concejo municipal*, the town council, prisoners. I have another report that a team of MDR fighters blew the Puente Internacional bridge and dropped it into the Uruguay River at Paso de los Libres. Ironic and fitting, since the town was named in honor of the heroes of one of our earlier battles to overthrow a dictator."

"And so it begins," Dillon murmured. Then he changed the subject, "Speaking of fighters, Jim Ward and Billy Joe Hunt are both showing improvement. It's going to be a while before they are up and running around, but Doc Cruz tells me that our two wounded frogs will be able to travel tomorrow."

"Frogs?" Manuelito replied, a look of confusion on his face.

Beaman laughed and chimed in. "That's what we SEALs call each other. 'Frogs,' since we live on both the land and the water. And most of us are really, really ugly."

It was Manuelito's turn to laugh. "Now that your mission is finished, I suppose you *ranas* must return to your own pond. In the morning, I will have some of my fighters escort you to the border. Calama is the nearest good hospital and airport. Your embassy can make arrangements there. As you might remember, it's a hard day's drive from here. With your two 'frogs' stretcher-bound, I would suggest a two- or three-day trip."

Beaman smiled. "That might be easier. At least no one should be shooting at us." Then he turned serious again. "And Guillermo, thank you for arranging for Winston's body to be sent home so quickly."

"He gave all for a cause in which he had no particular or specific stake, and for that, we honor his sacrifice," Manuelito said sadly.

"To the contrary, my friend," Beaman said. "The cause of freedom is something we SEALs willingly fight and die for. And if Don Winston were here with us right now, he'd tell you the same thing."

The men fell silent then, sipping their brews, watching the mounds of cottony clouds happily chase each other across a startlingly blue sky.

20

Commander Brian Edwards sat at his desk and reread the latest OPORD. Something had certainly gotten turned around back in the Pentagon. The mission was suddenly changed from slinking home while staying hidden from everyone, friend or foe—deliberately avoiding anything curious that screamed to be investigated—to getting busy and prosecuting a full-bore ASW barrier search against a Brazilian nuclear submarine. The *George Mason* was tasked with finding this submarine and then making sure that it did not get through and pose any kind of threat to the *Gerald Ford* strike group.

Edwards smiled and shook his head. Finally, someone actually wanted them to do a job that they trained for. Hell, that they *existed* to do! He picked up the phone and punched the button for the Officer-of-the-Deck. Aston Jennings answered almost immediately.

Edwards briskly ordered, "Mr. Jennings, deploy the thin-line towed array. Send your messenger to find the XO and Nav." The skipper glanced at his watch. "Have them meet me in control in ten minutes."

The thin-line array, the TB-29, used a long linear assemblage of ultra-sensitive sonar hydrophones towed several thousand yards behind the submarine to separate the hydrophones from the vessel's noise so it could listen for very low frequencies. Specifically, sounds made by another ship.

When Jackson Biddle and Jim Shupert arrived as summoned, Edwards was standing in front of the ECDIS, studying the navigation charts. He handed the tablet to Biddle with the new OPORD up on the display.

"XO, things have changed," the CO said. "Instead of going home, we're supposed to find that Brazilian sub we tangled with down south. SUBLANT has reliable reason to believe that he's coming north to play with the *Gerald Ford* strike group. And all this has to do with the blockade the Argentinians and Brazilians have decided to enforce against Uruguay for some damn reason. But that's neither here nor there. We got a new job to do."

Biddle looked up from the tablet screen and sideways at his CO, a grin on his face. "Roger on the new job."

Edwards turned to the ECDIS and fiddled with the controls to draw a square on the chart. The area covered was roughly parallel to the Uruguayan coast from Punta del Diablo to Punta del Este. Each side was one hundred miles long, with the nearest side twelve miles off the coast.

"The CSG is going to be MODLOCed in this box," he said, pointing to where the carrier strike group planned to conduct their "miscellaneous local operations," that is, steam back and forth in the box.

"Their mission all of a sudden is to keep the port of Montevideo and the Río de la Plata open, and to get nasty about it if the other parties don't back off. We need to set up a barrier search far enough away to allow us time to get in trail on this guy, ready to take him out if he so much as sneezes."

Edwards drew another line on the chart. This one ran east-west and was anchored just north of Mar del Plata, the city that housed the main Argentine naval base.

"This barrier here is two hundred miles south of the CSG box, which keeps us out from underfoot of whatever might go down up there. It also gives us plenty of time to dissuade this guy from doing anything ugly. And it allows us to keep an eye on the Argentines at the same time."

Shupert looked at where Edwards had drawn the barrier. "Skipper, we're almost there now."

"Yeah, I know. That's why I ordered the TB-29 deployed." He pointed at the line. "I figure we start at the west end and head east for twenty hours at fifteen knots, then we do a one-eighty and come back west. Just run back and forth until our friend shows his face and we can trail him."

Jackson Biddle studied the chart, rubbing his chin, a pronounced frown on his face. He looked up and said, "Skipper, good plan. I don't mean to throw a polecat in the gumbo, but I'm worried about those long search legs."

"What's the concern, XO? The sonar search program shows that the 29 can sweep the entire area at fifteen knots, no problem. Even if he's trying to slink through real quiet like, the probability of him slipping by undetected is, what, less than ten percent?"

Biddle nodded. He had seen the calculations and they looked correct. That was not the issue. "Skipper, you know we're limited to about twenty knots top speed since we only have one turbine generator. Intel rates this guy with an almost thirty-knot capability. If he's going flank and goes through one end of the barrier while we're way out there at the other end, he'll blow right past us. We'll see him coming all right, but before we can do anything about it, we'll see him going, too. That'll put us in a tail chase that we can't win."

Edwards nodded. "Good point, XO. If that happens, we'll have to turn him over to the carrier group ASW guys. Lord knows they have the equipment, and with our heads-up, they can fight back pretty well. Besides, we'll have him caught between us and the MH-60R ASW helos on the CSG and a whole bunch of *Arleigh Burke*s. And we won't have the risk of missing him out on the eastern end of the search."

Aston Jennings stepped over. "Excuse me, Skipper. The thin-line array is deployed. Coming left to course zero-nine-zero for the first leg. The array will be stable in fifteen minutes."

Edwards nodded. "Let's see if we can catch us a big fish."

The submarine came around and headed due east. Josh Hannon and his team of sonarmen settled in to search the frigid storm-tossed South Atlantic for the telltale sound signature of a nuclear submarine heading north. It was slow, boring work, mostly involving watching dots appear on a screen, hoping that they would develop into a submarine contact, only having them almost always turn into background noise or biologics. Snapping shrimp and whale farts.

It was monotonous work for everyone aboard. Steam three hundred miles away from the coast. Then turn around and head back. Twenty hours to a leg. Then, turn around and start the next leg. ASW was called "awfully slow warfare" for a reason.

They had just started their third leg, heading east once again, away from Mar del Plata, when Hannon called out, "Officer-of-the-Deck! Getting hits on the TB-29, four-point-five hertz. Equates to a Brazilian *João Cândido*-class nuclear submarine. Designate target as Sierra Two-Six. Gathering data. Best bearing right now is something to the south."

Jeff Otanga, the mid-watch OOD, happily put aside the pile of engineering records he had been reviewing and punched up the low-frequency passive display on the command console. It took him a minute before he could see the contact that Hannon was reporting, but there it was. Really faint, but certainly a submarine contact.

Jackson Biddle, the Command Duty Officer, suddenly appeared at Otanga's side, a steaming cup of coffee in hand. "Yep, Sierra Two-Six sure looks like our long-lost Brazilian friend. Eng, station the section tracking party. Let's go ahead and get a leg on him while we confirm our contact."

Otanga stared with undisguised envy at Biddle's mug of coffee. The duty messenger had been tied up all watch so there had not been a coffee run. He really needed a caffeine jolt.

Biddle noticed Otanga's stare. "Tell you what. While you get things set up here, I think I'll go brief the skipper. And I'll fetch you a cup of black-and-bitter."

Otanga smiled. Sometimes it seemed like the XO could read the minds of his crew.

The sonar watch standers and the section tracking party slowly but meticulously gathered data, grabbing each bit of information and analyzing it, like putting a puzzle together piece by piece. By the time Jackson Biddle returned with Otanga's cup of coffee, they were at least ninety percent certain that Sierra Two-Six was their prey, the Brazilian nuclear sub, and it was steaming directly toward them at a good clip.

"XO, you are a lifesaver," Otanga said with a grin before gratefully taking a sip of the hot liquid. "We have a leg on Sierra Two-Six. Best

214 GEORGE WALLACE & DON KEITH

bearing two-zero-five. Looks like a slight right-bearing drift, but it's hard to tell with all the data scatter. We're ready for a maneuver."

The team on the *George Mason* continued to work to solve the target motion analysis problem while Jeff Otanga drove their own submarine on shorter alternating legs to reduce the range. At the same time, he was getting into a position astern of Sierra Two-Six where they could shoot if necessary. But he had to be cautious. If they inadvertently got too close, that could allow the Brazilians to detect the *George Mason*. It was like being in a sword fight while blindfolded and miles apart, thrusting and parrying at a combatant in the next county.

By the time they had completed a couple of legs, Jackson Biddle was pretty sure that they had a good tracking solution on the sonar contact. Sierra Two-Six was still twenty miles to the southwest, heading north, making a beeline for the US carrier strike group. The problem was that he was making better than twenty-six knots and the current CPA—closest point of approach—was ten miles away to the west. Biddle played with a whole host of possible maneuvers to see if they could drive the *George Mason* close enough to the *João Cândido* to actually intercept it. Even if the *George Mason* were fully operational and could actually make her typical best speed, they would be hard-pressed to catch the speeding Brazilian. Now, limited to twenty knots, it was hopeless.

Then a thought struck him. Something he'd learned growing up back on the farm, where deer hunting was an important part of life for his rural family and venison actually helped fill the family larder. The deer could easily outrun and elude a single hunter. However, several hunters, with the help of a dog or two, could herd their prey to where one of them could get a good shot. Maybe they could herd Sierra Two-Six if they could convince the Brazilian submarine that he was being hunted by a whole slew of ASW ships.

That meant they needed to get the CSG involved in the game. Biddle found Brian Edwards in the wardroom, just finishing up his breakfast. After a short discussion, they headed back to control. Ten minutes later, Edwards finished his radio discussion with the FOXTROT XRAY, the destroyer squadron commodore on the strike group who was responsible for ASW protection. He was enthusiastic about the plan. But it would take a couple of hours to get all the players in place.

The *George Mason* would have to continue to work to keep contact on the Brazilian sub and detect any course change. Meanwhile, the rest of the crew had to ready themselves for anything that might happen.

Anything and everything.

Ψ

Chilean submarine captain Luis Alvite carefully steered the *O'Higgins* up through the narrow Canal Magdelena. He checked his watch. They were several hours behind schedule since they had parted company from their sister sub the *Carrera* at the north end of Isla Desolación. Snaking their way through the many rocks and islands dotting the Canal Cockburn had taken longer than anticipated. Then, dodging the Punta Arenas-Puerto William ferry as it made its regular trek down the canal—the slow-moving vessel completely oblivious to the submerged warship beneath her that was sneaking up toward the strait—added still more time to the journey. But the captain knew the delay really was not a problem. They still had plenty of time to get into position before the *Carrera* flushed any potential invading submarines and sent them toward the *O'Higgins*.

Alvite slowed the submarine to two knots. No reason to hurry. A deliberate, careful sonar search was more prudent than charging into the Paso Froward unawares. It was not lost on the captain just how odd it was that they were having to be so cautious in Chilean territorial waters. Their own sovereign territory. Sovereign territorial waters that were now patrolled and claimed by a foreign power, claimed to the point of taking innocent lives in an evil, unprovoked attack at sea and boldly invading the region's major city.

"Man battle stations torpedo," Alvite muttered angrily. It was a command he had been longing to issue for weeks now. "Make tubes one and two ready in all respects."

He was going to enter the arena with his guns loaded and cocked. He was ready to exact his revenge, for his brother, for his nation.

The *O'Higgins* slowly stuck its nose out from where the Canal Magdelena was squeezed between Isla Capitán Aracena to the west and a narrow finger of Tierra del Fuego to the east. The relatively open waters of Paso Froward stretched out for thirty kilometers ahead of them. It was only a matter of quietly slipping out into the Paso and waiting for his quarry to be chased toward Luis Alvite's waiting ambush.

Ψ

Capitán de Fragata Colas Lopez Alveras, commanding the Argentine Navy submarine *Santiago del Estero*, had long since grown bored with his monotonous duty. After the drama and excitement of sinking the two Chilean ships, his submarine had spent seemingly endless weeks slowly cruising up and down the Straits of Magellan, zigging and zagging like a steel ball in a watery pinball machine. He had done the transit so many times, and with precisely the same maneuvers, he felt that he could do it in his sleep. When the Paso Froward light was abeam to starboard, steer course three-zero-five; steam fifty kilometers, then steer course three-four-two for thirty kilometers to get around Isla Carlos III; turn to two-seven-zero for twelve kilometers; then three-four-two for sixty kilometers to the western approaches for the Straits. Turn around and head back southeast to the Paso Froward light. Rinse and repeat. The only deviation was when they needed to go around—or under—the numerous Chinese freighters that were using these confined waters. And a time or two maneuvering to avoid pods of humpback whales that seemed to believe they owned rights to that portion of the Straits.

The submarine had been patrolling this stretch of water long enough now that they were running seriously low on supplies. In a couple of days, the *Santiago del Estero* would have to pull into Punta Arenas for food and diesel fuel. Their supply of hydrogen for the fuel cell AIP system was also all but exhausted, with maybe an hour's worth of fuel onboard, but the small port would not have the facilities to refuel it. Until they could get back to Argentina—and who knew when that would be—Alveras had restricted use of the AIP system to emergencies only. Instead, they operated like a traditional diesel submarine. That meant they either surfaced or snorkeled often to keep the battery fully charged.

Alveras was gazing out the periscope, looking at the high bluffs that marked the southern end of Peninsula Brunswick. There was not anything else to see, except the nearly identical rough and rocky coastline of Isle Clarence five kilometers off the port beam. For the time being, he had the entire stretch of the Straits to himself.

But that quickly changed.

"Conn, sonar," came the call. "New sonar contact, bearing two-eight-zero. Probable submerged contact. He is close!"

Alveras spun the periscope around to the designated bearing, vainly hoping to see another Chinese freighter coming their way, misidentified as a submerged contact. The surface of the Straits of Magellan was empty as far as he could see. Whatever they were hearing, it was definitely underwater.

"Secure snorkeling!" he shouted. "Make your depth fifty meters! Man battle stations!" All this as he slapped the periscope handles up and spun the wheel to lower the scope.

He had craved a break in the routine. Now his wish had been granted. In spades!

The *Santiago del Estero* angled steeply down, clawing for the safety of the depths, crewmembers bracing themselves against anything they could grab for balance.

"Make tube two ready in all respects!" he called out. "Sonar, best bearing to the submarine?"

The answer was immediate. "Best bearing two-nine-two. He has opened his outer doors." Then, in a much higher-toned voice, "Torpedo in the water!"

Alveras knew he did not have time to work out a shooting solution on the other sub or even to hesitate while his battle stations team raced to their posts. He had to shoot now.

"Shoot tube two on the bearing to the submarine. Use minimum enable."

Down in the sub's torpedo room, the Black Shark heavyweight torpedo in tube two was impulsed out into the sea. Its electric motor immediately started and pushed it up to a speed of over fifty knots.

The captain knew that by firing so quickly without a better solution on the target, his chances of getting a hit were very small. Even so, having three hundred and fifty kilograms of high explosives racing toward the attacking vessel would certainly draw the enemy submarine's focus, hopefully preventing them from launching any more torpedoes their way.

Now it was time to duck.

"Ahead flank," Alveras ordered. "Left full rudder. Steady course one-zero-five."

"Own ship's weapon running normally," sonar called out. "Lost incoming weapon in the baffles, last bearing two-nine-one." The weapon hurtling their way was no longer visible, hidden in their sonar "blind spot." That was followed quickly by, "Lost own ship's weapon in the baffles."

Alveras knew that he was in a race with death. He and his crew had trained extensively for this predicament but had never experienced it for real.

The *Santiago del Estero* could go a little better than twenty knots at a flank bell. Assuming the attacker was Chilean—and who else would be shooting at them?—the incoming weapon was probably a Black Shark, identical to the one he had just launched in response. It could race at over fifty knots. If the other sub had shot from a couple of kilometers away and the torpedo was now maybe a kilometer astern, Alveras calculated they had two minutes to live.

His only hope was to trick the torpedo. He glanced at the chart. The steep bluffs of Peninsula Brunswick were only a kilometer away to their northeast. Maybe if he got the *Santiago del Estero* up closer to the cliffs, the reverb and sonar returns from the rocks would confuse the torpedo's guidance system.

There was no other choice. That would have to work.

Cavitation from along the planes and from the screw—the rattle of low-pressure bubbles forming and collapsing—sounded like the boat was being pelted by a heavy hailstorm. The noise was painful, but the only way to stop it was to either go deeper or slow down. Neither was an option if they were to dodge approaching death.

"Steer course zero-nine-zero," Alveras ordered. That would not point their bow directly at the cliffs, but it would skirt them up very close. Maybe even close enough. "Sonar, any contact?"

"No contact. Both weapons still in the baffles," was the reply.

"Loud explosion somewhere astern!" sonar called out. Before the report was finished, they could all hear and feel the blast. Though the *Santiago del Estero* rocked with a considerable jolt, they had not been hit. The big torpedo would have instantly destroyed the submarine. So, either the captain's maneuver to make for the cliffs had worked, or their own weapon had gotten a hit on their attacker. Either way, it was time to turn away from the rocks to avoid a collision with those immovable obstructions.

Alveras ordered, "Steer course one-zero-zero."

The sub had barely turned to its new direction when a massive explosion set hell loose. It lifted the boat's stern and brutally shoved it over onto its starboard side. Alveras went stumbling, thrown over against the switchboards on the starboard side of control. He smacked his head hard against one of the breakers. He was stunned for a few seconds, but when he stood up, shaking his head to clear the fog, he was amazed to realize that the *Santiago del Estero* seemed to still be afloat and not even seriously damaged.

Indeed, damage reports were already coming in and he was getting thumbs-up from crewmembers as he grabbed a greasy rag and wiped away the trickle of blood that ran down the side of his face. His boat was apparently undamaged and there were no reports of crew casualties other than scrapes and bruises. However, there was no way to know for sure what happened to the attacker. Maybe Alveras had gotten lucky and his mostly blind torpedo shot had taken the other boat out. Or perhaps that first, more distant explosion was a miss, just like this one was.

One thing was certain, though. He did not want to risk trying to learn those details right now. They would race around Paso Froward and then head up to Punta Arenas to refuel and check for undetected damage, all while trying not to allow the other sub—if it was still there—to get off another shot.

Alveras quickly checked the chart. "Steer course one-five-zero," he ordered. With no torpedo chasing them, there was no reason to risk running up on the rocks and allowing them to finish what the other vessel had started. Better for him to get out toward the middle of the Paso where there was plenty of open water to maneuver.

And to fight back, should it once again come to it.

Ψ

"Loud explosion to the northwest," the sonar operator on the *O'Higgins* called out. "Best bearing two-nine-zero. And a whole lot of reverb blanking the sonar." The excessive sound energy from whatever exploded up there was echoing and re-echoing off the granite sides of the Strait, saturating the submarine's passive sonar on that sector. It would continue until the ringing eventually died out.

Capitán Luis Alvite glanced quickly at the sonar repeater in the control room and then at the navigation chart. Two-nine-zero was almost directly up the Strait toward Isla Carlos III. Almost assuredly, that meant that the *Carrera* was at work up there. But who got hit? Was the Argentine sub now resting on the bottom? Or had *Carrera* been jumped before he could fire the first shot?

"Second loud explosion!" the sonar op called out. "Best bearing three-one-five."

So, there had been two torpedoes fired, Alvite surmised. One from each or both from the same vessel? Who lived and who died up there? There was nothing to do but wait and find out. Heading that way to investigate was not an option. He could not take the *O'Higgins* across the safety boundary at seventy-one degrees, ten minutes west longitude without risking being shot by *Carrera*, if the other Chilean submarine was the survivor. The predetermined boundary would not expire for another day. It was inviolable until then.

"Maintain course north and speed two knots," Alvite ordered. "Sonar, stay alert for a submerged submarine from the west-northwest." The commander found it surprisingly difficult to remain calm with this latest development. The killers who had taken Jorge, his natural brother, and all those other fellow naval brothers and sisters could already be dead. *Carrera*, victorious, might be coming down shortly to give him the good news.

Or the Argentine may have struck again.

Alvite forced himself to sit back and quietly sip his Nescafé, face impassive, demeanor noncommittal. It was imperative that the crew see a calm, in-control, and unconcerned façade.

"*Capitán*, we are hearing heavy cavitation," the sonar operator next reported. "Best bearing three-one-five. Submerged contact, moving fast."

The cavitation noise was the first indication that whichever sub was coming their way found speed much more important than stealth. Someone was running away.

Alvite jumped up and hurried over to see the sonar repeater, all pretense of a calm façade forgotten. The contact was certainly a submarine racing away from something, and it was headed straight toward the *O'Higgins*.

"Track the contact," Alvite ordered. "Assign it to the torpedo in tube one. If it crosses the safety boundary, we will let it generate for a kilometer to be certain. And then we shoot it."

Alvite double-checked the *O'Higgins*'s position. They were a little over a kilometer east of the safety line. He brought the boat around so that they were just east of the line and pointed north. When the submarine crossed their bow, it would be in the killing zone. If it stopped short or turned at the barrier, it was *Carrera*. If not, it was a target.

As they watched, the onrushing submarine dashed across the safety boundary without slowing, still pounding hard to the east. This was surely the Argentine submarine. And it was possible that the *Carrera* had been sunk or damaged.

Two minutes later, the racing sub crossed the bow of the *O'Higgins*. It was time to attack.

"Shoot tube one on the contact," Alvite calmly ordered. It was difficult for him to keep the malice from his voice.

He glanced at his watch and then at the firing solution. By his calculation, the men aboard the enemy submarine had a little over two minutes to live.

The Black Shark torpedo leaped from its tube and obediently sped away in the direction of its assigned target. The deadly fish had traveled five hundred yards when its sonar system activated. It then began searching in earnest for its prey.

The Argentine submarine painted a big, juicy picture for the torpedo. The weapon's onboard computer confirmed that the target met all the logic gates. It then shifted to attack and increased speed as it moved in for the kill.

The torpedo slammed into its target just behind the sail. The three hundred and fifty kilograms of high explosives detonated on impact, ripping the submarine apart. No one onboard had time to even register the hit in their consciousness. They died instantly.

Luis Alvite listened to the blast. To himself, he muttered, "*Bastardos! Eso es venganza por mi hermano!*"

"What was that, *Capitán*?" his Officer-of-the-Deck asked.

"Nothing. Maintain current position and listen for any signs of the *Carrera*. I will be in my quarters."

Alvite then turned away and stepped briskly to his stateroom. Once there, he sat and wept in quiet solitude.

21

Capitão de Fragata Bruno Ribeiro studied the navigation chart. It showed that the *João Cândido* was about midway across the Río de la Plata, the broad estuary formed by the Uruguay and Paraná Rivers and opening into the Atlantic. That put the two points of land generally considered the boundaries of the body of water about 115 kilometers northeast and southwest of their position, and the city of Montevideo about 80 kilometers to the north. They were almost to their assigned destination, ready to strike a mighty blow for their ally, Argentina.

Indeed, the latest intelligence message had plotted the *norteamericano* aircraft carrier they were racing to challenge to be fifty kilometers due east of the seaside town of La Paloma, Uruguay, just north of the entrance to the Río de la Plata. And the warship still deliberately steamed in their direction, obviously intending a show of force in support of Uruguay.

Ribeiro took a pair of dividers and carefully measured the distances. The Americans were about 250 kilometers away. It was time for the *João Cândido* to slow the mad dash, to resume the role of the hunter carefully stalking prey. Hurrying up from the south at better than twenty-six knots assured that the submarine's sonar was significantly affected. The flow noise prevented the sensitive hydrophones from hearing any contacts out beyond a few kilometers. Slowing to normal search speeds meant that they

could now detect ships at a much greater distance, on the order of fifty kilometers for something as big and noisy as an aircraft carrier and the other
vessels that were accompanying it.

Ribeiro turned and ordered, "Officer-of-the-Deck, slow to ahead-two-
thirds, come to course zero-six-zero, and commence a sonar search for the
norteamericano warships. They should be somewhere to the north-north-
east." He turned on a heel and strode out of the control room. "I will be in
my stateroom. Notify me at once when you have contact," he called back
over his shoulder. He was confident it would be several more hours before
they would detect the approaching group.

The captain had just sat down to enjoy a cup of coffee and read through
all the latest messages when his phone buzzed.

So soon? he thought.

"Captain," the Officer-of-the-Deck said, "We have detected three new
sonar contacts. They are classified warships with high-speed screws. Probably US Navy *Arleigh Burke*-class destroyers. Bearing zero-one-seven, zero-
two-six, and zero-three-eight."

Ribeiro frowned, surprised. He had not expected to detect any of the US
vessels for several more hours. His plan had been to sneak around well to
the east while he was still outside sonar range and then attack from deep
water. That would put the interlopers well within waters now claimed by
Argentina while trapping the warships up against the South American
coast. Their quarry would have much less room to run. So what were these
three destroyers doing this far south and probably less than fifty kilometers
away?

He played out the tactical picture in his mind. There was no reason to
think that the destroyers had any idea there would be a submarine in the
area. And there was no indication that they were performing any kind of
ASW search. And, as full of themselves as the *ianques* could be, they probably expected little to no challenge anyway. Their presence was surely
more for show than battle.

The destroyers' high-speed screws meant that they were sprinting
through the water. And because they were surface ships, their sonar was
even more limited by flow noise when the ships were transiting at such a
pace. Ribeiro had read reports on the TB-37 Multi-Function Towed Array

that some of the *Arleigh Burke*-class destroyers reportedly employed. The array was supposed to be very similar to the fat-line towed arrays that the US submarines used, giving the surface ships a greatly enhanced sonar search effectiveness. But, of course, even as sophisticated as it was, the equipment still required slow speed to be useful.

Ribeiro decided to give the destroyers a wide berth. He would turn west, into the much more shallow waters of the estuary, where the *norteamericanos* would not be willing to risk snagging their towed arrays on the bottom.

He grabbed the phone and buzzed the Officer-of-the-Deck.

The phone was answered immediately. "*Sí, Capitão!*"

"Come to course three-three-zero. We're going to sneak up the coast on the landward side of the American carrier."

Ψ

Fifty thousand yards south of the *João Cândido*, onboard the *George Mason*, STI Josh Hannon was carefully watching the dots stack up on the sonar display. The input to the display was the TB-29 thin line towed array and the dots were coming from Sierra Two-Six, the Brazilian nuclear submarine, the vessel they had been working so hard to track.

Hannon allowed the specks to dance around for several minutes, just to be sure of what he was seeing. Finally satisfied, he looked up and said, "Captain, possible contact zig on Sierra Two-Six. Shift across the line of sight. Best bearing three-five-five. New bearing-rate left point-zero-two degrees per minute. No change in received frequency."

Brian Edwards was standing back by the ECDIS table. He looked at the tactical plot and then flashed a broad grin in the direction of Jackson Biddle.

"Looks like he bit, XO. The dogs are driving the deer toward the hunters," the skipper said.

"Yeah, seems like we ought to blow a trumpet or something," Biddle responded.

"I think it's called a hunting horn. Speaking of horns, we'd better get FOXTROT XRAY on the horn and give him a heads-up."

The *George Mason* hurried up to periscope depth to inform the destroyer officer in charge of anti-submarine warfare what they had detected. The sub's low-profile photonics mast had barely broken the surface before they were all—submarine and the three destroyers—in sync on the LINK 16 and talking to FOXTROT XRAY on the MUOS satellite communications system. The LINK 16 gave everyone a common view of the information that the *George Mason* had on Sierra Two-Six. As long as they remained connected, the information was presented in real time. FOXTROT XRAY, the three destroyers, and everyone else involved could see exactly what the *George Mason* saw.

There was a flurry of activity. FOXTROT XRAY directed that the next leg of the trap be swung into place. He told the *George Mason* to stay active on the LINK so they could keep constant tabs on the Brazilian submarine. Brian Edwards agreed, even though that meant that his submarine would have to stay at periscope depth and would be slowed down even more. More worrisome, the *George Mason* would be vulnerable to anyone looking for a submarine in this part of the South Atlantic. The Argentine Navy was not particularly noted for their airborne ASW capability, but they did sport a couple of refurbished P-3C Orion aircraft—hand-me-downs from the US Navy—and one truly ancient S-2T Tracker plane. But even antique aircraft could get lucky and spot a sub so near the surface.

It was relatively easy for *George Mason* to tune the BLQ-10 ESM system to alert on the various radars carried by P-3Cs. However, it took quite a bit of research and some serious tweaking to set the system up to detect the old Tracker's outdated radar. And with his submarine's mast always exposed to the atmosphere above the wavetops, the Officer-of-the-Deck was continuously searching the skies for any low-flying aircraft. He imagined this must have been how it was for lookouts clinging to the rigging above the bridge —the "shears"—on the old diesel boats in World War II, scanning the horizon for Japanese aircraft while the boat, bobbing on the surface, ran their diesel engines to recharge the batteries.

Brian Edwards shook his head. All this throwback stuff reminded him of his days as a junior officer on the older boats. In those times, he had to spend entire watches "dancing with the fat lady," eye to eyepiece, constantly walking in a circle, using an old optical periscope. Jerry Billings, the current

OOD, only had to set his controller so that the photonics camera would automatically slowly rotate. Then he sat back and watched the big screen as if he was taking in a very boring TV show. Even if he missed seeing an airplane or something else of crucial importance, the contact recognition software built into the photonics system would alert him.

Brian Edwards punched up the LINK 16 tactical data display on the command console. He watched as the three destroyers maneuvered to their new tasking. Two of them, the *Delbert D. Black* and the *Thomas Hudner*, raced south to form a line with the *Jack H. Lucas* as the third warship slowed to anchor the north end of the formation. When the line stretched from twenty miles north of Sierra Two-Seven's plotted position to twenty miles south, the three destroyers pirouetted in perfect unison to head due west, directly at Sierra Two-Seven, now only fifteen miles away. Then they lit off their SQS-53C active sonars. Two hundred and fifty decibels of concentrated sound energy at a frequency of three kilohertz practically boiled the seawater. There was very little chance of actually getting a return from that blast of high-pitched racket. The submarine was still too far away. But the Brazilians on that boat would sure as hell hear it.

Edwards smiled. Watching the display was like observing a very large, very expensive video game. As soon as the destroyers went active with their sonars, Sierra Two-Six darted away from its previous steady course, obviously spooked and heading farther into the Río de la Plata.

Then a couple of blue, inverted half-circle symbols with bowties in them flitted across the screen from two of the destroyers, heading toward the bit of seaway that stretched from the Uruguayan coast out to the *Lucas*. The two MH-60R Seahawk helicopters had lifted off their ships and alternately gone into a hover. They were using their AQS-22 ALFS dipping sonar. The 3.5-kilohertz active sonar put 220 decibels of its own sound energy into the previously placid waters. As with the bedlam unleashed by the destroyers, there was not much chance of actually detecting the Brazilian sub, but they had effectively closed off the nuke boat's only route if he hoped to escape the onslaught and find the US Navy carrier by heading north.

Sierra Two-Six did not know it yet, but he was already boxed into the Río de la Plata.

Ψ

President Stan Smitherman greeted the carefully selected members of the media as they were ushered into the Oval Office and were handed a prepared press release by a staffer. Members of the Congressional leadership, each as deliberately handpicked as the journalists, were already scattered around the room in small conversational clusters. They had self-segregated into groups of three or four, divided without exception along strict party lines. Secretary of Defense Sebastien Aldo was over near the fireplace, along with the Attorney General, idly chatting about important subjects such as the unusually warm weather and the hopes for the Washington Commanders NFL team for the remainder of the season.

The president's press secretary held up a hand, and the room grew quiet.

"Let me remind you again," she said, looking at the assembled group. "Out of respect for the former vice president and his health concerns, and at the request of Ms. Dosetti, this will be a low-key event. Because of the president's extremely busy schedule, there will be no opportunity for questions today. Your handouts should be sufficient, and we will address any queries at tomorrow's regular press briefing. You will all be provided with pool video and still images within the hour." She ignored the few groans from the media members and motioned for the proceedings to commence.

Sandra Dosetti stood perfectly framed by the big windows that looked out toward the colonnade and iconic rose garden. Supreme Court Chief Justice Thurman Winston waited quietly off to one side in his black judicial robe, little more than another piece of archaic furniture.

Smitherman, standing behind his massive podium as if hiding there, muttered a few generic opening remarks that members of the press duly ignored. Then he signaled for Dosetti and the Chief Justice to join him in front of the Resolute desk. Winston held a well-worn Bible—the same one he had utilized at the inaugurations of four previous presidents, including Smitherman twice—and made use of it to administer the oath of office as he swore in Dosetti as the new vice president of the United States.

At the conclusion of the brief ceremony, the Chief Justice smiled, congratulated Dosetti, and promptly stepped away. There was polite applause from the members of Congress and curious stares from the reporters. None of this seemed right to them.

President Smitherman grabbed her hand and pumped it, loudly exclaiming, "Congratulations, Madame Vice President! It is wonderful to have you on my team, workin' hard for the American people."

"Well, Mr. President, I've been 'on the team' for almost seven years now . . ." she responded, forcing a smile.

Then, leaning in close, still tightly gripping her hand, his lips near her ear as if he might be apologizing for misspeaking, he whispered so only Dosetti could hear.

"Okay, bitch, when does the next shoe drop?"

Dosetti smiled, ignored the smell of whiskey on his breath, and quietly answered, "Soon. Very soon."

22

Luis Alvite heard a tentative tapping on his stateroom door. He glanced up at the clock and realized that he had been sitting here in a torpor for several hours now. He felt utterly drained, both physically and emotionally. The last several weeks had taken every ounce of commitment that he had to offer. But his major goal had been accomplished. Jorge had been avenged. The *asesinos* who had claimed his brother's life had been relegated to the watery grave they so well deserved.

The hate and the anger were gone, but they had been replaced with an emptiness. No relief, no emotion, nothing. Somehow, though, he would need to summon up the energy, the drive, to go back to work, to once again deal with the living, especially the men who crewed the submarine he commanded.

"*Ingresar,*" he growled at whoever was knocking. He was not sure he was yet ready to talk with anyone, but duty called.

His First Officer slowly opened the door and stuck his head in. "*Capitán,* are you alright?" His voice was hesitant. "The crew is concerned." Alvite nodded but did not speak.

The First Officer reported, "We have confirmed sinking the Argentine submarine. We located a large diesel oil spill and flotsam from the wreckage. I regret to report no contact with the *Carreras*. I fear that she has been sunk, too. We await your orders. What should we do now?"

Alvite slowly stood and stretched, trying to find relief from the painful stiffness in his back. He had been sitting for entirely too long. And the *O'Higgins* had been aimlessly circling, waiting for her captain while he mourned. Also for entirely too long. It was time for action, for him to lead his crew, his submarine, and make certain they did their jobs.

"We have a mission to complete," the captain said. "First Officer, set a course for Punta Arenas. We will report to headquarters on the way what has taken place here. Then I want to surveil the harbor at first light. We still have a war to win."

Alvite washed his face and straightened his uniform before he walked out into the darkened control room. As he allowed his eyes to adjust to the darkness, he felt the attention of the crew on him, felt their sympathy but also the niggling doubt that he was ready to lead them again. He glanced at the navigation chart. The *O'Higgins* had been making a meandering circle around the Paso Froward. He measured the distance to Punta Arenas and studied his watch. At four knots, they could easily be off the port town by first light, learning what was there and what was going on. The First Officer had already plotted the course and speed they would need. The submarine had just changed course to head that way. There was nothing for him to do but sit back and wait. Or even better, he could walk the boat and let the crew see that he was still full of fight and that their captain expected them to be as well.

Alvite was down in the torpedo room, inspecting one of the Black Shark torpedoes with the leading torpedoman when the voice on the boat's announcing system called out, "*¡Capitán, a controlar!*"

He was being summoned to control. Something was happening.

Alvite hurried up the ladder and walked quickly into the sub's control room. The Officer-of-the-Deck stepped back from the periscope and said, "*Capitán*, we have a sonar contact bearing zero-two-two. High speed screws. Sonar has classified it as a warship. I do not hold him visually yet."

Alvite stepped up to the periscope and, in a low voice that only the OOD could hear, told him, "Lower the periscope, *¡estúpido!* That is an enemy warship out there! Please demonstrate that you earned those dolphins that you are wearing." He moved back, took a breath, and calmed down a bit. Then he added, "That is probably one of the destroyers that are part of the invasion force at Punta Arenas. At night his radar will see our periscope long before you will see him. You do not leave our scope stuck up in the air any longer than absolutely necessary. Make your depth fifty meters. Let us do a submarine approach of him since we are, in fact, a submarine."

"*Sí, Capitán*," the duly chastised OOD responded.

Alvite turned and loudly announced, "Man battle stations. Make tube one ready in all respects. Assign the contact to the torpedo in tube one. We will get a shooting solution on sonar and then we will verify the contact from the periscope before we fire."

The *O'Higgins* crew surged with quiet, determined energy as they prepared for battle. The sub silently slipped down into the depths, ready for action.

Solving the firing solution was relatively simple since the narrow passage between Isla Dawson and Peninsula Brunswick severely limited the destroyer's maneuvering room. The only real problem was the need to positively identify it as an enemy warship before they shot. It really would not do to accidentally sink a cruise liner full of tourists on a whale-watching excursion.

Alvite slowly worked the *O'Higgins* over toward Isla Dawson where it would be more effectively veiled by the high bluffs and surf noise. It took almost an hour to maneuver into position and get set up to shoot when the target came into range. Finally, the fire control system showed that the vessel they were stalking was six thousand meters away, steaming a straight course of two-zero-one at a speed of fifteen knots. It was time to verify the target and, if it was the destroyer they thought it was, to shoot it.

The captain brought his submarine up to periscope depth and carefully raised the device so that it barely cleared the surface of the water. It was a dark, clear, moonless night. Isla Dawson was a black mass looming off to the east and Peninsula Brunswick was equally dark to the west.

Alvite could just make out the hazy outline of a ship to the northwest, where their target should be. He switched the periscope to infrared. The vessel's light gray outline appeared, painted against the inky background.

He recognized a Brazilian *Tamandaré*-class destroyer. This modern warship posed a real and lethal threat, carrying both the sensors to find their submarine and the weapons to launch an effective attack on them.

"Observation on the *Tamandaré*, number one scope!" he called out. They would juxtapose the latest sonar solution with what he was actually seeing up there. If they matched, it was time to shoot.

Alvite put the crosshairs of the scope amidships on the target. "Bearing mark!"

He pushed the button on the periscope to send the bearing directly to the fire control system.

"Range mark!" He pushed the button for the laser range finder. "Down scope!"

He stepped back confidently as the periscope slid down into its well.

The First Officer, bent over the fire control screen, called out, "Observation checks with solution. Ready to shoot!"

Despite the impassive look on his face, Alvite was satisfied that everything was ready for the attack. He ordered, "Shoot tube one at the *Tamandaré*!"

The Black Shark torpedo's electric motor immediately came up to speed after it was ejected from its tube, and that surge of propulsion sent the weapon dashing off toward the unsuspecting Brazilian warship. The hair-thin fiber optic wire connecting the torpedo to the *O'Higgins* gave Alvite a picture of what the torpedo saw and what it was doing. When it had traveled about halfway to its intended target, it began an active search. It detected the *Tamandaré* in its first search cycle and plowed in for the kill.

The 350-kilo warhead exploded directly beneath the ship's keel, ramming the vessel skyward like it was a toy boat kicked out of the water by a playful child. A split second later, the bubble of explosive gases unleashed by the blast collapsed, dropping the center of the ship into the vortex and snapping the keel in half. Almost immediately, the stern section slipped beneath the waves, even before much of the debris that had been shot skyward by the massive explosion could flutter back down into the water. A couple of minutes later, the bow section joined the other half of the destroyer on the way to the bottom.

Luis Alvite released a deep sigh. They were once again the victor in a very brief, very effective attack—not enough back-and-forth to even dub it a skirmish—but there was still more work for them to do.

"Officer-of-the-Deck, come to course zero-one-one and increase speed to standard. I still want to be off Punta Arenas at first light. We have four hours to get there."

Ψ

Bruno Ribeiro was one frustrated submarine captain. It seemed that those *norteamericanos* knew every move he was going to make before he even decided to make it. Their destroyers had flanked him and forced him to try to run up the Uruguayan coast if he had any hope of reaching the US Navy aircraft carrier.

But then, just as he committed to that course, the damnable helicopters showed up, blocking his northerly course with their dipping sonar. There had to be a way to escape this trap, to outsmart the *ianques*.

Ribeiro steered the *João Cândido* farther into the shallow estuary and into long-accepted Argentine territorial waters, not the ones now claimed by the politicians. That would be his best choice for remaining relatively safe. Not even the *norteamericanos* would consider attacking him here. However, it was impossible for him to accomplish his mission while he hid here like a frightened rabbit gone to ground. It was his duty to escape to the open ocean and head north again to halt the carrier's approach.

The water was so shallow that he was forced to bring his nuclear submarine to periscope depth. That was the only way for him to keep his vessel out of the mud and to dodge the constant stream of ships heading in and out of the busy port of Buenos Aires. But as was so often the case at this time of year, the river estuary was shrouded in thick fog.

"*Capitão*," the Officer-of-the-Deck called out as he kept his eye to the periscope. "I have a large merchant ship coming out of the fog and down channel. Range one thousand meters."

Ribeiro grabbed the scope and peered out. Sure enough, a giant ore carrier was bearing down on them. Even though the fog made visibility a kilometer or so, the ship was coming at them at better than fifteen knots. Its red-and-black-painted bow loomed high above them like a giant moving cliff. The letters painted up on the bow proclaimed it to be the *Ore Taijing*. It was one of the supersized Chinese ore haulers carrying Argentina's natural riches back to Shanghai. One of the vessels the *João Cândido* was duty-bound to protect.

"Right full rudder!" Ribeiro roared. "Come to course north. Ahead full! We'll try to slip by down her port side."

There were only a few meters for him to ease past without putting the *João Cândido* into the mud at the edge of the dredged channel, but better hitting bottom than getting run down by two hundred thousand tons of charging steel. The nuclear submarine jumped ahead. The onrushing ship cleared them by mere meters. It came so close that the *Ore Taijing*'s giant bow wave shoved the *João Cândido*'s sail over at a sharp angle as it steamed by. Everyone on the sub was forced to quickly grab and hang on to something to avoid being thrown to the deck or against a bulkhead.

As the mammoth vessel sailed on, totally oblivious to the nuclear submarine it had almost trampled, Ribeiro kept his boat hugging the side of the channel and thanked his lucky stars that they were not crushed and dead on the bottom. That would have been a very inglorious way for such a fine warship and its crew to meet a tragic end, under a giant ore hauler.

The thought struck him. Hiding under the ship. Here was their way out of the *ianque* trap! If he kept his submarine right up close beneath the giant ore hauler, they would never see him. Two hundred thousand tons of steel would hide the boat from anybody's sonar.

"Left full rudder," he abruptly ordered as he watched the *Ore Taijing*'s high, flat stern and frothy wake move away. "Steady course one-three-five." He watched through the periscope as the sub swung around to follow the outbound merchant ship. It took several minutes of precise shiphandling, particularly in the churning froth of the giant ship's wake, but he eventually fine-tuned the sub's course and speed so that they were pointed directly at the Chinese flag hanging over the stern of the vessel. They were so close that he had to aim the periscope upward to see that flag.

Now, it was only a matter of staying close behind the *Ore Taijing* until they were back in deeper water. Then they could slip directly beneath her and stay there until they were well clear of the destroyers. The *ianques* would never see them or even think to look there. And if somehow they did detect them, the *norteamericanos* would never dare to attack so close to a Chinese-flagged ship.

Bruno Ribeiro was quite proud of himself. He had concocted the perfect plan.

Ψ

Brian Edwards watched on the *George Mason*'s Common Tactical Picture display as the underwater chess match continued to play out. The CTP display, fed by the LINK 16 and correlating the data from all the players involved, was in turn being fed to the ECDIS electronic plot table so that FOXTROT XRAY's big picture of what was happening could be overlaid on the navigation display. That allowed Edwards to see the tactical picture superimposed on his submarine's navigation plot. Much better than the chart paper and colored pencils of the old days!

FOXTROT XRAY, orchestrating the ASW battle from aboard one of the US Navy *Arleigh Burke* destroyers, was leapfrogging his MH-60R helicopters with their dipping sonars farther and farther south. All the noise they were emitting was still effectively herding Sierra Two-Six—the Brazilian nuclear sub—inexorably southward, down to where the *George Mason* was waiting.

The three destroyers formed the seaward side of a chute that the target vessel was being guided down. The shallow waters of the Río de la Plata served as the muddy western boundary of that chute. The tactical data showed that two of the destroyers were now easily tracking Sierra Two-Six on their MFTA towed arrays. *George Mason*'s TB-29 was relegated to a slower and less accurate backup sensor.

Edwards studied the display for a few seconds before turning to Jackson Biddle. "XO, I'm thinking that we should mosey over and close the gate at the south end of that chute so our boy doesn't slip out somehow."

Biddle looked at the plot, gnawed on his lip, and finally shook his head. "Skipper, that water over there is real shallow and it skirts mighty close to the twelve-mile limit. The Argentines aren't going to like it if they find us even inside the thousand-mile boundary they're claiming. But if they find we've intruded into the twelve-mile limit, they're gonna have a real conniption fit."

Edwards chuckled. "Sometimes it's nice to be a submarine. If we happen to cross that line, we were never there. If anything happens, we were never there anyway, so we never did whatever it was that we did." The skipper studied the display for a moment. "But I agree with you about the shallow water part." He turned and called out to Jim Shupert, the on-watch OOD. "Nav, stow the TB-29. Come around to course two-nine-zero. Inform FOXTROT XRAY that we are going deep and moving in to close on Sierra Two-Six before he gets much farther down the chute."

Just then the sonar supervisor called out, "New sonar contact, bearing three-zero-five. Designate Sierra Five-Seven. Surface ship, by nature of sound. Looks to be a merchant and probably a big one."

No surprise. These waters were a busy shipping area, even with all the political and military focus lately. Edwards glanced at the ECDIS display and ran a line out on the bearing to this new contact.

"Makes sense," he said, "Merch in the Magdalena channel outbound, most likely from Buenos Aires. Nav, stay clear of him. Since he's sticking to that channel, he'll be a deep draft."

It took two hours for the *George Mason* to scoot over the twenty miles necessary to reposition themselves at the mouth of the Río de la Plata's Canal Magdalena navigation channel. The waterway was one of two accesses to Buenos Aries for deep-draft oceangoing ships. The other channel, the considerably older Canal Punta Indio, made a circuitous route through Uruguayan territorial waters up by Montevideo and was smack in the area of much tension between the two countries at the moment.

Sierra Five-Seven tracked right along the whole time. Once the *George Mason* arrived at the new position, it only took a few minutes to solve the passive sonar problem. The merchant ship was on course one-five-five at a speed of fifteen knots, hurrying down the Canal Magdalena outbound. Range was now twenty thousand yards and the big vessel was painting a very bright picture on the BYG-1 sonar screens.

But where was Sierra Two-Six? If the Brazilian submarine was doing what they all assumed he was doing—hustling down to escape the destroyer and chopper sonars—Edwards knew that the contact should have appeared on *George Mason*'s passive sonar screens by now.

But it was not there.

He decided to make a quick trip to periscope depth and sync with LINK 16. Maybe FOXTROT XRAY could vector the *George Mason* into regaining contact or had seen the Brazilian boat take some kind of dramatic turn. But to Edwards's dismay, FOXTROT XRAY reported that they had lost contact on Sierra Two-Six just after *George Mason* started its run over to the mouth of Canal Magdalena. The bearing line to the Brazilian sub had merged with Sierra Five-Seven—the big cargo ship—and never reappeared. Now out of sight for two hours, the missing sub could be almost anywhere. The complex hydrography of two rivers meeting, dumping millions of gallons of warm, silt-laden fresh water directly into the cold, polar Malvinas Current, was tailor-made for a submarine trying to hide. The dramatically different layers of water temperatures and salinities played havoc with even the most modern and sophisticated sonar.

Figuring that Sierra Two-Six could go a maximum of about fifty nautical miles in the two-hour time period, Edwards drew a circle around the Brazilian submarine's last known position. The ring stretched all the way from Cape San Antonio on the Argentine coast almost to Punta del Este, Uruguay. To the east and south, it reached out into the Atlantic very nearly to the continental shelf.

Edwards shook his head. This was a disaster! Finding Sierra Two-Six would be like finding a very quiet needle in a very large and noisy haystack. But Sierra Two-Six, even as quiet as it had proven to be, was not a ghost. The Brazilian had to be somewhere. The problem for Edwards and his crew was to figure out where. And to do it soon, because that circle was expanding very quickly. The sub they had so effectively chased down a well-designed chute had somehow escaped and could soon be threatening the approaching US carrier group they were all supposed to be protecting.

"Skipper, Sierra Five-Seven currently bears two-nine-six, range sixteen thousand," Jim Shupert reported. "CPA one thousand yards in thirty minutes. Recommend we come around to course zero-nine-zero to get off his track."

Edwards looked at the plot on the ECDIS table. The big merchant was still coming right at them. The skipper pushed a button so that AIS inputs appeared on the plot. AIS—or Automatic Identification System— tracked all commercial ships worldwide, designed primarily for aiding in search-

and-rescue should there be an emergency but also used to keep track of shipping. Each ship automatically broadcasted its name, location, course, speed, and destination on the network to anyone equipped to receive the information. A track labeled *Ore Taijing* appeared right where Sierra Five-Seven lay. Its course and speed matched *George Mason's* fire control solution very closely. Other than several ships anchored along the Canal Punta Indio and an inbound ship on the Canal Argentino, the *Ore Taijing* was the only ship AIS was showing anywhere close by.

Jim Shupert whistled softly. He had punched up Lloyd's Register on his screen. "That is one big momma," he said. "Lloyd's lists her at two hundred thousand tons. She's a Chinese-flagged ore carrier. Ninety-foot full load draft. She's a real bad submarine headache waiting to happen."

He spun the photonics mast around so that they could look at the ship as it came their way. Even seven miles away, the Chinese vessel looked huge. They eased the *George Mason* over to stay well clear of the ore carrier's route as it steamed toward them.

Jackson Biddle had been standing silently in the back of the control room. He was quiet but his mind was racing—"ruminatin'" was the exec's own Deep South description of what he was doing at such times—contemplating where Sierra Two-Six could be hiding. He was carefully looking at every possibility, analyzing it, then rejecting each one. One thing was obvious, though. The guy had to be hiding. Deliberately doing so. If he had decided to make a run for it, someone would have heard him race by.

Then a thought came to him. Could he be hiding and escaping at the same time? Biddle stepped over to where Edwards stood.

"Nuke it out, XO?" Edwards queried. It was the submariner's way of asking if the XO had solved the problem.

"Not sure, Skipper," Biddle answered. "But you know what Sherlock Holmes said. 'When you eliminate the impossible, whatever remains, however improbable, must be the truth.' I think I eliminated everything except Sierra Five-Seven. Two-Six has to be hiding under or right behind that big motha'. I'm thinking we ought to take a look."

Edwards laughed at first. Then he said, "Worth a shot. Let's mosey over and take a look up the *Ore Taijing's* skirts. Line up the chin and sail arrays to go active."

23

Bruno Ribeiro was on the edge of exhaustion. That only added to the danger of what he and his submarine were doing. Driving his boat this close to a massive surface ship for hours had been seriously hard work. He could feel sweat soaking his shirt. His arms ached from trying to hold the scope steady as it bucked and tossed in the churning wake of the merch they were shadowing. His head hurt from the eyepiece constantly pounding him. He was sure that he would have a nasty black eye tomorrow.

The *Ore Taijing* was only thirty meters ahead of the *João Cândido*, its massive bronze screw churning the water, threatening to slice his submarine open if they made even the slightest miscalculation. He did not dare step aside from the periscope and allow one of his officers to take over. This demanding chore belonged only to the captain of the boat.

Besides, Ribeiro knew they were only a couple of kilometers away from reaching deep water. Once they were out of this channel, they could slip down beneath the Chinese ore carrier, safely hide under it, and go as far out as they needed to before the ship inevitably turned south to make for the Straits of Magellan. By then, in even deeper water, he could dash around the *ianque* ASW ships and line up to hit the US Navy carrier.

He was close. Very close.

"*Capitão*, active sonar!" the sonar watch called out. "Twenty-three kilo-hertz. *Americano Virginia*-class submarine mine avoidance sonar!"

It took Ribeiro a second to process the information. Where had the American submarine come from, and why was it using a mine-hunting sonar? Then he realized the *ianques* were looking for him, of course, and they must have figured out his brilliant get-away plan. The mine-hunting sonar would certainly be able to separate the *João Cândido* from the *Ore Taijing*. After all, it was specially designed to work in shallow, muddy water, and discern subtle differences in hunks of metal.

If he was going to finish his mission, it was time to fight. He had no other option.

"Assign tube two to the *ianque* submarine! Make tube two ready in all respects!" he ordered, still not taking his eye away from the periscope and the high, looming stern of the Chinese ship chugging away in front of them.

"*Capitão*, the water is too shallow here. The torpedo will fall into the mud before it comes up to speed," the First Officer responded quietly, respectfully, not wishing to appear to be contradicting his captain and his order.

Ribeiro mentally kicked himself for not remembering that after being launched, torpedoes dropped about ten meters downward as they came up to speed. At the moment, the bottom was only five meters below the keel of his submarine.

He answered, "Of course I know that, First Officer. I am only getting ready. We are going to come up along the starboard side of our *grande amigo Chinês*, shoot, then dive back down and run out ahead while the *ianque* is busy avoiding our torpedo. Even if we miss, which is quite likely, by the time anyone realizes what is happening, we will be in deep water and long gone to the north to do our duty against the carrier."

"Of course, sir," the First Officer responded sheepishly. "I knew you would have a fine plan, sir."

Ψ

"Positive returns on two contacts," Josh Hannon called out. "Solid return between bearings two-two-zero and two-seven-three. Looks like a steel wall. Equates to Sierra Five-Seven. Much smaller solid return bearing two-seven-eight. Range twelve hundred yards."

Brian Edwards grinned broadly as he looked at the chin array screen. It appeared the XO's improbable truth had worked out. The smaller contact could easily be Sierra Two-Six, effectively hiding in the wake of the big merchant vessel, and not very deep at all. Now, the *George Mason* would see how the Brazilian captain responded to being prodded. And hope it would not be by the SOB deciding to throw a punch.

Hannon yelled, "Second contact just zigged. He has sped up and merged with the first. Can't separate the returns now."

Edwards was about to vent his frustration when Jackson Biddle said, "He doesn't know that we've lost him. Keep the sonar trained on him. He'll think we're still tracking and have a bead on him. I'm betting he'll flinch."

Edwards looked up. "Damn, XO! Remind me not to play poker with you."

Jim Shupert was peering at the photonics mast visual image on the large screen display. He suddenly called out, "Skipper, broached submarine close alongside the Chinese merch!" The distinctive black sail of the Brazilian nuclear submarine was clearly visible against the high gray sides of the ore carrier. The sub looked to be no more than a hundred feet away from the ship and was racing along toward its bow.

"Launch transients from Sierra Two-Six! Torpedo in the water!" Josh Hannon suddenly yelled. The sub they were watching, now on the surface, was shooting at them!

Edwards knew that he had only seconds to decide on what to do. His next few decisions would determine their life or death.

He could not go deep and run. The channel was too narrow, and the water outside the channel was much too shallow. It would be impossible to dodge an actively seeking torpedo with no room to maneuver.

"Ahead full!" he ordered. "Launch a pair of evasion devices!" He took a quick estimate of the bearing to the stern of the *Ore Taijing*. "Right full rudder, steady course two-two-six. Make your depth three-six feet."

Jackson Biddle glanced over at his captain, a confused look on his face.

Edwards flashed a quick, wry smile. "Don't worry, XO. I ain't gone suicidal yet," he told him. "Our big Chinese friend might make one hell of an evasion device."

"Bearing to the incoming weapon one-nine-nine," Josh Hanson called, his voice now a whole octave higher than normal. "It's gone active."

The incoming torpedo was looking for its target, the USS *George Mason*. At this range, and with no room for the submarine to duck, the deadly fish would almost certainly find it and kill them.

Edwards watched the visual display as the *George Mason* passed directly behind the Chinese ship. He could easily see crewmen up on the deck, several pointing down at his submarine. Some may have even realized by now that they were caught in the middle of a skirmish between two submerged warships.

"Torpedo bears one-nine-nine! Increasing speed!"

Of course it was. The weapon had found the US submarine and was homing in for the death blow.

Just as the *George Mason* was passing clear of the *Ore Taijing*, Edwards ordered, "Left full rudder, steady one-five-five."

"Torpedo bearing one-nine-nine! Range gating!" Hanson's voice was a squeak.

Edwards swore he could see the welds on the *Ore Taijing*'s hull as the *George Mason* turned to scoot along its starboard side.

The pounding jolt from a massive explosion suddenly tossed him to the deck. Dust, debris, and flying objects filled the air. The lights blinked off, then back on. The 2MC announcing system blared, "Reactor scram! Casualty assistance team lay aft! Loss of starboard turbine generator!"

Edwards was still shaking the cobwebs from his head and fully expecting the call of major flooding and reports of numerous casualties when he looked at the photonics screen. The *Ore Taijing*'s screw was not churning the water anymore. The giant ore carrier was rapidly losing headway though it was hard to judge since his submarine was also noticeably slowing. The *Ore Taijing* was also starting to alter direction—whether voluntarily or not—and drift toward the channel edge.

"Conn, Maneuvering, cause of the scram was shock from the nearby explosion. Commencing a fast recovery start-up. Turbine generator breaker tripped by the shock. Shut now. Electric plant in a normal half power line up on the starboard turbine generator."

The torpedo had not hit the *George Mason* after all. But it struck something close enough that the blast knocked the sub's nuclear reactor offline and tripped the turbine generator circuit breaker. It took ten minutes to regain propulsion and power back from the reactor and to get clear of the floundering Chinese vessel. By then, the ore ship had drifted well out of channel and appeared to be motionless, its nose stuck firmly in the muck.

It was clear that the Brazilian sub's torpedo had struck the ore carrier, not its intended target.

Edwards shook his head again, looked around, and said, "Now that we got power back, let's get the hell out of here and go find that Brazilian bastard that shot at us!"

Ψ

Vice President Sandra Dosetti and Secretary of Defense Sebastien Aldo sat in the Oval Office on two Sheraton settees separated by a low Federal-period-style coffee table. The settees and table had been moved so that they were directly in front of the president's desk. The table was piled high with briefing papers and messages.

President Stanley Smitherman sat behind the Resolute desk. It was clear of everything except a coffee cup bearing the presidential seal. And a half-empty whisky bottle.

Although Smitherman sat behind the desk, flanked by the US and presidential flags, Sandra Dosetti was clearly very much in charge of all that was going on this day. "Reports are pouring in that the dust-up down off Uruguay is growing hot," she said as she flipped through a briefing book to find a specific report. "We have confirmed reports that a Brazilian submarine fired on one of our boats in international waters without provocation."

"Dammit, I told you this would happen," the president said. "I told you to get that boat out of there. Damn thing's been a pain in the ass for weeks and I knew sooner or later it would—"

"Shut up, Stan," Dosetti interrupted. "Do you not understand that I will now tell you when to speak and what to say?"

The president frowned, took a big slug directly from the whisky bottle, then sat back in his chair, idly studying the wristwatch on his arm, a gift from the president of France.

Sebastien Aldo flipped out an 8x10 photo. The picture, probably taken from a helicopter or drone aircraft, showed a large ship sitting crosswise in the channel with its bow elevated, obviously aground in the shallows.

"This is the Chinese flagged ore carrier *Ore Taijing*," Aldo explained. "Reports are that it was hit by a torpedo and lost propulsion. Looks like the screw and rudder were blown clear off. The crew on the *Ore Taijing* took pictures of one of our submarines passing very close alongside just as the torpedo explosion happened. Those pictures are all over the web. The boat has been identified as one of our *Virginia*-class ships. We've confirmed it is the *George Mason*, but nobody else knows that for sure."

Aldo picked up another sheet of paper. "*George Mason* reported they detected a Brazilian nuclear submarine that was using the *Ore Taijing* for concealment. Intelligence reports identify the Brazilian boat as the *João Cândido*, which we believe was enforcing the unlawful blockade on Montevideo and other Uruguayan ports but could also be a threat to the carrier group we have on the way down there as a show of solidarity with Uruguay. At any rate, the Brazilian submarine fired on the *George Mason* as soon as it discovered that it had been found and was under surveillance. The *George Mason* captain reports that he ran up close to the *Ore Taijing* when he saw he was under attack, and the torpedo hit the merchant ship instead."

Smitherman raised his hand and opened his mouth to speak but thought better of it when Dosetti glared at him over the top of her reading glasses. She waited a second and then said, "We have already informed the Chinese and every other nation of exactly what happened. There will be propaganda and positioning, of course, especially from China, but everyone knows we are shooting straight. So to speak. Here is what we will do next. Mr. President, you will issue an order that this Brazilian submarine, this *João Cândido*, is declared hostile and is to be engaged by any of our warships in the area if detected." She flipped a sheet of paper onto the Resolute desk for Smitherman's signature. The order had already been written. She allowed a couple of seconds for that to sink in before she continued. "Then you will get that Brazilian strongman, Souza, on the phone. Tell him, in no uncertain terms, that he needs to get that boat and the rest of his silly little navy out of there, drop the blockade of Uruguay, and pose no threat to our carrier force or any other US or allied vessels in the area, or we will consider it to be an act of war and proceed accordingly. Make certain he understands that the time for pussyfooting around has now passed, since one of his vessels fired on a US ship in international waters."

"But I can't do—" Smitherman spluttered.

"Stan, I will be listening. You'd damn well better," Dosetti threatened. "Now, get on the phone and get it done before I am forced to email a couple of documents to some good friends of mine in the media who would love nothing more than getting their own cable news show at your miserable expense."

24

Bruno Ribeiro was well aware that he and his submarine were in a box. There was an American *Virginia*-class submarine somewhere astern. He had watched as his torpedo dutifully homed in on something and exploded at about the time he expected. But then the engines of the *Ore Taijing*, the huge Chinese vessel, had unexpectedly stopped and she veered out of channel. He could only assume that he had hit the wrong ship, which meant the American was still out there. In all likelihood, the sub was tracking the *João Cândido* right this instant. And he could hear the three *ianque* destroyers off to the northeast, still raising a fuss, banging away with their SQS-53 active sonars. He had to get past them to get within striking distance of that carrier. At least the helicopters were no longer buzzing around, contributing to the din. They had likely returned to their home ships for fuel but would soon return.

The real box the Brazilian sub captain was in was one made of time and distance. The clock was ticking. He had lost too many minutes trapped in the Río de la Plata by the damned *ianques* and their bell-ringing sonar. Then having to shoot his way out of their snare.

Ribeiro swung the *João Cândido* around and headed southeast, out into the broad and deep South Atlantic Ocean. Out there, he could more easily slip past the searching destroyers and then, once clear, turn north to approach and strike the unprotected aircraft carrier. It certainly looked easy on the navigation chart. But he was faced with a real quandary. There were two relatively safe tactics. He could either race far out into the Argentine Sea to move around the destroyers' ASW screen, or he could stealthily slip through the screen by running deep and slow. Either one would take far too long. His orders were to attack, and his president and military leaders expected those orders to be promptly executed. Or else.

The third approach was the direct one, play the *touro*, the bull, and charge straight through to the *matador*, the target. He would just run straight at the carrier and shoot anyone who got in his way. This bold plan offered the best chance of them successfully doing what they had been ordered to do, even if it bordered on suicidal.

Decision made, Ribeiro laid out a direct line to the last reported location of the American carrier and ordered, "Officer-of-the-Deck, steer course zero-three-three. Come to ahead full. Make your depth fifty meters."

Then the captain stood at the back of the control room and watched his team at work. He calculated that it would be a little over two hours before they were close enough to begin an attack. Time to get everything and everybody ready for battle.

At two hours, almost to the minute, the sonar operator called out, "*Capitão*, new sonar contact. Contact is bearing zero-two-two. Sounds like a deep draft contact with two four-bladed screws."

Ribeiro rushed over to the sonar output display. It appeared they had found the *ianque* carrier, but it was still a long way off. The signal strength was very low, almost below the threshold for detection.

He patted the sonarman on the shoulder and congratulated him. "Well done, Juan. A less expert sonarman would never have seen him. You will have a promotion when we return home."

Ribeiro maneuvered the *João Cândido* in for the kill. The best estimate on the range was thirty kilometers. The aircraft carrier, the *Gerald Ford*, was still over the horizon. He wanted to be close enough to get periscope pictures of the great ship as it sank, so he needed to cut that range by two thirds. It was an intricate dance to close the range on the unsuspecting surface ship while maneuvering to solve its course, speed, and range, all while driving to the best shooting point. And while looking over his shoulder to assure himself that the destroyers and submarine had not somehow managed to follow them.

"*Capitão*," Juan, the sonarman, called out. "New contact, bearing three-four-one. Sounds like an American destroyer using a Prairie-Masker. I hear a heavy rainstorm on that bearing, but there is no rain." There was a moment's pause, then, "*Capitão*, I think he is close, inside ten kilometers!"

Ribeiro looked at the solution on the *Gerald Ford*. The massive carrier was still at twenty-thousand meters. A shot at this range was possible, but with less chance of getting a hit. Better to gut it out and get closer, even if a *ianque* destroyer was stalking him.

Then the active sonar warning alarmed. Ribeiro saw that it indicated a three kilohertz pulse, an SQS-53. There was a destroyer out there and, based on the signal strength, he was close. The chances that this one had detected the *João Cândido* were very high. An American torpedo in the water could easily be the next thing they heard.

"Assign the destroyer to tube one!" he ordered. He could not hesitate. "Launch tube one!"

He felt the jolt and heard the rush of air as the Black Shark in tube one was impulsed out and away. He immediately shouted, "Assign tube two to the carrier! Launch tube two!"

"Torpedo from tube one running normally," the Weapons Officer announced. "Torpedo from tube two running normally."

"Ahead flank!" Ribeiro shouted. He had surely been discovered and there were certainly weapons heading toward him as well. He had pulled the trigger as he had been commanded to do. It was time to run.

He looked at the plot and suddenly, it was as if his escape plan was highlighted, clearly marked for him and his submarine.

The safest course was right beneath that destroyer.

"Come to course three-four-zero, make your depth four hundred meters."

Perhaps the plan was not so suicidal after all.

Ψ

Brian Edwards intently studied the tactical display on the ECDIS table.

The *George Mason* had not updated their picture of the COP from LINK 16 for over an hour, so the surface information was a little out of date. Still, sonar told most of the story.

The *Gerald Ford* was off to the northeast conducting an UNREP ("underway replenishment") with the *Rainier*, T-AOE-7. Edwards had to chuckle. The sophisticated nuclear-powered aircraft carrier was designed to steam for twenty-five years without refueling and carried over three million gallons of jet fuel for its contingent of aircraft. However, the crew could not go for even a week without fresh veggies.

The *Thomas Higginbotham*, a spanking-new *Arleigh Burke*-class destroyer, had drawn plane guard duty and was waiting for her turn alongside the T-AOE to take on her own load of fuel and groceries. The other three *Burkes* were still furiously ensonifying the ocean off to the southwest, searching fruitlessly for the once-again-lost Brazilian submarine.

"The *Higginbotham* has gone active on their 53," Josh Hannon reported just as the sonar intercept receiver alarmed as if to confirm the report. "Intense! Looks like a maximum-power search mode."

Aston Jennings, the Weapons Officer and the on-watch Officer-of-the-Deck, commented, "Something sure triggered the skimmer's interest. Pretty sure it ain't us, though."

"Captain, I hear launch transients on bearing zero-nine-one," Josh Hanson yelled. "Torpedoes in the water? Sounds like two of them."

Brian Edwards jumped from his seat and hurriedly glanced at the sonar display. Then he ordered, "Weps, man battle stations!"

Hanson announced, "First torpedo bears zero-eight-six. Second torpedo bears zero-eight-eight. Quick burst of suppressed cavitation bearing zero-nine-two. Sure sounds like a boat going to flank and then going deep."

Instantly Edwards ordered, "Snapshot tube two on the contact bearing zero-nine-two." If someone out there was shooting, it was time to get their own gun cocked and poised to shoot back.

"New sonar contact, bearing zero-nine-zero on the conformal array," Josh Hanson reported. "Designate Sierra Seven-Two, probable submerged submarine. First torpedo bears zero-eight-two. Second torpedo bears zero-seven-eight. Captain, neither weapon's coming toward us."

Edwards looked at the tactical display. Then he shouted, "Shit! The bastard's shooting at the *Higginbotham* and the *Ford!*" Then he yelled, "Weps, broach the ship, right now! Get up on the Battle Group Command Circuit and warn the *Ford* and *Higginbotham* about incoming torpedoes! With that tin can banging away on active sonar like that, they'll never hear 'em coming!"

The *George Mason* took a hard, hurried up angle to the surface. As soon as the sail was in the air, Jennings grabbed the red handset and relayed the warning about the incoming weapons to the surface ships.

The radio message elicited an immediate, panicked response from the two vessels. The *Gerald Ford* executed an emergency breakaway from the T-AOE. Both the flat-top and the replenishment vessel spun around and raced off in different directions. By the time the Black Shark torpedo was close enough to the original intercept point, the pair of ships were well out of its detection range and steaming away over the horizon. The torpedo kept on going—still vainly searching for its programmed target—until its battery died and it sank benignly to the bottom of the Atlantic Ocean.

The *Higginbotham* was not so lucky. Upon receiving the warning, it spun around with a full rudder. All four LM-2500 gas turbines pushed the twin screws up to maximum speed. The stern squatted as the screws threw up a pair of impressive rooster tails and shot the *Higginbotham* ahead. But the Black Shark had already detected the destroyer and was homing in for the kill. The race was on, but it was not a fair one. The thirty-knot ship was no match for the fifty-knot torpedo. Even the countermeasures the ship dumped into the water had no effect on the relentless weapon. It drove under the destroyer, satisfied its logic circuits with what it observed, and circled back around for the attack. Its three-hundred-and-fifty-kilo warhead detonated directly beneath the warship's keel, breaking it in half.

There was only one fortunate happenstance. The halves of the vessel lingered on the surface for several minutes. Miraculously, that allowed a major portion of the crew to abandon ship before the broken sections finally slipped beneath the waves.

The crew on the *George Mason* could hear and feel the explosion through the hull. It was obvious to them that an American warship had been attacked and probably sunk. That innocent lives were lost. That someone had the audacity to attack US Navy vessels in indisputable international waters. Not only was it time for some revenge, it was necessary for the submarine crew to do whatever it took to prevent the Brazilian sub from sinking anyone else.

"Skipper, I still have a tracking solution of Sierra Seven-Two," Jackson Biddle offered. "He has zigged around to the north. Looks like he's heading for the *Ford*."

"Okay, XO, what do you have?" Edwards asked Jackson Biddle.

"My best solution right now is range sixteen thousand yards, course north, speed twenty," the exec answered.

That put the enemy submarine roughly halfway between the *George Mason* and the carrier. The *Gerald Ford* and the *Rainier* were both wildly zigzagging to confuse the attacking submarine, but they were generally heading west and south at high speed.

Edwards quickly plotted an intercept course that cut off the legs of the triangle. It got them to a firing position just before the Brazilian could reasonably shoot another torpedo at the *Ford*. They would have to run at flank—or as close to flank speed as the *George Mason* could go with only one turbine generator—if they hoped to get there in time to prevent another hit.

The two nuclear submarines ran across the Argentine Sea, one seeking to destroy the *Gerald Ford*, the other striving to stop it. For over an hour they sprinted. Because of the shorter distance it had to go, the *George Mason* slowly gained on the *João Cândido*.

Edwards watched the contest play out. He calculated that they had another thirty minutes to get in the best firing position and that the Brazilian would most likely run for another forty-five minutes to get the range to the *Ford* down to five thousand yards or so. That would give them optimum stand-off distance to shoot an alerted surface ship.

"Possible contact zig on Sierra Seven-Two. Down shift in received frequency," Josh Hannon announced. "Contact has slowed."

"Damn," Jackson Biddle said softly as he looked at the fire control solution and the sonar inputs. He had a queasy feeling in the pit of his stomach. Then he called out, "Confirmed contact zig. Down doppler. Change in received frequency equates to seventeen knots in the line of sight. Set anchor range at ten thousand yards. Set new speed at six knots."

Brian Edwards looked over Biddle's shoulder. "What's he doing, XO?"

"Skipper, he has slowed way down. My guess is he's going to periscope depth to shoot. And real soon."

Edwards looked at the ECDIS tactical display and then smacked his forehead. "Of course! He's ten thousand meters from the *Ford*. He's coming to periscope depth to shoot! Way earlier than I would have, but he ain't me."

Edwards knew what that meant. It was time for them to shoot, even if doing so would only distract the Brazilian, making him duck instead of getting off a shot. "Firing point procedures, Sierra Seven-Two, tube two!"

Everyone involved had expected the order. In quick succession, Jackson Biddle reported, "Solution ready."

Then Jim Shupert, the battle stations OOD, sang out: "Ship ready."

Aston Jennings was last to pipe up. He confirmed, "Weapon ready."

Brian Edwards took one last look at the fire control solution, then he ordered, "Shoot on generated bearings."

Jennings jammed down on the button to launch the deadly torpedo. The fire control system sent the latest solution down to the ADCAP torpedo patiently waiting in tube two. Then the high-speed torpedo ejection pump came up to maximum RPMs and shoved the torpedo out of the tube. The otto-fuel-powered engine spun up and sent the torpedo racing toward Sierra Seven-Two.

Even running at sixty-five knots, the torpedo would not hit the Brazilian submarine for more than five minutes. That would give the attacker plenty of time to shoot at the *Ford*. Edwards knew he needed to play havoc with the other sub long enough for his torpedo to be effective. There was only one way, though that meant giving up stealth and very probably becoming a target himself. But there was no other choice.

"Sonar, line up to go active on Sierra Seven-Two!" Edwards ordered.

Putting two hundred and sixty decibels of acoustic energy in the water would certainly attract Sierra Seven-Two's attention. And most likely a torpedo, as well. But that would keep the Brazilian occupied with *George Mason* and not shooting at the *Ford*.

Hannon reported, "Ready to go active."

"Go active, maximum power, fifteen seconds ping interval," Edwards ordered.

"Skipper, at this range, ping return is thirty seconds," Hannon pointed out. "We won't get a valid response. The pings will overlap."

Edwards half smiled. "That's precisely what I want. Let the bastard think we are a lot closer than we really are."

"Own ship weapon running normally," Aston Jennings called out. "Normal wire clearance maneuver. Running at pre-enable speed."

The first ping showed on the sonar screen and, fifteen seconds later, it was followed by the second ping. Any return was lost in the jumble of outgoing pings.

"Launch transients, Sierra Seven Two!" Sonar announced. "Torpedo in the water!"

"Nav, broach up and warn the *Ford*," Edwards calmly ordered. "Then drop back down to one-five-zero and let's figure out who Seven Two's shooting at."

"Torpedo bearing zero-six-one!"

The *George Mason* once again zoomed to the surface and, for the second time that afternoon, the submarine warned the carrier of an incoming torpedo. Then it dropped back beneath the surface.

"Torpedo bears zero-six-one!"

"Own ship weapon enabled," Jennings called out. Their ADCAP torpedo had slowed and was now actively searching for the enemy submarine. Odds now were pretty good it would find what it was looking for.

"Torpedo bears zero-six-one! Torpedo has gone into active search!" Hannon called out, his voice rising noticeably. It was clear now who the other sub's target was. "Skipper, it has a zero bearing-rate and up doppler. He's shooting at us!"

Edwards calculated the timing and ordered, "Launch two evasion devices! Right full rudder, steady course zero-nine-zero. Make your depth one thousand feet."

It was time to get out of Dodge. They needed to drive out of the incoming torpedo's acquisition cone before it saw them. If the Black Shark torpedo was able to detect them, it would be very hard to lose it.

Two evasion devices blasted out of the dihedral launchers aft and immediately set up a wall of noise and bubbles that was hopefully enough to confuse the deadly fish. The *George Mason* angled down and accelerated as it headed east.

"Detect!" Aston Jennings yelled. Their weapon had successfully found the enemy submarine. "Detect! Acquisition! Terminal homing!" The ADCAP had acquired the Brazilian and was circling in to deliver the fatal blow.

"Inbound torpedo bearing zero-six-one! Still zero bearing-rate! It blasted past the evasion devices!"

Both submarines were now dancing with death.

"Inbound torpedo is range gating!" The Brazilian Black Shark had detected them and was rushing in to do what it had been built to do.

"Launch the CRAW from the port dihedral!" Edwards ordered with surprising calm. "Launch the CRAW from the starboard dihedral! Launch two more evasion devices!"

The pair of six-inch-diameter "compact rapid attack weapons"—actually small torpedoes originally designed as anti-torpedo weapons—were their last hope to destroy the incoming torpedo before it sent them all to a watery grave. The two mini torpedoes blasted out of the dihedrals. Their lithium-oxide-fueled SCEPS engines rammed them both up to better than seventy knots while their miniaturized sensor packages aimed them directly at the rapidly approaching torpedo.

"Loud explosion, bearing zero-five-two!" Josh Hanson shouted—though everyone aboard had clearly heard the blast—just as Aston Jennings yelled, "Loss of wire on own-ship weapon."

Sure enough, death had reached out and grabbed Sierra Seven-Two, the Brazilian submarine.

But the same fate was now homing in on the *George Mason*.

"Incoming torpedo bears zero-six-one! CRAWs both converging!" Josh Hanson's voice was up a couple of octaves.

"Lord, please! Come on. Come on. Come on! Do your thing, CRAWs!" Brian Edwards prayed under his breath.

The blast brutally rocked the American submarine. The skipper grabbed a stanchion, fully expecting to see a wall of seawater smashing in at him from all angles.

But nothing. No flooding. No fire. No reports of damage. No one injured. Or dead.

They all looked at each other. They had survived the attack! Prayers answered! The CRAWs had destroyed the inrushing torpedo!

All that pleading and praying—and those hours and hours of drilling—had worked after all.

25

Pedreira gently knocked and then, even without permission to enter, opened the massive doors just enough to slip through and into his boss's office. *Presidente* Cristiano Souza's ever-faithful aide and bodyguard was wary about disturbing his *patrono e chefe*, especially if the news he brought him was not good. And he was reasonably certain that this interruption would not be considered good news.

This would be another in a series of calamities—or near-calamities—that had cast a dark cloud over the Palacio de Planalto this week. Each of them served to ruin Souza's day. It had all begun when reports came in of another naval battle in the Straits. It seemed that one Chilean submarine had sunk all the Argentine and Brazilian warships still down there and single-handedly closed the Straits to all navigation. As if that were not bad enough, the self-styled Argentine strongman Bruno Martinez, Souza's partner in establishing a new political and economic order across South America, had called wailing about a minor skirmish somewhere up in the Andes that seemed to be causing unrest amongst his populace. The *camponeses* should have already been pacified and firmly under control by this time. Before Souza's blood pressure could return to normal, Admiral Barbosa called to inform him that the *norteamericano* Navy was preventing his fleet from returning to Brazil.

What the aide was about to tell his president might be the last straw. And Pedreira feared that another setback could really trigger the famously hotheaded Brazilian leader to do something earth-scorchingly irrational.

"Excuse me, *Excelência*," the big man said as he entered Souza's office. His boss was sitting in his oversized chair, his back to the door, staring out the window and watching the rain clouds hurry overhead as if they were fleeing something threatening beyond the horizon.

"Yes, Pedreira." Souza's voice was low but calm.

"The *norteamericano* president is on the phone for you. He demands to speak with you immediately. He says the matter is of utmost importance."

"What could that drunken blowhard possibly want this time?" Souza asked hotly, spinning around, no longer calm. "He dares demand anything more of me? He is bought and paid for, yet refuses to simply look the other way for a few weeks.!" He pounded the desk hard with a fist. "Probably wants to whine about the cost of his morning coffee. Or ask who to bet on in the World Cup."

"Let us hope," Pedreira responded. But he knew better.

Souza grabbed his phone and growled, "*Bom dia, senhor presidente.*"

But it was a distinctly female voice that replied. "Forget the diplomatic crap, Cristiano. And give me enough respect to at least speak English. This is Vice President Dosetti. I was just informed that one of your submarines attacked our ships in international waters off of Uruguay. It sank one of our destroyers, the *Thomas Higginbotham*, with loss of life."

Souza interrupted, spluttering, "Impossible! Your warships are—"

"Just shut up for once and listen to me," Dosetti told him, her voice ice cold. "Your submarine—our intelligence reports say it was the *João Cândido* —sank the *Thomas Higginbotham* and launched torpedoes aimed at the *Gerald Ford*, one of our nuclear aircraft carriers. The *João Cândido* was sunk as part of our counterattack before they could kill more innocent Americans. There were no survivors aboard your submarine."

"*Impossível!*" Souza shouted into the phone. Pedreira took a cautious step back. "This constitutes an act of war by the USA and—"

"You are quite right," Dosetti interrupted. "This is an act of war. But on the part of the Brazilian Navy, who attacked in international waters with no provocation whatsoever. Even you should be able to understand that neither the US nor the world's rational governments will tolerate this. Now, you have twelve hours to get every ship in that piss-ant navy of yours into a port somewhere. After that deadline, we will sink every single one of your ships we catch afloat. Any vessel that so much as sticks its nose outside the breakwater. And you can tell your Argentine partner, President Martinez, that the same thing applies to those rust buckets that he calls a navy. *Entender?*"

The call abruptly ended. The president of Brazil, mouth open, stared at a dead receiver.

Ψ

"Was that tone quite necessary?" Stan Smitherman asked peevishly.

He stood beside the Resolute desk while Sandra Dosetti, occupying his chair behind it, replaced the phone in its cradle and sat back, a pleased look on her face. She smiled and answered, "Yes, Stan, it was. The world, starting with those two idiots down there, needs to immediately understand that, to put it in your Texas vernacular, there's a new sheriff in town. Thanks to their idiocy, they gave me the perfect opportunity to prove it, and it'll all be legit. We don't even have to manufacture a crisis. Just like you gave us more blackmail material than we could ever have created on our own. Thank you."

"You're damned welcome," Smitherman said, but with little vigor.

She handed him two sheets of paper. "Here's the order to the Secretary of Defense to carry out operations against Brazil and Argentina, just as I outlined to *Presidente* Souza. And this is your report to Congress explaining your actions and how they clearly fall under the War Powers Act as a national emergency created by an attack upon the United States, its territories or possessions, or its armed forces. Not a bad legacy for your last act as commander in chief. The press will eat it up and you'll go down in history as a strong, decisive president. Which you and I know is a damnable lie."

Smitherman almost smiled, then realized what his new veep had just said. "Wait. What do you mean 'last act as commander in chief?'" But he still took the two papers from her and reached for his pen.

"Stan, I told you from the beginning how this was going down. It's time for you to exit stage left," Dosetti answered. She held up a bottle of pills and shook them. They sounded ominously like an angry rattlesnake. "We'll give you a choice, of course. You can either fake a heart attack, retire to that ranch of yours outside Austin, and sing cowboy songs to the cattle. Or we will, very soon and at a time you least suspect, actually give you a heart attack and your 'retirement' will be to a nice shady plot at Arlington National Cemetery. If you decide on option two, which I don't recommend, you will never be sure when you have taken your last bite of barbeque or your last slug of bourbon. But you will always know it's coming. Always, until it does."

The president's face was a washed-out shade of white as he put his signature—not quite so bold as usual—on both sheets of paper.

Ψ

The sun was shining high up in an iridescent blue sky when the pale green Land Rover Defender pulled into the circular driveway in front of the main entrance of the Hospital de Calama and stopped beneath the portico. Alston Jonas, the assistant naval attaché at the US embassy in Santiago, Chile, swung open the driver's door and jumped out. He stepped back to the left passenger door and helped Li Min Zhou-Ward climb out. Admiral Jon Ward hopped out of the right side and assisted his wife, Ellen, down from the lofty step. The high-clearance off-road vehicle presented a challenge to both women, even with its deployable sidestep.

Jonas pulled a card from his pocket and looked at it. "Admiral, Mrs. Ward—both of you—Commander Ward is in room three-twenty-seven in the trauma ward." He waved toward the entrance. "Shall we go on in?"

Jon Ward nodded toward the Land Rover. "Don't you need to park that tank somewhere where it won't get towed?"

Jonas chuckled and pointed to the diplomatic plates. "Says free parking."

The four walked into the hospital lobby to find a short, slightly pudgy man in a long white lab coat and light blue scrubs waiting for them just inside the doors. As if to confirm his status as a doctor, a stethoscope was draped around his neck.

"*Buen día*," he said as he approached the quartet. "I am Dr. Hernando Flores, Chief of Surgery." He extended his hand to Jon Ward and then to Alston Jonas. He bobbed his head in a slight bow as he greeted each. And a more formal bow to Ellen and Li Min. "Ladies. Welcome to Hospital de Calama. We are honored we have been able to care for your men after their injuries incurred while assisting our country. Come with me and I will escort you directly to Commander Ward and Chief Hurt's room."

"Thank you, Dr. Flores," Jon Ward told him.

The physician turned and walked toward a bank of elevators. "They are in our trauma ICU right now." He noticed the look of concern flash across the faces of both Ward women as they stepped into the elevator. "Do not be concerned. It is just hospital protocol with gunshot wounds. They are both progressing well and have a prognosis for a full recovery. But they will be with us for several more days as a precaution and to gain strength for the long trip home."

The elevator doors opened onto a busy, modern hospital ward. Nurses and doctors hurried about attending to patients. Dr. Flores led them past an open area nurse's station and to the doorway opening into a room. He entered ahead of them, but they could see around him to the patients in the two beds inside. Billy Joe Hurt lay in one of them, Jim Ward in the other. Both were connected to IV drips and sported bandages wrapped around their torsos. Various machines monitored their vital signs. The small room was crowded already with Bill Beaman, TJ Dillon, and the remaining two members of the SEAL Team, Chuck Jones and Gene LaCroix. The men were seated on every possible horizontal surface.

There was some scurrying among the SEALs as Dr. Flores appeared. He looked sternly at Beaman.

"*Señor* Beaman, we have discussed sneaking food into the hospital and our patients having so many visitors at a time. It is important that we control and monitor our patients' diets and rest."

Bill Beaman looked sheepish as he answered. "Shucks, Doc, these frogs need their sustenance, you know. They ain't gonna get no better eatin' green Jell-O." The former SEAL grabbed a chart and pretended to read it as he smiled broadly. "The patients were showing a concerning deficiency in their blood pizza level, you know."

"Ignore my medical advice at your own peril," the doc said with a slight grin. "Besides, I think I have the prescription that will make our patients feel much better. I bring visitors from—"

Li Min finally ignored the banter, rushing into the room, pushing past everyone to land on the bed and give Jim Ward a huge hug and passionate kiss. Then she smacked him on the chin. "Damn it, frog boy! When are you going to learn to duck?" She pulled back and looked into his eyes. There was an odd look on her face. "After all, how can you be a proper daddy of our child if you are always getting yourself shot up?"

It took a second for the meaning of her words to sink in. "The what? But . . . how?" he spluttered.

"You heard me, frog boy. You're going to be a daddy. I thought you would have figured out the 'how' part by now." She blushed and giggled.

Ward sat up, reaching to embrace his wife, but then groaned in pain and fell back onto the bed grimacing. "That was really not a good idea."

She had a sudden thought that caused her to frown. "Are you upset I told you the news here and now, in front of everybody?" she asked, glancing at the SEALs and others.

He looked at her, laughed, motioned that he wanted another kiss. She happily obliged.

"These are my brothers, darling," he told her. "Besides, I'm too happy to see you to ever be mad . . ."

Only then did he notice there were two other people who had now joined the crowd in the room. His mom and dad. And clearly this father-hood business was as much a surprise to them as it was for him. Ellen and Jon Ward appeared stunned, still processing the prospects of becoming grandparents. But both were grinning broadly.

Ellen ran over to give her son a hug as well but was careful not to be too vigorous in doing so. And his dad was still grinning goofily when he shook his boy's hand.

"You guys take the wrong exit off the Beltway?" the younger Ward asked.

"Naw, we just had some frequent flyer miles we needed to burn, so we came south to Chile for a few days," his dad answered. "But we didn't count on your wife dropping that happy bomb on us!"

They visited for a bit and got the full scoop on the baby situation while the others in the room pretended not to be listening. Then, inevitably, Jim Ward got serious. After all, he was the leader of a SEAL team just off a major mission on foreign soil in the midst of an international conflagration. His father was the Chief of Naval Intelligence. TJ Dillon was a CIA operative, on assignment. And Bill Beaman had been pulled out of retirement to help oversee this job. Clearly, they had business to discuss.

Chuck Jones and Gene LaCroix suddenly remembered they had something to do downstairs and dutifully filed out. Jonas, Beaman and Dillon remained. So did Li Min and Ellen Ward. Business or not, they weren't leaving Jim. Not just yet. And Li, ever mindful of useful intelligence data, had a vested interest in what was likely about to be discussed, though only her husband and father-in-law knew of her secondary reason for remaining in the room.

"Dad, when you all got here, Bill and TJ were just bringing Billy Joe and me up to speed on what's happening across the border in Argentina. As you know, we've both been pretty much out of it for the last several days. Since the assault by Kirkland's guys."

Admiral Ward looked to Bill Beaman. "It would be good to hear the intel straight for a change instead of getting it filtered by the weenies at the three-letter agencies." He nodded to TJ Dillon. "Present company excluded, of course." The admiral noticed the quizzical look on Alston Jonas's face as he glanced at Ellen and Li Min. "We're not going to talk about anything our wives haven't heard over dinner already. Bill?"

Beaman smiled. "This is straight from Guillermo Manuelito's people. In case you haven't heard the name, Guillermo is an olive grower who has found himself becoming pretty much the leader of the Argentine Movimiento de Resistencia, the MDR. It seems that the *trabajadores agrí-colas*, the farm workers, are rising up in a widespread general protest after seeing the success of the MDR. That's a big deal in an agriculture-based country like Argentina. The protests are spreading into the cities, too. Office and factory workers are moving to the front lines. Nobody likes what's going on with their government. There are indications that even the military may be swinging over to the MDR, at least behind the scenes. The people are refusing to use the *inútil*, that new funny money Bruno Martinez and his buddy Cristiano Souza cooked up to devalue the dollar and get them out of debt. You guys would know more about it than I do, but I'm hearing the black market in pesos is booming. Put it all together and my read is that Martinez's days as God's gift to Argentina are numbered."

Alston Jonas chimed in. "My sources in the Chilean military tell me that the Argentines are pulling back to the original border down in the Patagonian region. They're getting no international support after they claimed all that navigable water as their own. Even the Chinese, through back channels, are changing their allegiances. They've finally realized they picked the wrong horses to bet on this time. Chilean Army troops are set for an aerial assault on Punta Arenas in a couple of days, which they expect to be unopposed. Argentina has all but evacuated from that area."

Jon Ward nodded, taking it all in, matching it up mentally with other details he knew already. "That all pretty much jibes with my sources. And with Argentina going the way it's going and China getting cold feet, Brazil may just go along to get along, but they'll be a pain in our backside down the road so long as Souza is in office. If Martinez is quick on his feet, he may make it to Beijing for asylum. And maybe President Souza should consider following his buddy. Bad time to be head of state, I'd say. You may or may not have heard that our own president had a heart attack at Camp David yesterday and is going to resign for health reasons. Can't say I hate to see him go. He never seemed to understand what it was that we in the military do or why we do it. We'll see about the new vice president when she takes over. Word is she's running the show anyhow."

"Man, we do get behind on the news when we're off somewhere playing war, don't we?" Beaman exclaimed. "But that all seems odd, don't it? All taking place at the same time. The veep suddenly resigns for unspecified health reasons and POTUS has a heart attack while all this other crap is going on down here?"

Jon Ward and Li Min purposely avoided eye contact. But the admiral saw that the look on his daughter-in-law's face remained impassive as she idly stroked her husband's hand where it rested on her belly. The spot where the baby bump would soon be.

"All that's way above my pay grade, Double-B," the admiral said. But the savvy old SEAL grinned as he looked sideways at his longtime friend and former sub skipper. After so many SEAL/submarine ops in dangerous spots around the globe alongside the elder Ward, Beaman knew when he was being told to not ask questions because there would be no answers.

Jim Ward knew it, too. He turned to his dad and grinned. "Looks like we may actually pull victory from the jaws of defeat on this one ... Pawpaw!"

The dazed look on Admiral Jon Ward's face at the mention of his upcoming status was priceless. For the first time in a long, long while, everybody in the hospital room enjoyed a good laugh.

EPILOGUE

Brian Edwards stuck his head through the XO's stateroom door. The room was dark and the curtain on Jackson Biddle's rack was drawn shut.

"You see the message traffic yet?" he called out.

From behind the curtain came a mumbled, "Good morning to you, too, Skipper." Then the curtain was yanked open. Biddle was rubbing his eyes as he swung his feet out and onto the deck. "Naw, ain't seen the traffic yet. For some reason, I kind of thought I would sleep in this morning. At least until 0500, seeing how it's Sunday."

"Well, XO, grab your socks," Edwards told him. "It seems there's some sort of investigation of this whole Argentine-Brazilian thing. Big Navy is asking for any information that we might still have documenting their fleets moving against Chile. It seems that they 'lost' everything that we sent them. They're asking us to send them an officer who can explain the whole thing."

"Lemme guess. Little ole me."

"Yep, that's you. The helo will be here for a PERSTRAN at 0700. That'll give you just enough time to load your safe's contents into a briefcase, pack your seabag, and get topside."

"You got backups, too, Skipper, right? In case somebody loses our stuff again? Or that helo augers into the ocean."

"You know I do."

Biddle remained groggy, processing everything that was happening while still trying to sweep the cobwebs. "You gotta be kidding. This can't be real."

Edwards flipped the notebook over in front of his second-in-command so Biddle could see it for himself. "Orders right here. PERSTRAN to the *Gerald Ford*, where you and me and the rest of the crew of the *George Mason* are rock stars, by the way, for saving their asses twice. But you won't have much time to soak up all that adoration. It's onward from the carrier, routing to Carrasco International Airport, Montevideo, where they'd love you just as much if they had any idea what you did for them. Itinerary is United Airlines flight 7120 to Panama City, Panama, connecting to United flight 7156 to Dulles. Tickets waiting at the gate. Better get moving, XO. You just have time to enjoy one final submarine shower before you go."

Biddle shook his head. "There is too damn much to get done back here for me to be traipsing all over the world. What about the boat? Who's gonna herd the cats here for the rest of this op?"

Edwards chuckled. "I think the COB and I are pretty good at that chore by now. Besides, as soon as we chuck you over the side, we're heading north. Next stop, Portsmouth Naval Shipyard. That's the message below this one."

By the time Jackson Biddle had showered, dressed, packed his seabag, and stowed all of the copied patrol data in a locked satchel, he had just enough time to grab breakfast. Brian Edwards sat in his usual seat, finishing his powdered eggs and bacon. That was about all that was left this far into their prolonged run.

Wonder if they got a Waffle House in Montevideo yet? Jackson Biddle thought.

Biddle poured himself a cup of coffee and helped himself to a bowl of oatmeal. He slid a thick file to Edwards. "One more bit of bookkeeping, Skipper. Nav finished the JAGMAN investigation on the galley fire. I just finished reviewing it last night. It's ready for your review and endorsement."

"And?" Edwards questioned.

"He found that the fire was caused by improper maintenance. Looks like Cookie's team was gun-decking a lot of maintenance, and he probably knew about it. Nav is recommending that the possibility of charges be investigated. It's ready for your review and endorsement."

"Thanks, XO," Edwards said as he picked up the file. "I'll take a look, but it can probably wait until we get to Portsmouth. Nobody's going anywhere. Except you, of course."

"Helicopter transfer party, lay topside," the 1MC announced, interrupting their conversation at the most cogent point.

Edwards stood and held out his hand. "Safe travels, XO. See you in Portsmouth after they run you through the ringer."

Biddle shook the extended hand. "Thanks, Skipper. See you there. I'm guessing you'd better get to the bridge about now. And I need to scurry topside. Looks like my Uber is waiting."

Ψ

Sandra Dosetti's personal cell phone chirped. The sound of it startled her. The only people who had that number were her estranged husband—who would never call—and her two college-aged daughters—one at Princeton, one at Stanford—who would only reach out to her if they needed money or wanted to complain about the Secret Service guys who were now shadowing them. She considered allowing the call to go to voicemail but decided to at least pick up the device and read the screen.

"Caller unknown," it read, displaying a number she did not recognize. Wrong number? Telemarketer? Curiosity got the better of her. With trepidation, she answered, "Yes?"

"Madam Vice President, best of the day to you!" The voice was masculine and carried a tinge of an Oxford accent. It was maddeningly familiar, but she could not quite place it. Whoever it was did not wait for her to respond. "I understand that congratulations are in order. The People's Republic of China officially extends our best wishes on your upcoming inauguration as president of the United States of America, even as low-key as I am hearing it will be."

Chinese president Tan Yong, of course. It was the faint sneer in the otherwise pleasant enough voice that she should have recognized immediately. Dosetti carefully chose her next words.

"Mr. President, on behalf of the people of the United States, thank you for your good wishes. However, in the future, I would prefer that your calls to me be routed through the White House switchboard so that they can be properly logged and treated as official communications between our two nations."

Tan Yong chuckled. "I have been informed that you are quite cautious in your manner, and I see that is certainly the case. I specifically chose to make this a personal call rather than an official one, though. I find that having a warm, friendly personal relationship between heads of state makes international relationships so much more effective for all parties involved, without having to involve underlings and diplomats and legislative bodies. And, of course, the press. Understanding, cooperation, and sometimes even compromise are better enhanced by a one-to-one mutual understanding to the benefit of both of us, don't you think? Diplomatically, politically, and in other areas in which we can dispense with the trappings of diplomacy and get things done far more practically?"

Dosetti had surmised that the Chinese communist party head would eventually make some kind of approach now that Stan Smitherman was out of office, down on his Austin ranch "nursin' a bum ticker and workin' on my bass fishin' skills." But she had figured Tan Yong would at least wait until after the inauguration, allow time to pass, let some memories fade a bit, before he made contact. Clearly, he was not going to do that. Here he was, using a telephone number he should not even know to rather blatantly pitch a continuation of the old ways. And the moving company had hardly gotten Smitherman's possessions—or the fumigators the stench of cigar smoke—from the building.

"Mr. President," Dosetti responded, struggling to remain diplomatic but firm, falling back on her well-rehearsed response to the call she knew was coming. "I agree. A friendly, clear understanding between heads of state is essential for world peace and the safety and security of our nations. In that light, let me give you a friendly, clear description of how I view our relationship going forward. I will be candid. I know that you are well aware of the actual reasons for President Smitherman's hasty departure from the White House, and that it has nothing to do with his health. I am equally certain that your efforts led to those voluminous files finding their way to my desk, just as you intended. I have no desire to follow my predecessor down that path only to have someone blackmail me with incriminating eavesdropping tapes, digital images, or a list of offshore bank accounts and transaction records. Now, if you will excuse me, I have an inauguration address to write and a long list of proposed appearances to prepare for."

With that, Sandra Dosetti clicked the button to disconnect the call.

Ψ

A cold November wind was blowing down the Piscataqua River as the *George Mason* made the sharp turn to starboard, leaving the Atlantic behind, and threading the channel that separated Seavey's Island from Pierce Island. A darkening gray sky to the north, up beyond Kittery, Maine, carried the threat of the season's first snowfall. A dozen different varieties of seagulls wheeled and turned around the submarine, loudly calling their greetings or protests—impossible to determine which—to the large black intruder into their domain.

A pair of shipyard tugs spun the submarine around and proceeded to shove it toward the pier. Commander Brian Edwards stood up on top of the sail overseeing the docking. Next to him was the harbor pilot, Andy Cribbs, who was controlling the tugs. The pilot paused to point toward Seavey's Island and the sprawling Portsmouth Naval Shipyard that would be the *George Mason*'s new home port for the next two years.

"Captain, your arrival seems to have generated some excitement and drawn quite a crowd to these parts," Cribbs commented. "I'm not sure what you've been doing out there, but this is the first time I've ever seen the president of the United States out on our pier to welcome a boat into overhaul."

"The who?" Edwards questioned, caught totally off guard. Nobody had told him. Sure enough, there was a sizeable crowd gathered. Far more than the usual family members and base staff welcoming home a boat from a routine run.

"Yep, Ms. Dosetti herself," the pilot replied. "See her? Standing there on the pier. Yeah, it may all be for show, but she's out here in the wind welcoming home a boat that's been out there doing God knows what. That's your relief next to her, I think. And those other two . . ."

Sure enough, there she was. The new POTUS. Several unsmiling men in suits stood nearby. Secret Service. And to her left was the officer who would be Edwards's relief as CO.

Then he saw the other two people the pilot mentioned. A young man and woman, holding onto each other, smiling and waving a vigorous welcome to the *George Mason* as she settled against the pier.

Enrique Rivera and his wife, Julie Roth-Rivera. The young couple Edwards had married during the deployment, and who were MEDEVACed a few days later after she was badly burned fighting the galley fire. Edwards had already submitted the paperwork for a Navy Commendation Medal for her. He was thrilled they had come to Portsmouth to welcome home their boat. So too were the line handlers topside on the sub's deck, happily waving to the couple. The COB was alternating between profanely yelling at the line handlers to attend to their jobs and waving to the Riveras himself.

Then, concentrating once more on President Dosetti, Edwards noticed for the first time something odd. She appeared to be holding a bundle. A baby?

"Andy, is the president holding an infant?" he asked the pilot.

"Indeed, she is, Skipper. It's in all the news, but I guess they didn't tell you that either. That bundle she's holding is your youngest crew member, George Mason Rivera."

"Well, I'll be damned!"

"And they told the press that they're going to ask you to be his godfather. I thought you knew."

"Godfather?" He considered the thought for a moment. "Godfather, huh? Long as I don't have to change any diapers," Edwards said, breaking into a wide grin. "Excuse me, Andy. I gotta go meet my new godson!"

"And your new president, too," Cribbs reminded him.

But the skipper was gone.

THE GIBRALTAR AFFAIR

At the precipice of international conflict, the fate of the Mediterranean's "Cradle of Civilization" hangs by a thread. America's forces sailing out of Gibraltar are its last hope.

In the wake of Muammar Gaddafi's demise, the Mediterranean's strategic waters become the stage for a new power play. Ali Hakim Sherif, emerging as Libya's formidable strongman, dreams of resurrecting the glory of the Ottoman Empire. His eyes are set on the untapped oil riches of Egypt, and he's willing to employ brutal tactics and ancient claims to seize control. Sherif's quest for dominance finds eager allies in Russia, Iran, and Qatar, setting the stage for an explosive confrontation.

With global attention focused on the conflicts in the Middle East and Ukraine, the United States mobilizes clandestinely. Admiral Joe Glass, operating from the legendary Rock of Gibraltar, directs a covert mission involving two stealth submarines. Together with Commander Jim Ward and an elite SEAL team, they are America's first line of defense, tasked with supporting Egypt against an audacious adversary. In a race against time, American forces face the daunting challenge of preventing a new empire's rise while protecting a centerpiece of global commerce.

ABOUT GEORGE WALLACE

Commander George Wallace retired to the civilian business world in 1995, after twenty-two years of service on nuclear submarines. He served on two of Admiral Rickover's famous "Forty One for Freedom", the USS John Adams SSBN 620 and the USS Woodrow Wilson SSBN 624, during which time he made nine one-hundred-day deterrent patrols through the height of the Cold War.

Commander Wallace served as Executive Officer on the Sturgeon class nuclear attack submarine USS Spadefish, SSN 668. Spadefish and all her sisters were decommissioned during the downsizings that occurred in the 1990's. The passing of that great ship served as the inspiration for "Final Bearing."

Commander Wallace commanded the Los Angeles class nuclear attack submarine USS Houston, SSN 713 from February 1990 to August 1992. During this tour of duty that he worked extensively with the SEAL community developing SEAL/submarine tactics. Under Commander Wallace, the Houston was awarded the CIA Meritorious Unit Citation.

Commander Wallace lives with his wife, Penny, in Alexandria, Virginia.

Sign up for Wallace and Keith's newsletter at
severnriverbooks.com

ABOUT DON KEITH

Don Keith is a native Alabamian and attended the University of Alabama in Tuscaloosa where he received his degree in broadcast and film with a double major in literature. He has won numerous awards from the Associated Press and United Press International for news writing and reporting. He is also the only person to be named *Billboard Magazine* "Radio Personality of the Year" in two formats, country and contemporary. Keith was a broadcast personality for over twenty years and also owned his own consultancy, co-owned a Mobile, Alabama, radio station, and hosted and produced several nationally syndicated radio shows.

His first novel, "The Forever Season." was published in fall 1995 to commercial and critical success. It won the Alabama Library Association's "Fiction of the Year" award in 1997. His second novel, "Wizard of the Wind," was based on Keith's years in radio. Keith next released a series of young adult/men's adventure novels co-written with Kent Wright set in stock car racing, titled "The Rolling Thunder Stock Car Racing Series." Keith has most recently published several non-fiction historical works about World War II submarine history and co-authored "The Ice Diaries" with Captain William Anderson, the second skipper of USS *Nautilus*, the world's first nuclear submarine. Captain Anderson took the submarine on her historic trip across the top of the world and through the North Pole in August 1958.

Mr. Keith lives with his wife, Charlene, in Indian Springs Village, Alabama.

Sign up for Wallace and Keith's newsletter at
severnriverbooks.com

Printed in the United States
by Baker & Taylor Publisher Services